SHERRYL WOODS

With her roots firmly planted in the South, Sherryl Woods has written many of her more than one hundred books in that distinctive setting, whether it's her home state of Virginia, her adopted state, Florida, or her much-adored South Carolina. Now she's added North Carolina's Outer Banks to her list of favorite spots. And she remains partial to small towns, wherever they may be.

A member of Novelists Inc. and Sisters in Crime, Sherryl divides her time between her childhood summer home overlooking the Potomac River in Colonial Beach, Virginia, and her oceanfront home with its lighthouse view in Key Biscayne, Florida. "Wherever I am, if there's no water in sight, I get a little antsy," she says.

Sherryl also loves hearing from readers. You can join her at her blog, www.justbetweenfriendsblog.com, visit her website at www.sherrylwoods.com or contact her directly at Sherryl703@gmail.com.

RAEANNE THAYNE

Harlequin Special Edition author RaeAnne Thayne finds inspiration in the beautiful northern Utah mountains, where she lives with her family. Her books have won numerous honors, including three RITA® Award nominations from the Romance Writers of America and a Career Achievement Award from *RT Book Reviews* magazine. RaeAnne loves to hear from readers and can be reached through her website at www.raeannethayne.com.

New York Times Bestselling Author

SHERRYL WOODS

Never Let Go

HARLEQUIN® BESTSELLING AUTHOR COLLECTION

Recycling programs
for this product may
not exist in your area.

ISBN-13: 978-0-373-18073-8

NEVER LET GO
Copyright © 2013 by Harlequin Books S.A.

The publisher acknowledges the copyright holders of the individual works as follows:

NEVER LET GO
Copyright © 1998 by Sherryl Woods

A SOLDIER'S SECRET
Copyright © 2008 by RaeAnne Thayne

Printed in U.S.A.

CONTENTS

Good

Dear Friends,

It's been more than twenty years since I wrote *Never Let Go*, but the story still affects me as much now as it did back then. In 1988 I had just left my job at a Miami trauma hospital, far from patient care, but very aware of the miracles being performed every day. I also gained a few insights into the men and women who performed those miracles.

From that experience I created compassionate psychologist Mallory Blake, skilled-but-distant neurosurgeon Justin Whitmore and the little boy who brought them together with a shared cause—to make him whole again, physically and emotionally. To this day, child abuse of any kind tears at my soul.

I'm so glad that *Never Let Go* is back on store shelves. I hope you'll enjoy this emotional story and if you ever have a chance to step in to protect a child from harm, that you'll do it without hesitation. Blessings to all of you who love and protect your own children every single day.

All best,

Sherryl

NEVER LET GO

New York Times Bestselling Author

Sherryl Woods

To the dedicated physicians of The Miami Project.
May your research to cure paralysis be
blessed with success.

Prologue

The rumpled sheets on the on-call room's narrow bed felt as cool and welcome as satin when Dr. Justin Whitmore finally stretched out after nearly twenty-four straight hours on duty. His mind was numb, his thought processes dulled by an all-too-familiar exhaustion. His back ached from hours of standing in surgery bent over an operating table. His tired eyes burned and his stomach was knotted with hunger, but sleep was more important now than food. As his head hit the thin, lumpy pillow, the tensed muscles in his long legs and across his broad shoulders slowly began to relax and the deep furrow between his hazel eyes eased.

Just a half hour, he pleaded silently, as his eyes fluttered closed. A half hour of blessed sleep just might get him through the rest of the night and the day that stretched interminably ahead. Sometimes it seemed as though his residency had been an endless blur of such nights. Sleep tugged at him, luring him like a forbidden mistress, attracting him so thoroughly that it was several seconds before the piercing beep dragged him back.

"Hell," he muttered, leaping to his feet and pulling on his white lab coat as he took off down the hall with long strides.

He knew even before he pressed the beeper button for his message that it would be the emergency room. For a neurosurgeon at this hour it was always the emergency room and it was always trouble. He'd be needed by people on the edge of death, fighting not just to live, but to live with bodies and senses intact. There were times, like now, when that thought intimidated him. He thrived on the challenge, but the power he held in his hands humbled him, especially on a night like this. He feared his concentration wasn't sharp enough, his hands weren't quite as steady as they should be.

Double doors whooshed open automatically as he ran down the eerily silent halls, corridors that only a few hours from now would be teeming with doctors, nurses, technicians and visitors. Justin knew all too well that the middle of the night hush could be deceptive, hinting at serenity, only to erupt into well-orchestrated chaos once the ER was reached.

He arrived at the emergency center on the run, pausing only long enough for the triage nurse to point him toward the trauma area, where another nurse was waiting for him.

"Six-year-old male, head injury, possible fractured ribs, maybe a broken arm and internal injuries. His vital signs are shaky. The X-ray technician is in there now, and we've sent the blood work to the lab. I've called up for an operating room. You're going to need it," she summed up with a conciseness that Justin appreciated.

The trauma team nurses were exceptional. They were compassionate, but far more important in this setting they were skilled professionals. They never wasted a single second of time that could mean the difference between life and death.

"Thanks, Helen," he said, taking the chart and going into the room. The team of nurses, an intern from general surgery and the X-ray technician surrounding the patient all spoke in a terse medical shorthand. An intravenous line and portable monitors were already in place.

Justin moved into a space beside the table and asked the intern for a summary. The recitation of injuries and vital signs was ominous.

"What the hell happened?" Justin said, already going to work with skilled efficiency. Adrenaline pumped through his body, wakening him thoroughly and sharpening his senses.

"His mother says he fell down the stairs."

Justin's head snapped around, his gaze incredulous. "At four o'clock in the morning? Who's she trying to kid?"

"I recognize him, Dr. Whitmore. He's been here before," one of the veteran nurses offered. "Cuts and bruises, that sort of thing. Never anything quite this bad."

"How often?"

"I'd say a couple of times a year until recently. Lately, it's been more like once a month. Last time, I checked it out with social services. The social worker has filed reports with the state. They're trying to get him out of that house, but it seems his grandparents have a lot of clout. No one wants to take a chance that they might be wrong about what's going on."

Justin muttered a vicious expletive as he gazed down at the skinny little boy, who was lying so unnaturally still. The child's pale skin was already turning an angry shade of purple in splotches on his arms and legs. There was a nasty lump on his forehead and a deep cut on his scalp that had matted his curly blond hair to his head. The boy whimpered as Justin probed gently, and something inside the surgeon twisted into a hard knot as carefully blocked memories reawakened and washed through him. For just a second, his hands shook. Then he took a deep breath, fought for control and continued with the examination.

"It's okay, pal," he murmured soothingly as the boy moaned softly. "We're going to get you through this. I promise."

It was a terrible world that allowed a child to be mistreated like this. Repeated visits to the hospital, mysterious injuries always attributed to clumsiness and a system that didn't seem to give a damn. What would it take to end the child's suffering? His death?

The nurse who'd spoken seemed shaken by Justin's fierce expression and his heavy, heartfelt sigh as he scanned the X rays.

"Is he going to make it, Dr. Whitmore?" she asked hesitantly.

"With a little help from God, we might be able to save him one more time," he said, his voice raw-edged with a quiet fury. "Are the consents signed?" Helen nodded. He looked at the intern. "Okay, then, let's move it. Get him to the OR on the double, Frank. I'll meet you there."

He turned back to the head nurse. "Helen, see if you can rouse Dr. Hendricks at home and get him in here. He's the attending physician on tonight and we may need him. And have an orthopedic guy on call just in case that arm's broken, too."

Justin was out the door as he spoke, already racing for the elevator...racing against time.

Chapter 1

Afternoon sunlight spilled into the room, chasing away the gloomy shadows. Bright murals of children playing decorated the walls, the cheerful paintings a stark contrast to the sterile, high-tech machinery filling the room. A hand puppet, looking like a little boy, dressed in blue boxer shorts and a red-striped T-shirt poked its bandaged head between the high metal rails at the side of the hospital bed. The bed seemed much too big for the small patient it held.

"Hi, Davey," a soft voice said. "Remember me? I'm Joey. I was here yesterday."

The blond lashes that lay against pale cheeks fluttered, but the eyes of the boy in the bed didn't open. The only sound to break the expectant stillness was the steady beep of the cardiac monitor.

"I'd really like to have a friend," Joey said, waving one tiny hand hopefully. "Wouldn't you?"

This time there wasn't any sign at all that the injured child, his own head swathed in bandages, had heard.

Mallory Blake—and, thus, Joey—sighed.

She'd been at this for a week now, coming every day to spend a half hour or more at Davey Landers's bedside, hoping to penetrate the wall of silence that distanced him from the world. The nurses had told her he'd been like this ever since he came into pediatrics from intensive care. For nearly a month now he'd had no visitors except the staff, and few of them had time to sit with him and talk. He wasn't an assigned case, but Mallory was touched by Davey's desperate need for love and attention. She found the time for him in a schedule of rounds and appointments that grew more crowded each day she was at Fairview General.

She'd heard about the near-miraculous surgery that had saved Davey's life. She also knew it had been touch and go with him for a while in intensive care. Now, according to his chart, his physical condition was improving every day, but emotionally he couldn't be reached. His state of mind wasn't surprising, judging from his medical history and the bits of information she'd been able to pick up from the social worker on the case, but it saddened her just the same.

At first Mallory had simply talked during the visits to Davey, keeping her voice deliberately low and soothing. She had read him countless stories, asked him questions that were never answered. Because he refused to eat, he was still being fed by IV and she tried to tempt him by bringing in approved special treats. Not once did he even look at her, much less accept the offerings.

On one occasion she had tried foolishly to hold his hand, but he'd reacted so strongly to the gesture, his body tensing with fright, that she hadn't tried again. It wrenched her heart to see a six-year-old boy so terribly withdrawn, his psychological scars far deeper than his physical pain. She'd seen adults with no will to live, but never a child. She was determined to give him back that will, to see him laugh and play again.

For the past two days she'd brought Joey with her, hoping that Davey would respond to the puppet without the fear he obviously and understandably had of adults. In her practice, she often used puppets and dolls to help children get through the aftershocks of a trauma or to prepare them for surgery.

Joey, whose head had drooped while Mallory sat thinking, perked up and inched closer to the head of the bed for another try.

"Davey," he called beguilingly. "Won't you talk to me? I'm very lonely. I think this place is scary. If I had a friend, I'd get better faster. See, I've got bandages on my head, just like you."

There was the slightest rustling of the sheets as Davey moved. His eyes didn't open and he didn't speak, but Mallory rejoiced just the same. Davey had reacted and that was what counted. Maybe he was beginning to trust her. If only he would look at the puppet just once, he might discover it was less intimidating than he feared.

"Couldn't you look at me, Davey? I'd like to see what color eyes you have. Mine are brown. I wish I had blue eyes," the puppet said wistfully. "Somebody told me your eyes are blue. Is that true?"

Mallory waited breathlessly as Davey's eyes blinked

once. But before they could open, a harsh voice cut across Joey's gentle whisper like the fall of a rough-edged ax. "What the hell do you think you're doing?"

Davey's eyes clamped even more tightly shut, and he curled into a tight ball under the sheet. The moment of breakthrough was lost, and only concern for Davey kept Mallory from raising her voice in an outpouring of frustrated fury. She looked up to see hazel eyes burning with anger and a firm mouth tensing into a tight-lipped frown.

So, she thought, this had to be the infamous Dr. Justin Whitmore. Despite a day-old beard and a rumpled green scrub uniform, he was impressive and intimidating. Boldly masculine, he had an aura of confidence and strength about him that a military commander would envy and a woman would automatically swoon over. Mallory had always thought she was immune to sheer physical presence, but it was all she could do to keep from sighing aloud. Heaven knows what effect he could have on her in a suit and tie, with that square jaw of his clean-shaven.

Her reaction was absurd, especially since she'd been anticipating this meeting with dread ever since the nurses had called her in to help Davey. Mallory had been a child psychologist at Fairview General for less than three months and in that short time she'd heard a lot about Dr. Whitmore, the thirty-one-year-old chief resident in neurosurgery.

The kinder reports described him as driven and obsessed, a skilled, tireless surgeon who demanded perfection. Others called him arrogant, temperamental, cynical, even cruel, especially toward those who didn't live up to his impossibly high standards. The nurses in pediatrics had warned her that he had a low opinion of psychiatrists and psychologists and that he'd probably blow a fuse if he found out about their interference in one of his cases. Once she'd seen Davey, though, Mallory had been willing to risk the physician's wrath.

Besides, no one questioned Justin Whitmore's dedication to his patients. She was certain he would come around, once she could prove to him that Davey needed her. Now that he was here, though, glowering down at her, she wasn't so sure. He didn't look like an easy man to sway. He looked…indomitable, even more so than she'd expected.

Mallory had heard almost as much about the physician's attractiveness as she had about his attitude. No one, least of all the awed nurses, disputed the fact that he was wickedly handsome, in the style of a bold and rugged adventurer.

With the evidence staring her in the face, Mallory wasn't about to dispute it, either. He had a trace of prematurely gray hair intermingled with shaggy brown at his temples, eyes that could strip a woman bare and leave her trembling, and a scar at the corner of his mouth that could emphasize a cruel scowl or a sensual smile. Word had it, though, that the scowls were all too familiar, the sought-after smiles disappointingly rare.

He certainly wasn't bestowing one on her now. In fact, if looks could kill, Mallory figured they'd better start digging her grave.

"I asked you what you were doing?" he said again, his voice not one whit more mellow. His body unconsciously shifted to get between her and Davey, as if he felt the need to provide a protective shield for the boy.

"Talking to Davey," she said coolly, determined not

to be put off by the rude tone or the assessing gaze that seemed to strip her of her silk blouse and the lacy bra beneath it. Ironically, the boldness of his look didn't seem intentional, which made its effect on her pulse all the more disconcerting. She felt an urge to tug her lab coat more tightly around her, but sensed he would find the instinctive gesture irritating, if not amusing.

She held out her hand. "I'm Mallory Blake. *Dr.* Blake," she added, deciding that even though Justin Whitmore wouldn't be a full-fledged member of the staff until he completed his residency, he was the sort of man to consider status important.

Apparently he did, because he ignored her hand, looked her up and down and demanded disbelievingly, "What service?"

Nothing short of an outright lie would get her around that question, and Mallory wasn't about to try. "I'm not a medical doctor. I'm a child psychologist, a Ph.D."

His gaze narrowed. So much for status, Mallory thought. The nurses had been right. Hers clearly wasn't good enough. In fact, it only seemed to anger him further.

"Who brought you in on this case?" he demanded. "I'm Davey's doctor and I assure you I haven't placed a request for your services."

"The staff in the unit told me about Davey," she said. She decided it wouldn't serve any purpose to start casting the blame on the nurses who had to work with this man. Dr. Whitmore already had a reputation for having members of the staff written up at the slightest provocation. "They said he wasn't responding. I thought I might be able to help."

"Do you always butt in where you're not needed?"

Mallory's temper was slow to flare, but once it did, the Irish in her made it a spectacular sight to behold. It was beginning to flare right now. "I didn't consider it butting in," she said, her teeth clenched so tightly her jaw was starting to ache. "I considered it part of my duties, even though I acted unofficially."

"Look, Miss Blake—"

"Doctor," she corrected firmly.

"Whatever. This child doesn't need your sort of psychological mumbo jumbo. He needs time to heal. He won't get it with you in here pestering him."

Blue-green eyes flashed and full, sensual lips parted, then clamped shut as she whirled around, grabbed Dr. Justin Whitmore by his rock-solid arm and dragged him from the room. She was wise enough to know that at five-feet-two and 107 pounds she'd never have budged all six-feet plus of him if he hadn't been willing to follow. She wasn't sure whether it was curiosity or his own fully aroused anger, but at least he came.

In the hallway, she dropped her suddenly trembling hand to her side and stared defiantly at him. She tried very hard not to notice how exhausted he looked. It might have made her feel a stirring of sympathy for him and that was the last thing she needed if she was to put him quite properly and thoroughly in his place.

"I do not practice psychological mumbo jumbo, *doctor,*" she began indignantly, then tried to temper her tone to one of pure, straightforward professionalism. She met his challenging gaze with a direct, undaunted look of her own. It took every ounce of self-confidence she possessed not to duck and run for her life.

Justin gazed down at her and found himself admiring her guts despite himself. Not many people dared to

tell him off and he had no doubt that was what Miss—
no, *Dr.*—Mallory Blake was about to do. He hadn't in-
tentionally cultivated his domineering attitude but he'd
found it useful, and it usually kept people at a satisfac-
tory, respectful distance. This pint-size hellion was closing that distance and practically spitting fire in his eyes.
Yet her words were cool, calm and so damned reasonable he had trouble maintaining his anger.

"From everything I've seen, that child in there is suffering from a deep depression, in addition to whatever
physical injuries he sustained," she was saying.

"Do you blame him? It doesn't take a Ph.D. in psychology to figure out that kid has gone through hell,"
Justin snapped.

"Exactly," she said, and this time Mallory Blake's
fury mounted until it equaled his own. Her words lashed
across him with the force of a particularly nasty, well-
aimed whip. "And with every minute that his withdrawal continues, it's going to be harder and harder to
bring him back. If someone doesn't reach him soon, if
someone doesn't deal with the hurt that little boy is feeling, all your high-tech medicine won't do a damn bit
of good. You'll have saved him on that operating table,
only to lose him because you're too damned arrogant
to think he needs anyone's help but yours."

With her head tossed back, she glowered up at him,
her short black hair practically crackling with electricity. Much to his surprise, Justin found he was not immune to the effect she produced. Mallory Blake was
one hell of an attractive woman, even if she was pushy
and totally out of line. His body's instinctive response
would have told him that, even if he'd been too blind
or determinedly reluctant to see it.

Well, maybe she wasn't totally out of line, he finally conceded grudgingly. What she said was true to a certain extent. Davey wasn't getting any better. He needed attention, perhaps not a psychologist's, but certainly more attention than the staff could give him. His own scattered visits during the day were far too brief and unproductive. Aside from assessing the boy's physical state, he had no time for more. There was always another patient waiting, another surgery scheduled. In the dark, middle-of-the-night hours when he did have time, he didn't want to wake Davey. Usually at those times he just sat by the bed, sometimes falling asleep with the straight-backed chair tilted against the wall, hoping in some way that his mere presence would offer comfort.

Suddenly Justin's shoulders sagged in defeat and some of the fire went out of his eyes. Mallory Blake, Ph.D., apparently knew her business. She sensed a victory and promptly pressed her point. "Has he talked to you? Has he even looked at you?"

"No." It was a reluctant admission.

"Well, he was about to respond to me, when you came barging in there and confronted me. Not only did that interrupt the progress I was making, but it might have been a further setback. You saw how he reacted. The last thing that child needs is to hear more people arguing, especially people he might be learning to trust. He's obviously heard all too much of that."

Justin sighed and rubbed his eyes. "You're probably right," he conceded, though he didn't apologize.

"So, do I work with him or not? If it's not me, it will be some other psychologist assigned by the state."

Justin glanced toward the room, and Mallory recognized an astonishing depth of pain in his eyes. It intrigued her that a man who appeared so cold on the surface was capable of such powerful emotions. She wondered if anyone at Fairview General had even begun to understand the complexities of Dr. Justin Whitmore.

As soon as the thought crossed her mind, she brought herself up short. No way, she insisted stoutly. She wasn't going to be the one to try. Davey was her only concern, and as she waited out a seemingly interminable silence, Justin apparently came to some sort of decision. He uttered a resigned sigh.

"Do what you can," he said at last, the words so quietly spoken that she almost had to strain to hear him. "I'll write the order to make it official."

Then his gaze met hers and for one split, heart-stopping second, he and Mallory connected, electricity arcing between them. Mallory's breath caught in her throat, and the thanks she'd planned to give died on lips gone suddenly dry. She longed to moisten them with her tongue, but didn't dare for fear it would seem a blatant invitation for the kiss she suddenly yearned for. She swallowed nervously.

Then, as quickly as it had begun, the sensual tension vanished, and Justin's expression hardened again. "Just stay out of my way."

Inexplicably hurt by the abrupt return of his animosity, Mallory felt her own anger resurface. It sputtered to life, then died just as quickly when she looked in his eyes and saw those traces of pain again.

"Gladly, doctor," she retorted, but he was already gone, leaving her relieved, yet oddly puzzled and disturbingly intrigued. Outright, aim-for-the-shins fury would have been a more appropriate response.

"I'll work on it," she muttered to herself as she walked away in the opposite direction.

Chapter 2

Staying out of Justin Whitmore's way was easier said than done. Once Mallory had met the infuriating man, she saw him everywhere—in the halls, in the cafeteria, even in the parking lot, getting into a surprisingly battered old sports car. She would have expected a shiny new Jaguar at the very least. Residents might not make much money, but there was an aura surrounding Justin that suggested a wealthy background.

She was less puzzled by his choice of a car, though, than she was by his continued hostility toward her. His responses to her polite greetings were never more than a curt hello or nod of acknowledgment. Not once did he meet her gaze directly.

Nor did he stop her to ask about her progress with Davey, and though she wanted to, not once did she insist on discussing the case with him as she would have

with any other physician. The ground rules had been
firmly established, and the barriers were in place. She
found herself suspended in a sort of professional limbo
where Davey was concerned. It was a thoroughly frustrating position.

As the newest member of the psychology staff, she
also felt she couldn't go running to her boss for advice.
Dr. Joshua Marshall was a crusty old man who'd been
reluctant to hire a woman in the first place. The fact
that she was only thirty hadn't helped either. He seemed
to think white hair and wrinkles were among the appropriate qualifications for a staff psychologist. He'd
probably automatically chalk up her problems with Dr.
Whitmore to her inexperience and gender and simply
cluck disapprovingly. She didn't need someone just to
tell her to try harder to get along with the man.

Mallory was left to work out a solution on her own.
She spent an exorbitant amount of time doing it. Even
after meeting him, Mallory didn't understand Dr. Whitmore's antipathy toward psychologists in general any
more than she understood his attitude toward her spe-
cifically. It was clear he was only tolerating her for
Davey's sake, even though he obviously maintained his
private doubts that she would have any luck. She knew
he didn't actually want her to fail, but she was equally
certain he wouldn't be surprised if she did.

To her chagrin, his continuing coldness bothered her,
especially after that spark of excitement that had flared
between them. Admittedly, it might have been better
for their professional rapport if it had never happened.
An all-too-attractive element of danger had been added
to an already volatile situation. Justin clearly had withdrawn from such danger, while Mallory found herself

reluctantly and inevitably lured toward it. She felt like one of those moths that couldn't resist a fatal flame.

Late at night, as she lay alone in a bed that seemed suddenly too big and too empty, the image of Justin's piercing gaze would tease her senses. She could practically feel the strong caress of his long, tapered fingers and the sensation left her restless with a long-suppressed yearning. Then she determinedly swept away the disturbingly sensual thoughts by reminding herself of his demeaning, belittling attitude.

She wondered if he would have been quite so arrogant or distant had she been a male colleague. Maybe he was one of those chauvinists who, like Dr. Marshall, felt that women had no place in medicine. She'd been told that, although news that he was a bachelor had been circulated widely and optimistically upon his arrival at Fairview General several years earlier, no one had ever heard of Dr. Whitmore dating anyone around the hospital. Then again, perhaps he just kept his personal and professional lives separate. She certainly couldn't fault him for that, though once she'd found that working closely with someone she loved had given a special dimension to their relationship.

Whatever his problem, Mallory wasn't interested in having her friendly overtures rebuffed or her professional courtesy thrown back in her face. He'd told her she could work with his patient and for now she would try to be satisfied with that.

That didn't mean her curiosity wasn't piqued, though.

"What's the story on Dr. Whitmore?" she asked Rachel Jackson, a good friend who also happened to be the social worker on Davey's case. They'd run into each other in Davey's room and gone to the cafeteria for lunch.

Rachel couldn't contain her grin, but her tone held a note of warning. "Forget him, girl. He's a loner, a real type-A personality. Find yourself another man. The place is crawling with them."

"I'm not interested in him as a man," she retorted.

Rachel's hoot of disbelief rang through the cafeteria. "Then you're the only red-blooded female around here who's not. He's so cool to everybody, and that seems to present an irresistible challenge. I hear they're even taking bets on when the mighty will fall."

"Count me out. I'm not into masochism," Mallory swore, though she couldn't quite meet her friend's speculative gaze. "What kind of a doctor is he?"

"The best, according to the other docs on neurosurgery, and they're a tough bunch to impress. I hear he was the unanimous choice for chief resident, the best and brightest of the current crop. He's pulled some people through when even the trauma team was convinced they couldn't make it. Those hands of his ought to be insured for millions, like a pianist's or something. I hear it's worth buying tickets just to see him operate."

"Does he ever warm up?"

"Around here?" Rachel shrugged expressively. "Not that I've seen, though word is he was plenty hot under the collar when he called our department about Davey."

"He was the one who called?" Mallory was intrigued, but not particularly surprised. From the moment Justin had entered Davey's room and found her there, she'd sensed that his protectiveness toward the boy went beyond the concern of a doctor for his patient.

"He sure as hell did," Rachel said. "He blasted the

boss for not following through after the earlier incidents and didn't even pause long enough to listen to her explanations. He just said if that kid made it and he ever heard that Davey had been sent back to his mother, heads were going to roll. He didn't mention whose, but I doubt he planned to limit the bloodletting to the social work department. More than likely, a few state officials would be in line for that temper of his, too. In fact, that's how I ended up on the case. The boss was afraid Dr. Whitmore might go after Georgina if he saw her near Davey. He blames her for not getting the kid away from his parents and into protective custody before something like this happened. The boss figured maybe I could smooth his ruffled feathers, though why she thought that, I can't imagine. He's not one of my biggest fans."

"Odd, isn't it?" Mallory mused.

"What?"

"That he'd get so worked up over this particular case. I know everyone seems to feel very strongly about battered children but it was more than that. I thought I saw something in his eyes that day we met in Davey's room. He really cares about that kid."

"If he does, it's a first. One of the advantages of being a neurosurgeon is that your patients are asleep most of the time. When they come to, they're so grateful to be alive, you can get away with lousy bedside manners."

Mallory felt her indignation rise again. "But there's more to treating a patient than doing the surgery."

"Maybe so, but except in Davey's case Justin Whitmore isn't known for doing it. He considers saving a life his only objective. All the rest is frills."

"I gather you've had some rough encounters with him, too."

Rachel rolled her eyes. "No more. We declared a truce. I stay out of his way, and he stays out of mine."

"That's exactly what he suggested I do."

"Then, for once, I agree with his advice. Steer clear of him, honey. You'll get burned."

It was good advice, and Mallory knew it. Of course, despite her best intentions, she didn't take it. Puzzles of any kind fascinated her and this one was especially complex.

The next time she saw Justin in the cafeteria, it was barely 7:00 a.m., and he had three empty coffee cups lined up across the table in front of him. He was holding a fourth and still his eyelids were drooping. Thick brown lashes fluttered down, then blinked upward, only to go down again.

"Having trouble staying awake, doctor?" she asked. His hazel eyes snapped open and stared at her blankly for an instant, then seemed to register her identity with no particular pleasure. He blinked as if that action alone would clear away his exhaustion, but it didn't work. The shadows in his eyes were nearly as dark as those beneath. "Mind listening to a suggestion?"

"Can I help it?" he asked with a hint of the familiar asperity, but a contradictory and unexpected curve of amusement played about his lips.

Those lips, she thought dreamily. Those lips were just made for… She snapped herself back to the moment, appearing to ponder his question. Then she grinned. "Nope. I don't think so."

"Then get it over with."

"So you can go back to sleep?"

"I wasn't asleep," he said defensively.

"Then maybe you should have been. Wouldn't you be better off in the on-call room than in here pouring caffeine down your throat?"

"Not when I've been up all night and I have surgery in less than an hour."

Mallory knew that residents worked awful, mind-numbing schedules during their training, but she'd never before come face-to-face with one who was at the end of one of those thirty-six-hour shifts.

"You can't operate like that," she said, unable to keep the shock from her voice.

"Is that your medical opinion?" he asked sarcastically.

"I don't need an M.D. to recognize your symptoms. You're exhausted straight through to your arrogant bones. I've read enough studies of the effects of going without sleep to know that you're beyond your limits. You'll not only be risking your patient's life, but in case that doesn't mean anything to you, you'll be risking your career as well. Is it worth it?"

Her voice had risen with indignation, and Justin's hand suddenly snaked out and clamped around her wrist, pulling her down in the booth beside him. Though the seat was more than big enough for two, it seemed oppressively crowded with their thighs pressed together and his hand still tight around her wrist. It didn't take a degree in psychology to recognize the man's fury.

Nor did it take a lot of intuition to recognize the heat that swirled through her for what it was—plain, simple and totally irrational lust. On some traitorous level her body was responding with unerring accuracy to Justin Whitmore's blatant masculinity, to the feel of his heated flesh against hers. Mallory was still trying to puzzle out the reason for that particular phenomenon, when Justin put his anger into words.

"Do you realize if anyone overheard your touching little display of concern it could set me up for a malpractice suit, if something goes wrong in there this morning?"

Mallory's blue-green eyes widened. "Don't be absurd."

"I'm not the one who's being absurd. You don't even know me, lady, so where do you get off telling me my limits? If anyone's put my career at risk this morning, it's you."

At the sound of his raised voice, several heads turned to stare at them, and Mallory blanched under the impact of his outrage. Unfortunately, though she was tempted to argue the point, she knew he was right. She didn't know him. She only knew the statistics, the case studies on mistakes occurring because of extreme stress. If Justin Whitmore thought he was superhuman, who was she to dispute him? Obviously, this wasn't the first time he'd operated under such conditions, and she doubted it would be the last. With malpractice claims soaring, he was probably right about the odds of being sued as well.

"I apologize, doctor. I hope the operation goes well," she said tersely as she jerked free of his grasp, slipped from the booth and walked away feeling thoroughly chastised and publicly embarrassed. It was all the more humiliating because of the heat that had swirled through her at his touch.

Her mental recovery from the unexpected onslaught of sensations was not nearly as rapid as her physical escape. The memory lingered with her all day, sap-

ping her strength just as any nagging worry would. The
whole encounter had shaken her and not just because a
colleague had lashed out at her in anger. It had been a
very long time since she'd responded in such a violently
physical way to a man. That it had happened with a man
who so clearly disliked her seemed perverse.

Hours later she was sitting beside Davey's bed reading him a bedtime story, trying to concentrate on the
words that swam before her own tired eyes. She'd been
ending her days this way for nearly a week now, ever
since Justin had approved the visits. There had been
no further evidence of a breakthrough, but she wasn't
giving up. Sooner or later Davey would come to realize that he could trust her.

"Now you're the one who looks beat," a voice said
quietly, interrupting the soft cadence of her reading.
She turned and found Justin standing in the doorway.
For a change he was dressed in something other than
scrubs—tan slacks the exact same shade as his hair
and a blue oxford-cloth shirt. The shirt sleeves were
rolled up to reveal muscular forearms finely misted
with dark hairs. Her heart lurched in a purely feminine
response, sending blood roaring through her veins. Her
range of emotions around the great Dr. Whitmore was
becoming entirely too predictable, from lust to fury
and back again.

"If you came looking for another fight, doctor, I'm
not up for it," she whispered with an edge to her tone,
rising and walking away from the bed so they wouldn't
disturb Davey.

"No." He hesitated. "Actually, I…" His eyes, darkening in confusion, met hers. He sighed. "I came to
apologize. You were right this morning. I was too tired

to operate, but unfortunately the schedule makes no allowances for such human frailties."

Mallory had never been the type to hold grudges, particularly when part of the blame for an argument just possibly might have been her own. "Apology accepted," she said easily. "I was out of line, too. Did it go okay?"

"Yes. We were lucky. It wasn't very complicated, and I had a good assistant scrubbing with me."

"I'm glad."

"Relieved is more like it, I suspect," he said with a smile that came and went so quickly Mallory was sure she must have imagined it. While it softened the curve of his lips, though, it had been a wonderful sight. She wondered what it would take to get it back.

"How about dinner?" he said. "Have you eaten?" At her clearly startled expression, he added quickly, "You could tell me how it's going with Davey."

"Shouldn't you be getting some rest?"

"Prescribing again?" This time his smile was full-blown, lingering and devastating.

Mallory winced. "Sorry. Force of habit. In my family, we're all worriers. It's a trait my mother built into us. She taught us to call if we were going to be more than ten minutes late, to wear sunscreen when we went outdoors, to stay away from the pool unless an adult was with us, to get eight hours of sleep, to eat our vegetables and to take our vitamins. If we didn't follow the rules, all sorts of dire consequences were predicted, not the least of which was worrying her into an early grave. I can't even pass a display of vitamins without feeling the urge to pop one."

"It sounds like you had a happy childhood, though,"

he said with what sounded to Mallory like a surprising trace of envy.

"It was very happy. I think that's why I chose this career, so I could help other kids who aren't so lucky."

"Are you going to tell me more about it over dinner?" His voice was persuasive, but it was the look in his eyes that did her in. He looked, impossible as it seemed, vulnerable. Mallory was a sucker for a hint of vulnerability in a man as self-confident as Justin Whitmore. It was another layer to be noted, another hint of the man's startling complexity.

One of the pitfalls of being a psychologist was that she always found herself wanting to peel away those layers until she discovered the core of the human being beneath. She could just imagine how thrilled Justin would feel at being subjected to her professional scrutiny. Only in his case, she realized, it wouldn't be professional at all. It would be very personal. Thinking again about that foolhardy moth, she shrugged in resignation and accepted his invitation.

"Sure," she said at last. "Where shall I meet you?"

"Scared I'm so tired you wouldn't be safe riding with me?" he teased.

She reacted with an unaccustomed blush. "Sorry. I didn't mean that. I just figured it would be easier if we both had our own cars."

"To tell you the truth, I was hoping you would drive. I'm too beat to be behind the wheel. We'll go to the Thai Orchid, if that's okay. It's close, and you can drop me back here afterward."

"Perfect. I love Thai food. You give the directions, and I'll try to get us there in one piece."

It took less than ten minutes to reach the restaurant,

a tiny place, filled with pungent, tempting odors. Each table was decorated with a small branch of miniature orchids, the delicate blossoms creating a touch of elegance amid the informality. Mallory studied the varied menu with delight, ordering a salad and a shrimp dish, both of which had a three-star spiciness rating.

"Does that come with a fire extinguisher?" Justin asked, after he'd ordered his own milder dishes. "Or are you going to want something to drink?"

"Soda," Mallory said.

"Make that two," he told the waitress.

When she'd gone, he leaned back in his chair and studied the dark-haired woman opposite him. He wondered what it was about her that had convinced him to break his firm rule about avoiding personal relationships with all people—and especially women—at the hospital. He'd learned the hard way that they were complicated and often messy, especially when they ended. Even a dinner as casual as this one violated his longstanding code of behavior.

More important, he wondered why he'd let his guard down with a psychologist. Ever since his own tumultuous childhood, he'd had a well-founded distrust of anyone in that profession. There was something about Mallory Blake, though, that told him she might be different. There was fire and honesty in her eyes and compassion in her voice. Even when she'd snapped his head off, there had been an underlying gentleness about her that he trusted.

He didn't want to trust her. In fact, he viewed this dinner as nothing more than an extension of his earlier apology and a chance to hear how it was going with Davey.

"Tell me about our patient," he said. "Any signs of progress?"

Mallory sighed. "Not really. I keep thinking it will happen at any moment, but I'm afraid to push too hard. Sometimes, I get so frustrated, I just want to yell to provoke him into responding."

Justin's expression became instantly wary. "Don't you dare yell at that boy."

"Of course I'm not going to yell at him. I know in the long run it would only be counterproductive." Her wide-set, blue-green eyes watched him closely. "Why are you so concerned about Davey?"

"He's my patient."

"You have other patients. From what I've heard, you don't spend a lot of postsurgical time worrying about their problems."

Justin flinched as the barb struck home. He was well aware of his reputation for being aloof with his patients, and it rankled, even though he did nothing to change it. "My responsibility is to give them the best possible chance at survival with a decent quality of life, whether I'm dealing with a brain tumor or a spinal cord injury."

"If you've done that, you think you can just slip out of your scrubs, go home and rest easy?"

"Exactly," he said tightly, feeling a knot of tension form in his stomach. No matter what he said, though, he didn't rest easy. There were nights when, despite the exhaustion, he tossed and turned restlessly, wishing he could give more, but he couldn't. He needed that distance, worked at it. It was the only way he could do his job.

"Why did you become a doctor, if you don't care about the whole person? Don't you think you have an obligation to give them some moral support?" she persisted.

"I thought that was your business."

"In some instances with the kids I'm part of the team, yes. So are the social workers and nurses. That doesn't mean you can just walk away and go on to your next case."

"I have to. There's no time for anything more."

"That's an excuse. Other residents find the time."

"Check my schedule. Show me how to fit in any more."

"I'll take your word for it, but I ask you again: why is it different with Davey?"

Justin glowered at her, infuriated by her persistence. "I'm not on your couch, *Dr.* Blake."

"I'm just trying to make a little friendly conversation. Davey seems to be the one thing we have in common."

"Fine. We can talk all you want about Davey. Just leave my motivations out of it. If you can't do that, let's move on to the weather."

That glint of fire was back in her eyes. "Damn it, Justin Whitmore, you are the most impossible man I have ever met in my life. I thought when you suggested dinner, you might be mellowing toward me just a little, but you haven't, have you?"

"It depends on what you mean by mellowing," he said cautiously. "If you're referring to professional respect, maybe. If you're referring to trust, let's just say I'm still withholding judgment."

His lips curved into an unwilling smile. "If you're talking about my being attracted to you as a woman, I'd say I've definitely mellowed. In fact, if I weren't so damn tired, I'd spend the rest of the night showing you just how attracted I am." The admission, made lightly, was all too true. Even now, his body was responding to her in a way that he'd never intended.

If he wasn't particularly pleased about it, Mallory Blake was incensed. "Oh, no, you wouldn't, you pompous ass." She seethed with what he knew was thoroughly justifiable fury. He was surprised she didn't jump up and punch him in the nose. She looked as though she wanted to, but she settled for berating him verbally. "Do you honestly think I'm flattered that you're interested in my body, when you've just finished saying you *might* respect me and you *barely* trust me? Work on the respect and trust, doctor, and then we might have something to talk about."

"That's an intriguing invitation."

"It wasn't meant to be."

Justin chuckled, the knot in his stomach unraveling. "You are—"

Her eyes narrowed threateningly. "If you say one word about my being beautiful when I'm angry," she warned, "I will dump that entire chicken dinner on top of your overactive hormones."

He threw up his hands in mock surrender. "Never. I was simply going to say that you are the most fascinating woman I've ever known."

"Humph."

He regarded her warily. "Does that mean I can stop worrying about getting my lap doused with chicken and rice?"

"Maybe."

"When will I know for sure?"

Suddenly she grinned and that flashing smile made his heart thump crazily in his chest. One of the things he found so beguiling about her was her knack for letting go of her anger so readily, for saying exactly what was on her mind and then moving on. She was apparently one of those enviable souls who carried around no excess emotional baggage.

"When you've finished eating all the chicken," she said primly. Their laughter bubbled up and ended the moment of tension, if not the sizzling feeling of awareness.

For the rest of the meal, they stuck to safer topics, mostly focusing on Mallory. She described her childhood in Arizona, her two rambunctious brothers and devilish sister, her salt-of-the-earth mother and generous father.

"Dad blustered and threatened a lot, but he never once took a switch to any of us. He didn't have to. The minute he raised his voice, calling us by our full names, we knew the game was over. It was absolutely amazing how he could quiet a room, just by saying, 'Mallory Marie, Theodore James, David John, Heather Jane, that's enough now!'"

Something painful tugged at Justin's heart as he listened. Just when he sensed that Mallory was about to question him about his own childhood, he called for the check.

"Sorry to end this so early," he apologized. "I really am exhausted."

If Mallory was thrown by the abrupt end of their evening, she covered it well. "No problem," she said quickly. "I'm amazed you've made it this long."

As they approached the hospital, she asked, "Where's your car?"

"Don't worry about it. Just drop me at the front entrance."

Her expression was horrified. "You're not going back on duty, are you?"

Impulsively, Justin leaned across and brushed a kiss across her lips, which parted instantly in what he realized subconsciously was astonishment. He was every bit as shocked as she was, but it was something he admitted now that he'd been wanting to do all night, something he couldn't deny himself.

The kiss, for all its innocence and brevity, was everything he'd imagined it could be. Her softness was like velvet, her warmth like an autumn sun, tantalizing in its intensity. Heat surged through him, awakening his tired senses, and he was tempted to linger for more, but he knew the dangers were multiplying with every minute he spent in Mallory Blake's company.

"Thanks for worrying about me," he said softly, "but don't. I'm just going back in to say good-night to Davey."

"Oh," she said, her cheeks turning an attractive shade of pink. It intrigued him, seeing a woman so uncompromisingly sure of herself display a little sign of uncertainty.

"Thanks for dinner."

"See you around," he said in the most noncommittal tone he could manage. He moved quickly away before he could make the terrible mistake of setting an exact day and time for that next meeting to take place.

"Admit it," he muttered to himself as he made his

way slowly through the quiet corridors to Davey's room. "You weren't joking. You want that woman."

Worse, he knew that sooner or later he was going to do something about it. He shook his head. "Fool!"

Chapter 3

The dinner had only whetted her interest. As maddening as it was, Mallory found Justin Whitmore more seductive and alluring than ever. If it had been nothing more than professional curiosity about an intriguing enigma or even a healthy infatuation with a fascinating specimen of the opposite sex, it might not have been so worrisome. Something told her, however, that it was much more.

To be sure, she found him both complex and devastatingly attractive with an almost raw, primitive sexuality of which he seemed totally unaware. The hints of vulnerability, the gentleness with Davey, the respect accorded him by his colleagues gave him a substance that appealed to her. More than that, though, she also found him infuriating. She knew exactly what that implied—there was a potentially explosive chemistry between them.

Most men, even after weeks of trying, did not rouse her temper or passions to quite the heights that Justin had with just two short encounters and a kiss that had been so brief as to be almost elusive. He had reached a long-untouched spot in her heart and threatened to twist it in two before he was done.

No one since Alan had done that. Even now, with time and distance between them, the memory of Alan was enough to bring tears to her eyes. Her hand shook as she picked up the cup of black coffee from her tray and took a long swallow. The pain was as fresh as if it had been only yesterday that he'd left her facing a life from which all sunlight seemed to have vanished.

Alan had been as much a part of her childhood as her own family. When her brothers had scoffed at her, she'd served a besotted Alan mud pies with cactus on the side. He'd taught her how to handle a horse, and they'd ridden for hours through the desert, galloping toward the future in a rush of anticipation. She'd listened to his dreams, and he'd made hers come true. They were married when they finished college.

Alan had been a gentle boy, a decent man. What they had shared had been a once-in-a-lifetime experience. They had been soul mates in every sense of the word, understanding things that were never spoken, fulfilling needs that had been left unsaid.

Perhaps because their own communication had been so incredibly special, they had both been drawn to psychology as a profession. She had chosen to work with children, Alan with adults. Their practice in Phoenix had flourished until the day, more than a year ago one of Alan's patients, outraged at his lack of progress and blaming his psychologist for it, pulled out a gun and shot him. Horrified by the sharp, cracking sound that had ripped through the early-evening quiet, Mallory had run in from the next room to find Alan bleeding and dying, the patient sobbing in a chair with the gun pointed at himself.

Holding her husband in her arms, feeling the life ebb out of him, Mallory had instinctively talked Alan's killer out of committing suicide. The story had made national headlines, painting her alternately as some sort of saint or as a fool. She knew perfectly well she was no saint. She'd hated what happened to Alan and the man responsible, but she hadn't been able to bring herself to watch an anguished man die before her eyes. It wouldn't have saved Alan. Perhaps she'd done it simply because even in a crisis her training helped her to understand, if not forgive, him.

For months afterward, she had fought to maintain her own tenuous hold on sanity, questioning her profession, even the meaning of life itself. Finally, when she found she had nothing left inside to give to the troubled children who came to her, she had turned her practice over to a colleague. After the healing was done, she had chosen to leave Arizona, to relocate in San Francisco where no memories of Alan lurked in every whisper of the hot, dry breeze, in every brilliant setting of the desert sun.

In the end the experience, rather than destroying her, had made her even stronger. It had reaffirmed her conviction and Alan's that every moment of life was precious, not to be wasted on half-truths or self-pity or doubt. She would treasure her memories always, but she would not live with them as a constant companion. She had loved incredibly well before. She would again.

And when she did, she certainly would not fall in love with an uptight, contradictory man like Justin Whitmore, she reassured herself as she headed back to visit Davey one last time before going home. She'd find someone as open and caring as Alan, not a man who drove her to thoughts of mayhem.

The thought of how Justin would react to her trying to shake some sense into his stubborn head made her smile. She was still smiling when she walked into Davey's room and found Justin standing by the boy's bed, his arms resting on the high railing, his head bent in dejection as he tried to coax Davey to talk. His voice was low and tender.

"You know, pal, the sooner you get better, the sooner you and I can go to a ball game together. The season's about to start and I'm a big fan of the Giants. I might even be able to get tickets for opening day. Maybe when you're better you could play on a Little League team." There was a long hesitation before he added tentatively, "I've been thinking about signing up to coach one. We could do it together. How would you feel about that?"

There was a restless stirring on the bed, and Mallory held her breath as she watched from the doorway. Davey rolled toward Justin and opened huge blue eyes that stared solemnly up at the man above him. Mallory saw the exultant lift of Justin's shoulders and felt her eyes grow misty.

He reached out a gentle hand to brush the blond hair from Davey's forehead. The boy flinched, but kept his gaze fixed trustingly on the doctor. She could see Justin's normally steady fingers shake as they touched the pale skin. Under Justin's soothing touch, Davey relaxed at last.

"So," Justin said again, "what do you think? Want to go to that game?"

Davey nodded almost imperceptibly.

"That's my boy," Justin said, his voice soft and encouraging, but shaking slightly with justifiable excitement.

Davey's eyes closed and he drifted back to sleep, Justin still standing by his side. A deep, shuddering sigh rippled through the tall man as he watched the boy.

Mallory tiptoed into the room then and instinctively put her hand on top of Justin's. Startled, he looked down at her, and she realized for the first time that his eyes were bright with unshed tears. He tried to blink the tears away, glowering at her, and then he started from the room. Mallory caught him at the door and pushed it shut, determined not to allow yet another retreat, especially not at a moment like this.

"Why are you running away?" she demanded, brushing at her own freely falling tears. "Surely you're not afraid to let your emotions show." The taunt was deliberate, an appeal to what she suspected was a very macho self-image.

"I'm not running. I have things to do." After his display of sensitivity, he was all stiff-necked pride again, and the urge to shake him came back with a vengeance.

"You just got through to that little boy. Don't you feel like celebrating?"

"I feel..." He shrugged, apparently unable to express to her the mixture of joy and pain swirling through him. A smile tugged at his lips, even as his eyes brimmed with tears again.

"It's your victory, Justin," she said without a trace of jealousy. "You got through to him and you have every right to feel good about it. Damn it, you can even cry if you want to. Look at me. I'm a mess and I was only an observer."

She was not an especially competitive person. As long as Davey became whole again, it didn't matter to her which of them claimed the breakthrough. Davey would be the real winner. It was that way with all of her patients.

Justin refused to meet her gaze. "There's a long way to go. You should know that better than anyone," he said curtly.

"That doesn't mean you shouldn't be grateful for each step along the way. Today he responded. By tomorrow, maybe he'll talk to you."

Mallory was a toucher and without thinking about what she was doing, she put her hand on Justin's cheek as she spoke. The stubble of his beard was rough beneath her fingers, the flesh warm, the line of his jaw strong. The gesture would have been, under any other circumstances, between any other two people, an innocent expression of sympathy. Between them it was an explosive invitation.

Before she even recognized the touch for what it had been, Justin groaned and pulled her into his arms, his kiss desperate, yet gentle, possessive and yet uncertain. His lips slanted across hers persuasively, his tongue venturing a tentative touch that left her gasping and wanting more.

After the initial instant of shock, her arms crept up and circled his neck. Her body arched into his embrace until she could feel every solid inch of him pressed against her, and she knew for certain exactly how aroused he was. He was strength and tenderness, hungry passion and silent desperation. He was the flame and she, God help her, was drifting toward it with swift inevitability.

Then, before she could get burned, he was gone. She stood there staring after him, her heart thundering in her chest, heat sizzling through her to create an almost unbearable tension. With trembling fingers she reached up and touched her swollen lips, which had curved into a rueful smile.

"So, Mallory Marie, so much for good intentions. Like it or not, I guess that's your answer," she muttered wryly. "Now what the hell do you intend to do about it?"

The first thing she did after picking at a dinner she didn't want was to call home.

"Hi, Mom. How are you?"

"Mallory, sweetie, how are you? We miss you. Are you settling in okay?"

Mallory glanced around her half-empty apartment. She hadn't had her furniture shipped from home yet, and she was making do with a few rental pieces that were both nondescript and uncomfortable. "If you like an apartment that looks like it was furnished by a particularly inept and color-blind decorator, I suppose you can say I'm settled."

"You could have your things sent."

"I know. I'm still looking around for a better apartment, though. I'd like to buy something overlooking the water. After all those years in the desert, it seems I can't get enough of the Bay."

"I would have to go and have a child born under a

water sign, wouldn't I?" her mother said with a laugh. "It wasn't particularly good timing on my part."

It was an old joke between them. Her mother was a great believer in astrology. "I don't blame you, Mom. I could have held out for another couple of weeks and altered my chart."

"If you had, your daddy might never have forgiven you. I was mean as could be those last few weeks as it was. It was hotter than blazes here and I was so swollen up I could hardly move. I was darn glad you came early." There was a brief silence, then her mother said softly, "What's really on your mind, Mallory?"

"I don't know what you're talking about."

"Don't try to kid a kidder, girl. You never were any good at it. You're upset about something or you wouldn't be calling here at this hour on a weeknight."

Mallory groaned. "I never should have gotten into the habit of only calling home on Saturday morning. Now you'll think any other time I call, there's a crisis."

"Is there a crisis?" her mother persisted, then asked more gently, "Or are you just missing Alan?"

"Maybe that's it," Mallory said, seizing on the possibility as a way to make sense of her tangled feelings. Maybe this sense of confusion, this overwhelming attraction, was nothing more than loneliness.

"Maybe? You're a psychologist. Can't you figure out what's going on in your own head?"

"It's a whole lot easier to figure out what's going on in someone else's, and it is definitely easier to give advice than it is to take it."

"Have you been giving yourself some advice and ignoring it?"

"Something like that."

"Mind a little from me?"

"You don't even know what the issues are."

"Doesn't matter. I know you. You've got a good head on your shoulders. You're loaded with common sense and sensitivity. It's a wonderful combination. Trust your instincts."

"Thanks, Mom. Maybe you should be the psychologist," she said, feeling better somehow, though nothing had really changed. "I'll talk to you on Saturday."

Once she'd hung up, Mallory thought about her mother's advice to trust her instincts. The only problem was her instincts seemed to be all twisted up with her hormones this time, which left her right back where she'd started: wondering what to do.

What she intended to do, she decided at 4:00 a.m. after hours of restless tossing and turning, was to put a lid on her emotions. Rational thought protested valiantly that people did not fall in love in a couple of weeks, that it took longer to choose appropriately. She was definitely lonely. Other than Rachel she hadn't made any real friends yet. It was natural enough to feel a bond with a man who cared for Davey as she did. It would be crazy to think it was anything more. Thus satisfied that she had the whole thing in proper perspective, she slept soundly and dreamlessly.

Everything might have resolved itself exactly as she'd planned, if she hadn't run into Justin in the park on Saturday. Literally. The impact knocked the wind out of her and put her in his arms when he tried to steady her. Then she realized exactly who the lout was who'd come around the curve on the wrong side of the jogging path. She jumped away so quickly that she stumbled and found herself right back in his strong embrace.

"We have to stop meeting like this," he said dryly, and to Mallory's amazement she found there was a twinkle in his eyes as he pointedly reminded her of the last time they'd seen each other. He seemed to have gone out of his way to avoid her since that night in Davey's room when they'd kissed, and she was surprised to find him so completely at ease with her now. The fact that he seemed to be joking nonchalantly about an incident that had left her breathless with wonder was enough to rile her all over again.

Not to be outdone by his casual attitude, she searched for and found an equally light tone. "Have you thought of wearing a bell?"

His expression grave, he seemed to consider the idea. "I suppose that might work here, but it could be a little distracting at the hospital. The paging system is bad enough."

Steadier on her feet now and all-too-aware of the proximity of Justin's scantily clad body, Mallory tried to inch away from him, but his hands around her waist held firm. Those hands, so supple and powerful, made her feel incredibly delicate. When his thumbs absent-mindedly began a slow, up-and-down massage of her ribs, a jolt of electricity raced through her.

Whether by accident or design, her arms were wedged between her body and Justin's chest. He was wearing one of those jogging shirts that consisted of little more than a scrap of cloth and some sort of open-weave fabric. Mallory had always had difficulty deciding what to do with her hands under the best of conditions. With Justin's broad chest tempting her, she felt exactly the way Adam must have when Eve waved an apple under his nose.

Then she thought about how he'd walked away before, after kissing her practically senseless. If the man thought he could come on to her any time he liked and then vanish at the first sign of an honest emotion, he could just think again!

"Well, nice to see you," she said blithely, taking a determined step backward. "I suppose we'll run into each other at the hospital sooner or later. See you around."

She had taken exactly two strides in her pink sneakers, when a shadow loomed over her. Justin fell into step beside her, which wasn't the easiest thing in the world for him to do, considering the difference in the length of their legs. He probably could have crawled faster than she jogged.

"Mallory, about the other night."

She felt her throat go dry, and it had nothing to do with being parched from the heat. In fact, it was a lovely, cool day. "Yes," she said tightly.

"It shouldn't have happened."

"Probably not," she said agreeably, though her heart seemed to thud to a miserable halt at his declaration. "But it did."

"That doesn't mean it can happen again."

She stopped so quickly he almost tripped over her. Putting her hands on her hips, she glared at him furiously. "Exactly what are you trying to say, Dr. Whitmore? Do you object to the kiss itself, the location or the fact that it was me?"

"There can't be anything between us," he said stoutly, avoiding the specifics of her question.

"And exactly why not, doctor? Is a mere Ph.D. not good enough for you?"

"Damn it, that's not it at all. We're just not right for

each other." Justin glowered back at her, his body tense with a feeling of frustration and an unfamiliar longing that went counter to every hypocritical word he was uttering. He was trying to tell a woman who made the blood surge through his veins that there was nothing between them, when both of them knew perfectly well that there was. The fact that his jogging shorts were growing increasingly uncomfortable was proof enough of that.

But, he reminded himself, he had long since outgrown the days when you bedded a woman just because your body told you to. The irony for him, of course, was the fact that he didn't dare sleep with a woman who threatened his independence either. It made for a damn lonely existence, which was probably why he'd been doomed from the minute he'd run across this little hellcat. She was not about to let him take the easy way out.

Even now, she was saying, "Would you care to elaborate on that? If it's not my degree that's bothering you, is our difference in height the problem? Or maybe it's our backgrounds? Do you come from old money? Would your family look down on someone who works for a living?"

Suddenly Justin couldn't bear to hear another sarcastic word. Before he could think about what he was doing, his lips were on hers. She was still muttering accusations, which only made the kiss that much more provocative. She was also wriggling to get away from him, her body slippery and fluid as a snake's when she writhed in his arms.

"Damn it, hold still," he murmured harshly, holding her tight against him. His breath was coming in ragged gasps, but he was far more concerned about what a sudden departure would tell the world about the state of his libido.

"I will not hold still."

"Then I'll have to make you," he said ominously, slipping an arm across her bottom and tilting her into the cradle of his hips. Mallory stilled instantly, and he heard a tiny sigh whisper through her lips.

His voice went soft and became tinged with amusement. "That's better." Actually it was sheer torture. At this rate, he wouldn't be able to release her for hours.

They stood that way for what seemed an eternity, every muscle in his body tensed with rampaging desire. His conscience was at war with the rest of him, but eventually it won, and his body began to relax. He wasn't the least bit sure he was pleased about it. A lesser man might have given in, taken Mallory home and made love to her until both their passions were sated. Even as he loosened his hold on her, the idea seemed very attractive.

With a sigh, though, he let her go. "It seems I keep doing this, even when I swear I won't touch you again."

Surprisingly, the look he saw in her eyes now was amusement, rather than anger. In fact she looked exactly like a woman who was willing to concede the battle because she knew she was winning the war.

"Perhaps you should try some counseling to figure out why," she suggested.

He laughed. "I don't need counseling for that. Any old anatomy text would have all the answers."

"Ah, but would it tell you why you're resisting?"

"Perhaps not, but the reasons aren't all that important."

"That's where you're all wrong, doctor. I think they are."

"Don't push it, Mallory," he said, and a certain tone in his voice must have gotten through to her, because she didn't.

"How about getting something to drink?" she suggested instead. "I passed a stand a little way back."

Justin hesitated, then gave in. What possible harm could there be in simply having a soda with the woman?

They found the vendor, then took their cold drinks to a sunny patch of grass. They sprawled out side by side, staring up at the sky. Puffs of clouds played tag across the vivid blue.

"Do you run often?" Justin asked at last, just to break the silence. There was something far too companionable about not speaking. It made him yearn for things that couldn't be. It made him believe in possibilities.

"I aim for three or four times a week."

"Have you ever done a marathon?"

"Nope. I settle for my three miles. It makes me feel quite noble without seeming like a chore. What about you?"

"I'm afraid my running schedule is pretty irregular. I never know when I'm going to be away from the hospital long enough to do it. I'd hate to be called in for surgery when I'm out here, dripping wet and out of breath."

"You're not on call today?"

"Nope. Actually, it's the end of an enforced vacation. Dr. Hendricks told me to get my butt out of the hospital for four days whether I liked it or not."

"And did you?"

"Did I what?"

"Did you like it?"

Not before now, Justin wanted to say. Until this afternoon, he'd been going stir-crazy with too much time on his hands to think, too much empty space to crowd in on him. As much as he'd needed the sleep, as much as he knew he'd needed to relax, he had itched to get back in the operating room. Those long, stimulating hours of surgery, when every one of his senses seemed alert and responsive, were what he lived for. The time off had been an intrusion into his well-structured way of life.

"I survived it," he said stoically. "I didn't like it."

"Sounds as though you need to learn how to enjoy yourself."

"I do enjoy myself. I love my work."

"But all work and no play…"

"Don't finish that or I'll take back every nice thing I've ever thought about you."

Mallory propped herself on her elbow and gazed into his eyes, her expression quite serious. The look on her face teased him like a feather's touch. "I didn't think you ever thought nice things about me."

"All roads lead back to Rome," he muttered under his breath, furious with himself for giving her another opening.

Mallory just watched him and waited.

Those eyes of hers could make a saint do unpardonable things, he told himself. "Okay, I occasionally have thought nice things about you."

"Such as?"

"Lady, didn't anyone ever tell you it isn't nice to beg for compliments?"

"I'm not begging. I'm asking, sort of in the interest of research. Since so many of my qualities irritate you, I thought it might be nice if I could figure out what doesn't."

She looked incredibly pleased with herself for dreaming up that retort, and Justin couldn't help laughing.

"Okay. Okay. I applaud your clever tactics. I also respect your dedication. You appear to be kind and gentle and intelligent."

"Appear to be?"

"I don't know you all that well. I'd hate to make any claims I couldn't substantiate."

"We could work on that," she said softly, and Justin's heart flipped over at the wistful sound he detected in her voice. He hardened himself to it.

"No. We can't," he said flatly. He tipped up his soft drink and drained the can. "I've got to get going."

"Are you going back on duty tonight?"

"No. I have a date."

"Oh, I see." Averting her eyes, Mallory got to her feet. She threw her own half-filled can away, and then, with a determined lift of her head, she gave him a dazzling smile. The only thing spoiling the effect was the slight quiver of her chin. "Enjoy the rest of your weekend."

This time it was Mallory who ran away.

As he watched her go, Justin could have thrashed himself for lying to her, for hurting her, but he told himself he'd had to do it. He had to show her once and for all that it simply wouldn't work for them. He would never allow himself to fall in love and harm another human being the way he had been hurt. He'd thought once that perhaps it was possible to alter patterns, but then he'd learned otherwise. Things taught in childhood never left you, no matter how hard you tried to change.

Chapter 4

"Fool! Idiot!" Mallory repeated the words in time with her steps as she ran back to her car. "You asked for it, you jerk. The man told you he wasn't interested. How many ways do you want him to spell it out before you get the idea? He's obviously involved with another woman."

If anyone else had described the scene she'd just acted out with Justin, she'd have suggested they take the hint before they got hurt. Instead, she found herself trying to puzzle out why the man had lied to her.

He had lied. She knew it. She wasn't wildly experienced—there had been only a few dates with other men since Alan's death, virtually none before their marriage—but she knew kisses like those she'd shared with Justin didn't just happen unless there was a whole spectrum of emotions behind them. Justin was absolutely determined, though, to deny it. Maybe he was just fighting it out of loyalty to the other woman. That was certainly an admirable trait. She ought to feel terrific that he was so honorable.

She felt lousy.

She didn't buy that theory for a minute, anyway. There had to be some other explanation, but she was darned if she could think of one.

Whatever Justin's motivation, though, he either had to stop the denials or the kisses. She found herself praying she could get him to make the same choice she would, given the chance.

But what if she were only deluding herself, what if he were seriously involved, even engaged? She moaned as her imagination took flight again.

On the way home, she decided to make a quick detour by Rachel's. She simply couldn't bear the prospect of going back to her empty apartment where she'd spend the rest of the day analyzing Justin Whitmore or, worse, envisioning him in the arms of another woman. At the very least Rachel would give her a stern lecture on facing reality. Much better was the possibility that Rachel might go apartment-hunting with her.

A part of Mallory had been resisting getting a better place, knowing that it would mean a commitment to her new life. It was time, though, to either find somewhere she could really call her own or to pack it in and go back home. Suddenly she realized that Arizona was feeling less and less like home. She liked it here. She'd fallen in love with San Francisco. She liked the challenges of her work, the friends she was making, especially Rachel, who was levelheaded, funny and caring.

A new apartment would make the picture complete,

a home that would be bright with sunshine and maybe even have a fireplace. As an errant image of Justin in front of that fire flitted through her mind, she decided she probably ought to look for a place that needed a lot of work. It would keep her occupied and keep such wasted thoughts at bay.

She found Rachel in her backyard, pushing her three-year-old daughter, Deanne, on a swing, while Johnny, who was a year younger, tried to bury himself in a sandbox.

"Oh, thank God," Rachel murmured the instant she spotted Mallory rounding the corner of the house. "Another adult. My prayers have been answered."

"Bad day at the Jackson household?" Mallory inquired, taking over at the swing amid squeals of delight and pleas to go higher. Rachel sank down on a lawn chair and fanned herself with a paperback book she obviously hadn't had time to open.

"That, my dear, is an understatement. The washer broke down in the middle of doing a load of sheets. The repairman promised to be here within my lifetime at a cost equal to Hal's life insurance policy. The little one who is giggling so gleefully for you threw a temper tantrum when I refused to feed her hot dogs for breakfast. Cornflakes now cover the half of the kitchen that is not awash with overflowing soapsuds. Her father has threatened to send her to live with her grandparents until she's ready for college. He's hoping she'll be civilized by then."

Mallory couldn't help grinning at Rachel's recitation. "And your beachboy over there in the sandbox? What has Johnny done today to add to the chaos?"

"Other than getting up at 5:00 a.m. and shaking his

crib until I came to join him, not a thing. If the kid doesn't take a nap soon, though, I will not be responsible for my actions."

"Where's Hal? Did he run away from home?"

"I wouldn't blame him if he had, but no. He's actually out doing the grocery shopping. He promised to take over when he got back so that I could relax, prop my feet up and try to recall what life was like before these two entered it and brought me so much joy." There was a dry note in her voice, but her love for the children shone in her eyes. It made Mallory feel lonelier than ever.

"How would you feel about apartment-hunting with me, instead?"

Rachel's dark eyes gleamed. "You mean walk away from all of this? Maybe even stop for an uninterrupted dinner? Intelligent conversation?"

"I can't promise the latter, but we could give it a shot."

Rachel was on her feet before Mallory could complete the sentence. "If you'll watch the kids for a few minutes, I'll go and change right now, so I'll be ready the instant Hal walks in the door. If I'm already waiting in your car, he won't be able to back out of his promise."

Mallory chuckled at the edge of desperation in her friend's enthusiasm. Even though Rachel's life was crazy, Mallory felt a trace of envy. Rachel had all the things she'd expected to have with Alan—love, a home, children. She snapped herself back from what was destined to be a raging case of self-pity. "Go on," she said quickly. "I'll be fine here."

As soon as Rachel had left, Deanne tired of swinging. "Down," she demanded imperiously. Mallory lifted her off the seat and placed her on the ground.

The youngster popped a thumb into her own mouth, and regarded Mallory with wide brown eyes, as if trying to decide how much devilment this particular grown-up would tolerate.

While Deanne was working that out, Johnny wrapped his sandy arms around Mallory's legs and clung to her, wailing to be picked up.

"I think I'm beginning to see Rachel's problem," Mallory muttered as she hoisted Johnny up and grabbed Deanne by the hand.

"Okay, kids," she said brightly, "let's go inside."

Deanne planted her feet firmly where she stood and refused to budge. "Won't go."

"Don't you want to play a game with us?" Mallory improvised. Deanne's eyes brightened, then turned skeptical.

"Game?"

"Yep. Johnny and I are going to play a game. If you want to, you can play, too."

Deanne seemed to consider the offer from every angle. "Okay," she said at last.

Mallory took the two of them into the kitchen, which was every bit the mess Rachel had described. She put Johnny to work scooping bubbles into a pail. Thankfully, he seemed to consider it an extension of playing in the sandbox. Deanne, however, was not so easily fooled.

"I'll bet I can get more cornflakes into a dish than you can," Mallory taunted. Deanne eyed her warily. It was time for the big guns: outright bribery. "If you win, Mommy and I will bring you back ice cream."

Deanne began daintily picking cornflakes off the walls. With the kids occupied for the moment, if not actually helping much, Mallory searched for a mop and began cleaning up. The physical exertion felt good. It also kept her from thinking too much. She was still at it when Hal came in, his arms filled with groceries.

"Hi, there," he said cheerfully, brushing a kiss across her cheek. "Are you the new maid?"

"Not me. I'm just here to borrow your wife. She's going apartment-hunting with me."

"You mean I'm actually going to be left alone with these two terrors of hers?" He feigned a horrified expression.

One dark brow arched quizzically. "*Hers?* They're your children, too. Besides, I hear you promised."

"If you hadn't shown up, Rachel might have forgotten."

"I doubt it. She looked pretty determined to escape. If I hadn't stopped by, she might be heading for L.A., maybe even Hawaii. You should be grateful to me. I'll see that she comes home again."

Rachel appeared in the doorway just then. "Don't make promises you can't keep, Mallory. If I call home later and all of this isn't under control, I may stay away for days."

Hal swept his wife into his arms and kissed her soundly. "Could you stay away from that?" he teased.

"Would you consider meeting me at a motel?" she retorted.

"Not on your life. The beds are always too short. It's here or nothing."

Rachel's face was a study of indecision. She hesitated so long that Hal finally poked her. "Hey, you're making me feel insecure."

"You've never felt insecure a day in your life, Hal

Jackson. Maybe I should let you worry just a little. It might make you appreciate me more."

Hal turned to Mallory and warned, "You make sure she comes home tonight or I'll bring the kids over and leave them with you."

"She'll be home," Mallory promised so quickly that they all laughed.

"Come on," Rachel urged. "Before he changes his mind."

They drove to Mallory's apartment, so she could shower and change. When she emerged from the bedroom, Rachel had printed a list of ads for condominiums from the internet. "Any preference as to which side of the Golden Gate you're on?"

"Nope. Not as long as I can see the water."

"Then let's start on this side and finish in Sausalito. There's a restaurant over there I've been wanting to try, but Hal and I haven't managed a night out without the kids for weeks. I refuse to take them any place that actually has china and silverware. I can't afford to pay for damages."

"Then we'll live it up tonight. I'll even spring for a bottle of wine."

With the prospect of a quiet, elegant dinner ahead of her, Rachel's interest in the apartment search seemed to wane. She gave directions as they drove from building to building, but in between all she talked about was whether she'd order seafood or veal.

"Enough about food already," Mallory finally said with a laugh. "I missed lunch. If you keep this up, we'll be sitting down for dinner before five."

"That's fine with me."

"Rachel, I am going to find an apartment this afternoon or no dinner."

"Then drive faster."

An hour later Mallory found the perfect place. It had gleaming wood floors, a cheerful kitchen with cupboards galore, a fireplace, plenty of closets and, best of all, it had a huge bay window with a padded seat facing the water. It met every one of her requirements, with charm to spare. It was also more expensive than she felt she could afford.

"Mallory, you love the place. You have to buy it," Rachel said. "Bring tuna fish sandwiches for lunch if you have to. Don't stint when it comes to a place to live."

"Why are you so anxious to spend my money?"

"Once you've actually bought a place and started to put down some roots, you won't be so likely to leave. Good friends are hard to come by."

The sincerity in Rachel's words reminded Mallory of her earlier thoughts. She had found a friend and now a home. If only... She brought herself up short before the image of Justin could form clearly in her mind. She gave Rachel a hug and turned to the real estate agent. "Take my offer to the seller. If he accepts and I can get the financing, I'll take the apartment."

She was in high spirits when she and Rachel finally walked into the restaurant and were led to a table with a wonderful view across the Bay. When the wine had been poured, Rachel lifted her glass.

"To your new home."

Mallory joined in the toast. "Thanks for nudging me into it. I'm already beginning to arrange furniture in my mind."

Over dinner they talked about decorating possibilities, then wandered on to other topics. Rachel was filling her in on hospital gossip, when Mallory looked across the room and spotted Justin at the bar. Her heart seemed to stop, then pound more loudly than ever. With something that seemed suspiciously like jealousy nagging at her, she scanned the bar to look for his date.

"What on earth is the matter?" Rachel asked. "You look as though you've seen a ghost."

"Dr. Whitmore," Mallory said in a choked voice.

Rachel twisted in her chair to locate him. "I see," she said. Then looking at Mallory more closely, she moaned. "Oh, dear God in heaven, you didn't listen to me, did you?"

"What do you mean?"

"You went and fell for the man, even though I warned you not to."

There was no point in denying it. She'd always worn her heart on her sleeve for any perceptive person to read. "I didn't do it on purpose," Mallory grumbled.

"Well, as long as you're planning to rush in where angels fear to tread, why don't you go on over and say hello?"

"I can't. He has a date."

"There isn't a woman at that bar," Rachel said, then gasped. "You aren't suggesting…" Her voice trailed off.

"No, no."

"Then what is this nonsense about a date?"

"I ran into him earlier. He told me he had one tonight."

"Maybe she cancelled."

"Or maybe he never had one," Mallory said. She set her wineglass down so hard that the Chardonnay splattered all over the tablecloth. "Damn it, I knew it. He was lying to me."

"Why would he do that?"

"I don't know, but I intend to find out."

Tossing her napkin on the table, Mallory slipped out of her chair and marched across the restaurant. Justin glanced up from his drink just in time to see her coming. She was wearing a sexy little dress that clung to her curves. Her dark hair curled softly and provocatively around her face. He studied that face and swallowed nervously. She didn't look pleased to see him. In fact, she looked very much like a lady intent on mayhem. He was torn between trying to make peace and going on the defensive.

"So," she said amiably enough, sliding onto the bar stool beside him. He suspected the friendliness was deceptive, and he prepared to dodge the first blow. At least it was verbal.

"Where's your date?"

Guilt and well-deserved embarrassment rushed through Justin. "She couldn't make it," he muttered tightly, clenching his glass until his knuckles turned white.

"I'm sorry to hear that," she said. There was not one whit of sincerity in her voice.

He gazed directly into her eyes. She didn't bat an eyelash. "Are you really?" he said. "You don't sound like it."

"Oh, but I am. What was the problem? Flu? Pneumonia? A conflicting engagement?" Her blue-green eyes sparked with innocent interest.

Justin scowled at her, then sighed in resignation. She

already knew. He might as well admit it. "There was no date."

To his astonishment, she suddenly smiled brightly. "Thank you."

"What on earth for? For making a fool of myself?"

"No, for telling me the truth."

"You'd just have poked and prodded until you got to it. I figured I'd save us both the effort."

"Why did you lie in the first place?"

As always, her directness unnerved him. "I thought it was for the best," he murmured.

Mallory rolled her eyes in disbelief. "Please. Not that again."

He toughened his attitude. "Why won't you listen to me? It's the truth. You and I..." He gestured helplessly. "It just can't be. Accept it."

"Not on your life."

Suddenly he laughed at the incongruity of the situation. Here he was fighting like crazy to maintain his distance from the most attractive, beguiling woman he'd met in years. Maybe he should sleep with her and get her out of his system. Then go back to living the serene, if empty sort of bachelor life he'd had before she'd come along and turned his emotions all topsy-turvy. He looked into the depths of her clear blue-green eyes, saw the spark of humor, the intelligence, the bright flare of desire, and knew it would never end that simply.

"Mallory, what am I going to do with you?"

"I have some ideas."

"I'll just bet you do. It's probably best if you don't discuss them here. In fact, it's probably best if you sublimate them."

"Sublimation isn't healthy, and actually, I was only

going to suggest that you come join Rachel and me," she said primly. He felt the oppressive mass that had weighted his chest since he left her in the park begin to lift, even though Rachel's presence was a complication he hadn't counted on. Damn it all, he wanted to be with this woman.

"We're not exactly having a clandestine affair here, but in case you're worrying about the hospital rumor mill, Rachel knows how to keep her mouth shut," Mallory said, reading his mind. "She won't tell a soul that you sat down to dine with a couple of coworkers."

He capitulated all too easily. "In that case, I'd love to join you."

The atmosphere at the table was so pleasant and relaxing that Justin found himself wondering why he'd deprived himself of Mallory's company in the first place. Surely they could be friendly, have an occasional dinner, some casual conversation without it developing into anything complicated.

Mallory reached across just then and touched his hand. He'd lost track of the discussion even before she made the gesture, but with her fingers resting lightly on his, he couldn't think at all.

Friendly? Was that what he'd been telling himself? Not in a million years. If he and Mallory Blake were to spend ten minutes in a room alone, they'd generate enough spontaneous combustion to burn down an entire forest.

"I've got to be going," he said abruptly, his voice hoarse. He cleared his throat. "I'm going back on duty early tomorrow."

A protest formed on Mallory's lips, but she didn't voice it, thank goodness. He wasn't at all sure that he could walk away from her tonight as it was. If she asked him to stay for another drink, to drop by her apartment, the temptation would no doubt overcome every little bit of common sense he had left.

Instead, she said only, "We should be going, too."

Justin called for the check and insisted on paying for the dinner.

"That's hardly fair. You just had a couple of drinks," Rachel argued.

"I had good company, too. Lovely ladies. It's worth it. My own company was pretty lousy tonight." It was a telling remark and he knew it. From the smug look on Mallory's face, he guessed she knew exactly what he meant. Rachel, though, seemed unaware of the under-currents or was wise enough, at least, to ignore them.

"Hal and I will have you over for dinner soon," she said. "I assume you can tolerate kids."

"I can tolerate them," he said lightly. "It sounds nice."

"You haven't seen my kids," Rachel said and grabbed Mallory's valet parking ticket out of her hand. "I'll go get the car and meet you out front."

"Fine," Mallory said, her gaze locked with Justin's. She had accepted his retreat without a murmur, but keeping quiet was costing her. Her insides were tied in knots and she knew she was going to be awake long into the night, tossing and turning in frustration. She searched for a neutral topic, so she wouldn't stand on tiptoe and kiss the man. "You're going back on duty tomorrow?"

"At 7:00 a.m., unless I get beeped during the night."

"Will you see Davey?"

"First thing."

"He's probably missed you."

"Actually, I've stopped by every day, even though I've been off. I didn't want him to start feeling abandoned, just when we were seeing some sign of progress."

"Has he said any more to you?"

"Not much. At least he opens his eyes for me now and says hello."

"That's terrific."

"The first step, isn't that what you said?"

"That's right. It's always the hardest."

Suddenly it was very clear to Mallory that they were talking about far more than Davey. Justin was trying to say something to her about their relationship as well. Why was it so difficult for him to be direct? Why was he fighting the attraction so hard? Why couldn't he manage that first step that would take the two of them on to something more? She was all the more confused now that she knew with virtual certainty that there was no other woman.

Apparently it wasn't something she was likely to find out tonight, however. Outside he simply squeezed her hand, even though she'd turned her face up just a little in anticipation of a kiss. "I did enjoy dinner," he said softly, as he held the car door open for her.

"So did I."

He seemed to hesitate for an eternity before saying, "Maybe we could do it again sometime."

"I'd like that."

A heavy sigh shuddered through him then, and he closed the door and vanished without so much as a good-night to Rachel.

"Sorry," Mallory apologized. "Justin's manners could use a little work."

"He was a saint tonight, compared to most of the times I've had to deal with him. You're obviously good for him."

"I'm not sure he sees it that way."

Rachel laughed uproariously. "Oh, he sees it that way, girl. He's just fighting it." She grinned at her conspiratorially. "They all do, you know."

After picking up the promised ice cream for Deanne and dropping Rachel off, Mallory felt far too keyed up to go home herself. She decided to pay a late-night visit to Davey. More and more, she felt an urgent need to draw him back into the world, to see him smile. Besides, he was her link to Justin and if she couldn't be with him tonight, Davey was the next best thing.

She stopped at the nurses' station on her way to Davey's room and visited for a few minutes before wandering down the hall. Opening the door slowly, she found the room bathed in nighttime shadows. She tiptoed over to the bed and peered down at the still form. Davey was lying on his back, his arms and legs askew, the covers kicked aside. His bruises had faded now and his bandages were smaller. For once, he looked at peace.

Mallory pulled up a chair and sat by the bed, leaning her forehead against the railing. She closed her eyes and thought about Davey and what was in store for him, then about Justin and her own future.

Suddenly a high little voice whispered tentatively, "Where's Joey?"

Her eyes snapped open to see Davey staring at her solemnly. Her heart lurched unsteadily, and joy surged through her.

"I left him in his room sleeping," she said gently,

fighting for composure. "Which is what you should be doing, big guy. How come you're awake so late?"

He squeezed his eyes shut, and a tear rolled down his cheek. Mallory only just resisted the urge to reach over and brush it away. The moment was still too fragile.

"Scared." He mumbled the word so softly she could barely make it out.

"I get scared at night, too, sometimes," she confided. "What scared you?"

"I was bad. Mommy was going to hit me."

This time it was Mallory who closed her eyes and fought tears. "Davey, your mommy's not going to hit you anymore. We won't let that happen."

"Promise?" That single softly spoken word held such a mixture of hope and fear that it tore at her heart. Wide blue eyes gazed at her with the desperate appeal of a cornered animal.

"I promise, baby."

Mallory's fingers were curled tightly around the railing on the bed. Davey reached over tentatively and touched them, the way a child would stroke a beloved stuffed animal for comfort. Then with a whisper of a sigh he rolled on his side and went back to sleep.

Shaken, Mallory sat by the bed and let the tears—of relief, of sorrow, of joy—flow freely down her cheeks. At last she knew with certainty that despite the pain, Davey was going to get well. The emotional healing had finally begun. Davey was beginning to trust again. He was reaching out.

The burden of responsibility weighed heavily on her. It was up to her and Justin to see that they didn't let him down.

Chapter 5

"Dr. Blake, could I see you for a minute?" the head nurse from one of the surgical floors asked just as Mallory was getting ready to step into the elevator.

"Sure, Carol. What is it?"

"It's about Dr. Whitmore."

Mallory's breath caught in her throat. Surely the gossip mill hadn't latched onto news of those two innocent dinners so quickly. "What about him?" she asked warily.

"Well, you seem to have a way with him." At Mallory's startled expression, she added quickly, "I mean, I've heard you two are working together on that little boy's case up in pediatrics and I was wondering if maybe you could help me out."

"What's the problem?"

"I have a patient here scheduled for surgery in two

days and he's scared to death. He knows it's possible he'll be paralyzed. Actually I'm amazed he's holding up as well as he is. Anyway, I thought it would help if Dr. Whitmore talked to him, tried to give him the straight facts about his situation. All the wondering isn't good for him. I think he'd feel a whole lot more confident going into surgery, if he really knew his doctor was being honest with him."

Mallory sighed. Carol was absolutely right, but how was Justin going to feel about her interfering in another one of his cases, especially when the patient was an adult? Still, she couldn't ignore the situation, now that she knew about it. She believed too strongly in the healing power of communication between doctor and patient.

"What would you like me to do?"

"Couldn't you talk to Dr. Whitmore and persuade him to spend some time with the man? That's all. I just know it would help. I've tried, but he just brushes me off with promises that he'll do it later. At this rate, later will be after the guy's surgery."

"I'll talk to him, Carol," she agreed reluctantly, already envisioning the argument that would follow her mention of the case to Justin. "What's the patient's name?"

Carol's expression brightened measurably. "Harrison. He's in 615. He's a great guy, too. He got mangled in an auto accident, and they're trying to patch him up without damaging the nerves any further. He's only twenty-eight, and he's got these two little kids and the nicest wife you'd ever want to meet. They're all being so brave, even though I know they're worried sick about the surgery and paying the bills and all."

"I'll do what I can."

"Thanks, Dr. Blake."

An hour later Mallory ran into Justin in the corridor.

"Hi," she said cheerfully, her heart thumping right on cue. For a muscle, it was amazingly discerning since it only pounded like that when Justin appeared. For once he returned her smile without any apparent reservations. The effect was as powerful as an intimate caress. Her body seemed to sway toward him with a will of its own, until she caught herself and wrapped her arms around her middle in a gesture that any student of psychology would recognize as one of denial. It didn't do a thing to stop the thunder of her heart or the racing of her pulse, but it did keep her from reaching out to touch him.

"Do you have some time?" she asked, the words coming out in a nervous rush that made her want to bite her tongue and start the whole encounter over. Justin grinned at her knowingly, and she hurried on. "I have a couple of things I'd like to discuss with you."

Justin glanced at his watch. "Will a half hour do it? I have surgery again at two."

"A half hour's fine. Want to come to my office?"

"I'd rather try the coffee shop across the street. I haven't had anything to eat today and I'm not up to tuna fish in the cafeteria."

Mallory opened her mouth to protest his poor eating habits, but he silenced her with a look. "No lectures, doctor. It's the first break I've had all day."

She grinned back at him. "Sorry. Force of habit."

It was one of those gloomy San Francisco days, when the fog never seemed to lift and the air was damp and chilly. They hurried across the street and into the steamy warmth of the restaurant. Several nurses were just vacating a booth, and as Justin and Mallory approached, the women regarded her curiously. She could hear the interested buzz of speculation as they walked away.

As soon as Justin had ordered the homemade vegetable soup and a hamburger, he leaned back and asked, "Now, then, what's so important?"

"It's Davey."

Instantly his eyes were alert and his body tense. "What about him?"

"Calm down. It's good news. After I saw you Saturday night, I stopped by here. I didn't realize it when I first went into his room, but he was awake. He spoke to me. He asked about Joey."

"Who's Joey?"

"The puppet I've been using to try to reach him. He wanted to know why I didn't have him with me. Then he really began to open up. He admitted he was scared and he talked about his mother."

"What did he say?"

"That he was afraid of her. That he'd been bad and that she was going to hit him."

"Had he been having a dream or was he remembering a specific incident? That could be important when his case goes to court."

"It's hard to tell. A little of both, I imagine. Don't you see, though, now that it's out in the open, I can really begin to work with him."

Justin relaxed and grinned at her. "That's the best news you could have given me." His hand enveloped hers and squeezed, setting off tingles that raced through her and made her toes curl. She had to force herself to concentrate on what Justin was saying. "Maybe we make a pretty good team after all."

The words echoed in Mallory's head. If Justin had spent a lifetime searching for just the right thing to say, he couldn't have done any better. She just wondered when he'd let that professional trust expand to include the personal side of their relationship as well.

"So, what happens now?" he said as the waitress put his food down.

"We try to keep him talking and try to reassure him that not all adults behave the way his mother did. He has to understand that his mother has a kind of illness, that her behavior doesn't necessarily mean she doesn't love him."

Instantly Justin's lips curved down in an angry slash. "Do you really believe that hogwash?" he said incredulously, and she felt the fragile rapport between them begin to slip away. He released her hand and began eating his soup.

"Yes, I do, and it's more than hogwash," she said staunchly, ignoring his reaction. "Maybe she was an abused child herself. Maybe she's just responding the way she was taught to respond."

"You're saying you can't break the cycle, then?" Justin said in a voice gone suddenly flat. Mallory regarded him curiously.

"I didn't say that at all. I think she can be helped, given time. She has to understand what drove her to harm Davey. Once she does that, it's possible to break the pattern."

"I guarantee you, it'll never happen." He shoved the soup bowl away and grabbed his hamburger, biting into it angrily.

"What makes you so certain? You're not an expert

in this field, are you? Or have they added psychology to the neurosurgical program?"

"I know what I'm talking about," he said unequivocally, and his hazel eyes glittered dangerously. Mallory beat a hasty tactical retreat. It was not the time to fight this particular battle. She didn't want to upset him, when he had to go back into surgery in a few more minutes.

"Okay. Don't get angry."

"Who's getting angry?" His voice rose, and his eyes flashed.

Suddenly Mallory grinned at him and propped her chin in her hand. "Do you do impressions?"

"What?" The question came out hesitantly. He stared at her, wide-eyed, clearly baffled by the seemingly irrelevant question.

"You say you're not angry. I believe you. That must mean you're into doing an impression of an angry man."

Justin moaned at her attempt at humor, and his fierce expression faded instantly. "You win."

"Were we having another contest?" she inquired innocently.

"You won't even let me give in gracefully, will you?"

"Nope," she said sweetly. "I think maybe I like watching you squirm."

"You would. It's probably a defect in your character. Now what else did you want to talk to me about? You said you had a couple of things."

"You have a patient named Harrison."

Justin looked instantly wary. "What about him?"

"Carol says he's nervous about his surgery."

His shoulders visibly tensed again. "And why would Carol be telling you this?"

"I ran into her this morning. She wanted me to mention it to you."

"Damn it, I know the man is nervous. He's my patient. I don't need some nurse running to you to tell me what's going on with him. If she had something to say, she should have come directly to me."

"She said she had."

"Well, she should have tried again."

"Why? So you could yell at her?"

"I don't yell." His fist thumped angrily on the table, shaking the silverware and sending his coffee cup skittering toward the edge. Mallory saved it from certain disaster.

She grinned impishly. "Oh, this is just another of your impressions, then?"

Justin regarded her sheepishly. "I was yelling?"

She nodded.

"Sorry."

"So, have you talked to him?" she asked reasonably, determined not to allow his fit of temper to distract her from getting a promise from him.

"Of course, I've talked to him."

"And exactly what have you told him?" she asked. "Aside from the basics such as when his surgery is scheduled? Have you discussed the risks with him, told him his chances for a full recovery, reassured him at all?"

"Mallory, has anyone ever mentioned to you that nagging has destroyed many a relationship? I let you get involved with Davey because I thought he needed you. That doesn't mean you can start barging into the middle of all my cases."

"I am not barging in," she responded calmly. "I

haven't even seen the man. I'm just passing along a message."

"Fine," he grumbled. "Message received."

"Will it be acted on?"

His gaze swept over her angrily, then he shook his head. A faint smile appeared at the corners of his mouth. "You have the persistence of a gnat. I'll see the man this afternoon. Satisfied?"

She beamed at him. "Very." She laid a hand on his. "And you won't go back and yell at Carol for talking to me, right?"

"Right," he muttered, scowling at her. "You're going to ruin my reputation as a tyrant, you know."

"I'm trying."

"Care to celebrate your victory by going to a movie with me tomorrow? I'm not on duty and I could use a night out."

The invitation took her by surprise. She'd been sure they would ease into dating far more slowly, probably beginning with some chance encounter that would lead to casual meals. That Justin was apparently ready for more sent a sharp tingle of anticipation through her. She struggled to match his casual tone, when what she wanted to do was tap-dance on the tabletop. "Sounds good to me, as long as it's not a medical thriller. They hit too close to home."

"How about a Woody Allen film?"

"They usually hit pretty close to home, too."

"Yes, but at least they're funny," he said as he paid the check. They walked back to the hospital in companionable silence. As they entered the lobby, Justin noticed that the elevator door was about to close and he took off at a run. "Tomorrow," he called back over his shoulder. "I'll pick you up at seven."

At least half a dozen nurses turned to gaze at Mallory enviously. Holding back a grin, she admitted to herself that she didn't blame them one bit. The idea of finally going out on an official date with Dr. Justin Whitmore was enough to send the most resistant woman's pulse racing and she'd stopped resisting days ago.

The movie had been billed as funny and poignant, but it didn't stand a chance of competing with Justin for Mallory's attention. She found herself so conscious of him sitting next to her in the darkened theater, his arm draped casually across the back of her seat, his fingertips brushing her shoulder, that she couldn't have described the plot if someone had offered her a million bucks.

Fortunately, Justin was one of those people who liked to rehash every scene over coffee, so she had ample opportunity to learn all about the story line secondhand. She missed that, too. She was intent on studying the curve of his lips, when they were gentled by a laugh, and the spark in his eyes, when they lingered on her.

"Are you listening to me?" he finally asked, his voice laced with laughter.

"Umm."

"Mallory?"

She was thoroughly absorbed in contemplating the pulse that was beating in his neck. Her fingers practically itched to caress the column of flesh that promised heat and literally throbbed with life. "What?" she murmured absentmindedly.

"Are you with me here?"

"Umm."

"I was thinking it might be nice to go for a ride on the zebras at the zoo. What do you think?"

"Whatever you want." Suddenly his words registered, and she glanced at him in shock. "You want to ride the zebras?"

He chuckled and she flushed with embarrassment. "I'm glad I finally got through to you," he said. "Where have you been?"

She couldn't very well admit she'd been mentally assaulting the man's body. "Just thinking."

"Dare I ask what about?"

"The hospital, Davey, my schedule for tomorrow, stuff like that." The words spilled out too quickly, too unconvincingly. Only a very dense man would have believed her, and she knew perfectly well that Justin wasn't dense.

"Do you always get such a dreamy, faraway look in your eyes when you think about work?" he inquired with tolerant amusement.

That proved it. He knew exactly what she'd been thinking or had guessed at some particularly sensual variation of it. She gulped nervously. "Well, I do love my job," she said with a valiant attempt at bravado.

"So do I, but I guarantee you it never makes my pulse race."

"Who says my pulse was racing?"

"I do," he responded. "It pays to be a doctor, you know. When I took hold of your hand a minute ago— which was barely noticed, by the way—I took your pulse. I've had patients in the emergency room with a slower heartbeat."

She glared at him. "And just what do you think that proves?"

"That you want what I want." His voice was low and all too suggestive.

"Which is?" Her blood was flowing through her like warm honey, sweet and a little wild. She was going to force him to spell it out. It would do him good to be direct for once. To her amazement, he didn't bat an eye.

"To make love." If the statement had been the least bit crude, Mallory would have denied it with the last breath in her body. Instead the words were gently coaxing and more intoxicating than the finest French champagne.

"Oh," she said in a breathless whisper as heat swirled through her and practically melted her on the spot.

"Well?" His eyes met hers and wouldn't let go. She fought to cling to some lingering shred of reason, but the only reality was Justin—Justin and the white-hot flame of desire that was burning inside her.

"Why tonight?" she managed at last.

Justin heard the hesitation in her voice, saw the hope in her eyes and knew she wanted promises he wasn't prepared to make, answers he couldn't give because he didn't fully understand them himself. He sighed and settled for honesty, even though he knew it might cost him what he wanted more than anything. "Because tonight I need you more than I've ever needed anyone before."

She nodded solemnly. "Okay."

He regarded her in surprise. He'd been prepared for a battle, and she'd offered him a surrender. "That's it? Okay?"

There was just the slightest touch of defiance in the lift of her chin, but her voice was gentle. "Make no mistake about it, I want more from you, Justin Whitmore, but for now that's enough. I need you, too."

Her acceptance of his terms threw him at first. He'd never known a woman like Mallory before, a woman totally without guile, a woman willing to accept a relationship that was free of demands. No, that wasn't exactly true. He had known women who wanted nothing more than a pleasurable night in bed, but their easy ways had turned him off. Instinctively he knew that Mallory was different and that she was coming to him out of genuine caring. She was asking no more than he was prepared to give because it was the only way she could show him exactly how much she did care.

"My place or yours?" he said with a touch of irony. It was also a test of sorts. If she chose his, it would mean she was hoping for more than she was letting on. If she invited him to her place, she was allowing him the freedom to leave when he wanted.

"Mine," she said readily, and at that instant he realized he was a little bit in love with her. It terrified him, but he couldn't have changed the direction of the night now if he'd wanted to. His body ached with needing her. For days now he had wanted to know the feel of her beneath him, the scent of her surrounding him. He wondered how he could possibly last until they got to her apartment.

He did it by avoiding all contact with her, not even a hand on her elbow as she got out of his car or the most fleeting caress of her cheek. He knew that the tiniest spark could ignite a fire inside him that would rage until it burned itself out in her arms.

Her apartment was not at all what he'd expected. Except for the books scattered everywhere, it was bland and uninteresting. Mallory noted his surprised expression.

"Awful, isn't it?"

"It's just not you. It doesn't have any life to it."

"Thank you," she said, standing on tiptoe to press a kiss against his cheek. His arms went around her automatically and he pressed her head into his shoulder. A deep sigh of satisfaction rippled through him, followed by an utter sense of peace. Nothing had ever felt so right before. Despite his fear that he would rush things, he found now that he could wait. There was none of his usual sense of urgency, spawned by a need to get things over with so he could retreat to emotional safety. The desire that was building in him now was a gentler sort, a yearning to discover every nuance of this woman who was so still and quiet and patient in his embrace.

As he might have expected, though, it was Mallory who broke the silence. "You aren't going to sleep on me, are you, doctor?" she said lightly, her breath whispering past his ear.

He tilted her more intimately against him. "Does that answer your question?"

She wriggled with the slinky sensuality of a cat, and Justin gasped at the shock of pleasure that ripped through him. The blazing inferno wasn't nearly as far away as he'd thought. "Do that again, and I won't be able to stand up."

"Then I suggest we lie down," she said with the boldness that unnerved him, even as it drew him on.

She turned to lead him into the bedroom, but suddenly hesitant, he halted and stared deep into her eyes, searching for doubts. He saw none in the shining depths, but he asked anyway. "Are you absolutely sure this is what you want?"

"Absolutely," she said without hesitation. "What about you?"

The question was startling, and suddenly a part of him wanted to turn and run from this woman. She was giving him every chance to do just that, but freedom, he was discovering, was sometimes the most binding gift of all.

"I'm sure," he said with more conviction than he felt. He knew that this would be a night from which there might very well be no turning back, but it was an experience he wanted more than he'd ever wanted anything before. He sensed that if he ran, he'd be losing far more than a few hours of passion.

They shed their clothes by moonlight, taking turns so they could enjoy each moment. Mallory turned the undressing into a playful striptease that had him almost panting, his body hot and throbbing with the same urgency he'd been so certain earlier he couldn't control. He was hanging on now by the slightest thread.

Standing just out of his reach, Mallory was lovely, her pearly skin shimmering in the pale light, her body a rare combination of lush curves and fragility. He moved closer and his fingers trembled as they touched the surprising fullness of her breasts. She was as beautiful as a marble statue of the goddess of love, but her flesh was warm and supple and far more alluring. His tentative touch became strong and sure as he teased her nipples into rigid peaks and drew a ragged groan from her.

His lips followed, tasting the faint saltiness of her skin, tugging gently until she shivered against him and a low moan of pleasure sighed past her lips. Her head was thrown back, baring the slender column of her neck to his marauding mouth. His own muscles were tight with tension as her nails dug into his shoulders and she pulled him to her.

When at last his hands caressed the satin length of her legs, hesitating for what seemed an eternity on the heated flesh of her thighs, she trembled beneath him.

"Touch me, please," she urged, her eyes bright and shining as they stared directly into his with frankness and expectancy. "Please."

After that quiet plea, there was no holding back. His touch glided over her, lingering at places that made her practically purr with pleasure. With each soft gasp, his own excitement increased until his nerves were stretched taut, the muscles in his thighs and buttocks bunched tight.

She opened herself to him then and with a gentle thrust he was inside her, wrapped in her silken heat, swept away on a tide of passion so intense, so violent that he lay spent and shaken in its quiet aftermath. He wanted to weep at the joy of such a magnificent union, yet he trembled, instead, at its implications. Never before had he given himself so completely. Never before had any woman touched his soul.

Never before had he been so afraid.

Mallory curled herself contentedly into the welcoming shelter of his arms and ran her fingers across his damp chest. "There may be hope for you yet," she said with a tiny sigh of satisfaction.

"Really," he said with a touch of wry humor. "In what way? I thought this was pretty spectacular just the way it was."

"Exactly," she agreed, her gaze locked with his. "But you're a little like Davey."

Justin's breath caught in his throat as she continued, "Tonight was only the first step."

"Toward what?"

"Trust."

Justin sighed and drew her to him. He was startled at the depth of her understanding of him and he prayed she was right.

Maybe this time, he promised himself. Maybe this time, with this woman trust would come.

Chapter 6

Dr. Joshua Marshall was angry. Mallory could tell because his bushy eyebrows were knit together in a frown and he refused to look her straight in the eye. His tone, however, was extraordinarily civil, especially considering that it was barely eight in the morning. Outside the San Francisco fog had been swept away on an early breeze and Mallory had had high hopes for a gloriously happy day. Those hopes had just been effectively dashed.

"We have a problem, Dr. Blake," Dr. Marshall said in the voice of a man who found the thought of all problems, except those of a psychological nature, distasteful.

Mallory groaned mentally. After the wonderful night she had just spent in Justin's arms, this was no way to begin a new day, a promising new life. "What can I do to help?" she asked.

"There has been a complaint." He made the announcement as though the very possibility of anyone complaining about a member of his staff was extraordinary.

Mallory waited for more. He cleared his throat, put the tips of his fingers together to form a pyramid and stared at the fading print on the wall behind her. He seemed to expect her to guess the rest, but she wasn't about to play that game.

He cleared his throat again. "Yes, well, there are those who seem to feel you are spending too much time with one of your patients."

"Those?" she repeated. "Could you be more specific?"

"Actually, it was the mother of another patient who brought this to my attention."

"I see. And what is this mother's objection exactly?"

"She feels you are showing favoritism, that her own child is being neglected while you pursue an avid interest in one particular case."

"That one particular case being Davey Landers."

"Yes, I believe that was the name she mentioned." His gaze had drifted up to study the ceiling tiles, which were yellowing with age and stained by a leak from the water pipes. She knew perfectly well it was not the first time he'd seen them, so there was no reason for his sudden preoccupation with them.

Mallory bit her lip to keep from bellowing at him. She knew that was no way to reach a man who was deaf to anything but subservience. "Dr. Marshall, I'm terribly sorry if someone has complained to you about my conduct, but I assure you that the time I spend with Davey is not taking my attention away from my other duties. My appointments are carefully scheduled and logged. My charts are up-to-date. Beyond his arranged therapy session, I see Davey only on my own time at the end of the day."

Dr. Marshall took so long to answer, she wondered if he'd drifted off to sleep. His eyes certainly seemed to be closed. Perhaps he was praying for fortitude. "I see," he said finally. "Of course, I can't control what you do on your own time, Dr. Blake, but I must advise you that the appearance of preferential treatment is not good, not good at all."

He peered at her intently, his brown eyes shining through the thick lenses of his glasses. "I hope you understand what I'm saying."

"I think I do, Dr. Marshall."

He nodded in satisfaction. "Then we'll say no more about the subject." He began straightening the already tidy piles of paper on his desk. Clearly, he considered her dismissed. She didn't budge.

"Yes, we will say more, sir," Mallory contradicted politely, but firmly. His hands stilled, and he blinked at her. She wondered if anyone had ever challenged him before. "I will make every effort to see that none of my patients—or their mothers—feel slighted, but I will not refrain from spending my spare time with Davey. He is in far more desperate shape than the other children here, and I'm going to do everything in my power to help him. If you object to that, you can have my resignation right now."

Dr. Marshall's eyes had widened during her outburst. He seemed stunned, probably by the grim prospect of going through another long recruitment process to find her replacement. "Now, now, my dear, let's not be hasty.

I'm sure it's all just a misunderstanding. Of course, I want you to do what you think best for the patient."

"Thank you," she said and headed for the door.

"One last thing, though, Dr. Blake."

"Yes?"

"Try to remember the importance of objectivity. It's vital in our business."

Mallory wasn't absolutely certain, but there seemed to be the faintest suggestion of a smile on Dr. Marshall's face as she gently closed the door behind her. She had the most peculiar feeling she had just passed some sort of test.

Still, throughout the day, Dr. Marshall's reminder haunted her. Was she allowing herself to become too involved with Davey? Was it possible that she'd become too protective, almost motherly, rather than thinking as a professional about the hard decisions that had to be made about his future? Her doubts were put to the test later in the day.

She was in Davey's room late that afternoon listening to his hesitant little voice excitedly describing an outing Justin had promised him, when Rachel came to the door and beckoned to her. She nodded.

"Davey, I'll be right back. Mrs. Jackson needs to see me for a minute."

Blue eyes regarded her hopefully. "You will come back?"

"Promise, sport."

Outside, she discovered a tall, blond woman with the social worker, a woman so slender, polished and sophisticated she made Mallory feel dowdy. Mallory was compelled to remind herself that she was wearing perfectly stylish clothes and didn't have an ounce of extra flesh on her.

"Mallory, this is Jenny Landers."

Mallory's eyes widened incredulously and her heart thudded to a stop. "Davey's mother?"

The woman nodded, but didn't meet her gaze. Guilt and anguish made her face seem old beyond its years. Mallory could read the signs; the woman's nerves were stretched to the breaking point. Even now she was probably still struggling to understand how her life had veered so wildly out of control. Mallory tried very hard to reserve judgment, but she found herself wanting to strike the woman on the spot, to inflict some small measure of the pain she'd inflicted on Davey. So much for objectivity!

"She wants to see Davey," Rachel said as Mallory fought to keep her expression impassive. "What do you think? Protective services said it was fine as long as I got an okay from you and stayed with her. Is he ready to see her?"

Mallory longed to say no. All she wanted was to go back into that room, wrap her arms around Davey and make certain that no harm would come to him, that no bad memories would turn his dreams back into nightmares. He had only mentioned his mother a few times since that first night he'd spoken to Mallory, but each time his voice had quivered. Clearly, just the thought of his mother still terrified him.

Yet Mallory also knew that there would come a time when Jenny Landers and her son might be back together, when the courts would consider the woman well and able to care for Davey again. The healing needed to begin soon, and it was far better for the process to start with Rachel and her present.

"Okay," she said at last. "Let's play it by ear, though." She looked directly into Jenny Landers's blue eyes, which were so like Davey's. They were amazingly hesitant, in sharp contrast to her overall appearance, which projected cool self-assurance. If Mallory hadn't been trained to see beyond the surface, she would never have pegged Jenny Landers as anything other than a lovely, intelligent socialite. It was that veneer that had probably kept her from getting the help she and Davey had needed for so long.

"If Davey seems to be upset by your visit, I want you to go immediately."

"I understand," Mrs. Landers said in a soft, cultured voice that shook ever so slightly.

Mallory went in first. Davey was sitting up in bed, coloring with the crayons she had brought him earlier.

"Davey, there's someone special here to see you," she said, wishing she'd had more time to prepare him, more time to assess what his reaction might be. He looked up from the picture and started to lift it to show to her. Then his gaze fell on the woman standing in the doorway behind her and he seemed to withdraw into himself. He shoved the coloring book and crayons away angrily and curled up on his side, his back turned toward them. Mallory put her hand on his arm. Rather than recoiling, this time he took her hand and clung to it.

"It's okay, sweetie. I'm going to be right here. Your mom just wants to make sure you're doing okay." After a moment Davey rolled over.

Mrs. Landers stepped closer to the bed. She reached out with her hand, then flinched and withdrew it when she saw the look of terror in Davey's eyes. "I'm so sorry, baby," she said in a voice that was barely above a whisper and ragged with emotion. "Please, try to understand. I never meant to hurt you. Could I stay for a little while?"

Davey's gaze shot to Mallory for reassurance. At her nod, he sighed and visibly relaxed. Jenny Landers seemed to take that as permission to stay. She sat next to the bed and talked to him softly, fighting against tears the whole time. Mallory almost felt pity for her as she watched. The woman was trying very hard to make things right again, and Davey wasn't responding at all. Eventually, he turned on his side and closed his eyes, effectively shutting his mother out. It was impossible to tell whether he was asleep or only feigning.

The tension in the room was palpable, and the feeling was so intense that it seemed they'd been there an eternity. But only a short time had passed, while Jenny Landers stared helplessly at her motionless son before Justin strode through the door. From the violent look in his eyes, it was clear he'd already heard about Davey's visitor.

Justin took in the scene with a single, sweeping, furious glance, but before he could blow up, Mallory signaled to him, her face a mask of desperation. Only an extraordinary amount of willpower kept him from screaming at the lot of them, especially Mallory. What could she possibly have been thinking of to allow this to happen?

She came to his side, reaching out to him, then drawing back when she saw his expression. "Please," she whispered as he glared at her. All of the powerful, happy feelings of the night before abruptly vanished.

"Don't upset Davey. Don't let him see how angry you are," she pleaded. "He's handling this okay, and she'll be gone soon."

Justin swallowed the tirade he'd been planning all the way upstairs from the surgeons' lounge, where he'd been when one of the nurses had phoned him to tell him what was happening. Rage had overwhelmed him and sent him racing through the halls. His only thought was to protect Davey, to be there to reassure him. Never once had he considered the possibility that Mallory might already be present, that she might actually have condoned the visit.

With his fists clenched at his sides, he tried to understand the feeling of betrayal that swept through him upon discovering that Mallory was here. Over the past couple of weeks, especially after last night, he'd been starting to trust her, just as Davey had finally begun to reach out to him. In conspiring with Rachel to arrange this outrageous meeting between Davey and the mother who had repeatedly harmed him physically and emotionally, she had let them both down.

He gazed at Mallory and found he could hardly bear to look at her. It was as though he'd never seen her before, never realized the duplicity of which she was capable. At the same time, his body yearned for a repeat of her touch, for the comfort, gentleness and passion he'd found in her arms and in no one else's. His uncontrollable reaction only infuriated him more.

"I'll be outside," he said tersely and stormed out of the room. He wanted to leave the hospital, to pound on the walls, to throw things, but he didn't. He forced himself to remain in case Davey needed him.

He paced for what seemed like hours, but it was

only a short time later when Rachel and Jenny Landers came out of the room. Rachel cast a troubled glance in his direction, then hurried on with Davey's mother. It was another ten or fifteen minutes more before Mallory came into the hall and stood defiantly before him like an unrepentant child.

"Okay, Justin. Let's have it," she challenged. "I know you're just dying to tell me what a traitor I am."

At the sight of her facing him so spiritedly, as determined and beautiful as ever, all the fight drained out of him. "Just tell me why you did it."

"Justin, I didn't want to at first, but I had no choice."

"We always have a choice."

"Not this time. This was something that had to happen sooner or later. The courts would have insisted on it."

Fury raged through him all over again. "And you support the system above all else, is that it?" His angry gaze swept over her disdainfully. "It was the damn system that allowed this to happen to Davey in the first place. Are you planning to send him back to his mother the minute he's well enough to withstand another beating?"

"It's not my decision."

"That's a cop-out and you know it."

"No, it's not. It isn't my decision. The courts will decide."

"Mallory, come off it. You're a professional. Fool that I am, I allowed you on this case. You know perfectly well you will be asked to make a recommendation."

Mallory sighed heavily. "Possibly. If that happens, I'd have to know a lot more than I know now before I could decide what to say."

"What's to know? The woman has been abusing that child for months, probably years. Do you honestly expect her to stop now?"

"With counseling, it's possible," she said, stubborn to the end.

"You blasted shrinks are all alike, aren't you? You accused me once of being arrogant. What about you? Are you so sure that you or any other psychologist has the power to turn someone's behavior around so completely? Are you going to risk that boy's life to find out if the therapy has worked?" He shook his head. Her betrayal seeped into him and filled him with sorrow. "I don't understand how you could do this," he said wearily. "Especially after last night. Didn't that mean anything to you?"

"One thing has nothing to do with the other."

"Of course it does. It all has to do with trust. You said that yourself. You said you were on Davey's side. I believed you."

"I am."

"Like hell," he muttered angrily. He started to say more, then threw up his hands in disgust and walked away.

"Justin!"

He heard the hurt in her voice, the desperation, and knew exactly what she was going through. His own pain ran just as deep, perhaps even deeper because he'd allowed her to touch a part of him that had been unreachable for years. Once again he had come close to caring and once again it had ended in bitterness and regret.

"Justin, please, you have to listen to my side."

He turned then and stared at her, his expression cold

and implacable. He steeled himself against the injured look he knew he would see in her eyes.

"No," he said softly. "No, I don't."

A sob rose in Mallory's throat as she watched Justin walk away from her. She choked it back and kept herself from running after him, but just barely. They both needed to calm down. They both needed time to put the entire situation into perspective. She needed time, in fact, to figure out if there might not be some truth to what Justin had said.

Perhaps she was a bit of a Pollyanna, an eternal optimist. Not everyone could be helped. She'd be a fool not to realize that there were individuals who didn't want to change. There were others whose problems ran so deep that it would take years of analysis to discover the causes and even then change might not be possible without months, perhaps years more of therapy.

There was no way she could possibly know which category Jenny Landers fell into without spending time with the woman. She also needed more time with Davey. For her to make any judgments about the Landerses' future, she would need more than guesswork. She resolved to begin in the morning by asking Rachel to arrange an appointment with Jenny Landers. She would do it for Justin and for herself, but most of all, she would do it for Davey.

Still thinking about the horrible scene at the hospital, she walked into her apartment late that afternoon just as the phone began ringing. Maybe it was Justin, she thought, her heart slamming against her ribs as she picked it up.

"Mallory, it's Rachel. Are you okay?"

She closed her eyes in disappointment. "Fine," she said, her voice flat.

"You don't sound fine. I was worried about what happened at the hospital. Justin looked fit to kill. I wanted to talk to him, but I couldn't hang around. Did you all work things out after we left?"

"No. He thinks I betrayed him and Davey."

"I'm sorry. It's my fault. I should never have brought Jenny Landers there."

"Don't be crazy. That's your job. I just wish I'd had more warning. Maybe I could have done something to make things go more smoothly."

"For Davey or for Justin?"

"Both of them," she admitted ruefully.

"Do you think Davey's okay?"

"He was when I left. We talked a little, and he said he'd been scared when she first came in, but he wasn't afraid after that. You can do me a favor, though."

"What's that?"

"I'd like to meet with Mrs. Landers. There are a lot of unanswered questions. I don't even know what the situation is with Davey's father, for instance. Can you set up an appointment?"

"The court has already assigned a psychologist for her."

"I know, but I'd still like to talk to her. Off the record, if that's what it takes. It'll help me with Davey's therapy."

"Okay, girl. I'll see what I can do. You want to come over for dinner tonight? It's potluck, but we'd love to have you."

"Thanks, but no. I think I'll take a bath and get a good night's sleep."

"Who are you trying to kid? You won't sleep a wink. You're going to sit there and wait for the phone to ring."

Mallory gave a dry chuckle. "I'd forgotten that you probably took almost as many psychology courses as I did."

"Sure you won't change your mind and come over? I'll let you tell the kids a bedtime story."

"I'd probably put scary monsters in it, and they'd be awake all night. Thanks for the offer, but I'll take a rain check."

"Okay. I'll see you in the morning and I'll do what I can about that appointment."

As soon as she'd hung up, Mallory decided to make good on at least part of the excuse she'd given Rachel. She went into the bathroom and turned the water on full force and poured in a spoonful of bubbling bath crystals. While the tub filled, she fixed herself a glass of wine and turned the radio on.

Within minutes, she was lying back in the steaming, fragrant water, her eyes closed. It felt like heaven. She took a sip of wine and tried a little self-hypnosis, hoping to clear her head and improve her perspective on things.

From the beginning, her treatment of Davey had been shaded by Justin's attitude. She had approached the case cautiously, fearing that at the first sign of displeasure, Justin would ban her from the child's room. It was time she began thinking of herself as a professional again, doing what she thought was best, and Justin be damned. It was good advice, but she wondered if she'd have the strength to take it.

When she stepped out of the tub at last, she wrapped herself in a thick terry-cloth robe and glanced in the mirror. Her blue-green eyes were wide, her cheeks flushed. Her black hair framed her face in wispy curls. She looked sleepily sensual.

"What a waste," she muttered under her breath as she padded barefoot into the kitchen and fixed herself a plate of cheese and crackers.

The doorbell rang as she was heading for the bedroom and the mystery novel she'd been wanting to finish for days now. She peered through the peephole and saw a distorted image of Justin in the hallway. He was pacing nervously. Her heart lurched unsteadily at the sight of him, but she steeled herself to stick to her resolve to put their relationship on hold while she concentrated on what was best for Davey.

"What do you want?" she called through the door, knowing perfectly well that keeping it closed was a cowardly thing to do. But she was afraid that without that wooden barrier between them her resolve would melt.

"We need to talk."

"Hey, I wanted to talk earlier. You're the one who walked away."

"I don't want to talk through a damn door."

"Call for an appointment."

"Mallory, I know you're angry, and you probably have every right to be, but this is ridiculous. We're two intelligent adults. We should be able to talk this out."

"Oh, hell," she muttered and threw open the door. She positioned her body to block the entrance. "Talk."

"Inside."

"Here."

"Mallory!"

She glowered up at him until his determined gaze faltered.

"I'm sorry," he said at last.

"Thank you."

"Now can we please talk? Inside?"

Reluctantly, sensing that she was making a decision about more than conversation, Mallory stepped aside. Justin brushed past her so quickly it brought a half smile to her lips. Obviously, he wasn't taking any chances that she'd renege on the offer.

"Do you want something to drink?"

"Club soda, Perrier, whatever you have."

"With lime?"

"Fine."

Justin started to follow her into the tiny kitchen, then seemed to think better of it. He went into the living room and began to pace again, as he'd done outside her door. His shoulders were hunched, his hands jammed in his pockets. Mallory felt a twinge of sympathy and immediately gave herself a stern lecture. This was no time to go all soft and sentimental about the man. He owed her more of an apology than that cursory one he'd delivered a few minutes earlier.

She took his drink to him and settled herself in a chair, then gazed up at him expectantly. "I'm waiting."

He glanced at her in confusion. "Waiting?"

"You came here to talk."

"Right."

He stalked from one end of the tiny room to the other, which did nothing to soothe Mallory's nerves. She wanted to wrench the words out of him, but she sat patiently and waited.

"I still don't understand what happened this after-noon," he said at last. He sat down across from her, his knees splayed. He leaned toward her and studied her face as if by looking hard enough he could see into her soul.

Mallory returned his gaze evenly. "What don't you understand?"

"I just can't see where you're coming from. You're supposed to have Davey's best interests at heart."

"I do."

"Then how could you let that woman near him?"

"She's his mother. It will be better for everyone if we can bring the two of them back together eventually, but only, *only,* if Jenny Landers is ready to take responsibility for her actions, to bring her anger under control."

"That's just the problem. How do you know when that happens? Rationally, what you say makes sense. A child should be with his family, and everyone should try to work and make that happen."

"We're agreed on that much, then."

"My problem is that what the textbooks and the courts say should happen doesn't take into account the specific human beings. Not every family can be turned into a loving unit. Not every child is better off at home. Some of them would even be better off with strangers. They might be lonely, but at least they'd live."

Justin gazed at Mallory, pleading for her to understand. It was so important that she grasp his point of view, that she realize how much it mattered to him that Davey Landers should have a real chance to be a happy, healthy child. "Do you see what I'm saying?"

"Of course I do. I don't want to see Davey hurt again. I promise you I'll do everything in my power to see that doesn't happen. I've asked Rachel to make an appointment with his mother. Once I've talked to her, maybe we'll all have a better idea of where things stand."

Justin still wasn't satisfied, and he pressed harder. "Are you confident you'll be able to get a real fix on where she's coming from? A lot of people are good at faking their emotions."

"There are no guarantees. I could make a mistake. I'm only human, but I am trained to read what people don't say, as well as what they do. I don't think she'll be able to hide her real feelings from me."

"What did you think of her today?"

"On the surface, she's sophisticated, cool, self-confident. Underneath, she's a deeply troubled woman. She knows what she did was wrong, but I can't tell if she realizes why she did it. Maybe it was a cry for help. If so, then there's a real chance that therapy can make a difference."

Justin rubbed his tired eyes. "I hope to God you're right."

"We've talked about this before, but you've never really given me a straight answer. Davey really matters to you, doesn't he?"

"He's my patient."

"Justin, please, why can't you just say it? You care about him."

"Okay, damn it. Yes. I care about him."

"Was that so difficult?"

Difficult? A month, even a week ago, he would have found it impossible. He'd kept himself from having feelings for anyone, much less admitting to any. Now suddenly emotions were sweeping through him like a river that was flooding out of control. He met Mallory's gaze and saw the compassion and love shining there. It made him feel incredibly good inside, but it also terrified him.

Love was not an emotion with which he had much

familiarity. Since childhood, he'd distanced himself from people. To him, caring was equated with pain, and he'd learned to protect himself from it. The walls he'd built were so thick, they could have withstood an assault by tanks.

But they couldn't withstand the gentle smile on Mallory's lips. For the first time he became aware of what she was wearing—or rather not wearing. The robe, though thick enough to conceal her body, was held closed only by the belt tied around her waist. The V-neckline dipped low to expose a creamy curve of breast. The bottom parted to reveal an enticing expanse of slender thigh. Blood surged through him, his arousal so sudden and full it was almost painful.

"Come here," he whispered in a voice that was hoarse with longing. He thought he'd come merely to apologize, to extract a promise. He knew now that he wanted much more. It troubled him that he still needed her so badly after what she'd done, but he did. She'd brought something into his life that he now found irresistible.

To his astonishment and overpowering relief, Mallory was there for him. If she had questions, she didn't ask them. If she had doubts, she didn't voice them. She just gave—her body, her love, and he, God help him, took everything she offered.

Chapter 7

In the morning Mallory could practically feel Justin withdrawing from her, even before he took his arms away. He had come to her again last night in need, instinctively seeking her out, even though he felt she'd betrayed him. Vulnerable and in pain, he had reached out to her, trusting her to be there for him. It had told her what she needed to know without his having said a word. She wondered if he even recognized the significance of his actions.

More than likely, at some subconscious level he did, she decided. It would explain the subtle shift in his attitude this morning, the obvious regrets she could read in the depths of his eyes, the barriers that were slipping back into place. Justin might slowly be starting to care deeply about her, but he was going to go down fighting.

She wasn't about to allow him to run, though, not

without one hell of a battle. For better or worse, she seemed to share his fate. She had fallen in love with the impossible man and she had every intention of seeing that they got the chance they deserved.

She began her campaign to lure him back in one of the oldest ways known to women—appealing to the seemingly bottomless pit of his appetite, an appetite he never had time to fully satisfy. She made a hearty breakfast and had it on the table by the time he'd showered and dressed. She could see the indecision in his eyes as he looked at steaming coffee, crisp bacon, tempting French toast and warm maple syrup. Apparently his intuition told him that it came with what he would consider a particularly high price tag. Smart man, she thought, turning away with a smug grin, but all that intelligence wasn't going to do him a bit of good.

He regarded her warily. "I don't have much time."

"Surgery starts late today," she said, pouring coffee into his cup.

He grinned ruefully. "I knew it wasn't wise to get involved with a woman who knows the hospital schedule almost as well as I do."

"Are we involved?" she asked bluntly.

Justin straightened his tie with nervous deliberation and sank down in a chair. "I walked right into that one, didn't I?"

"Pretty much. Care to answer?"

"Do I have a choice?"

"We always have choices, isn't that what you told me yesterday?"

"My God, now you're going to throw my own words back in my face."

"Only because you're sometimes very wise."

"Don't start tossing compliments around. It's not your style."

"What is my style?"

"You tend to be brutally frank, at least with me."

"I've found it pays." She regarded him candidly. "Can you deal with that?"

"I don't know," he admitted. "As long as we're being so honest, it makes me nervous."

"Why?" She studied him closely, noted that he was toying with his French toast, cutting it into tiny pieces, but not lifting a single one to his lips. "Never mind. I think I can guess. Let me phrase it another way. Do you enjoy playing games, not knowing where you stand with people?"

"Of course not."

"Well, there you have it then. That's all I want for us. Honesty. I don't want to waste time playing hide-and-seek with a man who has no intention of letting me see beyond the superficial. To develop that kind of relationship involves trust. It involves risks. I'm willing to put my feelings on the line. Are you?"

Justin's fork clattered to his plate and he gazed at her despondently. She resisted a very strong urge to give the man a break.

"How can you be so damned sure of yourself?" he growled. "What makes you think this will work? The chemistry?"

"That's certainly part of it, but far from the whole thing. I can't explain it exactly. It's just something you know, something you feel in your heart."

"I can't even be sure what my feelings are. I've spent a lifetime hiding from them."

She was surprised at getting even that much of an

admission from him, and responded cautiously. "That's fair. I'm willing to take things one day at a time until you figure this out for yourself, but I want you to be clear about one thing. I had a very happy marriage once. I know what that kind of sharing can be like and I'm not about to have a casual fling. I think you're something pretty special, Justin, but I won't play games with you. I want as much honesty as you're capable of giving me all along the way and I'll give you the same thing." Her lips curved in a faint smile. "Whether you want to hear it or not."

Her eyes locked with his and she waited breathlessly for a reaction. Any reaction. Justin appeared too stunned to speak. It was as though he'd just been offered a vacation for two around the world and wasn't quite sure whether he dared accept since it would mean taking along a companion, someone who might get too close to him.

"Well," she said finally, the words formed through sheer bravado, "do we go on from here or not?"

"That all depends," he said slowly.

"On what?"

"How patient you're willing to be. I learned a long time ago to protect myself from betrayal. I don't trust easily. Yesterday you shattered the trust I was beginning to feel toward you."

"And last night? Why did you come here?"

He sighed. "I can't explain last night."

"Lust?"

"No, damn it. It was more than that."

"Thank you."

"That doesn't mean we can work things out. I'm no good at relationships."

"Because you don't want to be?"

"Maybe."

"Are you willing to walk out of here this morning and forget the closeness we've shared?"

He faced her defiantly, his eyes glittering. "I want to."

"Then go."

He pushed his chair back, and Mallory's breath caught in her throat. His eyes met hers and held. Time fell away until at last he said unevenly, "I don't think I can."

Mallory's heart, which she'd been certain would never function again, began to beat slowly. "I wish you sounded happier about that. What's made it so difficult for you to trust people, Justin? Is it your own judgment you really don't trust?"

"You're analyzing me again."

"Just trying to understand. Talk to me. Make me see what's made you so afraid to believe in anyone."

"Shall I take you back to my childhood, doctor? Isn't that where you all believe everything starts?" His tone was sarcastic and tinged with bitterness. Mallory refused to be goaded.

"For many people, yes. Is that when it began for you?"

She waited expectantly, sure that the breakthrough was coming, that the information she needed to truly understand him was about to come pouring out.

"I have to go," he said finally, and she only barely managed to conceal her frustration. This time, though, she let him go.

"Why don't we see Davey together this afternoon?"

she suggested. "You can see for yourself how he's taking that meeting with his mother."

Justin nodded. "I should be able to get there by five-thirty. Can you hang around that late?"

"I'll be there."

He stood hesitantly in the doorway, then came back and brushed a kiss across her forehead. Because of the tender promise it held, that gentle, fleeting touch meant more to Mallory than all the heated, unrestrained passion of the night before.

The day continued as the morning had begun, a blend of highs and lows that kept Mallory continually off balance.

Rachel had arranged the meeting with Jenny Landers for late morning, and it had been filled with revelations. Mallory felt as though she was beginning to understand what made the woman tick and she also felt confident that Davey's mother was on the road to recovery. Mrs. Landers had agreed to continue seeing her, as well as her own psychologist until Davey's future was resolved and her own day of reckoning before a judge was over.

Mallory had just come from that meeting, when she ran into Carol.

"You're a miracle worker," the head nurse proclaimed.

"And to think I don't even hold a degree in that," Mallory retorted. "What is this miracle you think I've worked."

"Dr. Whitmore. He spent nearly a half hour with Mr. Harrison this morning before his surgery. I can't tell you what a difference it made. Mr. Harrison was actually smiling when I went in to prep him for the operation. He thinks Dr. Whitmore is the greatest."

"I'm glad it worked out," Mallory said, more pleased than she was letting on. Not only was she delighted for Mr. Harrison's sake, but for Justin's. It was another chip out of that wall of reserve he'd built around himself. "You might mention it to Dr. Whitmore, when you see him. He'll be glad to know it made a difference."

"I already told him. Do you know the man actually walked off whistling?"

Mallory grinned as she walked away. Justin's reputation as a tyrant truly was tumbling down. She wondered if he was going to be furious about it.

She was still in an upbeat mood when she finally got back to pediatrics. It lasted until the head nurse there came running up. "Thank goodness you're here."

"What's the problem?"

"It's Davey. He's refusing to eat again and he's been throwing tantrums all day."

"Why didn't you call me before?"

"We tried to phone you, but you didn't respond. I thought maybe you weren't in the hospital."

Mallory pulled her phone from her purse and pressed a button. Nothing happened. "The battery's dead. I'll recharge it after I'm finished with Davey. Thanks."

"Sure. Good luck."

Even without the warning, Mallory would have sensed Davey's mood the minute she walked into the room. His whole body was tensed in anger and, though he glanced at her, he shut his eyes immediately and turned his back on her.

"So, sport, what's the problem? I hear you've been giving the staff a rough time today." She lifted the lid off the food on his dinner tray. "What's the matter with the food? I thought you loved hamburgers."

Davey drew his knees up to his chest. Mallory grasped his shoulders gently but firmly and turned him toward her.

"You have to eat, if you're going to get out of this place."

"Don't want to get out," he said as a tear slid down his cheek. Mallory brushed the tear away.

"How come?"

"Won't go home," he said stubbornly, but his lower lip trembled.

"Because of your mother?"

He nodded.

"You know, Davey, we won't make you go home unless we're very sure that nothing bad will ever happen to you there again."

"Can't I come home with you and Dr. Justin?" he begged.

Mallory ignored the way he had come to link the two of them together. "No, sweetie. But we can find another family for you, if it doesn't work out for you to go back with your mom."

His lip curled into a pout.

She hesitated, then asked gently, "Davey, how do you feel about your dad?"

She wasn't at all prepared for the violence of his reaction. Instantly he rolled away from her again and buried his face in the pillow. His thin shoulders shook with sobs.

"Davey, don't cry, sweetie. It's okay to miss your dad."

"My fault." The words were muffled.

"What's your fault? That your dad went away? That's not true."

"Mom said."

"She was just angry. She needed to blame somebody. It was not your fault. We talked today, and she told me all about it. Sometimes grown-ups have problems they don't know how to handle and they have to blame somebody else for them."

His shoulders stilled, and she could tell he was listening to her. "You know how you got mad today and took it out on the nurses? You weren't really mad at them, were you?"

He shook his head.

"You were mad at your mom and me and maybe even a little bit at yourself, weren't you? But you blamed the nurses and everybody else. That's sort of what your mom was doing when she said it was your fault that your dad went away. It hurt too much if she admitted it might be her fault."

"He didn't go because I was bad?"

"No. In fact, I talked to him myself this morning, and he's going to come to see you."

Davey turned to her then, his eyes wide and shimmering with tears. "He's really going to come?"

"He'll be here first thing in the morning. He's going to take a plane tonight."

"Why didn't he come before? I've been here a long time."

"He would have, but he didn't know you were sick." Jenny Landers hadn't had the nerve to call him, and her own parents were still trying to pretend none of it had happened. They were staunchly defending Jenny to the authorities.

"Will he take me away with him?"

"That's something we'll have to talk about more after

he gets here. He and your mom have a lot of things to work out."

"He's not mad 'cause I'm in the hospital?"

"Not at you."

A worried frown puckered his brow. "He won't yell at Mom, will he? They yelled all the time before he went away."

"How did that make you feel?"

"Sad," he said promptly. "And…and scared."

"I can understand that. I'll bet you even thought that was your fault, too."

He nodded. "I tried to be better, but it didn't change anything," he whispered sorrowfully.

"That's because they're the only ones who can make things change. You know something else? Even though they were mad at each other that didn't mean they were mad at you. When grown-ups have problems sometimes that gets pretty confusing, and you forget that they still love you in spite of everything."

Davey sighed. A glimmer of excitement flickered in his eyes. "My dad will really be here in the morning," he repeated as if he still couldn't quite believe it.

"Promise. Now how about some food? I'll get this warmed up for you."

"Okay."

As Mallory took the tray from the room, she found Justin leaning against the wall, his complexion ashen. Instantly worried, she touched his cheek.

"Are you all right?"

"Fine."

"You look lousy. Why don't you go sit down?"

"In a minute. Take the tray on down to the nurses' station and heat it. I'll be okay."

When she came back, he was with Davey, and the two of them were talking about baseball. Opening day was coming up soon, and Davey was planning to hold Justin to his promise that they could go. She sat back and listened to the excited chatter, watching Justin's face for some clue about what had upset him so earlier. There wasn't a single sign now that anything had been amiss. As he talked with Davey, he was animated, his pallor gone. She began to wonder if she'd only imagined the entire incident in the hallway.

Davey drew her into the conversation before her imagination could run wild, and for the next hour she put her confusion aside. Then she realized that Justin was prolonging his visit to avoid being alone with her. As Davey's eyelids fluttered down for the third time, she insisted that they leave.

Outside the room, she touched Justin's cheek gently. "You look beat. Was it a rough day?"

"It wasn't the greatest," he admitted. He seemed to struggle with something, then finally asked, "Do you have some time?"

"Sure."

"Let's go downstairs for some coffee. I could use someone to talk to."

Mallory's pulse pounded as ecstatically as if he'd just proposed a seduction in the linen room. Justin had actually turned to her openly, admitting that he had a problem and that he wanted to share it with her. She felt as if she'd been given a precious gift.

When they had their coffee and were settled in a booth at the back of the virtually empty cafeteria, Justin seemed to have difficulty finding the words he needed.

"You remember that patient of mine, Mr. Harrison?"

"Sure. Carol told me this morning you'd talked to him and that he was really optimistic. You must be feeling terrific about that."

"Terrific? Yeah, I feel just great," he said bitterly. "I built up the man's hopes, and now he's lying in an intensive care unit and may never walk again."

"What?" Mallory felt as though a cold, damp wind had rushed past and left her shivering. "I don't understand."

"His surgery was this afternoon. It was very tricky. The way it looks now, I'm not at all sure it worked. He could very well be paralyzed."

"Oh, Justin, I'm sorry. Are you sure? Is there any chance for him?"

He hesitated. "There's a chance, I guess. Call it instinct or whatever, but I just have a bad feeling about it," he said gloomily.

Mallory wanted to reach across the table and shake him. "Justin Whitmore, you stop that this very instant. As my mother would say, you're just borrowing trouble. I thought you actually knew he was paralyzed."

"I told you it's an instinct. I've done this procedure before. I know what to expect."

"Did one single thing go any differently than it has in the past?"

"No," he admitted. "The surgery went pretty smoothly. Dr. Hendricks was there and he's the best. He thought it went just fine."

"Has anything specific happened to indicate trouble?"

His voice faltered, but he met her gaze. "Not exactly."

She couldn't help it. She grinned at him. "You really must meet my mother."

"What does she have to do with this?"

"She can borrow trouble with the best of them. You can compare notes."

Before he could respond, his beeper went off and his expression turned somber. "It's the intensive care unit. It could be a problem with Mr. Harrison."

A shiver of dread ran along Mallory's spine, despite herself.

He gazed at her tentatively. "Wait here for me, will you?"

"You've got it." As he started away, she called after him. "Justin, no matter what happens, you're a damn good doctor."

He gave her a halfhearted thumbs-up gesture and took off at a run.

It was three frantic hours later when Justin wrapped things up. It hadn't been Mr. Harrison they had called him about after all, but another patient. After Justin had finished with him, he had checked on Mr. Harrison as well. He was halfway to the on-call room, when he remembered that he'd left Mallory in the cafeteria. He was sure she would have given up long ago and gone home, but he made a detour just to be sure.

He found her right where he'd left her, leaning back in a corner of the booth, her head drooping to one side. She looked cramped and uncomfortable and utterly desirable.

Gently, he lifted her legs and slid into the booth, then put her slender calves back down across his lap. She barely stirred. His hand resting on the curve of her leg, he sat watching her for several minutes, unable to believe that she was there for him again.

"Hey, lady," he murmured finally, running a finger lightly across her mouth. "Wake up. It's time to go home."

She smiled sleepily, her eyes still half-shut. "Hi. Is everything okay with Mr. Harrison?"

"It's looking pretty good," he said with cautious optimism.

"Does that mean the prognosis is better than you thought?"

"There's some evidence of feeling in his right leg. I'm still not so sure about the left, but I'm a whole lot more hopeful now than I was earlier."

She took his hand and lifted it to her lips. The kiss she brushed across his knuckles sent tremors through him.

"You've got great hands."

"Are you speaking from personal experience?" he inquired lightly.

A blush of pink stained her cheeks. "That, too, doctor, but I was thinking of something Rachel said. She said you were such a good surgeon, you ought to have your hands insured."

Justin was surprised. "Rachel said that? I didn't think she thought much of me. I can recall a few less than savory adjectives she applied to my character."

"She might have been referring to your bedside manner, which as we both know is improving tremendously."

"I wish I could go home with you now and work on it some more," he murmured, "but I'm on duty the rest of the night."

"Are you throwing me out?"

"It's late. You ought to get some sleep."

"That doesn't answer my question. Do you want me to go?"

He sighed. She was doing it again. She was backing him into a corner and, while a part of him rebelled, most of him felt an odd sense of relief. "No. Stay a bit and talk to me."

"Only if I can ask you a question."

"You never let up, do you?" he said resignedly. "Go on. Ask away."

"Was something else on your mind earlier? Something other than Mr. Harrison's condition?"

"Why would you ask that?"

"It's just that when I saw you outside Davey's room, you seemed so upset."

"You don't think worrying about Mr. Harrison was enough? I thought you wanted me to demonstrate more concern for my patients."

"If that's all it was, fine. I just have a feeling there was more."

He shook his head. "You and your feelings."

"So I'm wrong?"

He scowled at her. He'd hoped she hadn't noticed his mood, but he should have known better. "No, damn it. You're not wrong."

"Do you want to talk about it?"

"Since when have you given a hoot whether I wanted to talk about something?"

"That's not true, Justin Whitmore," she said indignantly. "Sometimes you just don't realize that you need to talk about certain things until I point it out to you."

He grinned feebly. "Oh, is that the way you see it?"

"Naturally."

"And you think I need to talk about this?"

"It wouldn't hurt," she said, her eyes widening with expectancy.

"Ah, but this time it might," he said, suddenly turning serious. He wanted to tell her. For the first time in his life, he actually wanted to be completely open, but he was afraid of ripping apart all the old wounds so they could fester again. Mallory waited until he found the words to begin. "I heard what you said to Davey."

"About his mother?"

"About both his parents."

"Why would that upset you? He needs to learn to understand what really happened to his family, that he wasn't to blame for any of it."

"I know that," he agreed, then added in a voice that was barely above a hoarse whisper, "I know it all too well."

Mallory grasped what he was really saying even more quickly than he'd anticipated. "Justin, how do you know?" she asked in a hushed tone.

"You're a very perceptive woman. I think you already have the answer to that."

Her hand was tight on his arm, her fingers digging into his flesh. "Say it, damn it. Just say it."

"Because I've been there," he said slowly, unable to meet her gaze. His voice was barely above a whisper. "I've been like Davey."

Chapter 8

For several minutes after Justin spoke, Mallory sat in stunned silence. Her heart grieved for this man she knew to be sensitive and gentle and kind beneath the harsh facade he maintained for the world. And she was angry, for she understood now why Justin had shut himself off from people, why he had been terrified to let anyone into his life. Those he had loved most as a child had done damage to his ability to trust that was possibly irreparable. It was also just as likely that they had warped his self-image in such a way that he felt he wasn't lovable.

Thinking back now, it all made sense—the impossibly high standards he set for himself and others, the distance he had kept from his patients, the special poignancy so evident in his relationship with Davey. All were the actions and attitudes of a man torn between wanting love and fearing it.

He was sitting next to her now, his jaw tightly clenched, his body rigid. Now that he'd said the words, he was clearly regretting them. He radiated tension as he waited for her response. When she started to put her hand on his, he jerked away, much as Davey had the first time she had reached out to him. With Justin, though, she didn't let go.

"Tell me about it," she said gently, her thumb grazing his whitened knuckles until his fingers finally relaxed.

He shook his head. "I can't talk about it."

"Not even to me?"

"Especially not to you."

"That doesn't make sense. You're obviously beginning to trust me. You've already told me it happened. Why not the rest?"

"I do trust you," he said, his gaze intense, trying to tell her far more than he could with words. "You, Mallory Blake, the woman."

Suddenly she understood and she uttered a soft sigh of regret. "But not Mallory Blake, Ph.D."

"Exactly."

"You can't separate the two, Justin. I am a psychologist." He had no idea how true that was, how ingrained the training was in her. Now was not the time for her to bring up her own personal tragedy.

"But right now, at this moment," she reassured him, "I am a woman who cares very much about you. No analysis, I promise. Just a friend who's willing to listen."

Whether it was because of the sincerity of her promise or the depth of his own need, Justin finally started talking. The words began slowly, like the first trickle of water that would later become a flood. For the next few hours the story poured out. It was not unlike Davey's.

Justin's mother, Karen Lewis, had been beautiful, socially ambitious and bright. She had been sent to the best schools, not so much for an education, but in the hope that she would find a suitable match. She had met Justin's father, heir to a large fortune in shipping, during her senior year. They had little in common, with the possible exception of an interest in his future. There had been a whirlwind courtship, which passed by in a blur of champagne and travel and parties. They were so rarely alone, it was little wonder that they didn't recognize their differences.

The marriage had been a disaster practically from the beginning. Suddenly Derrick Whitmore's playboy days were over. He was expected to settle in at the family business, and Karen was expected to remain at home and play the dutiful wife. It was a role for which she was particularly unsuited. She had loved every minute of the globe-trotting and partying. She had shone at social occasions planned by other people. Now that she was expected to entertain herself, she found it was work, and that tarnished the glitter. She became more and more absorbed with her friends at the country club, and Derrick Whitmore became more and more absorbed by his work. It was a marriage headed for divorce. The only thing that stood in the way was Karen's determination not to relinquish what she'd fought so hard to win— wealth. And Justin had been caught on the battlefield.

"She never wanted me. She got pregnant only to have something to use as leverage against my father. When it didn't work, she took it out on me. There wasn't a day that went by that she didn't remind me in one way or another how much trouble I was."

The words sent a hot spurt of outrage pouring through Mallory, followed by a swell of tenderness and compassion. She knew, though, that Justin wanted none of that from her. She waited silently for the rest.

"I was four the first time I had to go to the hospital," he said, his eyes focusing on something off in the distance, on stubborn, hateful memories that he couldn't let go. "I can't even remember how many times there were after that. My father wasn't interested enough to ask for explanations. In fact, he wasn't home long enough to even notice the bruises. He'd moved up in the company, and he was once again traveling all over the world. He took advantage of every opportunity to be on the road, and my mother resented me all the more because I kept her tied to home. It got so I dreaded my dad's trips out of town, not because I missed him, but because that's when she was angriest."

"But what about the authorities? After a few hospital visits, wouldn't someone catch on?"

"Ah, the system," he said with a wry grimace. "You still haven't given up on it, have you? Keep in mind that my mother was very smart. We rarely went to the same hospital twice in the same year. She always picked the busiest emergency rooms. If my grandmother hadn't walked in on one of her beatings, I doubt if anyone would have ever figured it out."

"What happened then?"

"My grandmother took me away and insisted that my mother get help. It was all kept very quiet. It would have been bad for the family business, for our exalted position in the community, if word had gotten out that my mother was a child abuser. I was never permitted to discuss it, not even with my grandparents. The lengths they went to to pretend that it had never happened were incredible. I stayed with my grandparents at their lake house for the summer. No one would question that. It was a child's dream vacation. After that, though, I was sent back home. My mother was supposed to be *better*."

"Was she? Did the treatment help?"

"It kept her occupied," he said with an ironic edge to his voice.

"What is that supposed to mean?"

"She had an affair with the shrink."

Mallory felt as though she wanted to be sick. No wonder Justin had such contempt for psychologists. "Was the man ever censured?"

"On whose word? That of a ten-year-old boy? We were already keeping the child abuse quiet. Why not add an affair to the list of secrets?"

Amid the outpouring of bitterness, Mallory heard the pain of a small, confused boy and, for once, was at a loss to know what to do about it. Words alone would never banish years and years of pent-up hatred and confusion and loneliness.

Before she could think of anything to say, Justin gave her a lopsided grin of sheer bravado. She had never loved him more. "Quite a tale, huh?" he said with a light touch he had to struggle to achieve.

"I'm sorry you had to go through that all alone."

"Don't be." He shrugged. "At least one good thing came out of it."

"What?"

"After all those trips to the hospital, I grew more and more fascinated with medicine. It was a way to make the hurt go away, and I wanted to do that. My father, who seemed to belatedly notice my existence, was only too glad to pay the expenses. He apparently considered it penance. It was only after I was already in school that I realized exactly what studying medicine meant, that I would have to get involved with the patients. I love neurosurgery and I'm good at it, but I chose it because I thought it would mean spending less time dealing with people directly. Pretty cowardly, don't you think?"

"If you'd really wanted to be cowardly, you could have chosen research. Surgery certainly didn't work as you'd planned, did it?"

He gave her a rueful half smile. "Actually it was working pretty well, until you came along and decided to prod my conscience."

"Maybe you're just ready to begin coming out of your shell."

"I suppose anything is possible."

Suddenly Mallory noticed that the cafeteria was getting busy. Then she noticed that the sky was turning gray.

"Justin Whitmore, do you realize we've been here all night? I can't remember the last time I stayed awake long enough to see the sunrise."

"I hope it was in a more romantic setting than this."

"Actually, I think it was when I was studying to take the oral examinations for my Ph.D."

"You really must come up with a better way to spend your nights," he remarked, his gaze roving suggestively over her, leaving a trail of fire in its wake.

"Any ideas?" she asked breathlessly.

"One or two. Would you like to start by going to a

ball game with Davey and me? I've promised him we could go to the Giants' opener today."

"He's well enough to leave the hospital?"

"Oh, I think I can arrange a pass, since he'll be with proper medical personnel. Actually, that's something I wanted to talk to you about, but I've been putting it off because I wasn't sure I wanted to hear the answer. Davey's really just about ready to get out of here. Has Rachel said any more about where he's likely to be sent? Have they found a foster home for him?"

"I don't know how much you heard earlier, but a foster home may not be necessary. His dad is coming in the morning. The court may want to look into sending Davey home with him, or there may even be a reconciliation. I know that's what Jenny Landers is hoping for."

At the scowl on Justin's face, Mallory added, "Now don't go getting all worked up again. Nothing's definite, and I promised you I wouldn't make any recommendation that wasn't in Davey's best interest."

"Okay, I'll withhold judgment for the moment, but I'm warning you…"

"Save it, doctor. I know where you're coming from. Now let me get out of here. I need a shower and some clean clothes before I face another day around this place." She rubbed her fingers across the stubble on his chin. Somehow it made him look even sexier. "I like the unshaved look, but I doubt if Dr. Hendricks would approve. You'd better get going, too."

Mallory started to nudge Justin from the booth, but he stopped her.

"Wait. Before we go, I want to thank you…for listening. You kept your promise, and I appreciate it."

"Anytime," she said softly. "I'll always be around, if you need me."

Hazel eyes met hers and held until her pulse, predictably, began to race. "I'm beginning to realize that."

They walked out of the cafeteria together, and Justin went with her as far as the front door. Suddenly she found herself backed against the wall, his body mere inches away. She could feel the heat emanating from him, smell his sharp, tangy male scent. It made her head reel and her blood sizzle. If he didn't move away, the oncoming shift was going to have enough gossip material to keep the hospital buzzing for a week.

"Justin," she said huskily. She cleared her throat and tried again. If she was going to object to his nearness, she would have to be more convincing than that. His eyes glittered back at her dangerously, the golden flecks in the hazel depths glinting like the eyes of a tiger.

"Yes," he said with feigned innocence. "Is there a problem?"

"You're crowding me." This time her voice squeaked.

"You've been crowding me since the day we met."

"Justin!"

He grinned at her then and before she could slide under one of his arms, he'd lowered his head and brushed his lips lightly across hers. She'd been in San Francisco long enough to know that the tremors he'd just set off were sufficient to rock the city, yet everyone else seemed to be going about their business as if there'd been no earthquake at all. In fact, many of the passersby seemed to be smirking with delight.

"What the hell," she muttered and lifted her head for the full-fledged kiss he was only too ready to bestow. The roughness of his cheeks tantalized her, his lips were firm and warm and hungry, his tongue teased until sensation overruled caution, and her arms slid around his neck. It was the only hope she had of staying on her feet. Her knees were trembling, and her entire body seemed all too languid.

"Shower," she finally mumbled, breaking free of the embrace. Justin was clearly startled as he came back to reality. He blinked and gazed around him, astonishment written all over his face.

"A cold shower," he echoed, suddenly grinning again. "It seems to have been a night full of surprises."

"Surprises?"

"No calls from the emergency room and now this." He seemed awfully pleased about the whole thing, while she was ready to die from embarrassment. Still, she wasn't going to let him see she couldn't take a passionate kiss in stride, even if it had taken place in a very public location.

She tried to brace her legs, convinced that they were about to fold right under her. "Later," she said with what she considered to be a reasonable amount of jauntiness.

"Six o'clock."

"Six o'clock?"

"The ball game. I'll meet you in Davey's room."

"Right. I'd almost forgotten." It probably didn't matter, she thought as she walked away in a daze of exhaustion, that she hated baseball. She'd probably sleep straight through the game anyway.

She was trying to sneak in a ten-minute nap in her office later that morning when Rachel wandered in.

"Ah, sleeping on the job. That's always the first sign. Could it be that our prize child psychologist is suffering from a common emotional disorder that tends to strike in the spring?" she teased as she sat down across from Mallory. Mallory glared back at her, but it didn't seem to daunt Rachel in the slightest. "Word has it that love is in the air, the mighty have fallen, and all's right with the world."

"Go to hell."

"Is that any way to treat your best friend?"

Mallory's head was back down on her desk. She muttered under her breath.

"What was that?" Rachel inquired cheerfully.

Mallory peered at her with one bleary eye. "I said you're going to be my former best friend, if you keep this up."

"Testiness. Another significant clue. Come on, girl, give. What's going on with you and the great doctor?"

"My impression is that you already know."

"Gossip," Rachel said, waving her hand dismissively. "I never listen to gossip."

"Then what brought you into my office?"

"A need for firsthand information. Now, talk, or I'll tell everybody that it's true the two of you spent the entire night making whoopee in the neurosurgery on-call room."

At that Mallory's eyes blinked fully open and her head came up. "Is that what's going around?"

"Well, not exactly. I added the part about the on-call room. Word is, though, that you were in the cafeteria together at some very late hours—and I do mean hours. A follow-up report has the two of you necking in the lobby at dawn. How's the accuracy so far?"

Mallory moaned. "On the mark."

"Oh my, I would pick today to come in late."

"Rachel, if you're not here for something constructive, buzz off."

"Constructive?"

"Like how am I going to live this down? I'm a professional. I do not go around *necking* in hospital lobbies, any more than I *make whoopee* in an on-call room."

"Apparently you do now. Justin's even better for you than I thought. I hate a woman who's not in touch with her emotions."

"Thank you for your kind moral support."

"You're welcome."

"Rachel, I'm serious. What am I going to do?"

"About Justin or the gossip?"

"At the moment, they seem to go hand in hand."

"Nothing."

Mallory looked at her incredulously. "My professional reputation is on the line here, and you think I should do nothing?"

"Hogwash. Your reputation is not on the line. If this place got uptight about every stolen kiss, we'd have a staff of ten, and none of them would be doctors. I take that back. Until this morning, Justin would have been among the ten."

"Terrific. I'm destroying his reputation, too."

Rachel's impish smile finally faltered as she caught on that Mallory didn't consider the incident to be a joking matter. "Mallory, you're making too much of this. What's really wrong?"

"Does the word terror suggest anything to you?"

Rachel peered at her, then erupted into laughter. "I see," she managed between giggles. "I love it. You've been so busy ensnaring Dr. Whitmore you never stopped to consider the implications. Now that he's in your arms—so to speak—you're beginning to panic."

"Bingo!"

"Like I said, you're making too much out of this. You're clearly in love with the man or you wouldn't be…"

"Don't say it."

"*…this upset,*" Rachel said, then added defiantly, "I was not going to say you wouldn't be necking with him in the lobby."

"Okay, yes. I am in love with him, but he's so much more complex than even I imagined. What if I can't deal with all of his problems?"

"Do you want to be his lover or his shrink? The way I see it, you're supposed to support him, not cure him."

"That's all very simplistic and wonderful, but I don't think you have the vaguest idea what I'm up against here."

"Mallory, there's not a man alive who's our age who doesn't come with a complicated past history. You accept the whole package. If it's flawed, you'd better know it going in. Apparently you do."

"That's precisely my point. What if I can't cope with the flaws?"

"Again, do you want to live with them or get rid of them? If it's the latter, don't count on it. If you want to live with them, you work at it. If some of them clear up along the way, so much the better."

"It sounds like you're talking about acne."

"I don't know what the hell I'm talking about," Rachel grumbled. "You've been babbling in riddles ever since I came in here. I'm just doing the best I can with what you've given me. I think I'm beginning to see why shrinks need shrinks."

"Me, too," Mallory said and put her head back down on her arms. "Go away. I'm going to take a nap. I have to go to a baseball game tonight. I haven't been to a ball game for years. Not since my father got the entire family thrown out of a Little League ballpark for threatening to kill the umpire if he ever called another strike on my little brother."

"Sounds like my kind of guy," Rachel enthused. "Why are you going if you hate baseball so much?" She sighed. "Never mind. It's one of those things we women do for the men we love, sort of like the way I go camping with Hal, even though I abhor bugs and fresh air."

"You've got it."

"Enjoy yourself," she kidded, then added seriously, "I mean that, Mallory, and I'm not just referring to tonight. Enjoy every minute of this time with Justin. You know better than anyone that time can go by all too quickly."

That was exactly what she'd needed to be reminded of, Mallory realized once Rachel had gone. This fleeting moment of panic was an anomaly. It would never come back. The love that had been building inside her for Justin was still there, as strong and sure as the beat of her heart. He was letting go of his past more and more every day she spent with him. It would be the ultimate irony if she were to become the one to cling to it, to fear its implications.

It was 6:05 when she got to Davey's room, and he was practically bouncing on his bed with impatience. He had a baseball cap perched rakishly on his blond hair and he was wearing a Giants warm-up jacket.

"Where have you been?" he said the instant she

walked in. "Dr. Justin just went to look for you. We're gonna be late."

She thought he looked feverish. "Are you sure you're up to this?" she asked, putting her hand on his forehead. "You seem a little warm to me."

Justin walked in just then. "Hey, who's the doctor around here? I've checked his vital signs. This kid could play first base tonight."

"Let's hope he doesn't have to."

"Come on, you guys. Let's go," Davey urged excitedly. "Come on."

"Okay, pal. We're on our way," Justin said and hoisted the boy up in his arms. "You've got a four-hour reprieve. Let's make the most of it."

When they reached the stadium, the parking lot was still practically empty. "Are we early?" Mallory said.

"Maybe a little, but I wanted to get a good parking space," Justin said, flashing her a secretive smile. The man was up to something, but she couldn't begin to imagine what. She was too busy trying to figure out why she hadn't thought to bring along a book to read.

When they reached the gate, the guard took one look at Justin and beamed. "Hey, doc, it's great to see you. I've been watching for you."

"How've you been, Louie?"

"Terrific, thanks to you. Never thought I'd be thanking somebody for drilling a hole in my head, but I ain't had a headache since you cut into me and took out that tumor. Had one of them fancy tests last week and everything's clear." He looked at Davey then. "So, this must be the big Giants fan you've been telling me about."

"This is Davey Landers, and this is my friend, Mallory Blake."

"If they're friends of yours, then they're okay in my book. Let's go on in. The guys are expecting you."

"The guys?" Mallory murmured under her breath. An idea was beginning to take shape in her mind, and suddenly she could hardly wait to see if she was right. If she was, Davey was going to be thrilled beyond belief.

Sure enough, Louie didn't lead them toward the stands, but instead took them through a maze until suddenly they were on the edge of the field where the teams were warming up. Davey's eyes were as round as giant blue marbles. He was staring around the stadium with an awed expression on his face.

Gradually the players began to trot toward the dugout, and every single one of them called out to Davey. Several of them even stopped to speak to him. Mallory would have expected the boy to be speechless, but he was chattering away with the aplomb of a seasoned politician. To the delight of the players, he even threw in a few batting averages from the previous season.

"Justin, how did you arrange this?" Mallory said, feeling a spirit of excitement steal over her in spite of herself.

"Don't give me any credit. I just made a call to Louie. He did the rest."

"Louie, you're incredible," she said, squeezing the old man's gnarled hand. "This is a night Davey will never forget."

"It ain't that much, miss, considering what the doc did for me. I owe him. You've got yourself a fine young man there."

Mallory's gaze locked with Justin's. "I know that," she said softly.

Louie took them to their seats then, and Davey insisted on giving them a detailed account of everything that had gone on in the dugout, as if they hadn't been there to see it for themselves.

"You're the best," he said. He threw his frail little arms around Justin's neck and squeezed. Mallory caught the shimmer of tears in Justin's eyes, then was enveloped in a hug herself. "I love you, too, Mallory."

"And I love you, sport. Now settle down a little. The game hasn't even started yet. You've still got a big night ahead."

Trying to calm Davey down was like trying to steer a rampaging herd of bulls back on course. For a little boy who had been through such an incredible ordeal, he seemed to have more energy than any ten children she'd ever seen before. She was worn out just watching him.

By the fifth inning, though, the activity was beginning to tell on him. His skin was pale, and his eyelids were drooping.

"I think this is about enough for tonight," Justin said.

"But the game's not over," Davey protested sleepily. "I'm okay."

"But you won't be okay if we don't get you back, and then I'll be in trouble. You can listen to the game on the car radio."

That seemed to satisfy him for the moment and by the time they'd driven back to Fairview General, he was sound asleep. Justin got him back into bed, checked his vital signs and recorded them on the chart.

Then he turned to Mallory. "And what about you? Are you worn out from all the excitement?"

"I just may be able to muster up enough energy to get home."

"Would you do better with a chauffeur?" he inquired lightly, but she could tell from the lines of tension around his mouth that asking made him nervous. He still seemed a little uncertain how she would react to what he'd told her the previous night, now that she'd had time to think about it.

"Much," she said, her voice thick with the sensual implication behind his question and her response.

They had barely gotten into Justin's car when Mallory's head fell back and her eyelids fluttered shut. She was still asleep when they arrived at her apartment. Justin switched off the ignition and just sat staring at her. Dark eyelashes fanned across her cheeks, and her hair was mussed. He loved it when her crisp, workday image fell away, and she became a vulnerable, incredibly sexy woman.

Her professionalism daunted him. She was so damn good at what she did that he sometimes feared she could read his mind, see into his soul. Only once before had he allowed anyone to get that close and it had ended in disaster. He had sworn never to let it happen again, but he hadn't counted on Mallory.

Apparently she had seen something in him that he'd kept carefully hidden from everyone else. She'd seen the sensitivity he held just out of reach and had climbed over the walls he'd built with the ease of a tomboy intent on reaching the top of a tree. She'd been nurturing him ever since, encouraging him to open up, to give as he'd always wanted but had learned early not to dare to do.

Tonight he'd wanted to give her back some of what she had given to him. He'd wanted to make love to her slowly and gently and with every part of his being. It was the risk he'd feared the most, and he was ready at last to take it.

He regarded her sleeping form with an ironic twist to his lips. Showing her would clearly have to wait for another night.

He eased her out of the car and carried her upstairs, but he was stymied at her door. Her key was buried in the depths of her purse, and he had no free hands with which to search for it. On top of that, she was snuggling into his neck, making soft little mewing sounds in her throat and it was driving him wild. It was a wonder he could stand at all. There was nothing to do but wake her up. Quickly.

"Mallory," he said softly, jiggling her in his arms. "Mal, come on, sweetheart, wake up."

She clung more tightly to his neck. "Dr. Blake!" he said crisply.

Her eyes opened immediately and she looked instantly alert. It was astonishing…and just a little disturbing.

"We're home. Could you dig around in your purse and find your key?"

She reached in and plucked it out with ease. "Why didn't you wake me before?"

"I thought I had this all organized until it came time to open the door."

"You could put me down now."

"I think I rather like having you under my control like this."

"I've got the key. You've got me. Which one of us is really in control?" she inquired tartly.

"You have a point." He shifted her weight in his arms. "Mallory, would you mind opening the door?"

"Am I heavy?"

He knew the trick in that question. "Nope, light as a feather."

She began nibbling on his neck and the arousal he'd just managed to bring under control came back with even greater urgency. "The door!"

Her tongue ran around the shell of his ear, then dipped inside. A tremor ripped through him. "Do that again, witch, and you're going to land on your bottom," he growled. "Now, open the door."

"Can I do it again inside?"

He shifted uneasily as his blood surged. "Mallory!"

"You haven't answered my question."

"You can do anything you want inside," he promised, his voice low and husky with anticipation. She gave him a thoroughly impish and absolutely beguiling grin.

"What a lovely prospect."

Chapter 9

Mallory's playful mood lasted for about thirty seconds after the door was closed. Then the atmosphere turned very serious indeed. Justin had had no idea that any woman could awaken so thoroughly so quickly.

She stood on tiptoe to link her fingers behind his neck. Her body swayed against him, the pressure just enough to make his flesh burn and his heart pound in his chest.

"Did I tell you how wonderful I think you are?" she murmured, her lips merely a hairbreadth away from his.

He wasn't one bit interested in her praise. He just wanted to capture more of her sweetness. He tried to close the distance, to lock his mouth over hers and slide his tongue inside for a taste of honeyed moistness, but she was having none of it. Why had he never realized how strong she was...or how much willpower she possessed? He could feel her body trembling in his arms and still she kept that infinitesimal distance between them. He realized then that he'd have to play out the scene on her terms.

"What did I do to convince you of my charms?"

"Your charms, as you put it, are not the issue." She loosened the arms she had clasped around his neck and poked him in the chest. "I'm referring to what's in here. You've got a big heart, Justin Whitmore, and never again will I allow you or anyone else to deny it. What you did tonight for Davey was incredible. I've never seen a kid so happy."

He returned her gaze, suddenly somber. "He deserves to be happy all the time."

"No one is ever happy all the time and, unfortunately, you and I are not the ones responsible for seeing to Davey's well-being. We can only hope to steer things in the right direction."

"Let's not get off on that subject again. I don't want to talk about Davey's future right now. I want to talk about ours."

He caught the startled expression in her eyes and cursed himself for a stupid slip of the tongue. He'd been thinking only of the immediate future, of the promising night ahead of them. She'd obviously thought he meant much more, and he wasn't ready for that yet. He'd made giant strides since meeting Mallory, but he might never be ready for marriage, for a commitment to a happily-ever-after he didn't believe existed. His dilemma was growing every day because he didn't think he could bear the thought of not having her in his life. Still, he wondered if he could correct the impression he'd just given her without seeming like a rat.

"For instance," he began suggestively, sneaking in a quick kiss to the line of her brow, then one to the tip of her nose, "what are you doing for the rest of the night?"

"You clearly have a rather shortsighted view of the future," she taunted, obviously seeing straight through him. Her remark wasn't made in anger, however, but rather with that wry amusement that delighted him. She was clearly the sort of woman who was confident enough to give a man the slack he needed, knowing that sooner or later she could reel him in.

"We'll talk about the future another time," he vowed solemnly.

"Then we do have something to talk about?"

"Yes," he murmured, running his hands along her sides until they rested on the curve of her hips. "I'm beginning to think maybe we do."

"Why does it sound as if all those positive words add up to a question, rather than a statement?"

Instead of answering, he tilted her body forward until it rested tightly against his. "I'm not much interested in talking about this right now. How about you?" He lowered his head to capture an already hardening nipple between his teeth. He heard her sharp gasp and felt the suddenly accelerated pace of her heart. Mallory's back arched as she sought the pressure of his mouth against her breasts, telling him silently that she, too, was beyond talking.

Suddenly he couldn't wait an instant longer to be inside her, to make her his in the only way he knew how, by pleasuring her, by lifting them both out of the present and into a world filled with possibilities. The patience he'd had all evening shattered and he shoved aside her clothes, then his own with a heated urgency.

His pants had barely dropped to the floor in a tangled heap, when he lifted her up and settled her on his throbbing manhood. She was as ready as he was. Her legs clamped around him and she buried her face against his chest, her lips burning him as they sought out his masculine nipples.

He leaned back against a wall for support and moved with a sort of frantic desperation, his eyes locked with hers. He watched the tension on her face change to surprise and delight as she shuddered in ecstasy, her head thrown back, her body shimmering with perspiration. Only then did he seek his own pleasure, thrusting deep into her silken warmth, feeling her muscles tighten around him and sheathe him in her love.

When the explosion rocked him, it seemed to last forever, a bursting of light and sound and sensation more spectacular than any fireworks display, more intoxicating than the finest champagne. Once more, as it had done only with Mallory, it touched not just his body, but the depths of his soul.

"I'm sorry. It wasn't supposed to be that way," he murmured in a voice that was thick and breathless.

"And what was wrong with it?" she inquired, peering at him indignantly, her eyes luminous.

"Not a thing, but I'd had every intention of taking you to bed and making love to you all night long."

She gazed at him with wide-eyed innocence. "What's stopping you?"

"You want more?"

"Shameless, aren't I?"

"And insatiable."

"Do you object."

"I don't, but you may, if I keep you awake two nights in a row."

"Try me."

The taunt was enough to get them as far as the bedroom, but exhaustion won out over desire, and they fell asleep still locked in the midst of a passionate embrace.

It'll be an interesting position from which to start, Justin thought as he drifted away on a sea of contentment.

In the morning, though, there was no time to recapture the wild tension, the reckless abandon and explosive promise of the night before. In their weariness, they hadn't set the alarm, and Justin awoke to the sound of his beeper going off. By the time Mallory got out of bed, he was on the phone to the hospital, being told by the scrub nurse on his team that he was already fifteen minutes late to prep for surgery.

It took him two minutes to shower and three to untangle his clothes and get into them, but it took him five to say goodbye. It would have taken longer, but Mallory at least had some sense—and indomitable willpower. With any luck he would make it to the operating room before the anesthesia was administered.

Mallory watched Justin rush through the door with a satisfied gleam in her eyes. He had just indicated very thoroughly that he was tempted to put her ahead of his work. She'd never let him do it—at least not at the cost of a scheduled surgery—but it was reassuring to know he would. It was another breakthrough to be logged on her rapidly lengthening list.

She had barely walked into her office an hour later when the phone rang. It was her real estate agent with the news that the closing on her condominium would be on Friday. "You can move in by the weekend, if you like."

"That's great news," she said, wondering how she'd managed to forget all about the apartment in recent days. She'd filled out the papers at the bank and pushed the whole thing out of her mind. Or, rather, Justin had. He'd kept her more than occupied physically and mentally for weeks now. She probably ought to thank him. In the past she'd have been worrying herself sick over every detail of the transaction. If she hadn't, her mother would have been.

Suddenly, she realized she hadn't even told her parents about the new place or asked them to send her furniture. On impulse, she picked up the phone and called her mother.

"Mallory Marie," her mother exclaimed the minute she heard her voice. "Where on earth have you been? And what are you doing calling at this hour on a weekday? Are you all right? I've called you the past two nights until late."

Guilt flowed over her in predictable waves, exactly as her mother intended. "Nothing's wrong, is it?"

"You tell me. You didn't call on Saturday. I haven't been able to reach you since. What's going on up there?"

"You mean there's nothing wrong at home?"

"Of course not. We're just fine, except for fretting about you."

Mallory groaned. "Mother, I'm a grown woman. You can't go into a panic every time you can't reach me. If you're really concerned, you could always call the hospital."

"I didn't want to bother you at work."

"If you thought I was in such terrible shape, what

makes you think I'd have been working? At least the hospital could have told you if I was being held by the authorities or locked away in a mental ward."

"Don't be cynical, Mallory. It doesn't become you. Why are you calling home in the middle of the week again, if nothing's wrong?"

"I called to tell you I've finally found a condo, the bank has approved the loan and we're closing on it on Friday."

Silence greeted the announcement.

"Mom, did you hear me?"

"I heard."

"What's wrong?"

There was a heavy sigh. "I guess I was just hoping you might not make this move permanent. You're so far away. We miss you."

"I miss you, too, but it's permanent. I like it in San Francisco, and Justin's here."

"Justin? Who's Justin? You haven't mentioned him before." The mention of a new man in her life would have distracted Mallory's mother from the impending arrival of a tornado.

"He's a friend, a doctor."

"Is it serious? It must be if you've been with him the past two nights."

She should only know, Mallory thought. Aloud, she said only, "I said he was a friend."

"You don't have male friends."

"Who says? Men and women can certainly be friends without it implying anything more about the relationship."

"Then there's nothing more to it?" Her mother's disappointment was obvious in the deflated tone of her voice.

"I didn't say that, either."

"Mallory, are you trying to drive me crazy?"

Mallory chuckled. "Sorry, Mom. Actually, I just called to tell you about the condo and to ask you to ship my furniture."

"On one condition."

"Don't even say it. I will tell you all about Justin when—or if—there's anything to tell. Just send the furniture. Saturday would be great if they can do it by then."

"Oh, all right. Sometimes you are absolutely impossible. I'll call you tonight and let you know the details. Will you be around?" she inquired pointedly.

"I'll be there," Mallory assured her.

She was, in fact, home and Justin was with her, when her mother called. He was rather ineptly trying to make a salad. Vegetables were scattered from one end of the kitchen counter to the other. On her way to the phone, Mallory skidded on a lettuce leaf that had fallen on the floor.

"If that's the extent of your skill with a scalpel, remind me to use another surgeon," she taunted him as she picked up the phone.

"If you had a decent knife, I wouldn't be having this problem," he retorted, as her mother said, "Who is that? Is that Justin?"

"Yes, Mother," she said, then cut short that particular line of questioning. "What's happening with the furniture?"

Her mother uttered a pained sigh that made Mallory smile. "I had your father call. He and Steve Falcone are bowling buddies. Steve promised to rush the shipment and get it to you on Saturday. He said it would probably be there by noon. I think your father has to buy the beers for the next six months."

"Thank Dad for me. Tell him I'll buy the beers."

"I'll hold you to that," her father said. Apparently he'd picked up the extension just in time to hear her promise.

Mallory chuckled. "Hi, Dad. Does this Falcone guy drink a lot? Should I take out another loan?"

"I think you'll be able to handle it. How's my girl?"

"Fine. Loving San Francisco more every day. You'll have to come visit, once I'm settled."

"Your mother tells me there's a new man in your life. Is he treating you okay? Does that have anything to do with your appreciation of San Francisco's finer points?"

"It might have a little something to do with it," she said, smiling as she watched the furrow of concentration on Justin's brow as he tried to dice the spring onions.

"I'm happy for you. Maybe we will take you up on that invitation one of these days. Your mother's already dying to give this guy a once-over. I'm surprised she hasn't ordered a check of his bank records and social standing."

"I'm sure she wants to," Mallory said dryly.

"Will you two stop making fun of me?" her mother said. "I'm just concerned about your welfare. You're my daughter."

"Right. Now let me go, so I can finish fixing dinner. Talk to you soon. Love to everyone."

When she'd hung up, Justin asked casually, "What was all that about furniture?"

"Good heavens, you mean I haven't told you, either?

My condo deal is going through this week. I'm going to move in on Saturday."

"Condo deal?" he asked with an unexpectedly ominous edge to his voice.

"Justin, don't go all vague on me. You were there the day I bought it, the night Rachel and I ran into you at that restaurant."

"You never mentioned that you'd bought a condo."

"But we were talking about decorating it," she argued, then her voice trailed off and she added weakly, "before you got there. Sorry. I guess I've had other things on my mind. I'd practically forgotten about it myself until the real estate agent called this morning."

Justin said very little after that, and she had the strangest sensation that he was angry. Finally she could stand it no longer.

"Justin, are you mad about something? Are you upset because I didn't tell you about the apartment?"

"Not exactly."

"Then what is it?"

"I'm not sure I can explain it."

"Try."

"It just seems like such a big step, and you never even mentioned it."

"But I've explained that. I'd practically forgotten it myself and at the time I actually found the place, you and I weren't exactly close."

"But what will you do with it, if you and I...I mean what if later..."

"Are you viewing this as some sort of rejection of you?"

"That's ridiculous."

"It certainly is. If, at some time in the future, things

change between us, I hardly think my owning my own condominium will matter. We could live in it, we could rent it or we could sell it…if we wanted to."

It was virtually impossible to have a sensible conversation when two people were stepping gingerly around the central issue. Justin hadn't been able to actually mention the word marriage, and she wasn't about to. The issue was left to float in the air like a ghost, whose presence was felt, but not spoken of.

She thought that their sidestepping of the topic had at least put the matter to rest for the moment, but after dinner Justin made up some flimsy excuse about needing to stop by the hospital and left.

He didn't bring the condo up again until Friday morning, when he caught her as she was about to run out of the hospital to get to the bank for the closing.

"Sorry about this week. It's been a little weird around here."

It certainly had been, but Mallory kept a lid on her sarcasm.

"Rachel says you're going to move tomorrow. Need any extra help? I've got the day off."

If this was his way of making amends, Mallory wasn't about to throw it back in his face. "I can always use a strong pair of arms," she said, letting the innuendo sink into him. It brought the grin she'd hoped for.

"Will any strong arms do?"

She paused thoughtfully. "No, I think I've grown accustomed to yours."

"It's a good thing," he said gruffly. "Now, what time do you need me? I'm on duty tonight, but I should be able to get out of here by 8:00 a.m. at the latest."

"Come on by my place then, unless you want to get some sleep before you come over."

"I'll see how it goes tonight and call you if there's a problem. If it's not too busy around here, I should be okay." He ran a finger along the curve of her jaw, then across her lips. The gesture produced as powerful a sensation as any kiss. "Good luck at the closing."

"Thanks, Justin," she said, more grateful than she should have been that he'd accepted the move. Despite her repeated reminders to herself that she was being absurd, his attitude had put a damper on her excitement. Now she could hardly wait to get the whole process started.

Two hours later she had the keys in her hand, a bag of cleaning supplies in her arms and a smile on her face as she walked up the steps to her apartment. When she stepped through the door, she felt astonishingly at peace. She dropped the bag of supplies on the kitchen counter and took a slow tour of the entire apartment, mentally arranging her furniture. She put her favorite woven Mexican carpet in front of the fireplace. In the bedroom, she envisioned her desk sitting beneath the window and her bed covered with a puffy down comforter in bold shades of blue, her favorite color. And everywhere she walked, she envisioned Justin beside her. The image stirred an aching need deep inside, and she wished with all her heart that he were here with her now, consecrating her house with their love.

"This is not getting the kitchen cleaned or the floors scrubbed," she chided herself and marched back to the kitchen. In the end, though, the first thing she did was to wash the bay windows in the living room. Kneeling on the padded window seat, she wiped away the layer of grime until the glass sparkled and sunlight poured into the room. She sat down and drew her knees up to her chest and gazed out at the Golden Gate Bridge in the distance and the snip of water she could see closer by. It was the sort of place for daydreams, and she let her mind wander, conjuring up visions of Justin again.

She could imagine him here, could feel the strength of his arms around her, but when it came to more, the picture wavered, then faded away. She saw no marriage, no children, and it was like an awful premonition. A chill raced down her spine. The moment, which had seemed so special, was spoiled by dark thoughts.

"Enough of this," she said aloud, just to break the gloomy spell. "You have work to do."

It took her the rest of the afternoon to do the major cleaning of the kitchen and bathrooms, to line the cupboard shelves and tackle the rest of the windows. The living room and bedroom floors needed waxing, but that was something she could do in the morning, while they waited for the furniture to arrive. For now she had to go home and pack up her belongings for the move.

She didn't pause for a break the rest of the evening, not even for dinner. She ate a sandwich while she put her books into the boxes she hadn't thrown away after the move from Arizona. At midnight she tumbled into bed, exhausted, only to waken from a dream she couldn't quite remember. The elusiveness haunted her almost as much as her strange sense of foreboding, a repeat of the odd sensation that had unnerved her earlier.

After another hour of tossing and turning, she finally gave up on getting any sleep, took a shower and dressed in jeans and a sweatshirt. She made herself a cup of strong coffee and wandered through the apartment to make sure she'd overlooked none of her own possessions when packing. Finally she sat down on the sofa and within minutes, despite the coffee, she was sound asleep.

Mallory was awakened by the pounding on her door. "Hey, lady, anybody in there?" Justin shouted with far more enthusiasm than was called for at—she glanced at her watch—barely 7:00 a.m. She was still yawning when she opened the door.

He looked disgustingly wide awake for a man who'd been on duty all night. He also had a box of doughnuts in his hand. Mallory reached for them like a drowning woman grasping for a lifeline.

"A kiss first," he insisted and pulled her close with his free arm. His lips captured and wooed her until she was breathless and thoroughly awake. He studied her with satisfaction. "Much better," he approved. "For a minute there, I thought you might not make it today. Did you sleep in those clothes?"

"As a matter of fact, I did," she said, grabbing the box and choosing a jelly-filled doughnut. Strawberry jam oozed out her mouth as she bit down and she caught it with her tongue. Justin seemed fascinated by the gesture. "Not that it should make any difference. I wasn't exactly dressing for style today, anyway."

"I wasn't commenting on the state of your clothes, my dear. It was obvious that I woke you, it took you only a minute or so to get to the door, therefore you must have slept in your clothes."

Mallory glowered at him. "I hate deductive reasoning at this hour."

"I thought you were a morning person."

"I am a morning person, when I have had eight

hours of sleep. When I have had virtually no sleep, I am a grouchy person. Ask Rachel. She got a dose of my grumpiness the other day after we spent the night in the hospital cafeteria."

"I'll try to remember that, next time I'm tempted to keep you awake too late. Now what needs to be done?"

"Couldn't you just sit down for five minutes and rest? All that energy is making me nervous."

"I could sit down," he said agreeably, perching on the sofa, too close to her. His thigh rested along hers, and heat arced between the two of them. "However, if I stay here in this precise position for very long, one of two things will happen. I will either rip those clothes off your body to the delight of Rachel and her husband, who should be arriving any minute, or I will fall asleep. Remember, I've been up all night, too."

"Good point," she said. "You can start putting the boxes into the car."

"I thought you'd see the wisdom of keeping me moving," he said with a decided trace of disappointment. "Any particular boxes first?"

"Nope. They're all marked, so it doesn't matter."

Rachel and Hal arrived as Justin was taking out the second load of boxes, and the activity began in earnest. To Mallory's amazement, it took barely an hour to load up all three cars.

"You all go on to the new place," Rachel suggested. "I'll stay here and vacuum and do a little of the cleaning. Hal can come back to get me."

"You're an angel," Mallory told her. "As soon as we've unloaded everything at the new place, I'll come back to help."

"Don't you dare. You and Justin start working over

there. Hal and I will finish up here and drop the keys off with the rental office."

Mallory led the caravan to her new apartment. She started up the steps, Justin on her heels. Hal seemed to have found a dozen things to do in the car.

"Why do I feel as though I should be carrying you across the threshold?" Justin said lightly as she turned the key in the lock.

Mallory's gaze caught with his. "Good question."

Suddenly he swept her into his arms. "If it feels right, do it, that's my motto," he said as he carried her in.

"Since when?" she demanded, laughing. "I think the lack of sleep is playing mind tricks on you."

"You don't like the new, improved Justin Whitmore?" He rocked her back and forth in the air as though readying himself to toss her right back out the door.

"I love him. I love him," she vowed solemnly. The swaying movement stopped, and she was locked against his chest.

"That's better," he said softly, his lips coming down to close gently over hers. "Much better."

Heat swirled through her, and the aching need for Justin that she had felt yesterday came back in a rush. Had it not been for the thought of Hal waiting outside, she would have followed through on that need. Unfortunately, a subtle cough whisked away the last remnant of temptation.

"Okay, you guys, if we get these boxes in here, I'll be out of your way and you can carry on," Hal said with a conspiratorial grin. "I'll even keep Rachel away."

"A man of taste and discretion," Justin said approvingly.

Mallory shook her head. "You'll never keep Rachel

away. The minute she guesses there is something she should be kept away from, she'll be over here."

Hal winked at her. "Don't worry about a thing. I'll promise her that afternoon in a motel she's always hinting around about."

"Whatever's going on around here this morning must be catching," Justin said. "I could probably win a Nobel Prize if I identified and cured it."

"Never, not if you cured it," Mallory countered. "This is one disease that should probably spread. A little more love in the world, and we wouldn't have war."

Justin quirked an eyebrow at her and went out to start unloading. When it was done, Hal left and Mallory and Justin distributed the boxes to the appropriate rooms.

"What now?" Justin asked.

"I'll put things away, if you'll wax the floors."

He looked at her incredulously. "For this, Hal left us alone?"

She patted his cheek. "I know it's a sorry substitute for what you had in mind, but if we don't get it done now, it'll be that much harder once the furniture's in place."

"Not really. Once the furniture's in, there'll be that much less floor to wax."

"Sorry. That's not the way it works."

"What do I know? I've never waxed a floor in my entire life."

"You're a neurosurgeon. Surely you can read the label on the wax and follow the directions."

"Okay," he grumbled. "They're your floors. Just one thing, though. I'm warning you now that I don't do windows."

"That's okay, love. I've already done them." She handed him the wax and a mop. "Go to it."

It was only a short time later when Mallory heard a plaintive call from the other part of the apartment. She walked through the living room and down the hall toward the bedrooms.

"Where are you?"

"In here."

"In where?"

"The master bedroom, I guess."

"Is this a trick?"

"Would I trick you?"

"It's been known to happen."

"Mallory, just get in here and tell me what to do."

She found him in the far corner of the room, sitting down.

"Don't step on the floor," he shouted when she started toward him.

"What's wrong?"

He glared at her. "I waxed everything, just like you told me."

"It looks terrific."

"Thank you. One thing, though." Mallory waited. "How the hell do I get out of here?"

She tried to keep a straight face. She really did, but it was impossible. Her lips twitched, then broke into a grin. Then came the laughter. Justin's scowl grew more fierce.

"It's not funny."

"Yes, it is. You should just see yourself."

"If I could get to a mirror, I'd take a look. Now get me out of here."

"No can do. You'll have to wait till the floor dries,

unless, of course, you'd like to tiptoe across it and redo all the parts you step on."

"I'll sit."

"Just be thankful it isn't raining."

"Why?"

"On a damp day, this could take forever to dry."

"That little piece of news has absolutely made my morning. Now go get me a book and throw it over here."

Mallory regarded him warily. "Are you sure you didn't plan this to get out of doing the rest of the waxing?"

He grinned at her. "You'll never know, will you?"

By the time the movers arrived, the floor had dried enough for Justin to come out of the bedroom. Thanks to her planning the day before, she knew exactly where she wanted every piece of furniture, and she directed the influx of her old familiar belongings like a choreographer. Everything was in place by late afternoon and already it felt like home. She kept wandering through the rooms, touching the wood, rubbing her fingers across the fabric of her chairs, testing the bed.

"Now that looks like a good idea," Justin said when he caught her bouncing on the edge of the king-size mattress.

"Oh, no, you don't," she said, jumping to her feet. "You're not getting out of any more work that way."

He held out his hand. "Then come with me."

She put her hand in his and allowed him to lead her into the living room, where the carpet had been unrolled in front of the fireplace. While she'd been wandering through the apartment, Justin had built a fire to ward off the early spring chill. He had also opened a bottle of wine and gotten two glasses from a box in the kitchen.

"I thought we should have a toast to your new home."

Mallory wondered if there was any added stress in his voice when he mentioned that it was her home, but the look in his eyes was warm, and no shadows lurked in the hazel depths.

They sat down on the carpet and Justin poured the wine, then touched his crystal goblet to hers. The clear pinging sound was a light and cheerful counterpoint to the low huskiness of his voice as he said, "May you always be happy here."

Only if you're here, Mallory wanted desperately to say, but sensed it was not the time for that sort of pressure. Justin had to reach his own conclusions about them, about their future. For the moment, it was enough that he was here at all, that he was sharing such a special beginning with her.

With a heavy sigh, he put down his glass and reached for her, cradling her against his chest.

"Do you like the apartment?" she asked hesitantly.

"I love it. It's like you, all brightness and sunshine."

She looked into his eyes, struck again by the urgent need to feel a part of him. "Make love to me, Justin," she pleaded. "Make love to me here, now. Make this a day I'll never forget."

Justin needed no further urging, and with the glow of the fire warming them and the pink-hued tint of the sunset splashing over them, they came together in an exquisite blending of familiar ecstasy and timeless passion. It was the loving they'd grown accustomed to, sharpened by the intensity of the present.

The only thing missing, Mallory thought as a tear of joy rolled down her cheek, was a hint of what lay ahead.

Chapter 10

After Justin left on Sunday Mallory worked compulsively around the apartment. In part she needed to feel the move was behind her, but in greater measure she was trying to keep at bay those odd, disturbing sensations about her relationship with Justin. Instinct told her it was teetering on the edge of a precipice, and an awful feeling in the pit of her stomach told her which way it was likely to go.

"You're going to wind up being just like your mother," she muttered to herself in disgust. "Borrowing trouble, worrying about things that might never happen."

Certainly there had been nothing she could put her finger on in Justin's attitude to stir such concern. He had been attentive and supportive the previous day. During the night he had held her in his arms, surrounding her with his warmth and with what she wanted to believe was his love. He had teased her all the next morning about her books, which ranged from ponderous scholarly publications to racy and tender romantic fiction.

"How can any one woman have such diverse tastes?" he'd asked with a shake of his head.

"I like to think of it as being well-rounded," she had retorted. "Besides, a good psychologist can learn all sorts of things about human behavior from reading fiction."

"What have you learned from these romances?" he asked teasingly, a wicked flame of desire sparking to life in his eyes.

"I could show you a few things," she offered and she did. Unpacking was forgotten as they indulged in a feast of sensuality, discovering again how in tune their bodies were.

She reminded herself of that incredible tenderness as she crawled into bed and picked up the intricately plotted popular mystery that she'd been trying to finish for days. Despite what she'd said to Justin about the allure of books, she couldn't get involved in this one. The characters no longer compelled her the way thoughts of Justin did. She finally tossed the book aside, pounded her pillow and tried to go to sleep. It was much harder to do without Justin's heavy leg draped across her thigh and his arm tucked protectively under her breasts. She missed the pressure of his solid length against her back.

In the morning she awoke with a throbbing headache. Every muscle and joint in her body seemed to hurt as well.

"It's back to the gym for you," she muttered as she stood under the shower, waiting for the hot spray to ease the aches. "If you can't even push a little furniture around without winding up in pain, you are definitely out of shape."

At the hospital she saw her early-morning patients, then retreated to her office. Usually she would have worked out all the kinks in her muscles by this time of day, but if anything she felt worse. She was leaning back in her chair, eyes closed, massaging her temples, when the door opened and Justin poked his head in.

"How about lunch? I know it's a little early, but it actually looks as though I have an hour free."

The thought of food turned her stomach, but she definitely needed some kind of relief. Perhaps lunch would do it after all. "Maybe that is what I need," she said without much enthusiasm. She got slowly to her feet. Justin regarded her worriedly.

"Are you okay? You look a little pale and you sound terrible. Did you have breakfast?"

"I wasn't hungry. I'm just tired and sore from all that moving. I'm sure I'll be fine by tomorrow."

He scowled. "I suppose you kept at it after I left."

"I just moved a few things and unpacked the rest of the boxes," she said defensively. "It wasn't all that much."

"I'm surprised you didn't paint the walls."

"Actually, I thought about it, but I didn't have the energy to run to the paint store."

He threw up his hands in a gesture of impatience. "Mallory, I was joking. Leave the damn walls. I'll help you next time I'm off. You don't have to be superdecorator on top of all you're doing around here."

"But I want it to be finished."

"And it will be. It doesn't have to be perfect within

seventy-two hours after you bought it. I've heard that some people even take months to decide exactly what color scheme they want. Slow down before you wear yourself out."

She opened her mouth to respond, but he held up his hand. "Check that. You're already worn out. No more until I can help. Promise?"

She felt too crummy to argue with him. She didn't feel one bit better as they stood in the hot food line in the cafeteria. She opened her mouth to say something to Justin, when a wave of dizziness washed over her and left her feeling cold and clammy.

"Justin." Her voice came out in a croak, and he gazed at her in alarm.

"Mallory, what is it? Are you okay?"

She shook her head. "Don't feel good," she mumbled and suddenly felt as though the lights were dimming. Then the whole world went dark. The last thing she was conscious of was Justin's muttered expletive and his arms catching her as she sank toward the floor.

When she came to, she was lying on a stretcher in the emergency room. There was an argument going on, and she felt as if both participants had been punching her in the stomach as she slept.

"Damn it, Justin," an unfamiliar voice said, "get out of here, so I can examine her."

"I'm a doctor. Why can't I stay?"

Mallory opened her mouth to agree, but suddenly she felt too exhausted to get even a whisper past her lips. Besides, the other doctor seemed adamant. She hoped he and Justin were friends. Otherwise, with Justin's temperament, the man was risking a bloody nose, even though he sounded as though he was trying very hard to be reasonable.

"Because in this instance you have no objectivity whatsoever," he said calmly, then added pointedly, "and you're in the way. Now move it."

Justin sent one last look of concern in Mallory's direction, then reluctantly left the cubicle and stalked up and down outside.

"Damn arrogant doctor," he muttered as he paced. He was about to march back through the curtains when he was paged. Cursing under his breath, he went to a phone.

"Your one o'clock patient is up here," his scrub nurse said. "Are you on your way?"

"Damn. Yeah, I'll be there in a minute. I've got an emergency down here. I just want to make sure it's under control."

He stuck his head back through the curtains around Mallory's cubicle. "Mack."

"Go away."

"Mack, I've got to get back up to surgery. How is she?"

"She'll be a lot better if I can finish checking her out. Go do your surgery."

Justin didn't want to leave. He wanted to stay right there until he knew exactly what was wrong with Mallory. She'd looked so pale and still against the white sheets. It had terrified him and left him feeling absolutely helpless. He was a doctor, after all. He should have been able to do something. Instead, he'd been forced to relinquish her care to Mack.

Mack was only a second-year resident, for heaven's sake. What did he know? Was he even running the right tests? She could have had some sort of brain hemor-rhage. Maybe there was even a tumor. He'd never even thought to ask her if she'd been having severe head-aches. Then again, there'd been no time to ask anything. One minute she'd been standing there talking to him and the next her knees had buckled and she'd started sinking slowly to the floor.

He reached the OR and found Dr. Hendricks already scrubbing. "What's this about an emergency?" the chief of neurosurgery asked. He'd been Justin's mentor ever since he'd joined the residency program, and the two of them had developed the sort of father-son affection and respect Justin had never experienced before.

"It's Dr. Blake," Justin blurted out anxiously as he began methodically lathering his arms. "She collapsed while we were standing in line in the cafeteria. She's down in the ER now, and Mack is checking her out. I don't know, though. He's awfully young, and he could miss something. What do you think? Should I call up one of the attending physicians?"

He caught the grin on Dr. Hendricks's face before the older man could hide it. "Justin, you've told me re-peatedly that Mack Davis is one of the best residents in internal medicine you've ever seen. A real genius for diagnosis, isn't that what you called him?"

"Yes, usually he's great, but he didn't know anything when I left down there. What if it takes him too long to figure out what's wrong with her? She could get worse."

"Exactly how long had he been working her up?"

"Fifteen, maybe twenty minutes," Justin admitted grudgingly, finally sensing the absurdity of his reaction.

"Maybe you should give him a little longer before making any judgments," Dr. Hendricks suggested. "Are you sure you're up to doing this case? I can get another resident to scrub, if you want to get back down to the ER. You won't be any good to me if you're distracted."

"No, I'll be okay once we get started. Mack won't let me near her anyway," he grumbled. "It'll be good for me to concentrate on something besides what's going on downstairs."

Fortunately, it was a relatively simple procedure, because, despite Justin's protestations, his mind kept wandering. It was two hours before he could get back to the emergency room. When he walked over to the cubicle where he'd left Mallory, she was gone. He ran to the desk.

"Dr. Blake? Where is she?" he demanded breathlessly, his heart thudding in his chest. Dear God, if anything had happened to her...

"Just a second, doctor. Let me check." The nurse ran over the list of the day's patients as he drummed his fingers impatiently on the counter. "It says here she went home."

"Went home?" he said incredulously. "How did she get home? She certainly couldn't drive. She should have been admitted. Where the hell is Mack?"

"It says here that Rachel Jackson came by to give her a ride home, and I think Dr. Davis is on rounds on the fourth floor. Do you want me to page him?"

"Never mind."

Justin found another resident to cover the rest of his shift for him and raced out of the hospital. His thoughts were in such turmoil, he was hardly aware of time passing as he drove to Mallory's apartment. What could Mack have been thinking of? Why hadn't he waited to consult with him before discharging Mallory? She had no business being home all alone. What if she had a relapse? If she did, he would personally break every bone in Mack's body.

Rachel opened the front door within seconds after he knocked.

"Don't beat the door down," she admonished. "You'll wake Mallory."

"Is she okay? What's wrong with her?"

"After the fuss I heard you raised earlier, I'm surprised you didn't read the chart in the ER."

"I didn't stop long enough to do it, and Mack wasn't around. He never should have sent her home without running more tests and keeping her in the hospital for observation. The woman passed out, for God's sake."

Suddenly he realized that Rachel was grinning at him, exactly the same way Dr. Hendricks had. "Getting a taste of your own brand of medicine, doctor?" she taunted with delight.

He had started toward the bedroom, but Rachel's words caused him to halt in his tracks and whirl around to stare at her. "What the hell is that supposed to mean?"

"Now you have some idea of how your patients and their families feel when you don't stop long enough to give them a complete picture."

The barb struck home. "Okay. You've made your point, but this is no time for lectures. You still haven't said how she's doing. I want to check on her."

"Get back in here and let her sleep. She ought to be just fine in another forty-eight hours or so. She has the flu."

Justin blinked. "The flu?" he muttered disbelievingly.

"That's it. Sorry to disappoint you."

He came back into the living room, sank down on the sofa and put his head in his hands. Relief flooded through him. "That's it? You're absolutely sure?"

"That's it. It's going around. In fact, I wouldn't be too surprised if you don't wind up with it as well, considering the amount of time you two have been spending with each other."

He quirked one brow at her. "You sound almost pleased about that."

"Which part?"

"That I might wind up with the flu, too."

"Why, Dr. Whitmore, I would never wish you ill health." Rachel hesitated thoughtfully. "Unless, of course, I thought it might do you some good to see things from the other side of the fence."

"Don't start on me again." He gazed at her plaintively. "Do you have any idea how worried I was?"

Rachel sighed then and sat down next to him. This time the teasing tone was gone as she touched his hand gently. The expression in her eyes was compassionate. "I think I do. I'm sorry I gave you such a rough time and I'm really very glad you care so much. Does she know?"

"That I care? I don't know. I've been fighting it so hard, I'm not sure even I realized it until this afternoon. When she passed out on me, practically in midsentence, I thought I'd go crazy."

"Why don't you tell her that, when she wakes up? It would probably be the best medicine she could have." Rachel got up and picked up her purse. "As for me, I'm out of here. If you need help, give me a call."

"I'll be able to handle things until tomorrow at least. I've got someone covering for me at the hospital."

When Mallory awoke, Justin was sitting in a chair

beside the bed, his eyes closed. He looked as though he'd been through a battle and wound up on the losing side.

"Are you okay?" she croaked.

His eyes snapped open and finally focused on her. "You're awake."

"Not by choice. If I'd known I was going to feel this lousy, I'd have stayed asleep."

"Can I get you anything?"

"Maybe a little water."

Justin brought her a glassful and lifted her shoulders off the pillow, while she took several sips. She waited for a moment to see what effect drinking would have on her stomach. So far, so good.

"Enough," she said finally, not wanting to press her luck.

"Why didn't you tell me you weren't feeling well this morning?"

"I didn't know it was anything serious. I just thought I'd overdone it this weekend."

"You scared the living daylights out of me." He sat on the edge of the bed and took her hand in his. Despite the chills that had her shivering under the covers, the look in Justin's eyes warmed her. "I realized today how lost I would be without you. I just want you to know…"

She watched him struggling with the unfamiliar emotions and squeezed his hand. "You don't have to say any more. I understand."

"No. I have to say this. I still don't know what to do about it, but I love you. I want you to know that. I'm not sure I can give you everything you deserve, but I know now that I have to try."

He was staring at the comforter, but finally he lifted

his head and met her gaze evenly. "Maybe, when I finish my residency this summer, we should think about getting married."

Mallory had had one proposal in her life before, and it had been delivered with ardent affection at the blazing height of a glorious desert sunset. This one, tentatively spoken as she lay pale and wan in her bed, was every bit as romantic, perhaps simply because it had cost Justin so much to make it.

For that very reason, she knew she couldn't accept it.

She searched for a way to explain it to him. "Justin, you know how much I love you," she said gently. "And what you just said means more to me than you can possibly realize, but I don't think we're ready to start talking about marriage."

His expression grew puzzled, then indignant. "Why not? You just said you love me. I love you. What more do you want?"

"I want you to be ready to make a commitment, not just afraid of losing me. I want you to see marriage as the next logical step for us, the only choice, because it feels right and good."

"But it does. Maybe I didn't say it right. Hell, I never thought I'd be saying it at all. Don't hold it against me just because I didn't get all flowery and sentimental."

"Oh, Justin, don't you see? I don't want you to get all flowery and sentimental. There was absolutely nothing wrong with the words you used or the way you said them. Maybe it's just the timing. You had a scare today. Apparently it startled you into making some sort of a grand gesture, but it wasn't necessary. I love you enough to wait for as long as it takes. We can go on the way we have been, until you're really ready for a commitment."

"I am ready. I asked you to marry me, didn't I?"

"Can you look me in the eye and honestly tell me that the idea of marriage doesn't terrify you?"

Stubbornly, he met her gaze, opened his mouth to speak, then looked away and sighed. "I'm sorry."

"Don't be sorry. I believe with all my heart that the day will come when it's right for us to be together."

He gave her a rueful smile. "If I couldn't even get you to marry me when you're lying here in this weakened condition, what makes you think I'll be able to convince you later?"

She grinned back at him. "I'm not the one who has to be convinced," she reminded him. "Now go on home and get some rest. There's no point in your hanging around here and catching this bug I've got."

"I'm not going off and leaving you here alone. You might need something during the night." He reached out and gently stroked a tendril of hair away from her face. "Go back to sleep. I'll be around if you need me."

She wanted to protest, but suddenly she was much too tired to argue. She drifted asleep, content in the knowledge that once again Justin hadn't run away when she'd given him the chance.

It was morning before she awoke again. While she still felt as though a truck had run a wheel back and forth across her middle, she also thought that she might survive the ordeal. To her disappointment there was no sign of Justin, but then she heard the clatter of pots and pans in the kitchen. Several minutes later he appeared in the doorway proudly bearing a breakfast tray. He'd taken one of the fresh flowers she'd picked up at the grocery store on Sunday and put it into a glass.

"Think you're up to a little food?"

The thought made her stomach flip over, and she was sure her complexion had turned green, but she tried for an enthusiastic nod. He brought the tray to her.

"Flu is a little out of my area of expertise, but I seem to remember something about tea and dry toast," he said, staring at the plate worriedly. "It doesn't look very appetizing."

"It does to me," she reassured him. "I was dreading the prospect of finding an egg staring back at me."

"I have to get to the hospital. Want me to come back at lunchtime or will you be able to manage until I can get here later?"

"I'll manage. I may not do any sprints around the house today, but I should be able to get to the kitchen if starvation sets in. Besides, you need to spend some time with Davey. Neither one of us saw him yesterday. Stop in and give him my love, too."

Justin nodded. "I'll bring you a full report tonight, and I'll try to call you later to see if there's anything special you'd like for dinner. Can you get to the phone?"

"Justin, stop fussing. It is less than a foot away. I can reach it without budging from the bed. Now, go. If you're late for another surgery, Dr. Hendricks will have your hide."

"I've already talked to him this morning. He knows I'm with you. He told me to take as much time as I needed." He pressed a kiss to her forehead. "Take care of yourself today."

After he'd gone Mallory sank back against the pillows in amazement. Justin had actually told his boss about her, had gotten permission to stay with her. If he was willing to share his feelings so openly with Dr. Hendricks, maybe she'd been wrong to turn down that proposal so hastily. Maybe he was more ready to make a commitment than she'd realized, even though he hadn't fought very hard when she'd said no.

Before she could make herself crazy trying to analyze what all of that meant, the phone rang.

"Hey, girl, how're you feeling?" Rachel asked cheerfully. "Still have your own personal physician in residence?"

"Nope. I just sent him off to the hospital."

"You must be feeling better then."

"I'll live."

"How'd it go last night?"

"How did what go?"

The question was met with silence.

"Rachel, you answer me this instant. How did what go?"

"Maybe I should have kept my big mouth shut for a change."

"Well, you didn't, so you might as well spill the rest of it."

"I just had the feeling when I left there that Justin was going to tell you how he felt about you."

Mallory had a queasy feeling in the pit of her stomach, and this time it had nothing to do with any virus. "He told you that?"

"Not exactly. I mean he told me how he felt—or rather I guessed, since he was acting like a lunatic—and I said he ought to tell you and I thought he was going to. Oh, dear, I've really put my foot into it this time."

"No," Mallory said with a sigh. "I'm the one who's a fool. The man asked me to marry him, and I turned him down."

"You what!" The screech nearly shattered Mallory's eardrum. "Are you crazy?"

"I thought he was just caught up in the moment. I knew he'd been scared when I keeled over. I figured his feelings had just gotten a little out of hand temporarily. I was sure when he had time to think about it, he'd regret being so impulsive."

"You don't give the man much credit for knowing his own mind. Did you ever stop to think that maybe it just took a jolt like that to wake him up to his real feelings?"

"That's more or less what he said."

"Then I suggest you figure out a way to retract your refusal in a hurry. Justin may not be the type to get up his nerve more than once."

It was hard for Mallory to envision Justin being nervous about anything. He was the strongest, most self-confident man she'd ever known.

Except when it comes to love, you idiot, she chided herself. That's the one area in which he hasn't had any practice, and Rachel was right: it could take him forever to get up the courage to broach the subject again.

She wondered if candles on the table, roses and a negligee trimmed in lace would be enough to get him back in the right frame of mind.

Chapter 11

Midway through the afternoon, Mallory realized that her plan was probably sheer folly. It was certainly badly timed. She could barely stay on her feet long enough to set the table. She'd called the florist and a nearby restaurant from bed, and they'd promised to deliver the flowers and the meal by three. It took every ounce of strength she possessed to answer the door when they came.

After a two-minute shower that first revived, then weakened her, she took her makeup to bed, and tried to apply it while leaning back against the pillows. Her hands were so shaky that she gave up after putting a streak of blush on each cheek and a touch of lipstick on her mouth. The effort required a thirty minute nap.

She was still asleep when Justin came into the bedroom. Her eyes snapped open when she felt the mattress dip down beside her.

"Hi, sleepyhead. What's all this?" he asked, gesturing at the array of makeup scattered across the covers.

"I was trying to get all spruced up for you."

"And the feast in the kitchen?"

"I thought you deserved a nice dinner for taking care of me last night." She gave him a wobbly grin. "I had to order it, though."

"Are you feeling any better?"

"Some. I was doing pretty well until I had to set the table. If you give me a few more minutes, I should be able to get dinner in the oven."

Justin shook his head in exasperation. "Will you stop this nonsense? I will get dinner in the oven and I'll bring a table in here. You're obviously not ready to bounce around the house. Mack said you should probably stay in bed for the rest of the week."

"Are you sure you didn't put that idea into his head?" she asked suspiciously.

"No, but now that you mention it, I certainly am all in favor of it. Now, give me this junk and go back to sleep." He began gathering up the cosmetics.

"But I wanted tonight to be special."

His eyes glittered at her wickedly. "You don't think I consider being in a bedroom with you special?"

"Not when we're in here because I'm sick."

"You'd be just as sick in the dining room," he pointed out reasonably.

Mallory sighed and gave up the fight. If he'd proposed in the bedroom once, the setting was probably good enough for a repeat performance.

Justin brought a small table into the bedroom, set it

with the silver and crystal and put the arrangement of roses on her bedside nightstand. An hour later he had dinner ready as well, but Mallory couldn't eat a bite of the delicious meal. Even if she hadn't been sick, nervousness would have prevented her from keeping down a morsel of food.

Justin cast suspicious looks at her as he ate. When he'd finally finished, he sat back and said, "Okay, what's the real story here?"

"I don't know what you mean."

He grinned at her. "Don't give me that. You're clearly up to something. No woman who's as sick as you've been takes time out to plan an intimate little dinner, especially when she knows perfectly well that she's not going to feel like eating a bite of it. Maybe if you'd prepared broth, I'd buy it, but you ordered Italian, my favorite."

"I like Italian, too."

"Maybe so, but it's hardly the right meal for a woman with the flu. You're the great believer in directness. Talk. What's this all about?"

Mallory hadn't quite expected this turn of events. She'd been hoping in some sort of irrational way, no doubt brought on by her fever, that the setting would simply lead Justin around to making his proposal again. Now she saw how absurd that was, which left her with two choices—she could dream up some fantastic tale to explain this evening or she could propose herself. She wasn't wild about either option. And her head was starting to pound again, too.

She tried clearing her throat, and Justin's waiting expression changed to one of concern. "Want some water?"

"No, really. I'm fine." She wondered if she could manage to faint again, since it seemed to have brought out the best in Justin before. Finally, she realized there was no point in delaying the inevitable. There were times when Justin could manage to display astonishing patience, and this appeared to be one of them. "Actually…" She cleared her throat again. "Umm, what I wanted to talk to you about is…umm, I thought maybe we should discuss…"

"Mallory, you're not being particularly coherent. Are you sure you're feeling all right?"

"Fine. More or less, anyway. I'm just having a little trouble figuring out how to get into this."

"Into what? If you have something to say, say it. That's what you're always telling me."

She took a deep breath and blurted quickly, "I was thinking maybe I was a little hasty in turning down your marriage proposal last night, and I wondered if we could talk about it again, I mean, if you still want to. Do you?" She ran out of breath and peeked to see how Justin was taking her announcement. He didn't look like a man who was feeling trapped or even particularly stunned. In fact, he was actually grinning at her.

"What changed your mind?"

"Dr. Hendricks."

"The head of neurosurgery? You don't know the man, do you?"

"Not personally."

"Then what on earth does he have to do with this?"

"It's a little hard to explain."

"Try."

"Well, you mentioned that you'd told him about me being sick, and it made me realize that you must really care about me, if you actually talked to him about me. Then Rachel called…"

"And what did Rachel have to say on this subject?" His voice seemed to be rising dangerously. Mallory met his gaze with a mutinous expression.

"Don't go getting all huffy. She just said you'd been acting like a lunatic yesterday and that you were going to tell me how you felt. Then I realized I'd gone and spoiled it by analyzing you and making assumptions about how you really felt, so I thought I'd better try to make things right before I lost you. I mean you might not be the type to bring this up a second time."

He shook his head and moved to the side of the bed. He reached over and touched her cheek. Heat swirled through her and this time it most definitely was not flu-related. "Are you going to stop babbling now and give me a chance?"

"Sure," she said and sank back on the pillows. "I'm a little worn out anyway."

"Try to stay awake for this part."

"I'll try," she said demurely and waited, trying not to notice that his fingers were drifting along her neck and down to the lace-trimmed edge of her nightgown. She was very glad she'd managed to get out of the Mickey Mouse T-shirt she'd worn during the day and into something a little sexier.

"I meant everything I said last night," he began slowly. "I nearly went crazy yesterday when I thought you might really be sick."

"I was really sick."

"You know what I mean. Don't interrupt," he said, putting a finger to her lips. She wanted his hand back where it had been, just a tantalizing inch or so from the aching peak of her breast. "I'll finish my residency this summer. If you want to, it might be a good time to get married. I'll be going into private practice with a guy who finished up at Fairview last year, and it might be a little rough at first, but I think we could manage."

Mallory had a puzzled frown on her face. "Now I remember what it was that stopped me last night. It was all this *might* stuff. You're the one who doesn't sound convinced. Are you really sure this is what you want?"

"Here we go again," he said with a resigned sigh. "I know I love you. I know that the idea of living without you hurts deep inside. I'll admit that I'm afraid. I don't have a lot of experience with commitment. I can't be sure I can give you the sort of marriage you deserve. You'll be taking a risk, if you say yes. I may never be able to change."

"What does marriage mean to you? Explain it in terms of you and me."

"The two of us together, sharing our lives, being there for each other, laughing together, making love— just the way we have been the past couple of months."

Words, Mallory thought. He was saying all the right words. He was even saying them with conviction, but there was something wrong.

"What about a family, Justin? Do you want children?"

The caress of his fingers stilled, and a shadow darkened the light that had been shining in his eyes. He shook his head. "I never really thought about it," he said evasively. "What about you?"

"I do, Justin. I want kids, who'll be a part of you and me. Can you see yourself ever wanting that?"

He stood up and began to pace. He raked his fingers

through his thick brown hair until it was thoroughly mussed. "I can't do it, Mallory," he said finally. "I can't have kids. Not ever."

"You can't."

"All right, I won't, damn it," he said savagely. The words seemed to be wrenched from some anguished place deep inside him. "I'll never be a father. Never."

There was such finality in his tone that it shook her. "Why not?"

"You know my past. You know why I don't dare be around kids. How can you even ask that? I'll be damned if I'm going to wind up some day beating my kids the way my mother did, or neglecting them the way my father did."

"Justin, you know the risk. That's three-fourths of the battle. There's no reason to believe you can't stop the cycle. Your children would be safe and you'd probably be the most attentive father in the world, just to make up for what you missed."

"The issue isn't open for discussion." He was adamant, and her heart sank. "If you want marriage, fine, but there won't be any kids." He sat down next to her again, but he wouldn't look at her.

"If I want marriage?" Her temper was beginning to flare. She waved a finger indignantly under his nose just to be sure she had his attention. "You started this discussion last night, Justin Whitmore, not me. Maybe we ought to just forget the whole thing. We were doing fine with things the way they were."

"No, we weren't. We were kidding ourselves. Or at least I was. I thought that what we had would be enough for you. At least I wanted it to be. Then I honestly thought marriage might be okay. We love each other, that should be enough. Now I see how foolish I was. You have every right to want children. I just can't be the one to give them to you."

Damn, Mallory thought, near tears and furious. They had come so close and now it was all falling apart. She couldn't bear to see it all wind up in ashes. Damn it, she wouldn't let it. "There's more to it than that, isn't there? There's something you haven't told me. You're far too intelligent to allow your childhood to ruin your future—our future—this way. Tell me now. I have to understand why you're doing this. One minute you want to get married, then I bring up kids, and all of a sudden all bets are off. What is it with you? Tell me."

"There's nothing to tell."

"Don't lie to me, Justin. I know you too well." She forced him to meet her gaze, challenging him. She'd sit here all night if she had to until he talked. Apparently he realized it because he finally gave a sigh of resignation.

"Okay. I'll tell you, and then you'll hate me and that will put the whole thing to rest once and for all."

Justin stood up, his hands clenched at his sides. He started to pace again, then finally sank down in a chair beside her. But he couldn't look her in the eyes. He couldn't bear the thought of what he would see there, the contempt, the betrayal. How could he tell her this?

Mallory waited, gazing at him expectantly, and finally, knowing it was useless to put it off, he began.

"Years ago, when I was still in medical school, I met a woman. She was a nurse at the hospital affiliated with the school, and she was a couple of years older than I was. Like you, she made me believe in possibilities. She'd been married before and had a little girl." He shut his eyes against the images, but they were all in his head and they wouldn't go away. "Amy. That was her name. She was such a pretty little kid. She had all these blond curls and these blue eyes. She was like someone you'd see in a painting."

"What was her mother's name?"

"Linda." Just saying the name still brought a smile to his lips. She had been a lovely, gentle woman and she'd begun a healing process inside him.

"What happened? What happened with Linda and Amy to convince you that you should never have a family?"

"To understand, you have to know what it was like in medical school. I was always so tired back then. In some ways it was even worse than it is now. The schedule was crazy, and there was a tremendous amount of pressure. Maybe I just felt it more, because I wanted so badly to be the best at something. I suppose I was still trying to be the perfect son, the one who didn't deserve those beatings."

A shudder ran through him as the memories flooded back. "There's no excuse for what happened. Amy was just a kid. She couldn't possibly know that she was driving me crazy. Every time I went over there she seemed to throw some sort of a tantrum. I couldn't study. I couldn't relax. I didn't feel I had any right to discipline her and Linda was lenient, the way mothers are after a divorce. The tension just built and built until one day I finally exploded. The next thing I knew Amy was screaming and crying, and Linda was taking her to her room. I hated myself at that moment, more than I'd ever thought was possible. I don't know if you can even comprehend that kind of self-loathing. I'll never forget the look on that child's face or the way it made me feel."

"Did you and Linda talk about what happened?"

"I couldn't. I couldn't even look at her. All I could see was that I was going to be just like my parents. It made me sick. Before she could come back into the living room, I left. I avoided her at the hospital, hung up on her when she called. I know it was cowardly, but I simply couldn't face her."

"Did she know about your childhood?"

Justin nodded.

"Then don't you think she might have understood what you were going through? Certainly she would have understood about the pressure. Nurses see it all the time."

He was on his feet again, a restless energy unleashed in him. "Don't you see, it didn't matter. I'm the one who doesn't understand. I was an adult. I'm the one who should have known how to handle the pressure and I didn't. I just blew up and hurt an innocent little girl."

"Did you actually hit her?"

Justin blinked and stared at Mallory. "Hit her? No," he said hesitantly, then shook his head. "That's not the important thing. I wanted to. God, how I wanted to." He shuddered. "Never again. Never again."

He realized then that Mallory was trying to struggle to her feet. "No," he said, urging her back. "Leave it alone. Leave me alone. I was wrong to think you and I could make it work. I should have realized how you would feel about having kids. You're a child psychologist. Of course, you'd want children of your own. I'm sorry."

He wanted to touch her one last time, but he was sure if he did, he'd never be able to leave and he knew he had to leave. It was the only choice. "I'm so sorry."

Tears were running down his cheeks, but he was hardly aware of them as he backed toward the door. He gazed at Mallory as though he could imprint an image of her on his mind forever. Not this one, his head shouted, not this image of her staring at him as though he'd delivered a cruel blow. He wanted to remember her laughing. He wanted to remember how she'd felt in his arms.

And then he thought, as he ran out of the apartment, he didn't want to remember at all.

Mallory wasn't nearly as startled as she once would have been when Justin began avoiding her. She'd even expected it after the revelations he had made to her. She could analyze his behavior with a calm, rational professionalism that would have made her college professors proud. She understood exactly why he had run, exactly what his fears were, but she found it hurt just the same.

It hurt even more when she tried to force the issue, to make him face it so they could go on. He practically told her to get lost.

"There's no point in discussing this anymore. It won't change anything."

"I won't just let it die. I love you too much. I know if we work together, we can resolve this. We can't do a damn thing if you won't even see me," she snapped when she finally managed to corner him alone in an elevator. She pulled the emergency stop button and halted it between floors.

"What the hell are you doing?" He pushed the button back in. The elevator jerked to a start.

"Trying to talk some sense into you." She yanked on the button again.

"If I want to go into analysis, I'll pay the two hundred dollars an hour for it." He hit the emergency button, and the elevator reached her floor before she could stop it again.

"You are a stubborn fool, Justin Whitmore," she said as the doors slid open. "You're just going to throw this away, aren't you?"

She stalked off furiously, determined not to be the one to make the next move. Justin didn't want Mallory Blake, the Ph.D., who could understand what he was going through, who could help him deal with it. He only wanted the woman and right now Mallory Blake, the woman, was ready to tear the man in two. It would be just as well if they kept as much distance between the two of them as possible until she could bring that Irish temper of hers under control.

It was Davey who drew them back together again. He was beginning to make astonishing progress, now that his father was there to see him every day. He even seemed to accept his mother's infrequent visits with a certain childish stoicism. It looked to Mallory as though his father would be granted custody, and that there would be no reconciliation between Jenny Landers and her husband. It didn't surprise her. She didn't believe in reconciliations anymore.

Every evening either Mallory or Justin took Davey for walks around the hospital grounds or to the playroom. They were astonishingly successful at seeing that their visits never coincided.

One night, though, Davey insisted that the three of them go out for hamburgers at the coffee shop across the street.

"Dr. Justin said I could," he announced with a stubborn pout when Mallory hesitated.

"Then I'm sure he'll take you," she said.

"I want you to come, too." His eyes filled with tears that were amazingly timely. "Please," he begged, and Mallory was lost. Damn the kid!

If Justin was surprised to see her when he came to get Davey, he hid it well. His greeting was polite, if not effusive. Dinner was an uncomfortable affair at first, but Davey's enthusiastic chatter gradually overcame their initial reticence, and soon the three of them were laughing like any of the other families in the restaurant. For Mallory it was an all-too-tempting image, bittersweet because of what it said about the future she was finally accepting would never be hers. Justin's glance caught hers across the table, and the old touch of magic and fire was in his eyes. It was Mallory who blinked and looked away.

After dinner, they took Davey back to his room and said good-night.

"Come on," Justin said. "I'll walk you to your car."

"That's not necessary."

"Necessity has nothing to do with it," he said, already walking along with her. "I'm sorry if Davey forced you into this."

Mallory shrugged indifferently. "You're the one who called it quits. I wanted to keep on seeing you, to try to work things out."

She could see Justin's jaw working. "I'd like to see you again. I've missed you," he said, and her heart rose with excitement, only to plummet in the next instant. "I don't want to lose you as a friend."

As a friend. The words seemed to stick in Mallory's

throat, and she wanted to choke. She wanted to wring his neck, but she managed to smile. "Why not?" she said with a bravado she didn't feel. Never let it be said that Mallory Blake was a coward. Mature, rational adults, who had been as close as she and Justin, ought to be able to remain friends after the love affair ended. "We can always give it a try."

"Want to go to a picnic with me on Saturday? The residents are playing ball against the guys from radiology."

"Sounds like fun." It sounded like sheer, unadulterated torture. It was also doomed to failure. Mallory should have known that, and so should Justin.

Instead, they blithely set off for the park on Saturday, a picnic hamper in the back seat of the car, friendly smiles plastered on their faces. Mallory was smiling so hard her jaw hurt.

"So, is this game for men only?"

"As far as I know."

"Sounds a bit chauvinistic. Are the women supposed to stand on the sidelines and cheer dutifully or are we relegated to the food detail?"

He cast a sharp glance in her direction. "You don't really want to play, do you?"

Actually, it was the last thing she wanted to do, but there seemed to be a principle involved and suddenly she was stubbornly determined to defend it. "Why not? I used to play ball with my brothers." Only after dire threats and promises of unlimited ice cream in return.

Justin shrugged. "Let's see what's happening when we get there."

When they arrived at the park, they found that there were more than enough residents to play, but the radiology group was a little short and was willing to be an equal-opportunity team. Mallory was given a glove and sent to the outfield on the theory that most of the doctors were out of shape and would never hit a ball that far. She trotted past Justin, shooting him a triumphant smile.

It felt good to be outdoors with the sun beating down on her bare shoulders. The sky was a vivid blue, and white puffs of clouds skittered by overhead. She was so busy enjoying it all that she nearly missed a play. She heard the crack of the bat against the ball and looked up just in time to see the ball whizzing in her direction.

"Oh, dear heaven," she muttered as she moved backward in an attempt to get in position.

"Go for it, Mallory! You've got it."

She was encouraged by all the shouts and stretched up to make the catch. She took one last step back—into a hole. Her ankle twisted and down she went with a sickening thud, arms askew. No one was more astonished than she was when she heard the soft *thunk* of the ball in her glove and a roar of triumph from her teammates.

She got to her feet and trotted in, trying to ignore the strange look of approval she caught in Justin's eyes. If the catch had been her only moment of glory, she would have considered the day a success. Instead, she had a chance to put her team ahead.

With two men out and players on first and third, it was her turn at bat. She hadn't made a hit all day and had no reason to expect anything to change. The pitcher seemed to take uncommon delight in whizzing the balls past her so quickly she rarely even saw them. This time she simply closed her eyes and put the bat somewhere in the middle of the strike zone. There was a dull *thwack,* her hands started to sting, and her teammates screamed at her to run toward first.

Mallory took off, hardly aware of the fact that the ball was dribbling slowly down the baseline in the same direction she was headed. She was focused entirely on where she was going, and when Justin suddenly loomed up in front of her, there wasn't time to stop, much less to avoid him. She ran headlong into the solid mass of his body and practically knocked herself out.

His arms went around her, and every inch of her body went instantly weak as her pulse skipped crazily. She never noticed that he had the ball in his hand, that the umpire had called her out or that her teammates were trailing off dejectedly. All she knew was that she was in the arms of the man she loved more than anything.

"Are you okay?" His voice seemed choked. She could only manage a nod as her eyes locked with his.

"Justin…"

He closed his eyes. "Don't say it, Mallory. Don't say anything." He held her cradled against his chest, where she could feel the rapid beat of his heart and smell the sharp, tangy male scent of him. His shirt was damp under her cheek and it felt so damn good. She sighed.

"This isn't working," he said at last, forcing himself to let go of her. He had to use every bit of self-restraint to keep from hauling her to some secluded section of the park, stripping off her ridiculous tank top and sexy shorts and making love to her until they were both unable to think of anything but the present.

It was the future that had gotten them into trouble. If only they could live for the moment, things would be just fine. But that wasn't the kind of woman Mallory was, and he wasn't going to ruin her chances of finding someone else.

"This was a mistake."

"Getting me out at first? I'll say it was. I may never forgive you. It was the closest I came to a hit all day."

"Don't try to make jokes about it, Mallory. You know exactly what I mean. We'd better stop seeing each other."

"Again?"

He smiled apologetically. "I know. I'm the one who came back, but I was wrong to think we could have some sort of friendly, platonic relationship. I can't spend ten minutes with you without wanting to hold you, to touch you." His voice was husky with emotion.

"What's stopping you?"

"For all my faults, I do have a few scruples left. I won't let you waste your life on me."

"I don't consider it a waste of time."

"It is, Mallory. We both know it. I'll never be able to give you that marriage and family bit, not the way you want. If I try to do it your way, they'll probably have to lock me away somewhere. If you try to do it my way, you'll only wind up resenting me. I don't think I could stand that."

"So, it's adios, have a good life, take care of yourself and all that?"

"I think so. It's for the best." He kissed her, desperately needing one last taste of her lips. "I'll drive you home."

"The condemned woman doesn't even get lunch?"

"Do you really want to eat?"

"No. I guess not. I'd probably choke on the chicken." They were quiet during the ride to her apartment.

Justin couldn't stand the silence, but he had no idea what he could say that would matter at this point. He'd selfishly wanted to keep her near him, even if just as a friend, but it would never work. It had been foolish to think it might.

"This is for the best," he repeated when he pulled to a stop in front of her apartment. He didn't shut off the engine, not wanting to draw the painful moment out. He saw the hurt in her eyes and pressed a shaking finger to her mouth in a farewell gesture, feeling the tremor of her lips. It nearly broke his heart—and his resolve.

"You think you're so smart, Justin Whitmore," she muttered as she got out of the car and slammed the door. "But you don't know a damn thing about love."

Yes, he contradicted mentally as he pulled away. *It's taken me a long time, but, thanks to you, I do. I know enough to give you your freedom.*

Chapter 12

Once more it was Davey who provided their solace, though separately. Mallory knew of Justin's visits because Davey talked about them, but Justin was careful to avoid her. She also knew he was pouring himself into his work, taking longer and longer shifts. She heard the rumblings about his reversion to tyrannical fits of temper, and she was doing the same thing, snapping at everyone. She had added on patients so that by the end of the day she was emotionally spent and too exhausted to even think about her breakup with Justin. Davey was the one bright spot in her life.

He was flourishing now. As the court wrestled with a decision over custody, he remained at the hospital. Though he was physically fine, it had been decided that he would be better off there for a few extra days or even weeks, than if he were put into a temporary foster home.

His father had had to return to his job, but was coming back into town each weekend to give Davey as much support as possible. He had even indicated to the court a willingness to return to San Francisco permanently, if that would influence the custody decision.

A tutor came to see Davey several times a week and Mallory worked with him as well. He was reading far beyond a first grade level, going through the storybooks in the playroom at a speed that astonished and delighted her. She took pride in every accomplishment and had several pieces of his colorful artwork on the walls in her office. The nurses, Davey's father and even Jenny Landers had commented on how well Davey had responded to her.

"It was just a matter of giving him some attention," she told Jenny Landers late one afternoon.

"It was more than that. You gave him love, something I haven't done very well. I hope to God he'll be able to forgive me some day."

"I'm sure he will. Just give him time."

"I just want you to know how much I appreciate everything you've done," Jenny said. "We're all very grateful."

Feeling especially good after that conversation, Mallory was unprepared when Dr. Marshall called her into his office a few minutes later and began to reprimand her again for becoming overly involved with her patient. Mallory sat and stared at him blankly. First Justin and now this? She was going to quietly lose her mind.

"I thought we'd settled this," she said when she could open her mouth without shouting.

"I must say I had thought the same thing, Dr. Blake.

I warned you about this several weeks ago. Apparently you didn't take that warning seriously."

"Have there been more complaints? I swear to you that I've kept my promise. I'm only working with Davey in my spare time. His parents are very pleased with the progress he's making. I just talked to his mother today."

"That's not the point."

"Then what is?"

"You've allowed yourself to become too involved with this child."

Mallory couldn't honestly dispute that fact. She adored Davey, and he'd begun treating her almost like a mother. "Do you think it's clouded my judgment?" she asked cautiously.

"Perhaps not. The court seems to value your input highly and, as you say, his parents have nothing but praise for you, but I am going to have to recommend that you be taken off the case."

"You can't do that now," she protested, her heart beating wildly as anxiety surged through her. "The court will be making a decision soon. I'll need to be there."

"You've filed your statements. If they require more, you will be permitted to comply with any requests, but I want you out of that boy's room beginning now." His tone was crisp and decisive, and it cut straight through to her heart.

"Please, Dr. Marshall, don't do this. It will be bad for Davey."

"Bad for Davey?" He regarded her knowingly, but not without compassion. "Or bad for you?"

"I don't understand."

"I think you do, Dr. Blake. Whether you believe it or

not, I am concerned about you. You're far too involved with that little boy. I've observed the two of you together myself. There's a bond there that goes far beyond the doctor-patient relationship."

Mallory felt a sharp ache in her heart. "Is that so awful?"

"Oh, my dear, that's not the issue. Speaking as a human being, I can well understand your fondness for Davey. I can also see why he would become so attached to you. You're a kind, generous young woman. But speaking as a psychologist, I have to tell you it's wrong. I think you know that as well as I do."

"I don't know that," she argued, but she knew from the look in his eyes it was futile.

"Let me just ask you one question. What will you do when he leaves here?"

The prospect of Davey no longer being a part of her day was something Mallory had considered and pushed aside time and again. Dr. Marshall was forcing her to confront it and she didn't like what she saw...emptiness of a sort she hadn't faced since she'd lost her husband. With Justin already out of her life, the thought of losing Davey, too, terrified her. Apparently her fear was written all over her face.

"I think you'd better take some time off and get this case back into perspective," Dr. Marshall said, and this time his voice was gentle, his brown eyes filled with kindness. "You're a good psychologist, Dr. Blake. Don't allow one case to ruin a very promising career."

"I won't allow that," she vowed. "I swear to you that I can get Davey's situation in perspective. He still needs the attention I've been able to give him."

"Perhaps he did, at first. Now he needs to get ready

to leave here. He won't be able to do that if he's too attached to you and you to him. Give him his freedom,
my dear."

"Are you suggesting for one minute that I've ham-
pered his progress for my own selfish reasons?"

"Of course not," he replied. "But it's time to let go.
Think it over, and I know you'll see that I'm right. Say
your goodbyes now."

Mallory thought about little else all night. In the end,
she admitted that there was far too much truth in Dr.
Marshall's assessment of her relationship with Davey
for her peace of mind. He was an appealing little boy
and he had needed her. It was no wonder he was becoming the child she'd never had during her marriage,
the child she might never have with Justin. It wasn't a
healthy situation for either one of them.

The next morning she asked the psychology chief
for some time off. He readily granted her a three-week
leave, clearly pleased by her decision to act on his advice. By the time she came back, Davey would very
likely be home again, perhaps even in another city with
his father.

It was late in the afternoon when she went to break
the news that she wouldn't be seeing him anymore.

"Hiya, sport. How's it going?" she asked when she
found him in the playroom, finger paints streaked
across his cheeks. The tip of his tongue peeked out of
the corner of his mouth as he concentrated on the picture he was drawing of a mother, father and little boy
standing in front of a house. A wobbly sun shone down
on the scene and a three-legged dog was being completed in the bottom corner. "Nice picture."

Davey gave her a lopsided grin. "It's for Mommy.

Rachel told me tomorrow's her birthday." A frown puckered his brow. "Do you think she'll want a present from me?"

"She'll love it," Mallory said with forced enthusiasm.

Davey smiled at her response, then gave her one of his very wise looks. "Are you sad?"

"A little bit."

"Why?"

"I have to go away for a little while."

The smile on Davey's face faded, and tears promptly formed. "No," he said adamantly.

"I have to, sport."

"Was I bad?"

The question was entirely predictable, but for some reason she hadn't anticipated it. It broke her heart. She gathered him close, ignoring the paints that got smeared all over her. "No. Absolutely not. You are my very favorite person in the whole world, and I'm going to miss you like crazy."

She choked back a sob. "When I get back, you may be at home again, just like in the picture. Remember, we've been talking about that for a long time now. Right now we don't know if you'll be with your dad or your mom, but I don't want you to be afraid. If you're with your mom, it won't be like it was before. She's much better now."

"Will you come to see me?"

"I'll try," she promised. "But if I don't get there for a while, you just remember that I'll always love you and that you'll always be right here." She pointed at her heart, then at his. "And you can keep me right there inside you, too."

That was the way Justin found them, holding on to

each other. Mallory was trying her darnedest not to cry, but it was a wasted effort. Davey was sobbing furiously.

She looked up and saw Justin in the doorway, and he caught the mute appeal in her red-rimmed eyes. With a fear greater than any he'd ever felt before, he went into the room and picked the little boy up, trying to comfort him. Then he had to watch as Mallory ran from the room and, he knew instinctively, out of his life, this time possibly for good.

It took him an hour to calm Davey down. It wasn't until the child's father came that he felt he could leave the boy and go after Mallory. The decision to go had been made without conscious thought. His determination to stay aloof had vanished instantly at the sight of her holding Davey, clearly deeply distressed.

He found her packing.

"What the devil is going on? Why were you saying goodbye to Davey? Is he being released?"

"Probably quite soon, but that wasn't it. You might as well know, I'm going away for a while. Dr. Marshall pretty much insisted on it."

The news hit him like a sharp blow to his midsection. "Why?"

"He seems to feel I've lost my objectivity, and I think he's right. I've turned Davey into a substitute for everything I don't have in my own life."

"So you're running away?"

"I suppose that's one way of looking at it."

"How can you leave now?"

"There's really no reason to stay. There's no one here for me. I need to get away, try to get things together for myself."

"And then you'll be back?"

"Justin, why does it matter to you? You broke things off. I should think you'd be delighted to know I won't be around. It'll give you some space, too."

"Why do I suddenly feel as though space is the last thing I want?"

"I can't answer that one for you."

"Maybe I was wrong about all this. Maybe we can work it out. The past couple of weeks have been hell. I thought I could just pick up with my life the way it was before we met, but I haven't been able to do that. It's like a part of me has died. I don't want to lose you."

"Maybes aren't good enough, not for a marriage, Justin. And what about kids? We feel very differently about that. It's a real problem. It's not exactly something we can compromise on. We can't have kids on alternate weeks or keep them in a separate house."

"I'll try to change."

"I don't want you to do something you're uncomfortable with for me. You have to do it for yourself."

"I'm not sure if I can. After what happened with Linda's daughter, I don't know if I'll ever be able to trust myself around kids. I'll always be terrified that I'll explode and take my anger out on them."

Mallory gazed at him and sighed. She had wanted so desperately to believe they had a future together, but not this way, not with Justin struggling to fight demons every step of the way. If only he could see how wrong he was about himself, about his ability to love, to be a good parent. She made one last attempt to reach him.

"I understand your fears. I really do, but what about all these weeks with Davey? You've been patient and loving and gentle with him, even when he's been a little terror."

"Davey was different."

"Why?"

"I identified with him."

Mallory smiled at him. "You still can't say it, can you? You love him. One word, Justin, and it makes all the difference to everything." She sighed and snapped the suitcase shut. He still didn't understand, and perhaps he never would.

"I'm glad you stopped by before I left. As long as I'm saying goodbyes today, I might as well include you."

"Mallory, no. It's not over for us." He pulled her roughly into his arms and slanted his mouth across hers with brutal urgency. His lips were warm and demanding, and fire raced through her veins as he tried to master her. The desperate attempt almost worked. She felt herself weakening, melting in his embrace, and then she glimpsed the future. What he was offering wasn't nearly enough.

There were tears in her eyes when she finally broke free. Her voice shook. "Yes, it is. We'll both be better off. You've been telling me that from the first."

"Damn it, I will not be better off. You've finally shown me that I can't go through life without people, without you. You can't just leave now."

"I have to," she said gently and walked to the door. Justin didn't follow, so she called over her shoulder as she went out, "Lock up when you leave, okay?"

She was sobbing by the time she reached her car, but she tilted her chin bravely and got in. With every remaining ounce of strength she had, she turned on the ignition and, with a last look up at the light burning in her living room window, she put the car in gear and drove away.

Three blocks later, she stopped and cried some more. By the time she reached the freeway, she'd made three more stops, used an entire box of tissues and picked up a bottle of eye drops. She doubted if, despite the claims, they would ever get the red out of her eyes.

"Not if you keep thinking about him," she muttered. "Think happy thoughts. Think about going home. Think about sitting on the patio sipping lemonade and watching the sun go down."

She was actually doing better until that last thought. It reminded her of sitting on the floor of her living room, Justin's arms around her, as a pink-hued sunset spilled through the window and splashed across their damp, bare flesh with a magical glow. The vision started a fresh bout of tears.

"You walked out, you dummy. He wanted you to stay. This time you were the one who said this was for the best." The words echoed hollowly through the car. Now she recognized the lie. It wasn't for the best. Nothing that hurt this much could be for the best.

She felt like swinging the car around and heading straight back to her apartment, where she had a feeling Justin would still be waiting. Pride and sheer force of will kept her driving south. They were lousy companions.

He has to come to you, she told herself. *He did.* But he has to be ready for a commitment. *He asked you to marry him. What more do you want?* He has to mean it. *Give me a break.*

Mallory wasn't certain where this other voice was coming from, but she wished it would shut up. It was obviously losing patience with her.

She was still talking to herself and still not finding

that she liked the answers when she finally pulled into her parents' driveway the next day. She had stopped at a motel in a futile attempt to get some rest. She had watched every cable channel available all through the endless night and had even considered calling in to order one of those unbelievable vegetable choppers that could slice and dice and probably perform miracles.

She had barely opened the door of the car, when her mother came bursting through the front door and ran down the sidewalk. "Mallory Marie, are you okay? What are you doing here? Your phone's turned off and I've been worried sick all night."

Mallory gazed at her in confusion. "Why were you worried? You didn't even know I was coming."

"Justin's been calling since late yesterday. He seemed to think you were much too upset to be on the road and, judging from the looks of you, he was right to worry. You look absolutely terrible."

"Just the ego boost I needed, Mom."

"Sorry. It's not that I'm not glad to see you. Your father's going to be thrilled. I'll call your sister and your brothers, too. I'm sure they'll all want to come right over. How long will you be here?"

"If you call in the troops, about fifteen minutes. Please, Mom, leave it alone. Give me a day or two to pull my act together before you convene the family council."

Her mother looked hurt. "I just wasn't sure how long you planned to stay. I wanted to be sure everyone had a chance to visit with you."

Mallory relented. "I'll probably be here a couple of weeks. I don't know. I'm just so tired."

That immediately put her mother on another track

entirely. "Well, of course you are. What am I thinking of? You go right on back to your room and take a nap. I'll have a nice dinner ready when you come out."

Mallory gave her mother a hug and wandered down the hall in a daze. When she came out of the bedroom a few hours later, she heard her mother's hushed voice.

"I don't know what's the matter with her. She won't say a word, but that man from San Francisco's been calling all day. Maybe they had a fight. No. Don't come over. She says she doesn't want to see anyone quite yet. Yes, dear, I'll try not to worry."

Mallory poked her head through the kitchen doorway.

"Oh, my, well, she's up now," her mother said brightly. "I've got to go." She cast a hopeful look in Mallory's direction. "Would you like to talk to your sister?"

"Tell her hello and that I'll call her later." Mallory was not up to an inquisition. She was not up to much of anything. In fact, she felt as though she might very well spend the next couple of weeks in bed with the covers pulled over her head. With any luck, she'd suffocate.

When her mother had hung up, Mallory offered to help with the dinner preparations. She reached for a knife to slice the carrots, but it was snatched out of her reach. Apparently her mother didn't think she was ready to be trusted with sharp objects. "I was just going to cut the carrots," Mallory grumbled.

"There's no need, dear. Not on your first night home. Just sit here and talk to me."

"How's Dad?"

"Your father's fine. I'm a little concerned about this heat, though. It seems to take a lot out of him."

"You've been saying that for the past twenty years."

"Well, it's been true for the past twenty years," she said, clearly miffed by the observation. "As people get older things like that affect them more."

"I see."

The knife clattered to the table, and the carrots were pushed aside. Mallory knew a serious moment when she saw it coming. Her mother had lost patience and was about to launch an all-out assault until she got some straight answers.

"So," she began innocently enough, "tell me more about this Justin. You've only mentioned him once or twice on the phone, but I could tell he was someone important in your life, even before he started calling here every half hour."

"Mother!"

"Aren't I supposed to ask personal questions?"

"Can't we just leave it alone for tonight?"

"Not when I see you sitting there with circles under your eyes—you could use some eye drops, by the way— and a glum expression. You haven't looked this way since…" Her voice trailed off in confusion.

"Since Alan died." Mallory completed the thought for her. She sighed. "I know. I haven't felt this way since then."

"Don't you want to talk about it?" her mother urged. "You're the great believer in talking. People pay you a fortune to listen to them talk about their problems. I won't even charge."

"I don't know where to begin. I think this is one time I need to muddle through on my own. Maybe when I've had some time to sort it all out, I'll be able to talk about it. Okay?"

Her mother hugged her. It felt good, but it didn't

make the pain go away the way hugs had when she was a child.

"I'll be here, whenever you're ready," her mother promised just as the phone rang.

"Oh, hello, Justin," her mother said, staring at her pointedly. Mallory's heart did a traitorous flip, but she shook her head. "Yes, she's here. She got in a few hours ago, but she's resting. Yes, of course, dear, I'll tell her you called. Would you like me to have her call you back? I see. Okay, then. Goodbye, Justin."

She regarded Mallory peculiarly. "He doesn't want you to call back."

"I'm not surprised."

"Then why has he been calling here, if he didn't want to talk to you? Did he do something to upset you, Mallory?"

How did you explain to your mother that the man you loved had asked you to marry him, then rescinded the offer, made it again, only to rescind it yet another time when the subject of kids came up? How did you tell her that the man you loved was an absolute fool, who had no idea of all the good qualities he possessed? How did you say any of that without giving entirely the wrong impression of the man or of your own good sense? Mallory had no idea, so she kept her mouth clamped firmly shut.

Justin hung up the phone and sat staring at it blankly. Thank God, Mallory had finally gotten home. He hadn't been absolutely certain that that was where she was headed, but instinct told him she'd want the security and love of her family when she was going through an emotional upheaval. If she hadn't been there, he'd have turned the entire state of California upside down until he found her.

Then what?

Then he'd have sat telling himself he was an idiot for letting the woman get away, just as he was doing now. He was also telling himself he couldn't go after her. Not until he worked through all these conflicting emotions that were tearing at his insides. The only thing he knew for certain was that he loved Mallory Blake more than he'd ever imagined he could love anyone. That truth shone through all the others and made him want to try like crazy to make sense of the rest.

He would have preferred to do that with her nearby. At least knowing that she was in the hospital, catching an occasional glimpse of her moving briskly through the halls, had kept him going. Damn it all. It was Dr. Marshall's fault that she was gone. What had the man been thinking of to suggest that there was something unprofessional in her caring so much for Davey? Mallory should never be made to question the depth of her concern for her patients. It was what made her such a good psychologist.

With that thought in mind, he leaped to his feet and tore through the hospital in search of the psychology chief. He found him in his stuffy, dark office on the third floor.

Justin had only met Dr. Marshall once or twice at faculty-resident functions, but he'd always struck Justin as a bit of a pompous jerk. In fact, he'd reminded him all too much of the overbearing, self-indulgent psychologist who'd gotten involved with Justin's mother, when he was supposed to be treating her.

"Dr. Marshall, I think there are a few things you and I need to discuss."

The man's head snapped up and he blinked furiously at Justin. "Who are you?"

"I'm Dr. Whitmore, neurosurgery. Davey Landers is my patient."

"Of course. Of course. I've heard a great deal about your extraordinary efforts to save that boy's life. I congratulate you. I hear he has made a remarkable recovery." The words of praise seemed genuine, which momentarily startled Justin.

"Thank you. But that's not what I wanted to talk to you about. Why did you take Dr. Blake off that case?"

"I felt it was best for the boy...." He raised a silencing hand when Justin would have interrupted. "And for Dr. Blake."

"I'm not buying it. There was no reason to remove her. She was doing an excellent job with Davey. He's a happy, stable little boy again, thanks to her."

Dr. Marshall leaned back in his chair and to Justin's amazement, his eyes were twinkling. "I see. I seem to recall hearing that you don't have much use for psychologists, Dr. Whitmore. What changed your mind with regard to Dr. Blake?"

"I just told you. I've watched her work with Davey. She's very good. You'll never find a psychologist who cares more about the well-being of her patients."

"I think that's probably true. Unfortunately, I'm not so sure she was thinking quite enough about herself in this case."

"I don't understand."

"Dr. Whitmore, I'm going to be frank with you. It's evident to me that you—" he hesitated a fraction of a second as he chose his next word carefully "—*respect* Dr. Blake a great deal. I have to wonder, though, how well you really know her."

"Quite well, I think."

"Perhaps. Are you aware that she lost her husband little more than a year ago?"

"She's mentioned it, yes. What does that have to do with Davey?"

"It's human nature, Dr. Whitmore, to attempt to fill a void. Davey needed someone like Dr. Blake, but no more than she needed him. She was growing far too attached to the child. In suggesting that she take some time off, I was merely trying to get her to recognize that attachment, to take action to prevent her from suffering another loss. That is what it would have come to had she not been the one to let go. Davey will leave this hospital soon, either with a member of his family or a court-appointed guardian. It would not have been good for either one of them to hold on to each other."

Justin listened to what the psychologist was saying and felt all of the fight drain out of him. He had come up here to tell off an enemy and had found, instead, an ally, a man whose respect for Mallory equaled his own, a man far more compassionate than he'd expected.

"Then you weren't trying to tell Mallory that she was a bad psychologist?"

"Quite the contrary. I think she's one of the best we've ever had on staff. I wanted to be sure she'd learn to save some of herself for future patients. No doctor— whether psychologist or even neurosurgeon—can afford to share too much of himself with his patients. You have to hold a little back in order to survive. It doesn't

mean you don't care, only that you know how to pre-
serve your objectivity."

Justin stood then and held out his hand. "Thank you,
Dr. Marshall. You have no idea how much this talk has
meant to me. Do you know when Dr. Blake will be
coming back?"

"She took a three-week leave. I'd say we can expect
her here by the end of the month."

Three weeks, Justin thought as he walked away. It
seemed like an eternity. Would it be nearly enough time
for him to get his own life in perspective?

Chapter 13

Ever since his talk with Dr. Marshall, Justin had wandered around the hospital in a daze. He had performed skillfully in the operating room. If anything, he was more obsessed than ever with his work, but he wasn't happy. It no longer brought him the fulfillment it once had. He missed sharing his triumphs and his concerns with the one woman who had ever loved him totally and without reserve.

It still astonished him that a woman as wonderfully sensitive, bright and attractive as Mallory could know all of his flaws and love him just the same. Wasn't it about time, then, that he learned to love himself?

As a child he'd been convinced that he couldn't possibly have any good qualities, that he wasn't worthy of love, but that was the reaction of a boy to a situation that was beyond his understanding. He was an adult now and, damn it all, he did have good qualities. It had taken Mallory to bring them out, to nurture them until he believed in himself, not just as a surgeon, but as a man.

He loved her, for giving him that new sense of confidence and self-worth and for so much more. He loved her for the joy, the laughter, even the persistent nagging she had brought into his life. The latter, as irritating as it sometimes had been, was only a sign of the depth of her caring. He was all the stronger because of it. He wished she were here now, so he could tell her in person just how much she had given him.

Still, he told himself it was better that she was gone. Despite his desire to put the past behind him, to build a new future with Mallory, too much of the past lingered to torment him. What if he and Mallory married and had children and he found that he was incapable of being a kind, loving parent, the type of father he'd always wanted? Certainly his experience with Linda's daughter had shown him that he was far too short on patience. It was a fact that he didn't dare to ignore. It was the one stumbling block that kept him from going after Mallory.

He was sitting in the staff lounge near the recovery room waiting to check on a postsurgical patient, when he heard a familiar laugh and looked up to see an almost-forgotten smile, a smile he once had loved. Now it sent a chill through him.

Linda! Dear God, why now? Was it an omen, a reminder of all he was incapable of being? How could he put the past behind him when it was staring him in the face?

Linda's smile brightened instantly when she spotted

him, wavered and then faded as she saw the scowl on his face and realized it was meant for her.

"Justin, how are you?" Her voice was soft, with just the slightest hint of restraint.

"Hello, Linda," he said stiffly. "It's been a long time."

"Eight years."

"What are you doing here?"

She gestured at her own scrubs. "Come now. You were always an astute man. What does it look like?"

"You've transferred to Fairview?" He couldn't begin to hide his dismay. "Why? I thought you were happy with your old job."

Her faint grin was rueful. "That's just it. After all those years it had grown too old, too familiar. I needed a challenge. I'll be supervising the afternoon shift here, with a good chance to move up to director of nursing for the operating room in a couple of years."

"Congratulations," Justin said, though the word seemed to catch in his throat. The thought of running into her every day, of working with her, of dredging up old memories time after time made a hard knot form in his stomach.

She was regarding him perceptively. "You always were a lousy liar, Justin. You're not one bit happy to see me or to hear that I'm going to be around for a while. Want to talk about it?"

"There's nothing to say. We said it all eight years ago."

"No," she contradicted. "You walked out on me and when I tried to find out why, you said a lot of things that didn't make any sense. I've never really understood what happened. If we're going to have to work together here—and I don't see any way around that—then we'd better put the past behind us."

The words echoed hollowly in his head. It was all he had wanted, too, and he knew it could never happen. "I have to go check on a patient," he said, moving toward the door. She put a restraining hand on his arm.

"Justin, don't run from this. Have lunch with me, get things out in the open."

He regarded her curiously. "Why, Linda? Why is this so important to you?"

She chuckled, obviously amused by the caution in his voice. "I'm not trying to start things up again, if that's what you're afraid of. I'm married now. Happily, I might add. But you meant a lot to me once, and I'd like to end the tension. I'd also like to understand what went wrong. You know me—I never was one to like any loose threads dangling around in my life."

He nodded curtly, relieved on one level, yet still troubled. Linda might very well have answers for him, insights into his personality that no one else had. Would they be the answers he wanted to hear? If there was to be any hope for him and Mallory, he had to find out.

"Noon," he said at last. "There's a coffee shop across the street. I'll meet you there."

The rest of the morning seemed interminable, touched by an unlikely combination of anticipation and dread. Justin felt as though he were on a singularly unstable plank across a deep chasm, his whole life in the balance. On one side, the future was bright with possibilities. Mallory's face danced before his eyes. She beckoned to him, and his body tightened with arousal as it always did at the merest thought of her. On the other side of the chasm was emptiness, years of loneliness that stretched endlessly ahead.

Linda was waiting for him when he finally raced across the street and into the crowded coffee shop at 12:15. A cup of coffee and a chef's salad were already on the table at his place. He smiled despite himself.

"Reading my mind again?"

"Nope. Just figuring that some things aren't likely to change much. Still take your Russian dressing on the side?"

"Yes."

She shook her head. "I've never figured out why. You dump every bit of it onto the salad anyway. Why not let them do it in the kitchen?"

"It's the closest I ever get to cooking."

"I'm amazed you haven't starved." She studied him closely. "Or is there a woman in your life to do the cooking?"

He sighed. "There was...until recently."

"What happened?"

"She went away, and I didn't try hard enough to stop her."

"Why not?"

"I couldn't. She deserves much more than I could give her."

"Your decision or hers?"

"Mine mostly."

"Still playing God with other people's emotions, I see."

"What's that supposed to mean?"

"You always did put your own interpretation on a situation and to hell with what anyone else thought or felt. That's what you did with me, anyway."

"How can you say that after what I did to Amy?"

To Justin's amazement, Linda's expression was incredulous. "What you did to Amy? Exactly what do you think you did to her?"

"I yelled at her." He hesitated, and Linda waited expectantly.

"That's it?"

It took every bit of his strength, and still the words seemed to be wrenched from him. "I wanted to hit her."

"She deserved it," Linda said very quietly.

Justin's eyes widened, and his heart began to pound. "What are you saying?"

Linda reached across and touched his hand. The gesture was compassionate and filled with regret. "Oh, Justin, is that what this is all about? You've been torturing yourself because you got angry at a little girl? Don't you realize that not a parent alive doesn't get furious with their kids at one time or another?"

"But I wanted to hit her, damn it. I almost did."

"But you didn't. Even though she deserved it, you didn't touch her. You just yelled. I'm the one who spanked her for drawing all over your term paper. I'm the one who sent her to her room. I'm astonished you held out as long as you did. From the minute you came into my life, she was abominable to you. She thought you were trying to take the place of her daddy and she did everything a six-year-old could think of to make sure that didn't happen. She set you up, Justin, and you fell into the trap."

"You mean…"

"I mean that Amy would have driven a saint to the edge. She behaved like an absolute brat, and all the talks

I had with her only seemed to make matters worse. It wasn't your fault, Justin."

He closed his eyes and felt a sigh of relief well up from the depths of his soul. "I was so sure I was going to repeat the pattern I had grown up with. I was terrified of it."

Linda gazed at him with eyes brimming with understanding. "God help me, I should have realized. I knew what you'd been through, but I had no idea you'd overreact like that, that you'd blame yourself."

"It's tortured me for the past eight years. You can't imagine what a weight it is off my chest to know that you don't hold me responsible."

"Hold you responsible? For what? Getting angry? It's a human emotion, Justin. Want to know what I think? I think you're not capable of hurting anyone, certainly not physically. You may be the gentlest man I've ever known. In fact, I suspect the only person you've ever hurt has been yourself. You've got so damn much stubborn pride, Justin. It's always kept you from taking chances, even when the odds are on your side. If you love her, go after this woman. Make things right."

Justin stood up quickly, practically knocking over his chair in his rush. He started away from the table, then came back and brushed a hasty kiss across Linda's brow and tossed some money on the table. "I'll invite you to dance at my wedding," he promised with a grin as he took off at a run.

It took him twenty-four hours to arrange it, but by Friday morning he was on a plane to Phoenix. He called the Blakes' house from the airport and got directions from Mallory's mother.

"It shouldn't take you more than fifteen or twenty

minutes to get here." She chuckled then. "I should be able to dream up an errand at the shopping mall that will require my urgent attention."

"Just be sure it's not something Mallory will volunteer to do for you."

"No problem. Mallory absolutely hates to shop. How any daughter of mine could feel that way, I don't know. Must be her father's influence."

Justin had no trouble at all following the directions. What he had trouble with was working up his courage to make the last turn onto the Blakes' street. Would Mallory want to see him or was she finally tired of his behavior, thankful it was all over between them?

"You're not going to get any answers sitting in a car half a block away," he finally muttered and made the turn just in time to see a car shoot out of the driveway with a woman who had to be Mallory's mother at the wheel. She was alone.

Justin parked in front of the house and walked slowly to the door. It was several long minutes after he rang the bell before he heard the sound of footsteps, then sensed a presence on the other side of the door.

"What are you doing here?" The words were muffled by the Spanish-style wooden door, but he recognized the feisty, indignant tone.

"I want to see you."

"What's the point? Go on back to San Francisco."

"Mallory Marie, your mother would be appalled by your manners."

"Probably so," she admitted. "I suppose she knew you were coming."

"Why would you think that?"

"Because she went scooting out of here so fast, she

forgot to take off her fuzzy pink bedroom slippers. She ought to be a real hit at the mall."

"Are you going to open the door or not?"

"I don't think so."

Justin shrugged. "Okay, it may be a little unconventional, but we'll do it your way."

"Do what my way?" she asked suspiciously.

"Never mind. Have you got a decent view through that peephole?"

"A decent view? Justin, what are you up to?"

"I'm down on my knees. Can you see me?"

"No, I can't see you." Her voice was exasperated. "What are you doing?"

He moved back a bit, then knelt down again. "What about now? Can you see me yet?"

"Justin, this is ridiculous. Why are you down on one knee on my sidewalk?"

"For a bright lady, you're very slow today. It must be the heat. No one will ever convince me ninety-seven degrees isn't hot, just because it's dry heat."

"Justin!"

"Okay, don't get impatient." He dug around in his pocket until his fingers found the little velvet box. He took it out and flipped it open. "I hope you can see this. It kind of glares in the sun."

"What is it?"

"A ring."

Instantly the door opened a crack, and blue-green eyes peered around the edge. "What kind of a ring?"

"An engagement ring. I was sort of hoping to do this a little more romantically, maybe even without sweat streaming down my back, but what the heck. A proposal's a proposal, right? Mallory Marie Blake, Ph.D., will you do me the honor of becoming Mrs. Justin Whitmore? If you want to stay Mallory Blake for professional reasons, I suppose that would be okay, too, as long as we're married. It may be a little confusing for the children, but I'll explain it so they understand and don't think they're illegitimate or something."

The door opened all the way at that, and startled eyes stared at him. "You want to get married," she breathed softly. "And have children?"

He nodded. "Preferably before my knees are welded to this sidewalk," he said.

"What changed your mind?"

"It's a long story and if you don't mind, I really would prefer not to tell it out here. Not that I'm not prepared to give you almost anything you want to get you to agree to marry me, but my brain is frying."

"Come in."

Air-conditioning had never felt so good to him in his life. He wanted to stand in front of one of the vents until his muscles froze, but Mallory was regarding him with such a light shining in her eyes that he quickly forgot his discomfort.

"Would you like some iced tea?" she asked politely.

"What I would like very much is a kiss. Is that possible?"

"It is definitely possible," she said and moved into his arms. If he had his way, she'd stay there forever. He buried his face in her hair, then tilted her chin up so he could slant his mouth across hers. The touch set off a brushfire inside him that no air-conditioning could cool. "God, Mallory, don't ever leave me again."

"I didn't leave you."

"Then why are you in Phoenix?"

"I'm thinking."

"That's not the same as leaving?"

"Not when you're still in love with a man who seemed to be too damn stubborn to realize what he was giving up."

"That reminds me, you haven't answered me yet," he said. "Will you marry me?"

Her arms were tight around his waist, but the look in her eyes was suddenly hesitant. "Are you absolutely, positively sure this is what you want? I'm not sure I can go through another one of these on-again, off-again things."

"More than anything."

"You couldn't say that a week or so ago. What changed your mind?"

"A week or so ago, I hadn't chased away the last of the demons. Linda helped me to do that."

"You saw her?"

"Funny thing. She turned up at Fairview, working in the OR. We had a long talk about what had happened, and she made me see it in a different light. She broke the last of my ties to the past. I'm ready to move forward now...with you, if you'll have me."

"No more fears and doubts?"

"I suppose I'll always have fears, but I know now you and I can work through just about anything. How many men are lucky enough to have their own personal psychologist around when the going gets rough?"

"Then you're reconciled to my profession, too?"

"Actually, it seems I'm a rather staunch defender. I gave Dr. Marshall a piece of my mind for sending you away."

She frowned at him, then chuckled in spite of herself. He could see the laughter coming into her eyes. "Oh, Justin, you didn't? What did he say?"

"Actually, it seems he's one of your biggest fans, but I think he was impressed with the persuasiveness of my argument."

"I'll just bet he was."

"Don't you care that I stood up for you?"

"Of course. But after everything you've said in the past, I have to wonder why you did it."

"You didn't deserve to be reprimanded for being good at your job."

"And?"

"And I finally admitted to myself it wasn't what you did at the hospital that made me so angry. It was my own fears."

"Explain."

"Do you really have to ask?"

She grinned. "No. But you need to answer."

"That's exactly what I was afraid of. You know me too well."

"Don't you see, though, that's not just because I'm a psychologist. It's because I love you. Do you understand everything about me?"

"Now that you mention it, no."

"Really? What don't you understand?"

"Why it's taking you so long to answer my question. Will you marry me?"

"I think you already know the answer."

This time it was Justin whose eyes were filled with humor. "But I want to hear you say it."

"Then, yes, my love. Yes."

When Mallory's mother came sneaking through the front door in her slippers an hour later, Justin and Mallory were necking on the sofa.

"Mallory Marie!" she said indignantly, but there was a decided sparkle in her eyes.

"Go away, Mother," Mallory murmured, still dropping kisses along Justin's jaw and at the tender spot just beneath his right ear.

"Aren't you going to introduce me?"

"Not right this minute."

"You'll be sorry," her mother responded, and Mallory's head snapped up. She looked toward the doorway, just in time to see her mother vanishing toward the kitchen.

"Why will we be sorry?" Justin asked nervously. "Has she gone after a shotgun?"

"My guess is she's headed for the phone."

"Why?"

"I would say that within the next fifteen minutes we'll be surrounded by curious relatives."

"It's an interesting technique for keeping you out of a man's arms. Did she do that back in high school or did she use the more traditional method of flashing the porch lights?"

"She waited on the porch and, for your information, she is not one bit interested in keeping me out of your arms. She wants my relatives here, just in case we're interested in getting married."

"We are interested in getting married."

"Were you prepared to do it today?"

"You mean…"

"I mean that right after she calls my father, brothers and sister and assorted cousins, she'll be on the phone to the family minister."

Justin chuckled. "She's definitely a woman who

doesn't leave anything to chance. What if we weren't planning to get married?"

"Then we'd all have a lovely dinner and an assortment of testimonials on the advantages of wedded bliss."

"As opposed to necking in the living room?"

"Exactly."

"How do you feel about giving her what she wants?"

"You mean a wedding? Here? Now?"

"Why not?"

Mallory saw the love—and commitment—shining in Justin's eyes and felt as though her heart might very well explode with sheer joy. "Why not, indeed."

"Just make me one promise."

"What's that?"

"That we'll never stop necking in the living room."

"You've got it, doctor," she said, linking her arms behind his neck and drawing him down for a kiss that left them both breathless.

When the doorbell began ringing a few minutes later, they looked at each other and chuckled.

"I guess you'd better go find something to wear to your wedding, Dr. Blake."

* * * * *

Dear Reader,

I am so pleased to give readers another chance to become familiar with two of my favorite characters, Abigail Dandridge and her wonderful dog, Conan. Through the more than forty books I've written, I have created countless characters and have come to love them all (except the villains, of course!). But I don't think I have ever cared for any as much as the benevolent octogenarian free spirit and her matchmaking dog, who inhabit the pages of *A Soldier's Secret* and the other books in Harlequin Special Edition's The Women of Brambleberry House series. I truly hated to say goodbye to them when I finished *A Soldier's Secret*.

I'm not sure where I stand on the subject of ghosts—though I must confess that while we lived in our 1904 Victorian, I often heard a baby cry when I was in the shower. I don't know if it was the old pipes complaining or a trick of acoustics or just my own new-mother paranoia, but many times I had to turn off the water and go check on my children, who were invariably sleeping. It always gave me a bit of a shiver. But when it comes to ghosts, I probably lean more toward the skeptical perspective of Anna Galvez, the heroine of this book. After I created Abigail, though, I could only wish I had such a kindhearted friend, even one on the other side!

All my very best,

RaeAnne

A SOLDIER'S SECRET

USA TODAY Bestselling Author

RaeAnne Thayne

To my brothers, Maj. Brad Robinson, U.S. Air Force, and high-school teacher and coach Mike Robinson. Both of you are heroes!

Chapter One

Lights were on in her attic—lights that definitely hadn't been gleaming when she left that morning.

A cold early March breeze blew off the ocean, sending dead leaves skittering across the road in front of her headlights and twisting and yanking the boughs of the Sitka spruce around Brambleberry House as Anna Galvez pulled into the driveway, behind an unfamiliar vehicle.

The lights and the vehicle could only mean one thing.

Her new tenant had arrived.

She sighed. She *so* didn't need this right now. Exhaustion pressed on her shoulders with heavy, punishing hands and she wanted nothing but to slip into a warm bath with a mind-numbing glass of wine.

The day had been beyond ghastly. She could imagine few activities more miserable than spending an entire humiliating day sitting in a Lincoln City courtroom being confronted with the unavoidable evidence of her own stupidity.

And now, despite her battered ego and fragile psyche, she had to go inside and make nice with a stranger who wouldn't even be renting the top floor of Brambleberry House if not for the tangled financial mess that stupidity had caused.

In the backseat, Conan gave one sharp bark, though she didn't know if he was anxious at the unfamiliar vehicle parked in front of them or just needed to answer the call of nature.

Since they had been driving for an hour, she opted for the latter and hurried out into the wet cold to open the sliding door of her minivan. The big shaggy beast she inherited nearly a year earlier, along with the rambling Victorian in front of her, leaped out in one powerful lunge.

Tail wagging, he rushed immediately to sniff around the SUV that dared to enter his territory without his permission. He lifted his leg before she could kick-start her brain and Anna winced.

"Conan, get away from there," she called sternly. He sent her a quizzical look, then gave a disgruntled snort before lowering his leg and heading to one of his favorite trees instead.

She really hoped her new tenant didn't mind dogs.

She hated the idea of a stranger in Sage's apartment. If she had her way, she would keep it empty, even though Sage and her husband and stepdaughter had their own beach house now a half mile down the shore for their frequent visits to Cannon Beach from their San Francisco home.

But after Anna vehemently refused to accept financial help from Sage and Eben, Sage had insisted she at least rent out her apartment to help defray costs.

The two of them were co-owners of the house and Sage's opinion certainly had weight. Besides, Anna was nothing if not practical. The apartment was empty, she had a fierce, unavoidable need for income and she knew many people were willing to pay a premium for furnished beachfront living space.

Army Lieutenant Harry Maxwell among them.

She gazed up at the lights cutting through the twilight from the third-story window. She was going to have to go up there and welcome him to Brambleberry House. No question. It was the right thing to do, even if the long, exhausting day in that courtroom had left her as bedraggled and wrung-out as one of Conan's tennis balls after a good hard game of fetch on the beach.

She might want to do nothing but climb into her bed, yank the covers over her head and weep for her shattered dreams and her own stupidity, but she had to put all that aside for now and do the polite thing.

She grabbed her laptop case from the passenger seat just as her cell phone rang. Anna swallowed a groan when she saw the name and phone number.

She wasn't sure what was worse—making nice with a stranger now living in her home or being forced to carry on a conversation with the bubbly real estate agent who had facilitated the whole deal.

With grim resignation, she opened her phone and connected the call. "Anna Galvez speaking."

"Anna! It's Tracy Harder!"

Even if she hadn't already noted Tracy's information

on the caller ID, she would have recognized the other woman's perky enthusiasm in an instant.

"So have you seen him yet?" Tracy asked.

Anna screwed her eyes shut as if she could just make those upstairs lights—and Tracy—disappear. "I just pulled up to the house, Tracy. I've been in Lincoln City all day. I haven't had a chance to even walk into the house yet. So, no, I haven't seen him. I'm planning to go up to say hello in a moment."

"You are the luckiest woman in town right now. I mean it! You have absolutely *no* idea."

"You're right," she said, unable to keep the dry note out of her voice. "But I'm willing to bet you're about to enlighten me."

Tracy gave a low, sultry laugh. "I know we didn't mention a finder's fee on top of my usual property management commission, but you just might want to kick a bonus over my way after you meet him. The man is gorgeous. Yum, that's all I have to say. *Yum!*"

Just what she needed. A player who would probably be entertaining a long string of model types at all hours of the day and night. "As long as he pays his rent on time and only needs a two-month lease, I don't care what he looks like."

"That's because you haven't met him yet. How much longer will Julia Blair and her kids be renting the second floor? I might be interested when she moves out— I'd love to be beneath that man."

Anna couldn't help her groan, both at Tracy's not so subtle sexual innuendo and at the idea of the real estate agent's wild boys living in the second-floor apartment.

"Julia and Will aren't getting married until June," she answered. With any luck, Lieutenant Maxwell would be long gone by then, leaving behind only his nice fat rental check.

"When she moves out, let me know. That might be a good time for us to talk about a more long-term solution to Brambleberry House. You can't keep taking in temporary renters to pay for the repairs on it. The place is a black hole that will suck away every penny you have."

Didn't she just know it? Anna let herself in the front door, noting that the paint on the porch was starting to crack and peel.

Replacing the furnace the month before had taken just about her last dime of discretionary income—not that she had much of that, as she tried to shore up her faltering business amid scandal and chicanery. The house needed a new roof, which was going to cost more than buying a brand-new car.

"Now listen," Tracy went on in her ear as Anna opened the door to her apartment to set down her laptop, Conan on her heels. "I told you I've got several fabulous potential buyers on the hook with both the cash and the interest in a great old Victorian on the coast. You need to think about it, Anna. I mean it."

"I guess I didn't realize there was such a market for big black holes these day."

Tracy laughed. "When you have enough money, no hole is too big or too black."

And when you had none, even a pothole could feel like an insurmountable obstacle. Anna swallowed another sigh. "I appreciate the offer and your help finding a tenant for the attic apartment."

"But you're not interested in selling." Tracy's voice was resigned.

"Not right now."

"You're as stubborn as Abigail was. I'm telling you, Anna, you're sitting on a gold mine."

"I know." She sat down in Abigail's favorite armchair. "But for now it's my gold mine. Mine and Sage's."

"All right, but when you change your mind, you know where to find me. And I want you to call me after you meet our Lieutenant Maxwell."

As far as Anna was concerned, the man wasn't *our* anything. Tracy was welcome to him. "Thanks again for dealing with the details of the rental agreement," she answered. "I'll let you know how things are going in a week or two. 'Bye, Tracy."

She ended the call and set down her phone, then leaned her head back against the floral upholstery. Conan sat beside her and, like the master manipulator he was, nudged one of her hands off the armrest and onto his head.

She scratched him between the ears for a moment, trying to let the peace she usually found at Brambleberry House seep through her. After a few moments— just when her eyelids were drifting closed—Conan slid away from her and moved to the door. He planted his haunches there and watched her expectantly.

"Yeah, I know, already," she grumbled. "I plan to go upstairs and say hello. I don't need you nagging me about it. I just need a minute to work up to it."

Still, she climbed out of the chair. After a check in the mirror above the hall tree, she did a quick repair of her French twist, grabbed Conan's leash off the hook by the door and put it on him, then headed up the stairs to meet her new neighbor.

As she trailed her fingers on the railing worn smooth by a hundred years of Dandridge hands, she reviewed what she knew about the man. Though Tracy had handled the details, Anna knew Lieutenant Maxwell had impeccable references.

He was an army helicopter pilot who had just served two tours of duty in the Middle East. He was currently on medical leave, recovering from injuries sustained in a hard landing in the midst of enemy fire.

He was single, thirty-five years old and willing to pay a great deal of money to rent her attic for only a few months.

When Tracy told her his background, Anna wanted to reduce the rent. She was squeamish about charging full price to an injured war veteran, but he refused to accept any concession.

Fine, she thought now as she paused on the third-floor landing. But she could still be gracious and welcoming to the man and hope that he would find the healing and peace at Brambleberry House that she usually did.

Outside his door, the scent of freesia curled around her and she closed her eyes for a moment, missing Abigail with a fierce ache. Conan didn't let her wallow in it. He gave a sharp bark and started wagging his tail furiously.

With a sigh, Anna knocked on the door. A moment later, it swung open and she forgot all about being kind and welcoming.

Tracy had told the God's-honest truth.

Yum.

Lieutenant Maxwell was tall—perhaps six-two—with hair the color of aged whiskey and chiseled, lean features. He wore a burgundy cotton shirt and faded jeans with a small, fraying hole below the knee.

He had a small scar on the outside of his right eye that only made him look vaguely piratelike and his right arm was encased in a dark blue sling.

The man was definitely gorgeous, but there was something more to it. If she had passed him on the street, she would have called him compelling, especially his eyes. She gazed into their hazel depths and felt an odd tug of recognition. For a brief, flickering moment, he seemed so familiar she wondered if they had met before.

The question registered for all of maybe two seconds before Conan suddenly began barking an enthusiastic welcome and lunged for Lieutenant Maxwell as if they were lifelong friends.

"Conan, sit," she ordered, disconcerted by her dog's reaction. He wasn't one for jumping all over strangers. Despite his moods and his uncanny intelligence, Conan was usually well-mannered, but just now he strained against the leash as if he wanted to knock her new tenant to the ground and lick his face off.

"Sit!" she ordered, more sternly this time. Conan gave her a disgruntled look, then plopped his butt to the floor.

"Good dog. I'm sorry," she said, feeling flustered. "Hi. You must be Harry Maxwell, right?"

Something flashed in his eyes, too quickly for her to identify it, but she thought he looked uncomfortable.

After a moment, he nodded. "Yeah."

With that single syllable, he sounded as cold and remote as Tillamook Rock. She blinked, not quite sure how to respond. He obviously didn't want to be best friends here, he was only renting her empty apartment, she reminded herself.

Despite Conan's sudden ardor, it was probably better all the way around if they all maintained a careful distance during the duration of Harry Maxwell's rental agreement. He was only here for a short time and then he would probably head back to active duty. No need for unnecessarily messy entanglements.

Taking her cue from his own reaction, she forced her voice to be brisk, professional. "I'm Anna Galvez, one of the owners of Brambleberry House. This is my dog, Conan. I don't know what's come over him. I'm sorry. He's not usually so...ardent...with strangers. Every once in a while he greets somebody like an old friend. I can't explain it but I'm very sorry if his exuberance makes you uncomfortable."

He unbent enough to reach down and scratch the dog's chin, which had the beast's tail thumping against the floor in ecstasy.

"Conan? Like the barbarian?" he asked.

"Actually, like the talk-show host. It's a long story."

One he obviously wasn't interested in hearing about, if the remote expression on his handsome features was any indication.

She tugged Conan's leash when he tried to wrap himself around the soldier's legs and after another disgruntled moment, the dog condescended enough to sit beside her. "I'm sorry I wasn't here when you arrived so I could show you around. I wasn't expecting you for a day or two."

"My plans changed. I was released from the military hospital a few days earlier than I expected. Since I didn't have anywhere else to go right now, I decided to head out here."

How sad, she thought. Didn't he have any family eager to give him a hero's welcome?

"Since I was early, I planned to get a hotel room for a couple days," he added, "but the property management company said the apartment was ready and available."

"It is. Everything's fine. I'm just sorry I wasn't here."

"The real estate agent handled everything."

Not everything Tracy probably *wanted* to handle, Anna mused, then was slightly ashamed of herself for the base thought.

This whole situation felt so awkward, so out of her comfort zone.

"You were able to find everything you needed?" she asked. "Towels, sheets, whatever?"

He shrugged. "So far."

"The kitchen is fully stocked with cookware and so forth but if you can't find something, let me know."

"I'll do that."

Despite his terse responses, Anna was disconcerted by her awareness of him. He was so big, so overwhelmingly male. She would be glad when the few months were up, though apparently Conan was infatuated with the man.

She had a sudden fierce wish that Tracy had found a nice older lady to rent the attic apartment to, but somehow she doubted too many older ladies were interested in climbing forty steps to get to their apartment.

Thinking of the steps reminded her of his injury and she nodded toward the sling on his shoulder. "I'm really sorry I wasn't here to help you carry up boxes. I guess you managed all right."

"I don't have much. A duffel and a suitcase. I'm only here for a short time."

"I know, but it's still two long flights of stairs."

She thought annoyance flickered in his eyes, as if he didn't like being reminded of his injury, but he quickly hid it.

"I handled things," he said.

"Well, if you ever need help carrying groceries up or anything or if you would just like the name of a good doctor around here, just let me know."

"I'm fine. I don't need anything. Just a quiet place to hang for a while until I'm fit to return to my unit."

She had the impression Lieutenant Harry Maxwell wasn't a man who liked being in any kind of position to need help. She supposed she probably shouldn't be holding her breath waiting for him to ask for it.

"I'm afraid I can't promise you complete quiet. Conan is mostly well-behaved but he does bark once in a while. I should also warn you if Tracy didn't mention it that there are children living in the second-floor apartment. Seven-year-old twins."

"They bark, too?"

She searched his face for any sign of a sense of humor but his expression revealed nothing. Still, she couldn't help smiling. "No, but they can be a little… energetic…at times. Mostly in the afternoons. They're gone most of the day at school and then they're usually pretty quiet in the evenings."

"That's something, then."

"In any case, they won't be here at all for several days. Their mother, Julia, is a teacher. Since they're all out of school right now for spring break, they've gone back to visit her family."

Before Lieutenant Maxwell could respond, Conan broke free of both the *sit* command and her hold on the leash and lunged for him again, dancing around his legs with excitement.

Anna reached for him again. "Conan, stop it right now. That's enough! I'm so sorry," she said to her new tenant, flustered at the negative impression they must be making.

"No worries. I'm not completely helpless. I think I can still manage to handle one high-strung mutt."

"Conan is not like most dogs," she muttered. "Most of the time we forget he even *is* a canine."

"The dog breath doesn't give him away?"

She smiled at his dry tone. So some sense of humor did lurk under that tough shell. That was a good sign. Brambleberry House and all its quirks demanded a strong constitution of its occupants.

"There is that," she answered. "We'll get out of your way and let you settle in. Again, if you need anything, don't hesitate to call. My phone number is right next to the phone or you can just call down the stairs and I'll usually hear you."

"I'll do that," he murmured, his mouth lifting slightly from its austere lines into what almost passed for a smile.

Just that minimal smile sent her pulse racing. With effort, she wrenched her gaze away from the dangerously masculine appeal of his features and tugged a reluctant Conan behind her as she headed back down the stairs.

Nerves zinging through her, Anna cursed to herself as she let herself back in to her apartment. She did *not* need this right now, she reminded herself sternly.

Her life was already a snarl of complications. She certainly didn't need to add into the mix a wounded war hero with gorgeous eyes, lean features and a mouth that looked made for trouble.

He forgot about the damn dog.

Max shut the door behind the two of them—Anna Galvez and Conan. His last glimpse of the dog was of him quivering with a mix of excitement and friendly welcome and a bit of *why-aren't-you-happier-to-see-me?* confusion as she yanked his leash to tug him behind her down the stairs.

It had been shortsighted of him not to think of Abigail's mutt and his possible reaction to seeing Max again. He hadn't even given Conan a single thought—just more evidence of how completely the news of Abigail's death had knocked him off his pins.

The dog had only been a pup the last time he'd seen him before he shipped to the Middle East for his first tour of duty. During those last few days he had spent at Brambleberry House, Max had played hard with Conan. They'd run for miles on the beach, hiked up and down the coast range and played hours of fetch in the yard.

Had it really been four years? That was the last time he had had a chance to spend any length of time here, a realization that caused him no small amount of guilt.

Conan should have been one of the first things on his mind after he found out about Abigail's death—several months after the fact. He could only blame his injuries and the long months of recovery for sending any thoughts of the dog scattering. It looked as if he was well-fed and taken care of. He supposed he had to give points to the woman—Anna Galvez—for that, at least.

He wasn't willing to concede victory to her, simply because she seemed affectionate to Abigail's mutt.

Anna Galvez. Now there was a strange woman, at least on first impressions. He couldn't quite get a handle on her. She was starchy and stiff, with her hair scraped back in a knot and the almost-masculine business suit and skirt she wore.

He would have considered her completely unappealing, except when she smiled, her entire face lit up as if somebody had just turned on a thousand-watt spotlight and aimed it right at her.

Only then did he notice her glossy dark hair, the huge, thick-lashed eyes, the high, elegant cheekbones. Underneath the layers of starch, she was a beautiful woman, he had realized with surprise, one that in other circumstances he might be interested in pursuing.

Didn't matter. She could be a supermodel and it wouldn't make a damn bit of difference to him. He had to focus on the two important things in his life right now—healing his shattered arm and digging for information.

He wasn't looking to make friends, he wasn't here to win any popularity contests, and he certainly wasn't interested in a quick fling with one of the women of Brambleberry House.

Chapter Two

She could never get enough of the coast.

Anna walked along the shore early the next morning while Conan jumped around in the sand, chasing grebes and dancing through the baby breakers.

The cool March wind whipped the waves into a froth and tangled her hair, making her grateful for the gloves and hat Abigail had knitted her last year. Offshore, the seastacks stood sturdy and resolute against the sea and overhead gulls wheeled and dived in the pale, early morning sky.

It all seemed worlds away from growing up in the high desert valleys of Utah but she loved it here. After four years of living in Oregon, she still felt incredibly blessed to be able to wake up to the soft music of the sea every single day.

Abigail had loved beachcombing in the mornings.

She knew every inlet, every cliff, every tide table. She could spot a California gray whale's spout from a mile away during the migration season and could identify every bird and most of the sea life nearly as well as Sage, who was a biologist and naturalist by profession.

Oh, Anna missed Abigail. She could hardly believe it had been nearly a year since her friend's death. She still sometimes found herself in By-the-Wind—the book and gift store in town she first managed for Abigail and then purchased from her—looking out the window and expecting Abigail to stop by on one of her regular visits.

I know the store is yours now but you can't blame an old woman for wanting to check on things now and again, Abigail would say with that mischievous smile of hers.

Anna's circumstances had taken a dramatic shift since Abigail's death. She had been living in a small two-room apartment in Seaside and driving down every day to work in the store. Now she lived in the most gorgeous house on the north coast and had made two dear friends in the process.

She smiled, thinking of Sage and Julia and the changes in all their lives the past year. When she first met Sage, right after the two of them inherited Brambleberry House, she had thought she would never have anything in common with the other woman. Sage was a vegetarian, a save-the-planet sort, and Anna was, well, focused on her business.

But they had developed an unlikely friendship. Then when Julia moved into the second-floor apartment the next fall with her darling twins, Anna and Sage had both been immediately drawn to her. Many late-night gabfests later, both women felt like the sisters she had always wanted.

Now Sage was married to Eben Spencer and had a new stepdaughter, and Julia was engaged to Will Garrett and would be marrying him as soon as school was out in June, then moving out to live in his house only a few doors down from Brambleberry House.

Both of them were deliriously happy, and Anna was thrilled for them. They were wonderful women who deserved happiness and had found it with two men she was enormously fond of.

If their happy endings only served to emphasize the mess she had made of her own life, she supposed she only had herself to blame.

She sighed, thinking of Grayson Fletcher and her own stupidity and the tangled mess he had left behind.

She supposed one bright spot from the latest fiasco in her love life was that Julia and Sage seemed to have put any matchmaking efforts on hiatus. They must have accepted the grim truth that had become painfully obvious to her—she had absolutely no judgment when it came to men.

She trusted the wrong ones. She had been making the same mistake since the time she fell hard for Todd Ashman in second grade, who gave her underdog pushes on the playground as well as her first kiss, a sloppy affair on the cheek. Todd told her he loved her then conned her out of her milk money for a week. She would probably still be paying him if her brothers hadn't found out and made the little weasel leave her alone.

She sighed as Conan sniffed a coiled ball of seaweed and twigs and grasses formed by the rolling action of the sea. That milk money had been the first of several things she had let men take from her.

Her pride. Her self-respect. Her reputation.

If she needed further proof, she only had to think about her schedule for the rest of the day. In a few hours, she was in for the dubious joy of spending another delightful day sitting in that Lincoln City courtroom while Grayson Fletcher provided unavoidable evidence of her overwhelming stupidity in business and in men.

She jerked her mind away from that painful route. She wasn't allowed to think about her mistakes on these morning walks with Conan. They were supposed to be therapy, her way to soothe her soul, to recharge her energy for the day ahead. She would defeat the entire purpose by spending the entire time looking back and cataloguing all her faults.

She forced herself to breathe deeply, inhaling the mingled scents of the sea and sand and early spring. Since Sage had married and moved out and she'd taken over sole responsibility of Conan's morning walks, she had come to truly savor and appreciate the diversity of coastal mornings. From rainy and cold to unseasonably warm to so brilliantly clear she could swear she could see the curve of the earth offshore.

Each reminded her of how blessed she was to live here. Cannon Beach had become her home. She had never intended it to happen, had only escaped here after her first major romantic debacle, looking for a place far away from her rural Utah home to lick her wounds and hide away from all her friends and family.

She had another mess on her hands now, complete with all the public humiliation she could endure. This time she wasn't about to run. Cannon Beach was her home, no matter what, and she couldn't imagine living anywhere else.

They had walked only a mile south from Brambleberry House when Conan suddenly barked with excitement. Anna shifted her gaze from the fascination of the ocean to see a runner approaching them, heading in the direction they had come.

Conan became increasingly animated the closer the runner approached, until it was all Anna could do to hang on to his leash.

She guessed his identity even before he was close enough for her to see clearly. The curious one-handed gait was a clear giveaway but his long, lean strength and brown hair was distinctive enough she was quite certain she would have figured out it was Harry Maxwell long before she could spy the sling on his arm.

To her annoyance, her stomach did an uncomfortable little twirl as he drew closer. The man was just too darn good-looking, with those lean, masculine features and the intense hazel eyes. It didn't help that he somehow looked rakishly gorgeous with his arm in a sling. An injured warrior still soldiering on.

She told herself she would have preferred things if he just kept on running but Conan made that impossible, barking and straining at his leash with such eager enthusiasm that Lieutenant Maxwell couldn't help but stop to greet him.

Maybe he wasn't quite the dour, humorless man he had appeared the day before, she thought as he scratched Conan's favorite spot, just above his shoulders. Nobody could be all bad if they were so intuitive with animals, she decided.

Only after he had sufficiently given the love to Conan did he turn in her direction.

"Morning," he said, a weird flash of what almost looked like unease in his eyes. Why would he possibly seem uncomfortable with her? She wasn't the one who practically oozed sex appeal this early in the morning.

"Hi," she answered. "Should you be doing that?"

He raised one dark eyebrow. "Petting your dog?"

"No. Running. I just wondered if all the jostling bothers your arm."

His mouth tightened a little and she had the impression again that he didn't like discussing his injury. "I hate the sling but it does a good job of keeping it from being shaken around when I'm doing anything remotely strenuous."

"It must still be uncomfortable, though."

"I'm fine."

Back off, in other words. His curtness was a clear signal she had overstepped.

"I'm sorry. Not my business, is it?"

He sighed. "I'm the one who's sorry. I'm a little frustrated at the whole thing. I'm not a very good patient and I'm afraid I don't handle limitations on my activities very well."

She sensed that was information he didn't share easily and though she knew he was only being polite she was still touched that he would confide in her. "I'm not a good patient, either. If I were in your shoes, I would be more than just a little frustrated."

Some of the stiffness seemed to ease from his posture. "Well, it's a whole lot more fun flying a helicopter than riding a hospital bed, I can tell you that much."

They lapsed into silence and she would have expected him to resume his jog but he seemed content to pet Conan and gaze out at the seething, churning waves.

It hardly seemed fair that, even injured as he was and just out of rehab, he didn't seem at all winded from the run. She would have been gasping for breath and ready for a little oxygen infusion.

"It looks like it's shaping up to be a gorgeous day, doesn't it?" she said. "Forecasters are saying we should have clear and sunny weather for the next few days. You picked a great time of year to visit Cannon Beach."

"That's good."

"I don't know if you've had a chance to notice this yet but on one of the bookshelves in the living room, I left you a welcome packet. I forgot to mention it when I stopped to say hello last night."

"I didn't see it. What kind of welcome packet?"

"Not much. Just a loose-leaf notebook, really, with some local sightseeing information. Maps of the area, trail guides, tide tables. I've also included several menus from my favorite restaurants if you want to try some of the local cuisine, as well as a couple of guidebooks from my store."

She had spent an entire evening gathering and collating the information, printing out pages from the internet and marking some of her favorite spots in the guide books. All right, it was a nerdy, overachiever thing to do, she realized now as she stood next to this man who simmered with such blatant male energy.

She really needed to get a life.

Still, he didn't look displeased by the effort. If she didn't know better, she would suspect him of being perilously close to a surprised smile. "Thank you. That was…nice."

She made a face. "A little over-the-top, I know. Sorry. I tend to be a bit obsessive about those kinds of things."

"No, it sounds perfect. I'll be sure to look through it as soon as I get a chance. Maybe you can tell me the best place for breakfast around here. I haven't had much chance to go shopping."

"The Lazy Susan is always great or any of the B and Bs, really."

Or you could invite him to breakfast.

The thought whispered through her mind and she blinked, wondering where in the world it came from. That just wasn't the sort of thing she did. Now, Abigail would have done it in a heartbeat, and Sage probably would have as well, but Anna wasn't nearly as audacious.

But the thought persisted, growing stronger and stronger. Finally the words seemed to just blurt from her mouth. "Look, I'd be happy to fix something for you. I was in the mood for French toast anyway and it's silly to make it just for me."

He stared at her for a long moment, his eyes wide with surprise. The silence dragged on a painfully long time, until heat soaked her cheeks and she wanted to dive into the cold waves to escape.

"Sorry. Forget it. Stupid suggestion."

"No. No, it wasn't. I was just surprised, that's all. Breakfast would be great, if you're sure it's not too much trouble."

"Not at all. Can you give me about forty-five minutes to finish with Conan's morning walk?"

"No problem. That will give me a chance to finish my run and take a shower."

Now there was a visual she didn't need etched into

her brain like acid on glass. She let out a breath. "Great. I'll see you then."

With a wave of his arm, sling and all, he headed back up the beach toward Brambleberry House.

With strict discipline, she forced herself not to watch after him. Instead, she gripped Conan's leash tightly so he wouldn't follow his new best friend and forced him to come with her by walking with firm determination in the other direction.

What just happened there? She had to be completely insane. Temporarily possessed by the spirit of Abigail that Sage and Julia seemed convinced still lingered at Brambleberry House.

She faced what was undoubtedly shaping up to be another miserable day sitting in the courtroom listening to more evidence of her own foolishness. And because she felt compelled to attend every moment of the trial, she had tons of work awaiting her at both the Cannon Beach and Lincoln City stores.

So what was she thinking? She had absolutely no business inviting a sexy injured war veteran to breakfast.

Remember your abysmal judgment when it comes to men, she reminded herself sternly.

It was just breakfast, though. He was her tenant and it was her duty to get to know the man living upstairs in her home. She was just being a responsible landlady.

Still, she couldn't control the excited little bump of anticipation. Nor could she ignore the realization that she was looking forward to the day more than she had anything else since before Christmas, when everything safe and secure she thought she had built for herself crashed apart like a house built on the shifting, unstable sands of Cannon Beach.

This might be easier than he thought.

Fresh from the shower, Max pulled a shirt out of his duffel, grateful it was at least moderately unwrinkled. It wouldn't hurt to make a good impression on his new landlady. So far she didn't seem suspicious of him—he doubted she would have invited him to breakfast otherwise.

Now *there* was an odd turn of events. He had to admit, he was puzzled as all hell by the invitation. Why had she issued it? And so reluctantly, too. She had looked as shocked by it as he had been.

The woman baffled him. She seemed a contradiction. Yesterday she had been all prim and proper in her business suit, today she had appeared fresh and lovely as a spring morning and far too young to own a seaside mansion and two businesses.

He didn't understand her yet. But he would, he vowed.

Not so difficult to puzzle out had been his own reaction to her. When he had seen her walking and had recognized Conan, he had been stunned and more than a little disconcerted by the instant heat pooling in his gut.

Rather inconvenient, that surge of lust. His unwilling attraction to Anna Galvez. He would no doubt have a much easier time focusing on his goal without that particular complication.

How, exactly, was he supposed to figure out if Ms. Galvez had conned a sweet old lady when he couldn't seem to wrap his feeble male brain around anything but pulling all that thick, glossy hair out of its constraints, burying his fingers in it and devouring her mouth with his?

He yanked off the pain-in-the-ass waterproof covering he had to use to protect his most recent cast from yet another reconstructive surgery and carefully eased his arm through the sleeve of the shirt. He was almost—but not quite—accustomed to the pain that still buzzed across his nerve endings whenever he moved the arm.

It wasn't as bad as it used to be. After more than a dozen surgeries in six months, he could have a little mobility now without scorching agony.

He had to admit, he couldn't say he was completely sorry about his unexpected attraction to Anna Galvez. In some ways it was even a relief. He hadn't been able to summon even a speck of interest in a woman since the crash, not even to flirt with the pretty army nurses at the hospital in Germany and then later at Walter Reed.

He had worried that something internal might have been permanently damaged in the crash, since what he had always considered a relatively healthy libido seemed to have dried up like a wadi in a sandstorm.

He had even swallowed his pride and asked one of the doctors about it just before his discharge and had been told not to worry about it. He'd been assured that his body had only been a little busy trying to heal, just as his mind had been struggling with his guilt over the deaths of two members of his flight crew.

When the time was right, he'd been told, all the plumbing would probably work just as it had before.

It might be inconvenient that he was attracted to Anna Galvez, inconvenient and more than a little odd, since he had never been attracted to the prim, focused sort of woman before, but he couldn't truly say he was sorry about it.

And if he needed a reminder of why he couldn't pursue the attraction, he only needed to look around him at the familiar walls of Brambleberry House.

For all he knew, Anna Galvez was the sneaky, conniving swindler his mother believed her to be, working her wiles to gull his elderly aunt out of this house and its contents, all the valuable antiques and keepsakes that had been in his father's family for generations.

He wouldn't know until he had run a little reconnaissance here to see where things stood.

His father had been the only child of Abigail's solitary sibling, her sister Suzanna, which made Max Abigail's only living relative.

Though he hadn't really given it much thought—mostly because he didn't like thinking about his beloved great-aunt's inevitable passing—he supposed he had always expected to inherit Brambleberry House someday.

Finding out she had left the house to two strangers had been more than a little bit surprising.

She must not have loved you enough.

The thought slithered through his mind, cold and mean, but he pushed it away. Abigail had loved him. He could never doubt that. For some inexplicable reason, she had decided to give the house to two strangers and he was determined to find out why.

And this morning provided a perfect opportunity to give Anna Galvez a little closer scrutiny, so he'd better get on with things.

Buttoning a shirt with one good hand genuinely sucked, he had discovered over the last six months, but it wasn't nearly as tough as trying to maneuver an arm that didn't want to cooperate through the unwieldy holes in a T-shirt or, heaven forbid, a long-sleeved sweater, so he persevered.

When he finished, he put the blasted sling on again, ran a comb through his hair awkwardly with his left hand, then headed for the stairs, his hand on the banister he remembered Abigail waxing to a lustrous sheen just so he could slide down it when he was a boy.

Delicious smells greeted him the moment he headed downstairs—coffee, bacon, hash browns and something sweet and yeasty. His stomach rumbled but he reminded himself he was a soldier, trained to withstand temptation.

No matter how seemingly irresistible.

He paused outside Abigail's door, a little astounded at the sudden nerves zinging through him.

It was one thing to inhabit the top floor of Brambleberry House. It was quite another, he discovered, to return to Abigail's private sanctuary, the place he had loved so dearly.

The rooms beyond this door had been his haven when he was a kid. The one safe anchor in a tumultuous, unstable childhood—not the house, he supposed, as much as the woman who had been so much a part of it.

No matter what might be happening in his regular life—whether his mother was between husbands or flushed with the glow of new love that made her forget his existence or at the bitter, ugly end of another marriage—Abigail had always represented safety and security to him.

She had been fun and kind and loving and he had craved his visits here like a drunk needed rotgut. He had looked forward to the two weeks his mother allowed him with fierce anticipation the other fifty weeks of the year. Whenever he walked through this door, he had felt instantly wrapped in warm, loving arms.

And now a stranger lived here. A woman who had somehow managed to convince an old woman to leave her this house.

No matter how lovely Anna Galvez might be, he couldn't forget that she had usurped Abigail's place in this house.

It was hers now and he damn well intended to find out why.

He drew in a deep breath, adjusted his sling one more time, then reached out to knock on Abigail's door.

Chapter Three

She opened the door wearing one of his aunt's old ruffled bib aprons.

He recognized it instantly, pink flowers and all, and had a sudden image of Abigail in the kitchen, bedecked with jewels as always, grinning and telling jokes as she cooked up a batch of her famous French toast that dripped with caramel and brown sugar and pralines.

He had to admit he found the dichotomy a little disconcerting. Whether Anna was a con artist or simply a modern businesswoman, he wouldn't have expected her to be wearing something so softly worn and old-fashioned.

He doubted Abigail had ever looked quite as appealing in that apron. Anna Galvez's skin had a rosy glow to it and the friendly pink flowers made her look exotically beautiful in contrast.

"Good morning again," she said, her smile polite, perhaps even a little distant.

Maybe he ought to forget this whole thing, he thought. Just head back out the door and up the stairs. He could always grab a granola bar and a cola for breakfast.

He wasn't sure he was ready to face Abigail's apartment just yet, and especially not with this woman looking on.

"Something smells delicious in here, like you've gone to a whole lot of work. I hope this isn't a big inconvenience for you."

Her smile seemed a little warmer. "Not at all. I enjoy cooking, I just don't get the chance very often. Come in."

She held the door open for him and he couldn't figure out a gracious way to back out. Doing his best to hide his sudden reluctance, he stepped through the threshold.

He shouldn't have worried.

Nothing was as he remembered. When Abigail was alive, these rooms had been funky and cluttered, much like his aunt, with shelves piled high with everything from pieces of driftwood to beautifully crafted art pottery to cheap plastic garage-sale trinkets.

Abigail had possessed her own sense of style. If she liked something, she had no compunction about displaying it. And she had liked a wide variety of things.

The fussy wallpaper he remembered was gone and the room had been painted a crisp, clean white. Even more significant, a few of the major walls had been removed to open up the space. The thick, dramatic trim around the windows and ceiling was still there and nothing jarred with the historic tone of the house but he had to admit the space looked much brighter. Cleaner.

Elegant, even.

He had only a moment to absorb the changes before a plaintive whine echoed through the space. He followed the sound and discovered Conan just on the other side of the long sofa that was canted across the living room.

The dog gazed at him with longing in his eyes and though he practically knocked the sofa cushions off with his quivering, he made no move to lunge at him.

Max blinked at the canine. "All right. What's with the dog? Did somebody glue his haunches to the sofa?"

She made a face. "No. We're working on obedience. I gave him a strict *sit-stay* command before I opened the door. I'm afraid it's not going to last, as much as he wants to be good. I'm sorry."

"I don't mind. I like dogs."

He particularly liked this one and had since Conan was a pup Abigail had rescued from the pound, though he certainly couldn't tell her that.

She took pity on the dog and released him from the position with a simple "Okay."

Conan immediately rushed for Max, nudging at him with that big furry red-gold head, just as a timer sounded through the room.

"Perfect. That's everything. Do you mind eating in the kitchen? I have a great view of the ocean from there."

"Not at all."

He didn't add that Abigail's small kitchen, busy and cluttered as it was, had always been his favorite room of the house, the very essence of what made Bramble-berry House so very appealing.

He found the small round table set with Abigail's rose-covered china and sunny yellow napkins. A vase of fresh flowers sent sweet smells to mingle with the delicious culinary scents.

"Can I do anything?"

"No, everything's all finished. I just need to pull it from the oven. You can go ahead and sit down."

He sat at one of the place settings where he had a beautiful view of the sand and the sea and the haystacks offshore. He poured coffee for both of them while Conan perched at his feet and he could swear the dog was grinning at him with male camaraderie, as if they shared some secret.

Which, of course, they did.

In a moment, Anna returned to the table with a casserole dish. She set it down then removed covers from the other plates on the table and his mouth watered again at the crispy strips of bacon and mound of scrambled eggs.

"This is enough to feed my entire platoon, ma'am."

She grimaced. "I haven't cooked for anyone else in a while. I'm afraid I got a little carried away. I hope you're hungry."

"Starving, actually."

He was astonished to find it was true. The sea air must be agreeing with him. He'd lost twenty pounds in the hospital and though the doctors had been strictly urging him to do something about putting it back on, he hadn't been able to work up much enthusiasm to eat anything.

Nice to know *all* his appetites seemed to be returning.

He took several slices of bacon and a hefty mound of

scrambled eggs then scooped some of the sweet-smelling concoction from the glass casserole dish.

The moment he lifted the fork to his mouth, a hundred memories came flooding back of other mornings spent in this kitchen, eating this very thing for breakfast. It had been his favorite as long as he could remember and he had always asked for it.

"This is—" *Aunt Abigail's famous French toast,* he almost said, but caught himself just in time. "Delicious. Really delicious."

When she smiled, she looked almost as delectable as the thick, caramel-covered toast, and just as edible. "Thank you. It was a specialty of a dear friend of mine. Every time I make it, it reminds me of her."

He slanted her a searching look across the table. She sounded sincere—maybe *too* sincere. He wanted to take her apparent affection for Abigail at face value but he couldn't help wondering if his cover had been blown. For all he knew, she had seen a picture of him in Abigail's things and guessed why he was here.

If she truly were a con artist and knew he was Abigail's nephew come to check things out, wouldn't she lay it on thick about how much she adored his aunt to allay his suspicions?

"That's nice," he finally said. "It sounds like you cared about her a lot."

She didn't answer for several seconds, long enough that he wondered if she were being deliberately evasive. He felt as if he were tap-dancing through a damn minefield.

"I did," she finally answered.

Conan whined a little and settled his chin on his forepaws, just as if he somehow understood exactly whom they were talking about and still missed Abigail.

Impossible, Max thought. The dog was smart but not *that* smart.

"I've heard horror stories about army food," Anna said, changing the subject. "Is it as awful as they say?"

Even as he applied himself to the delicious breakfast, his mind couldn't seem to stop shifting through the nuances and implications of every word she said and he wondered why she suddenly seemed reluctant to discuss Abigail after she had been the one to bring her into the conversation. Still, he decided not to push her. He would let her play things her way for now while he tried to figure out the angles.

"Army food's not bad," he said, focusing on her question. "Army hospital food, that's another story. This is gourmet dining to me after the last few months."

"How long were you in the hospital?"

Just as she didn't want to talk about Abigail, he sure as hell didn't want to discuss his time in the hospital.

"Too damn long," he answered, then because his voice sounded so harsh, he tried to amend his tone. "Six months, on and off, with rehab and surgeries and everything."

Her eyes widened and she set down her own fork. "Oh, my word! Tracy—the real estate agent with the property management company—told me you had been hurt in Iraq but I had no idea your injuries were so severe!"

He fidgeted a little, wishing they hadn't landed on this topic. He hated thinking about the crash or his injuries—or the future that stretched out ahead of him, darkly uncertain.

"I wasn't in the hospital the entire time. A month the first time, mostly in the burn unit, but I needed several surgeries after that to repair my shoulder and arm then skin grafts and so on. All of it took time. And then I picked up a staph infection in the meantime and that meant another few weeks in the hospital. Throw in a month or so of rehab before they'd release me and here we are."

"Oh, I'm so sorry. It sounds truly awful."

He chewed a mouthful of fluffy scrambled eggs that suddenly tasted like foam peanuts. He knew he was lucky to make it out alive after the fiery hard landing. That inescapable fact had been drilled into his head constantly since the crash, by himself and by those around him.

For several tense moments after they had been hit by a rocket-fired grenade as they were picking up an injured soldier that October day to medevac, he had been quite certain this was the end for him and for the four others on his Black Hawk.

He thought he was going to be a grim statistic, another one of those poor bastards who bit it just a week before their tour ended and they were due to head home.

But somehow he had survived. Two of his crew hadn't been so lucky, despite his frantic efforts and those of the other surviving crew member. They had saved the injured Humvee driver, so that was something.

That first month had been a blur, especially the first few days after the crash. The medical transport to Kuwait and then to Germany, the excruciating pain from his shattered arm and shoulder and from the second-and third-degree burns on the right side of his body…and the even more excruciating anguish that still cramped in his gut when he thought about his lost crew members.

He was aware, suddenly, that Conan had risen from the floor to sit beside him, resting his chin on Max's thigh.

He found enormous comfort from the soft, furry weight and from the surprising compassion in the dog's eyes.

"How are you now?" Anna asked. "Have the doctors given you an estimate of what kind of recovery you're looking at?"

"It's all a waiting game right now to see how things heal after the last surgery." He raised his arm with the cast. "I've got to wear this for another month."

"I can't imagine how frustrating that must be for you. I don't know about you, but I'm not the most patient person in the world. I'm afraid I would want results immediately."

They definitely had that much in common. Though his instincts warned him to filter every word through his suspicions about her, he had to admit he found her concern rather sweet and unexpected.

"I do," he admitted. "But I was in the hospital long enough to see exactly what happened to those who tried to rush the healing process. Several of them pushed too hard and ended up right back where they started, in much worse shape. I won't let that happen. It will take as long as it takes."

"Smart words," she said with an odd look and only then did he realize that it had been one of his aunt's favorite phrases, whether she was talking about the time it took for cookies to bake or for the berries to pop out on her raspberry canes out back.

He quickly tried to turn the conversation back to her. "What about you? For a woman who claims she's impatient for results, you've picked a major project here, renovating this big house on your own."

"Brambleberry House belonged to a dear friend of mine. Actually, the one whose French toast recipe you're eating." She smiled a little. "When she died last year, she left it to me and to another of her lost sheep, Sage Benedetto. Sage Benedetto-Spencer, actually. She's married now and lives in San Francisco with her husband and stepdaughter. In fact, you're living in what used to be her apartment."

He knew all about Sage. He'd been hearing about her for years from Abigail. When his aunt told him she had taken on a new tenant for the empty third floor several years ago, he had instantly been suspicious and had run a full background check on the woman, though he hadn't revealed that information to Abigail.

Nothing untoward had showed up. She worked at the nature center in town and had seemed to be exactly as she appeared, a hardworking biologist in need of a clean place to live.

But five years later, she was now one of the owners of that clean abode—and she had recently married into money.

That in itself had raised his suspicions. Maybe she and Anna had a whole racket going on. First they conned Abigail, then Sage set her sights on Eben Spencer and tricked him into marrying her. What other explanation could there be? Why would a hotel magnate like Spencer marry a hippie nature girl like Sage Benedetto?

"So you live down here and rent out the top two floors?"

She sipped her coffee. "For now. It's a lot of space for one woman and the upkeep on the place isn't cheap. I had to replace the heating system this year, which took a huge chunk out of the remodeling budget."

There was one element of this whole thing that didn't jibe with his mother's speculation that they were gold-digging scam artists, Max admitted. If they were only in this for the money, wouldn't they have flipped the house, taken their equity and split Cannon Beach?

It didn't make sense and made him more inclined to believe she and Sage Benedetto truly had cared for Abigail, though he wasn't ready to concede anything at this point.

"The real estate agent who arranged the rental agreement with me mentioned you own a couple of shops on the coast but she didn't go into detail."

If he hadn't been watching her so carefully, he might have missed the sudden glumness in her eyes or the subtle tightening of her lovely, exotic features.

He had obviously touched on a sore subject, and from his preliminary internet search of her and Sage, he was quite certain he knew why.

"Yes," she finally said, stirring her scrambled eggs around on her plate. "My store here in town is near the post office. It's called By-the-Wind Books and Gifts."

"By-the-Wind? Like the jellyfish?" he asked.

"Right. By-the-wind sailors. My friend Abigail loved them. The store was hers and she named it after a cross-wind one year sent hundreds of thousands of them washing up on the shore of Cannon Beach. I started out managing the store for her when I first came to town. A few years ago when she hit seventy-eight she decided she was ready to slow down a little, so I made an offer for the store and she sold it to me."

Abigail had adored her store as much as she loved this house. She wasn't the most savvy of business-women but she loved any excuse to engage a stranger in conversation.

"So you've opened a second store now," he asked.

She shifted in her seat, her hands clenching and un-clenching around the napkin in her lap. "Yes. Last summer I opened one in Lincoln City. By-the-Wind Two."

She didn't seem nearly as eager to talk about her second store and he found her reaction interesting and filed it away to add to his growing impressions about Anna Galvez.

He had limited information about the situation but his internet search had turned up several hits from the Lincoln City newspaper about her store manager being arrested some months ago and charged with embezzle-ment and credit card fraud.

Max knew from his research that the man was cur-rently on trial. He didn't, however, have any idea at all if Anna was the innocent victim the newspapers had portrayed or if she perhaps had deeper involvement in the fraud.

Before coming back to Brambleberry House, he had been all too willing to believe she might have been in-volved, that she had managed to find a convenient way to turn her manager into the scapegoat.

It was a little harder to believe that when he was sitting across the table from her and could smell the delicate scent of her drifting across the table, when he could feel the warmth of her just a few feet away, when he could reach out and touch the softness of her skin...

He jerked his mind from that dangerous road. "You must be doing well if you've got two stores. Any plans to expand to a third? Maybe up north in Astoria or farther south in Newport?"

"No. Not anytime in the near future. Or even in the not-so-near future." She forced a smile that stopped just short of genuine. "Would you like more French toast?"

He decided to allow her to sidetrack him for now, though he wasn't at all finished with this line of questioning. Instead, he served up another slice of the French pastry.

Being here in this kitchen like this was oddly surreal and he almost expected Abigail to bustle in from another part of the house with her smile gleaming even above the mounds of jewelry she always wore.

She wouldn't be bustling in from anywhere, he reminded himself. Grief clawed at him again, the overwhelming sense of loss that seemed so much more acute here in this house.

Oh, he missed her.

He suddenly felt a weird brush of something against his cheek and he had a sudden hideous fear he might be crying. He did a quick finger-sweep but didn't feel any wetness. But he was quite certain he smelled something flowery and sweet.

Out of nowhere, the dog suddenly wagged his tail and gave one happy bark. Max thought he saw something out of the corner of his gaze but when he turned around he saw only a curtain fluttering in the other room from one of the house's famous drafts.

He turned back to find Anna Galvez watching him, her eyes wary and concerned at the same time.

"Is everything okay, Lieutenant Maxwell," she asked.

He shook off the weird sensation, certain he must just be tired and a little overwhelmed about being back here. *Lieutenant Maxwell,* she had called him. Discomfort burned under his skin at the fake name. This whole thing just felt wrong somehow, especially sitting here in Abigail's kitchen. He wanted to just tell her the truth but some instinct held him back. Not yet. He would let the situation play out a little longer, see what she did.

But he couldn't have her calling him another man's name, he decided. "You don't have to call me Lieutenant Maxwell. You can call me Max. That's what most people do."

A puzzled frown played around that luscious mouth. "They call you Max and not Harry?"

"Um, yeah. It's a military thing. Nicknames, you know?"

The explanation sounded lame, even to him, but she appeared to buy it without blinking. In fact, she gifted him with a particular sweet smile. "All right. Max it is. You may, of course, call me Anna."

He absolutely was *not* going to let himself get lost in that smile, no matter his inclination, so he forced himself to continue with his subtle interrogation. "Are you from around here?"

She shook her head. "I grew up in a small town in the mountains of Utah."

He raised an eyebrow, certain he hadn't unearthed that little tidbit of information in his research. "Utah seems like a long way from here. What brought you to the Oregon coast?"

Her eyes took on that evasive film again. "Oh, you know. I was ready for a change. Wanted to stretch my wings a little. That sort of thing."

He had become pretty good over the years at picking up when someone wasn't being completely honest with him and his lie radar was suddenly blinking like crazy.

She was hiding something and he wanted to know what.

"Do you have family back in Utah still?"

The tension in her shoulders eased a little. "Two of my older brothers are still close to Moose Springs. That's where we grew up. One's the sheriff, actually. The other is a contractor, then I have one other brother who's a research scientist in Costa Rica."

"No sisters?"

"Just brothers. I'm the baby."

"You were probably spoiled rotten, right?"

Her laugh was so infectious that even Conan looked up and grinned. "More like endlessly tormented. I was always excluded from their cool boy stuff like campouts and fishing trips. Being the only girl and the youngest Galvez was a double curse, one I'm still trying to figure out how to break."

This, at least, was genuine. She glowed when she talked about her family—her eyes seemed brighter, her features more animated. She looked so delicious, it was all he could do not to reach across the table and kiss her right here over his aunt's French toast.

Her next words quickly quashed the bloom of desire better than a cold Oregon downpour.

"What about you?" she asked. "Do you have family somewhere?"

How could he answer that without giving away his

identity? He decided to stick to the bare facts and hope Abigail hadn't talked about his particular twisted branch of the family tree.

"My father died when I was too young to remember him. My mother remarried several times so I've got a few stepbrothers and stepsisters scattered here and there but that's it."

He didn't add that he didn't even know some of their names since none of the marriages had lasted long.

"So where's home?" she asked.

"Right now it's two flights of stairs above you."

She made a face. "What about before you moved upstairs?"

Brambleberry House was the place he had always considered home, even though he only spent a week or two here each year. Life with his mother had never been exactly stable as she moved from boyfriend to boyfriend, husband to husband. Before he had been sent to military school when he was thirteen, he had attended a dozen different schools.

Abigail had been the rock in his insecure existence. But he certainly couldn't tell that to Anna Galvez. Instead, he shrugged.

"I'm career army, ma'am. I'm based out of Virginia but I've been in the Middle East for two tours of duty. I've been there the last four years. That feels as much home as anywhere else, I guess."

Chapter Four

Oh, the poor man.

Imagine considering some military base a home. She couldn't quite fathom it and she felt enormously blessed suddenly for her safe, happy childhood.

Her family might have been what most people would consider dirt-poor. Her parents were illegal immigrants who had tried to live below the radar. As a result, her father had never been paid his full worth and when he had been killed in a construction accident, the company he worked for had used his illegal immigrant status as an excuse not to pay any compensation to his widow or children.

Yes, her family might not have had much when she was a kid but she had never lived a single moment of her childhood when she didn't feel her home was a sanctuary where she could always be certain she would find love and acceptance.

Later, maybe, she had come to doubt her worth, but none of that stemmed from her girlhood.

And now she had Brambleberry House to return to at the end of the day. No matter how stressful her life might seem sometimes, this house welcomed her back every night, solid and strong and immovable.

It saddened her to think of Harry Maxwell moving from place to place with the military, never having anything to anchor him in place.

"I suppose if you had a wife and children, you would probably be recovering with them instead of at some drafty rented house on the Oregon shore."

"No wife, no kids. Never married." He paused, giving her a careful look. "What about you?"

She had always wanted a big, rambunctious family just like the one she'd known as a girl but those childhood dreams spun in the tiny bedroom of that Moose Springs house seemed far away now.

Her life hadn't worked out at all the way she planned. And though there were a few things in her life she wouldn't mind a do-over on—especially more recent events—she couldn't regret all the paths she had followed that had led her to this place.

"Same goes. I was engaged once but…it didn't work out."

Before he could respond, Conan lumbered to his feet and headed for the door.

"That's a signal," she said with a smile. "Time for him to go out and if I don't move on it, we'll all be sorry. Excuse me, won't you?"

Though he had a doggie door to use when she wasn't

home, Conan much preferred to be waited on and to go out through the regular door like the rest of the higher beings. She opened her apartment door and then the main door into the house for him and watched him bound eagerly to his favorite corner of the yard.

When she returned to the kitchen, she found Lieutenant Maxwell clearing dishes from the table.

"That was delicious. It was very kind of you to invite me. A little unexpected, but kind nonetheless."

"You're welcome. I'll be honest, it's not the sort of thing I usually do but...well, it *is* the sort of thing Abigail would have done. She was always striking up conversations with people and taking them to lunch or whatever. I had the strangest feeling this morning on the beach that she would want me to invite you to breakfast."

She heard the absurdity of her own words and made a face. "That probably sounds completely insane to you."

"Not completely," he murmured.

"No, it is. But I'm not sorry. I enjoyed making breakfast and I suppose it's only fitting that I know at least a little about the person living upstairs. At least now you don't feel like a stranger."

"Well, I appreciate the effort and the French toast. It's been...a long time since I've had anything as good."

He gave her a hesitant smile and at the sight of it on those solemnly handsome features, her stomach seemed to do a long, slow roll.

Oh, bad idea. She had no business at all being attracted to the man. He was her tenant, and a temporary one at that. Beyond that, the timing was abysmal. She had far too much on her plate right now trying to save By-the-Wind Two and see that Grayson Fletcher received well-deserved justice. She couldn't afford any distractions, especially not one as tempting as Lieutenant Harry Maxwell.

"I'm glad you enjoyed it," she said, forcing her voice to be brisk and businesslike.

Conan came back inside before he could answer. He headed straight for the lieutenant, who reached down to pet him. The absent gesture reminded her of another detail she meant to discuss with him.

"I'm afraid I'm going to be tied up in Lincoln City most of today. Some days I can take Conan with me since I have arrangements with a kennel in town but they were full today so he has to stay home. I hope he doesn't make a pest of himself."

"I doubt he'll bother me."

"With the dog door, he can come as he likes. I should probably tell you, he thinks he owns the house. He's used to going up the stairs to visit either Sage when she lived here or Julia and the twins. If he whines outside your door, just send him back downstairs."

"He won't bother me. If he whines, I'll invite him inside. He's welcome to hang out upstairs. I don't mind the company."

He petted the dog with an unfeigned affection that warmed her, though she knew it shouldn't. Most people liked Conan, though Grayson Fletcher never had. That in itself should have been all the red flags she needed that the man was trouble.

"Well, don't feel obligated to entertain him. I would just ask that you close the gate behind you if you leave so he can't leave the yard. He tends to take off if there's a stray cat in the neighborhood."

"I'll do that." He paused. "Would you have any objection if I take Conan along if I go anywhere? He kind of reminds me of a…dog I once knew."

At the sound of his name, the dog barked eagerly, his tail wagging a mile a minute.

Conan would adore any outing, she knew, but she couldn't contain a few misgivings.

"Conan can be a little energetic when he wants to be. Are you certain you can restrain him on the leash if he decides to take off after a squirrel or something?"

"Because of this, you mean?" he asked stiffly, gesturing to the sling. "My other arm still works fine."

She nodded, feeling foolish. "Of course. In that case, I'm sure Conan would love to go along with you anywhere. He loves riding in the car and he's crazy about any excuse to get some exercise. I'm afraid my schedule doesn't allow me to give him as much as he would like. Here, let me grab his leash for you just in case."

She headed for the hook by the door but Conan had heard the magic word—*leash*—and he bounded in front of her, nearly dancing out of his fur with excitement.

Caught off balance by seventy-five pounds of dog suddenly in her way, she stumbled a little and would have fallen into an ignominious heap if Lieutenant Maxwell hadn't reached out with his uninjured arm to help steady her.

Instant heat leaped through her, wild and shocking. She was painfully cognizant of the hard male strength of him, of his mouth just inches away, of those hazel eyes watching her with a glittery expression.

She didn't think she had ever, in her entire existence, been so physically aware of a man. Of his scent, freshwashed and clean, of the muscles that held her so securely, of the strong curve of his jawline.

She might have stayed there half the morning, caught in the odd lassitude seeping through her, except she suddenly was quite certain she smelled freesia as she had earlier during breakfast.

The scent eddied around them, subtle and sweet, but it was enough to break the spell.

She jerked away from him before she could do something abysmally stupid like kiss the man.

"I'm sorry," she exclaimed. "I'm so clumsy sometimes. Are you all right? Did I hurt you?"

A muscle worked in his jaw, though that strange light lingered in his eyes. "I'm not breakable, Anna. Don't worry about it."

Despite his words, she was quite certain she saw lines of pain bracketing his mouth. With three older brothers, though, she had learned enough about the male psyche to sense he wouldn't appreciate her concern.

She let out a long breath. This had to be the strangest morning of her life.

"Here's the leash," she said. "If you decide to take Conan with you, just call his name and rattle this outside my door and he should come running in an instant."

He nodded. For a moment, she thought he might say something about the surge of heat between them just now, but then he seemed to change his mind.

"Thanks again for breakfast," he said. "I would offer to return the favor but I'm afraid you'd end up with cold cereal."

She managed a smile, though she was certain it wasn't much of one. He gazed at her for a long moment, his features unreadable, then he headed for the door.

Conan danced around behind him, his attention

glued to the leash, but she managed to close the door before the dog could escape to follow him up the stairs.

He whined and slumped against the door and she leaned against it, absently rubbing the dog's ears as that freesia scent drifted through the apartment again.

"Cut it out, Abigail," she spoke aloud. Lieutenant Maxwell would surely think she was crazy if he heard her talking to a woman who had been dead nearly a year.

Still, there had been that strange moment at breakfast when she had been almost positive he sensed something in the kitchen. His eyes had widened and he had seemed almost disconcerted.

Ridiculous. There had been nothing there for him to sense. Abigail was gone, as much as she might wish otherwise. She was just too prosaic to believe Sage and Julia's theory that their friend still lingered here at Brambleberry House.

And even if she did buy the theory, why would Abigail possibly make herself known to Harry Maxwell? It made no sense.

Sage believed Abigail had played a hand in her relationship with Eben, that she had carefully orchestrated events so they would both finally be forced to admit they belonged together.

Though Julia didn't take things quite that far, she also seemed to believe Abigail had helped her and Will find their happily-ever-after.

But Abigail had never even met Harry Maxwell. Why on earth would she want to hook him up with Anna?

She heard the ludicrous direction of her thoughts and shook her head. She had far too much to do today to spend any more time speculating on the motives of an imaginary matchmaking ghost.

She wasn't about to let herself fall prey to any beyond-the-grave romantic maneuvering between her and a certain wounded soldier with tired, suspicious eyes.

Max returned to his third-floor aerie to be greeted by his cell phone belting out his mother's ringtone.

He winced and made a mental note to change it before she caught wind of the song one of his bunkmates at Walter Reed had programmed as a joke after Meredith's single visit to see him in the six months after the crash.

His mother wouldn't be thrilled to know he heard Heart singing "Barracuda" every time she called.

When he was on painkillers, he had found it mildly amusing—mostly because it was right on the money. Now he just found it rather sad. For much the same reason.

He thought about ignoring her but he knew Meredith well enough to be sure she would simply keep calling him until he grew tired of putting her off, so he finally picked it up.

With a sigh, he opened his phone. "Hi, Mom," he greeted, feeling slightly childish in the knowledge that he only used the word because he knew it annoyed her.

She had been insisting since several years before he hit adolescence that he must call her Meredith but he still stubbornly refused.

"Where were you, Maxwell? I've been calling you for an hour." Her voice had that prim, tight tone he hated.

"I was at breakfast. I must have left my phone here."

He decided to keep to himself the information that he was downstairs eating Abigail's French toast with Anna Galvez.

"You said you would call me when you arrived."

"You're right. That's what I said."

He left his sentence hanging between them, yet another strategy he had learned early in his dealings with her mother. She wouldn't listen to explanations anyway so he might as well save them both the time and energy of offering.

The silence dragged on but he held his ground. Finally she heaved a long-suffering sigh and surrendered.

"What have you found?" she asked. "Have those women gutted the house and sold everything in it?"

He gazed around at the apartment with its new coat of paint and kitchen cabinets and he thought of the downstairs apartment, with its spacious new floor plan.

"I wouldn't exactly say that."

"Brambleberry House was filled with priceless antiques. Some of them were family heirlooms that should have gone to you. I can't believe Abigail didn't do a better job of preserving them for you. You're her only living relative and those family items should be yours."

Since she had backed down first, he let her ramble on about the injustice of it all—as if Meredith cared about anyone's history beyond her own.

"I was apparently mistaken to let you visit her all those summers. When I think of the expense and time involved in sending you there, I just get furious all over again."

He happened to know Abigail had paid for every plane ticket and Meredith had looked on those two weeks as her vacation from the ordeal of motherhood but he decided to let that one slide, too.

"She must have been crazy at the end," Meredith finally wound down to say. "That's the only explanation that makes sense. Why else would she leave the house to a couple of strangers when she could have left it to her favorite—and only—nephew?"

"We've had this conversation before," he said slowly. "I can't answer that, Mom."

"What do you intend to do, then? Have you spoken with an attorney yet about contesting the will?"

"It's been nearly a year since Abigail died. I can't just show up out of nowhere and start fighting over the house."

He didn't need Brambleberry House. What did he care about some decaying old house on the coast? He certainly didn't need any inheritance from Abigail. His father had been a wealthy, successful land developer.

Though he died suddenly, he had been conscientious—or perhaps grimly aware of his wife's expensive habits. He had left his young son an inviolable trust fund that Meredith couldn't touch.

Through wise investments over the years, Max had parlayed that inheritance into more money than one man—or ten—could spend in a lifetime.

The money didn't matter to him. Abigail did. She had been his rock through childhood and he owed her at least some token effort to make sure she had been competent in her last wishes.

"You most certainly can fight over it! That house should belong to you, Maxwell. You're entitled to it."

He rolled his eyes. "I'm not entitled to anything."

"That's nonsense," Meredith snapped. "You have

far more claim on Brambleberry House than a couple of grubby little gold diggers. Did you contact Abigail's attorney yet?"

He sighed, ready to pull the old bad-connection bit so he could end the call. "I've been in town less than twenty-four hours, Mom. I haven't had a chance yet."

"You have to swear you'll contact me the moment you know anything. The very *moment*."

He had a fleeting, futile wish that his mother had been as concerned when her son was shot down by enemy fire as she apparently was about two strangers inheriting a house she had despised.

The moment the thought registered, he pushed it quickly away. He had made peace a long time ago with the reality that his mother had a toxic, self-absorbed personality.

He couldn't change that at thirty-five any more than he had been able to when he was eight.

For the most part, both of them rubbed together tolerably well as long as they were able to stay out of the other's way.

"I'll do that. Goodbye, Mom."

He hung up a second later and gazed at the phone for a long moment, aware she hadn't once asked about his arm. Just like Meredith. She preferred to pretend anything inconvenient or unpleasant just didn't exist in her perfect little world.

If Brambleberry House had been some worthless shack somewhere, she wouldn't have given a damn about it. She certainly wouldn't have bothered to push him so hard to check into the situation.

And he likely would have ignored her diatribes about the house if not for his own sense of, well, *hurt* that

Abigail hadn't bothered to leave him so much as a teacup in her will.

It made no sense to him. She had loved him. Her Jamie, she called him, a nickname he had rolled his eyes at. James had been his father's name and it was his middle name. Abigail seemed to get a kick out of being the only one to ever call him that.

They had carried on a lively email correspondence no matter where he was stationed and he thought she might have mentioned sometime in all that some reason why she was cutting him out of her will.

He had allowed his mother to half convince him Sage Benedetto and Anna Galvez must have somehow finagled their way into Abigail's world and conned her into leaving the house and its contents to them. It now seemed a silly notion. Abigail had been sharp as a tack. She would have seen through obvious gold-digging.

But she was also very softhearted. Perhaps the women had played on her sympathy somehow.

Or maybe she just had come to love two strangers more than she loved her own nephew.

He sighed, disgusted with the pathetic, self-pitying direction of his thoughts.

After spending the last hour with Anna Galvez, he wasn't sure what to think. She seemed a woman of many contradictions. Tough, hard-as-nails businesswoman one moment, softly feminine chef with an edge of vulnerability the next.

It could all be an act, he reminded himself. Still, he couldn't deny his attraction to her. She was a lovely woman and he was instinctively drawn to her.

Under other circumstances, he might have even liked her.

He heard a vehicle start up below and moved to the window overlooking the driveway. He saw her white, rather bland minivan carefully back out of the driveway then head south toward Lincoln City.

The woman was a mystery, one he was suddenly eager to solve.

Chapter Five

This was a stupid idea.

Just after noon, Max slipped into the condiment aisle of the small grocery store in town, cursing his bad luck—and whatever idiotic impulse had led him to ever think he could get away with assuming a false identity in this town.

He must have been suffering the lingering effects of the damn painkillers. That was the only explanation that made sense.

It had seemed like such a simple plan. Just slip into town incognito, then back out again without anybody paying him any mind.

The idea should have worked. Cannon Beach was a tourist town, after all, and he figured he would be considered just one more tourist.

He had forgotten his aunt had known every permanent resident in town. Scratch that. Abigail probably had known every single person along the entire northern coast.

He felt ridiculous, hovering among the ketchup and steak sauce and salad dressing bottles. He peeked around the corner again, trying to figure out how he could get out of the store without being caught by the woman with the short, steel-gray hair and trendy tortoiseshell glasses.

Betsy Wardle had been one of Abigail's closest friends. He knew the two of them used to play Bunco on a regular basis. If Betsy recognized him, the entire jig would be up.

He had met her several times before, as recently as four years earlier, the last time he stayed with his aunt.

He couldn't see any way to avoid having her recognize him now. The worst of it was, Betsy was an inveterate gossip. Word would be out all over town that Abigail's nephew was back, and of course that word would be quick to travel in Anna's direction.

He had two choices, as he saw it. He could either leave his half-full grocery cart right here and do his best to hightail it out of the store without being caught or he could just play duck-and-run and try to avoid her until she paid for her groceries and left.

He shoved on his sunglasses and averted his face just in time as she rounded the corner with her cart. He pushed past her, hoping like hell she was too busy picking out gourmet mustard to pay him any attention.

To be on the safe side, he turned in the direction she had just come and would have headed several aisles away but he suddenly heard an even more dreaded sound than Betsy Wardle's soft southern drawl.

Anna Galvez was suddenly greeting the older woman with warm friendliness.

He groaned and closed his eyes. Exactly the last person he needed to see right now when Betsy could expose him at any second. What was she doing here? Wasn't she supposed to be in Lincoln City right now?

He definitely needed to figure out a way out of here fast. He started to head toward the door when Betsy's words stopped him and he paused, pretending to compare the nutritional content of two different kinds of soy chips while he listened to their conversation one aisle over.

"How is your court case going against that awful man?" Betsy was asking.

"Who knows?" Anna answered with a discouraged-sounding sigh.

"The whole thing is terrible. Unconscionable. That's what I say. I just can't believe that man would work so hard to gain your trust and then take advantage of a darling girl like you. It's just not fair."

"Oh, Betsy. Thank you. I appreciate the support of you and Abigail's other friends. It means the world to me."

He wished he could see through the aisle to read her expression. She sounded sincere but he couldn't tell just by hearing her voice.

"I know I've told you this before and you've turned me down but I mean it. If you need me to testify on your behalf or anything, you just say the word. Why, when I think of how much you did for Abigail in her last years, it just breaks my heart that you're suffering so now. You were always at Brambleberry House helping with her taxes or paying bills for her or whatever she needed. You're a darling girl and I wouldn't hesitate a minute to tell that Lincoln City jury that very thing."

"Thank you, Mrs. Wardle," Anna answered. "While, again, I appreciate your offer, I don't think it will come to that. I'm not the one on trial, Grayson Fletcher is."

"I know that, honey, but from what I've read in the papers, it sounds like it's mostly his word against yours. I'm just saying I'm happy to step up if you need it."

"You're a dear, Mrs. Wardle. Thank you. I'll be sure to let the prosecutor know."

They chatted for a moment longer, about books and gardening and the best time to plant rhododendron bushes. Just as he was thinking again about trying to escape the store without being identified, he heard Anna say goodbye to the other woman. Out of the corner of his eye, he saw Betsy heading to the checkout counter that was at the end of his aisle.

He turned blindly to head in the other direction and suddenly ran smack into another cart.

"Oh!" exclaimed Anna Galvez.

"Sorry," he mumbled, keeping his head down and hoping she was too distracted to notice him.

No such luck. She immediately saw through the sunglasses. "Lieutenant Maxwell! Hello!"

"Oh. Hi. I didn't see you there," he lied. "This is a surprise. I thought you were going to be out of town today."

Her warm smile chilled at the edges. "My, uh, obligation was postponed for the rest of the afternoon. So instead I'm buying refreshments for one of the teen book clubs that meets after school at By-the-Wind. They're discussing a vampire romance so I'm serving tomato juice and red velvet cake. A weird combination, I know, but they have teenage stomachs so I figured they could handle it."

"Don't forget the deviled eggs."

She laughed. "What a great idea! I wish I'd thought of it in time to make some last night."

When she smiled, she looked soft and approachable and so desirable he forgot all about keeping a low profile. All he wanted to do was kiss her right there next to the organic soup cans.

He jerked his gaze away. "I guess I'd better let you get back to the shopping then. Your vampirettes await."

"Right."

He paused. "Listen, after I'm done here, I was thinking about taking a quick hike this afternoon. I know you said your dog could hang out with me but since you're here, maybe I'd better check that it's still okay with you."

"Absolutely. He'll be in dog heaven to have somebody else pay attention to him."

"Thanks. I'll bring him home about six or so."

"Take your time. I probably won't be done at the store until then anyway."

She smiled again, and it was much more warm and open than the other smiles she'd given him. He could swear it went straight to his gut.

"In truth," she went on, "this will take a big weight off my shoulders. I worry about Conan when I have to work long hours. Sometimes I take him into By-the-Wind with me since he loves being around people, but that's not always the easiest thing with a big dog like Conan. You're very sweet to think of including him."

Sweet? She thought he was *sweet*? He was a lieutenant with the U.S. Army who had been shot down by enemy fire. The last thing he felt was sweet.

"I just wanted a little company. That's all."

He didn't realize his words came out a growl until he saw that soft, terrifying smile of hers fade.

"Of course. And I'm sure he'll enjoy it very much. Have fun, then. I believe there were several area trail guides among the travel information I left in your apartment. If you don't find what you're looking for, we have several others in the store."

"I just figured I would take the Neah-Kah-Nie Mountain trail."

She stared at him in surprise. "You sound like you're familiar with the area. I don't know why, but for some reason, I assumed you hadn't been to Cannon Beach before."

He cursed the slip of his tongue. He was going to have to watch himself or he would be blurting out some of the other hikes he'd gone on with Aunt Abigail over the years.

"It's been a while," he answered truthfully enough. "I'm sure everything has changed since I was here last. A good trail guide will still come in handy, I'm sure. I'll be sure to grab it back at the house before I leave."

"If you get lost, just let Conan lead the way out for you. He'll head for food every time."

"I'll keep that in mind."

He smiled, hoping she wouldn't focus too much on his past experience in Cannon Beach. "Have fun with your reading group."

"I'll do that. Enjoy your hike."

With a last little finger wave, she pushed her cart toward the checkout. He watched her go, wondering how she could manage to look so very delicious in a conservative gray skirt and plain white blouse.

This was a stupid idea, he echoed his thought of earlier, for a multitude of reasons. Not the least of which was the disturbing realization that each time he was with her, he found himself more drawn to her.

How was he supposed to accomplish his mission here to check out the situation at Brambleberry House when all his self-protective instincts were shouting at him to keep as much distance as possible between him and Anna Galvez?

They were late.

Anna sat at her home office computer, pretending to work with her spreadsheet program while she kept one eye out the window that overlooked the still-empty driveway.

Worry was a hard, tangled knot in her gut. It was nearly seven-thirty and she had watched the sun set over the Pacific an hour earlier. They should have been home long before now.

Without Conan, the house seemed to echo with silence. She had always thought that an odd turn of phrase but she could swear even the sound of her breathing sounded oddly magnified as she sat alone in her office gazing out the window and fretting.

She worried for her dog, yes. But she also worried about a certain wounded soldier with sad, distant eyes.

They were fine, she told herself. He had assured her he could handle Conan even at his most rambunctious. He was a helicopter pilot, used to situations where he had to be calm under pressure and he was no doubt more than capable of coping with any difficulty.

Still, a hundred different scenarios raced through her brain, each one more grim than the last.

Anything could have happened out there. Neah-Kah-Nie Mountain had stunning views of the coastline but the steep switchbacks on the trail could be treacherous, especially this time of year when the ground was soaked.

She pushed the worry away and focused on her computer again. After only a few moments, though, her thoughts drifted back to Harry Maxwell.

How odd that it had never occurred to her that he might have visited Cannon Beach before. Is that why he seemed so familiar? Had he come into By-the-Wind at some point?

But if he had, wouldn't he have mentioned it at breakfast when she had talked about buying the store from Abigail?

It bothered her that she couldn't quite place how he seemed so familiar. She usually had a great memory for faces. But thousands of customers walked through By-the-Wind in a given year. There was no logical reason she would remember one man, no matter how compelling.

And he was compelling. She couldn't deny her attraction for him, though she knew it was completely ridiculous.

He was her tenant. That's all she could allow him to be at this complicated time in her life—not that he had offered any kind of indication he was interested in anything else.

Breakfast had been a crazy impulse and she could see now how foolish. It created this false sense of intimacy, as if an hour or so together made them friends somehow, when in reality he had only been at Bramble-berry House a day.

No more breakfasts. No more chance encounters on the beach, no more bumping into him at the supermarket. When he and Conan returned safely from their hike—as she assured herself they would—she would politely thank him for taking her dog along with him, then for the rest of his time at Brambleberry House, she intended to do her absolute best to pretend the upstairs apartment was still empty.

It was a worthy goal and sometime later, when her pulse ratcheted up a notch at the sight of headlights pulling into the driveway, she told herself her reaction was only one of relief and maybe a little annoyance that he had left her to worry so long.

She forgot all about keeping her distance, though, when she saw him in the pale moonlight as he gingerly climbed out of his SUV then leaned on Conan as he limped his way toward the house.

Chapter Six

She burst through her apartment into the foyer just as he opened the front door, Conan plodding just ahead of him.

Max looked up with surprise at her urgent entrance, then she saw something that looked very much like resignation flash in his expression before her attention was caught by his bedraggled condition. Mud covered his Levi's and he had a long, ugly scrape on his cheek.

"Oh, my word! Are you all right? What happened?"

He let out a long breath and she thought for a moment he would choose not to answer her.

"I'm fine. Nothing to worry about."

"Nothing to worry about?" she exclaimed. "Are you crazy? You look like you fell off a cliff."

He raised an eyebrow but said nothing and she could swear her heart stuttered to a stop.

"That's not really what happened. Surely you didn't fall off a cliff, did you?"

"Not much of one."

"Not much of one! What kind of answer is that? Either you fell off a cliff or you didn't."

"I slid on a some loose rocks and fell. It was only about twenty feet, though."

Only twenty feet. She tried to imagine falling twenty feet and then calmly talking about it as if she had merely stumbled over a curb. It was too big a stretch for her and her mind couldn't quite get past it.

"I'm so sorry! Did you hurt your arm when you fell?"

He shrugged. "I might have jostled it a little when I was trying to catch a handhold but I managed to stay off it for the most part and land on my left side."

"Please, just tell me Conan didn't trip you or something to make you fall."

He gave a rough laugh and she realized with some shock this was the first time she had heard him laugh. Smile, yes. Laugh, not until just this moment, when he was battered and bleeding and looking like something one of Conan's feline nemeses would drag in.

He reached down to scratch the dog's ears. "Not at all. He was off the leash about five meters ahead of me at the time I slipped. You should be very proud of him, actually. He's a real hero."

"Conan? My Conan?"

"If not for him, I probably would have slipped farther down the scree and gone off the cliff," he answered. "I don't know how he did it, as steep as that thing was, but he made it down the hill where I had fallen and practically dragged me back up, through the mud and the rocks and everything. With my stupid arm and shoulder, I'm not sure I could have climbed back up on my own."

She shuddered at the picture he painted, which sounded far worse than anything she had been conjuring up in her imagination before they arrived home. Twenty feet! It was a wonder he didn't have a couple dozen broken bones!

"I'm so glad you're both okay!"

"I shouldn't be," he admitted. "It was luck, pure and simple. I should never have gone across that rock field. I could tell it wasn't stable but I went anyway. I don't blame you if you don't trust me to take your dog again. But I have to tell you, if not for Conan, I'm not sure I would be here right now. The dog is amazing."

Conan grinned at both of them with no trace of humility. She shook her head, fighting the urge to wrap her arms around her brave, wonderful dog and hold on tight.

"It was lucky you took him, then. And of course you can take him again. Anytime. Maybe he's your guardian angel."

Conan barked as if he agreed completely with that sentiment.

"Or at least helping him out," Max said with a rueful smile.

"You're so certain your guardian angel is a man?"

He made a face. "I haven't really given it much thought. Most women I know would have knocked me to the ground before I could take a step across dangerous terrain in the first place. A preemptive strike, you know?"

"Sounds like you know some interesting women, Lieutenant Maxwell."

"I had an…older relative who taught me most women

are interesting if a man is wise enough to allow them room to be."

She blinked. Now there was something Abigail might have said. She wouldn't have expected the philosophy to be echoed by a completely, thoroughly masculine man like Harry Maxwell but she was beginning to think there was more to the helicopter pilot than she'd begun to guess at.

"We could stand out here in the hall having this interesting discussion but why don't you come inside instead and let me help you clean up and put some medicine and bandages on those cuts on your face?"

As she might have predicted, he looked less than thrilled at the prospect. He even limped for the stairs and she felt terrible she had kept him standing even for these few moments.

"Thanks, but that's not necessary. I can handle it."

She raised an eyebrow. "One-handed?"

He paused on the bottom stair with a frustrated sigh. "There is that."

"Come on, Max. I'm happy to do it."

"I don't want to put you to any trouble."

"I had three rough-and-tumble older brothers and always seemed the permanently designated medic. I think I spent half my childhood bandaging some scrape or other. I'm not squeamish at the sight of blood and I have a fairly steady hand with a bottle of antiseptic. You could do worse, Lieutenant Maxwell."

He studied her for a moment, then sighed again and she knew she had won when he stepped gingerly down from the bottom stairs.

"I'm sorry you have to do this. First your dog and

now you. The inhabitants of Brambleberry House are determined to look out for me, aren't you?"

Somebody has to do it, she almost said, but wisely held her tongue while Conan barked his own answer as Max followed her into her living room.

Anna Galvez intrigued him more every time he saw her.

Earlier in the grocery store she had worn that slim gray skirt and white blouse with her hair tucked away and had looked as neat and tidy as a row of newly sharpened pencils.

Tonight, as she led the way into her apartment he was entranced by her unrestrained hair as it shivered and gleamed under the overhead lights in a luscious cloud that reached past her shoulders.

She had on the same white blouse from earlier—or at least he thought it was the same one. But she had traded the skirt for a pair of jeans and she was barefoot except for a flirty pair of turquoise flip-flop slippers.

As she led him inside Abigail's apartment, he caught sight of just a hint of pale coral toenail polish peeking through and he found the contrast of that with her slim brown feet enormously sexy.

If he were wise, he would turn right around and race up the stairs as fast as he could go with his now gimpy foot from the ankle he was certain he twisted in the fall.

The hard reality was he wouldn't be going anywhere fast. He hesitated to take off his hiking boot for fear the whole ankle would balloon to the size of a basketball the moment he did. It had ached like crazy the whole way down the mountain and he had a feeling he'd only made it home because his SUV was an automatic and his right leg was fine to work the gas pedal and the brake.

Like it or not, he was stuck in this apartment with Anna for the time being. He could probably do a credible job of washing the worst of the dirt and tiny pieces of mountain from his face but he had a couple of scrapes on his left arm that would be impossible for him to reach very well while the right was still in the damn sling.

It was Anna or the clinic in town and after all the time he'd spent being poked and prodded by medical types over the last six months, Anna was definitely the lesser of two evils.

"Sit down," she ordered in a drill-sergeant sort of voice.

He gave her a mocking salute but was grateful enough to take the weight off his ankle and the throbbing pain. He tried his level best not to wince as he eased onto her couch, feeling a hundred years old, like some kind of damn invalid in a nursing home.

She watched him out of those careful, miss-nothing eyes and he saw her mouth firm into a tight line. He suspected he wasn't fooling her for a moment.

"I just have to gather up a few first-aid supplies and I'll be right back," she said.

"I'm not going anywhere," he answered, which was the absolute truth.

Conan had disappeared into the kitchen—probably to find his Dog Chow, Max figured. If he'd been thinking straight, he should have stopped off and picked up the juiciest, meatiest steak he could find for the hero of the hour.

He leaned back against the sofa cushions and closed

his eyes, ready for a little of the calm and peace he had always found in these rooms.

An elusive effort, he discovered, especially since the scent of Anna seemed to surround him here, sweet and sultry at the same time.

He allowed himself the tiny indulgence of savoring that delectable combination for only a moment before she bustled back with her arms loaded down by bandages and antiseptic.

"I don't need all that. Do I really look that terrible?"

She gave him a sidelong look and for just a moment, he sensed something in her gaze that stunned him to the core, a thin thread of attraction that seemed to tug and curl between them.

She was the first one to look away, busying herself with the first-aid supplies. "You want the truth, you look like you just tangled with a mountain lion."

He ordered his pulse to settle down and reminded himself of all the dozens of reasons there could be nothing between them. "Nope," he answered, trying for a light tone. "Just the mountain."

She smiled a little, then reached for the iodine. "Let's take care of the cut on your face first and then I'll check out your arm."

"I can do the face. I just need a mirror for that. I, uh, would appreciate a little help with the arm, though."

For a moment, she looked as if she wanted to argue and he wasn't sure if he was relieved or disappointed when she finally reached for his arm.

Her fingers were deliciously warm on his skin. Sensation rippled from his fingertips to his shoulder and to his vast chagrin, his heartbeat accelerated with the same thick jolt of adrenaline that hit him just as his bird lifted into the air.

Anna was some seriously potent medicine. One touch and he completely forgot about all his other aches and pains.

She gripped his arm firmly with one hand while she used her other hand to dab antiseptic on the scrapes along his forearm. He welcomed the cold, bracing sting of the medicine to counterbalance her heat.

His sudden hunger was a normal response to a lovely woman, he knew. It had been just too long and she was just too pretty for him to sit here without any reaction to her soft curves and silky skin.

"Tell me if I'm hurting you," she said after a moment.

Oh, you have no idea. Max choked down the words.

"Don't worry about it," he muttered instead.

"I mean it. You don't have to be some kind of tough-guy, stoic soldier. If this stings or I'm not careful enough, just tell me to stop."

"I'll be fine," he said gruffly, though it was a bald-faced lie. He couldn't tell her just how badly he wanted to close his eyes and lean into the gentleness of her touch.

What the hell was wrong with him? He had been fussed and fretted over by soft, pretty nurses for the last six months and none of them had ever sparked this kind of reaction in him.

He tried to tell himself it was just a delayed reaction to the adrenaline buzz of his fall—a sort of spit-in-the-face-of-death response. But he wasn't quite buying it.

Her sweep of hair brushed his skin as she bent over his arm and he wondered if she could see the goose bumps rising there.

She didn't appear to notice as she reached for a tube of antibiotic cream and slathered it on with the same slow, careful movements she seemed to do everything.

"You have a choice," she said after a moment.

"Do I?" he murmured.

"I can leave it like this or I can put bandages on the scrapes to protect them for a few days. It's up to you. I would recommend the bandage to keep things clean but it's your decision."

He wanted to tell her to stop but after he had spent several extra weeks in the hospital from a bad infection, he knew he couldn't afford to take any chances.

"Go ahead and wrap it. I might as well look like something out of a horror movie."

She smiled. "Wise choice, Lieutenant."

She pulled out gauze from her kit and wound it carefully around his arm. "If you need me to rewrap this anytime," she said as she worked, "I've got plenty."

"Right."

He figured he'd rather gnaw off his arm than endure this again.

He caught a flicker of movement in the room. Grateful for any distraction, he shifted his gaze and found Conan watching him with what looked like a definite smirk in his eyes, as if he knew exactly how tough this was for Max.

He gave the dog a stern look. *Thanks for the backup.*

When she finished his arm, she stepped back. "Are you sure you don't want me to take care of your face while you're here and all the stuff is out?"

"No. Thanks anyway."

Just the thought of her touching his face with

those soft, competent fingers sent shivers rippling through him.

"Anywhere else on you I need to take care of?"

Though his mind instantly flashed a number of inappropriate thoughts, he clamped down on all of them.

"Nope. I'm good. Thanks for the patch job. I appreciate it."

He rose and took only one step toward the door when her voice stopped him.

"You were limping when you came in and you still seem hesitant to put weight on your left foot. What's that all about?"

He turned back warily. "Nothing. I twisted my ankle a little when I fell but it's really fine. Just a little tender."

"You twisted your ankle and then you hiked back down to the trailhead and drove all the way here? Why didn't you say something? We need to put some ice on it."

He had to be the world's clumsiest idiot and right now he just needed to put a little space between himself and the enticing Anna Galvez before he did something he couldn't take back.

"It's really not a big deal. I can take care of it upstairs. You've done enough already."

More than enough. Or at least more than I can handle!

"Oh, stop it! How can you possibly take care of it when you can't use your shoulder?" she pointed out with implacable logic. "I'm willing to bet your foot is swollen enough that you won't be able to even take off your boot by yourself, even if you didn't have your shoulder to contend with as well."

He knew she was right but he wasn't willing to concede defeat, damn it. He'd figure out a way, even if he had to slice the boot off with a hacksaw.

With his eye firmly on his objective—escape—he took another few steps for the door. "You can stop worrying about me anytime now. I can take care of myself."

"I'm sure you can. But you don't always have to," she answered.

He had no response to that so he took a few more steps, thinking if he could only make it to the door, he was home free. She couldn't physically restrain him, not even in his current pitiful condition.

But Abigail's blasted dog had other plans. Before he could take another step, Conan magically appeared in front of him and planted his haunches between Max and the doorway, looking as if he had absolutely no intention of letting him leave the apartment.

He faced the dog down. "Move," he ordered.

Conan simply made a sound low in his throat, not quite a growl but a definite challenge.

"You might as well come back," Anna said, and he heard a thread of barely suppressed laughter in her voice. "Between the two of us, we're here to make sure you take care of that ankle."

He gave Anna a dark look. "Are you really prepared for the consequences of kidnapping an officer in the United States Army, ma'am?"

She laughed out loud at that. "You don't scare me, Lieutenant."

I should, he thought. *I damn well should.*

Once again, he felt foolish for being so churlish when she was only trying to help. He could spend an hour trying to wrestle the boot one-handed or he could let her help him and be done in five minutes.

He sighed. "I would appreciate it if you would help me take off the boot. I can handle the rest from there. I've got ice upstairs."

"Of course. Come back and sit down."

He ignored Conan's look of triumph as he slowly returned to his spot on the sofa. Instead, he cursed his stupid arm and shoulder all over again.

If not for the crash and his subsequent injury, none of this would be happening. He would still be carrying out his duty, he would be flying, he would be in control of his world instead of here in Oregon wondering what the hell he was going to do with the rest of his life.

She knelt on the floor and worked the laces of his hiking boot. Her delicious scent swirled around him again and he told himself the fact that his mouth was watering had more to do with missing dinner than anything else.

Conan seemed inordinately interested in the proceedings. The dog plopped down beside Anna, watching the whole thing out of curious eyes.

The dog was spooky. Max couldn't think of another word for it. Though he felt slightly crazy for even contemplating the idea, he was quite certain Conan understood him perfectly well.

Throughout the day he had carried on a running commentary with him and Conan barked at all the proper places.

He was trying to distract himself, thinking about the dog. It wasn't quite working. He still couldn't seem to avoid noticing the curve of Anna's jawline or the little frown of concentration on her forehead as she tried to ease his tight hiking boot over his swollen ankle.

He jerked his gaze away and his attention was suddenly caught by an open doorway and the contents lined up on shelves inside.

"You kept…" His voice trailed off and he realized he couldn't just blurt out his surprise that she had kept his aunt's extensive doll collection without revealing that he knew about the collection in the first place.

"Yes?"

He couldn't seem to hang on to any thought at all when she gazed at him out of those big dark eyes.

"Sorry. I, um, was just thinking that it, uh, looks like you've kept the original woodwork in the house."

"Actually, not in this room. There was some old water damage and rot issues in here and the trim was beyond saving. I was able to find a decent oak pattern that was a close imitation, though not exact."

"You wouldn't know it's not original to the house."

"I have an excellent carpenter."

"You must have to keep him on retainer with a house of this size."

She made a face, tugging a little harder on the stubborn boot. "Just about. It helps that he only lives a few houses down. And he's marrying Julia Blair, the woman who lives on the second floor."

As she spoke, she finally managed to tug the boot off his ankle.

Before he could jerk his foot away, she rolled the sock down and then gasped. "Oh, Max. That looks horrible! Are you sure it's not broken?"

His entire ankle was swollen to the size of a small cantaloupe and it was already turning a lovely array of colors. He felt like a graceless idiot all over again.

"It's only a little sprain. I just need to wrap it and everything will be fine. Thanks again for your help."

He was determined this time he would make it out of the apartment as he picked up his boot and leaned forward to rise to his feet.

"Max—" she started to argue, and he decided he just couldn't take another word.

Driven by the slow, steady hunger of the last half hour and his own frustration at himself, he bent his head and captured her mouth with his, knowing just a moment's satisfaction that at least he had discovered an effective way of shutting her up.

Okay, it was just about the craziest thing he had ever done in a lifetime of crazy stunts but he couldn't regret it. Not when her mouth was soft and slightly open with surprise and when she tasted like cinnamon and sugar.

Before this moment, he would have thought a kiss where only two sets of lips connected would lack the fire and excitement of a deep, full-body embrace, when he could feel a woman's soft curves against him, the silky smoothness of her skin, each pulse of her heart.

But standing in Anna Galvez's living room with every muscle in his body aching like a son of a bitch, simply touching her mouth with his was the most intense kiss he had ever experienced.

He felt the electrifying heat of it singe through him like a lightning strike, as if he stood atop Neah-Kah-Nie Mountain with his arms outstretched in the middle of a thunderstorm, daring the elements.

Hunger surged through him, a vast, aching need, and he couldn't seem to think straight around it.

This wild heat made no sense to him and contradicted every ounce of common sense he possessed.

If she wasn't a con artist, she was at least an opportunist. She struck him as tight and contained. Buttoned-down, even. Very much not the sort of woman to engage in a wild, fiery romance with a wounded soldier who would be leaving in a few weeks' time.

Despite what logic was telling him, he couldn't ignore her reaction to his kiss. Instead of jerking away—or even slapping his face—she made a breathy kind of sound and leaned in closer.

That tiny gesture was all it took to send his control out the window and he pulled her closer, suddenly desperate for more.

Chapter Seven

Some tiny, logical corner of her brain that could still function knew this was completely insane.

What was she thinking to be here kissing Harry Maxwell—she barely knew him, he was her tenant, and right now the man couldn't even stand upright, for heaven's sake!

Usually she tried to listen to that common-sense corner of her mind but right now she found it impossible to focus on anything but the heat of him and his strong, commanding mouth on hers.

As he pulled her closer, she wrapped her arms around his waist. This was a little like she imagined it would feel to stand in the midst of the battering force of a hurricane, holding tight to the hard, immovable strength of a centuries-old lighthouse. His body was all heat and hard muscles and she wanted to lean into him and not let go.

She closed her eyes and savored the taste of him, heady and male, and the thrum of her blood as his mouth explored hers.

The house faded around her and she was lost to everything but the moment. Right now she wasn't a struggling businesswoman or an out-of-her-league homeowner. She wasn't a failure or the victim of fraud or an unwilling dupe.

She was only Anna and at this frozen moment in time she felt beautiful and feminine and *wanted.*

She didn't know how long they kissed, wrapped together in her living room with the sounds of their mingled breathing and the creaks and sighs of the old house settling around them.

She would have been quite willing to stand there forever. But that still-functioning corner of her mind was aware of him shifting his weight slightly and then of his sudden discordant intake of breath.

Awareness washed over her like the bitter cold of a January sneaker wave and she froze, blinking out of what felt like a particularly delicious dream into harsh reality.

What was wrong with her? He was a stranger, for heaven's sake! She'd known him for all of twenty-four hours and here she was entangled in his arms.

She knew nothing about this man other than that he could be kind to her dog and he disliked being fussed over.

This absolutely was not like her. She always tried to be so careful with men, taking her time to get to know them, to give careful thought to a man's positive and negative attributes before even considering a date with him.

And wasn't that course of action working out just great for her? a snide little voice sneered in her mind.

She pushed it away. She barely knew the man. Not only that, but he was injured! He could barely stand up and here she was throwing herself at him. She couldn't even bring herself to meet his gaze, mortified at her instant, feverishly inexplicable reaction to a simple kiss.

Why had he kissed her, though? That was the real question. One moment she had been urging him to take it easy with his sprained ankle—okay, nagging him— and the next moment his mouth had been stealing her breath, and whatever good sense she possessed along with it.

This sort of thing did *not* happen to her.

Still, she found some consolation that he looked as baffled and thunderstruck as she was.

In fact, the only one in the room who didn't look like the house had just imploded around them all was Conan, who sat watching the two of them with an expression that bordered on smug delight, oddly enough.

Max was the first one to break the awkward silence.

"Well, your nursing methods might be a little unorthodox, but I suddenly feel a hell of a lot better."

Her flush deepened. "I'm so sorry. I don't know what…I shouldn't have…"

He held up a hand. "Stop. I was trying to make a stupid joke. I completely started it, Anna. I kissed you. You have nothing to apologize about."

She tried to remember the steps in the circle breathing Sage was always trying to make her practice but her mind was too scrambled to focus on the calming method. She also still couldn't quite force herself to meet his gaze.

"I was way out of line," he added. "I don't know quite what to say, other than you can be sure it won't happen again."

"It won't?" Now why did that make her feel so blasted depressed?

"I don't make it a habit of accosting people who are only trying to help me."

"You didn't accost me," she mumbled. "It was just a kiss."

Just a kiss that still seemed to sing through her body, moments later. A kiss she could still taste on her lips and feel in her racing pulse.

"Right," he said after a moment. "Uh, I'd better get out of your way and let you get back to…whatever you were doing before we showed up."

She fiercely wanted him gone so she could try to regain a little badly needed equilibrium. At the same time, she couldn't help worrying about his injuries.

"Are you sure you'll be able to make it up the stairs?"

"Unless Conan stands in my way again."

"He won't," she promised. If she had to, she would lock the dog in her bedroom to keep him from causing any more trouble.

He paused at her door. "Good night, then. And thank you again for all your help."

A shadow of something hot and intense still lingered in the hazel depths of his eyes.

She told herself she shouldn't be flattered by it. But her ego had taken a beating the last few months with the trial and Gray Fletcher's perfidy. She felt stupid and incompetent and ugly in the knowledge that Gray had only pursued her so arduously to distract her from his shady dealings at her company—and that she had been idiot enough to fall for it.

Harry Maxwell didn't work for her, he didn't want anything from her. He seemed as discomfited by the heat they generated as she was.

At the same time, the fact that this gorgeous man was at least interested enough in her to kiss her out of the blue with such heat and passion was a soothing balm to her scraped psyche.

He grabbed his boot and headed into the foyer. Though she knew his ankle had to be killing him, he barely limped as he headed up the stairs.

Abigail would have followed him right upstairs with cold compresses and ibuprofen for his ankle, no matter what the stubborn man might have to say about it.

But Anna wasn't Abigail. She never could be. Yes, she might invite the man over to breakfast to make him feel more welcome in Cannon Beach and she might fill his room with guidebooks and put a little first-aid ointment on his scrapes.

But Abigail had possessed unfailing instincts about people. She didn't make the kinds of mistakes Anna did, putting her trust in the completely wrong people who invariably ended up hurting her....

Though she knew he wouldn't appreciate her concern, she waited until she heard the door close up on the third floor before returning to her living room.

She closed the door and sagged into Abigail's favorite chair, ignoring Conan's interested look as she pressed a hand to her mouth.

What just happened here? She had no idea a simple kiss could be so devastatingly intense.

She had certainly kissed men before. She'd been engaged, for heaven's sake. She had enjoyed those kisses
and even the few times she and her fiancé had gone
further than kisses.

But she had always thought something was a little
wrong with her in that department. While she enjoyed
the closeness, she had never experienced the raw, heart-
pounding desire, the wild churn in her stomach, that
other women talked about.

Until tonight.

Just another reason why her reaction to a wounded
soldier was both unreasonable and dangerous. She
wanted to throw every caution to the wind and just
enjoy the moment with him.

How on earth was she going to make it through the
next few months with him living just upstairs?

Julia and the twins would be back in a week. Their
presence would at least provide a buffer between her
and Max.

Whether she wanted it or not.

She didn't see Max Saturday morning before she left
for the store. His SUV was gone and the lights were
off on the third floor, she saw with some relief as she
backed her van out through a misting rain that clung
to her windshield and shimmered on the boughs of the
Sitka spruce around Brambleberry House.

He must have left while she was in the shower, since
his vehicle had been parked in the driveway next to hers
when she returned with Conan from their morning walk
on the beach earlier.

She spent a moment as she drove to By-the-Wind
wondering where he might have gone for the day.

Maybe the Portland Saturday Market? That was one of her favorite outings when she had the time and she was almost certain this was the opening weekend of the season. But would Lieutenant Maxwell really enjoy wandering through stalls of produce and flowers and local handicrafts? She couldn't quite imagine it.

Whatever he had chosen to do with his Saturday was none of her business, she reminded herself. She only hoped he didn't overdo.

She had fretted half the night that he wouldn't be able to get up and down the stairs with his ankle, that he would be trapped up on the third floor with no way of calling for help.

It was ridiculous, she knew. The man was a trained army helicopter pilot who had survived a crash, for heaven's sake, and she had no idea what else during his service in the Middle East. A twisted ankle was probably nothing to someone who had spent several months in the hospital recovering from his injuries.

Her worry was obviously all for nothing. With no help whatsoever from her or Conan, he had managed to get down the stairs, obviously, and even behind the wheel of his vehicle.

Since he was apparently mobile, she needed to stop worrying about the man, especially since she had a million other things within her control she could be stressing over.

She barely had time to even think about Max throughout the morning. Helen Lansing, her wonderful assistant manager who led the weekly preschool story hour on Saturday mornings—complete with elaborate puppets and endless energy—called in tears, with a terrible migraine.

"Don't worry about it," Anna told her as she mentally reshuffled her day. "Just go lie down in a quiet, dark room until you feel better. Michael and I can handle story hour."

The rain—or probably their parents' cabin fever—brought a larger than average crowd to the story hour. It might have been not quite as slick and polished as Helen's shows usually were but the children still seemed to enjoy it—and as a business owner, she certainly enjoyed the sales generated by their parents as they waited for their little ones.

By the time the last child left just before lunch, she was ready for a little quiet.

"I'll be in the office for a few moments working on invoices," she told Michael and Kae, her two clerks. "Yell if you need help."

She had just settled into her desk chair when her office phone rang. She didn't recognize the number and she answered rather impatiently.

"Sorry. Is this a bad time?"

Her mood instantly lifted at the voice on the other end of the line. "Sage! No, of course it's not a bad time. It's never a bad time when you call. How are you? How are Eben and Chloe?"

There was an odd delay on the line, as if the signal had to travel a long distance, though the reception was clear enough.

"Wonderful. Guess where I'm calling from?"

Eben owned a chain of hotels around the world and he and Sage frequently traveled between them, taking his daughter, Chloe.

Last month Sage had called her from Denmark and the month before had been Japan.

"Um, New York City?" she guessed.

"A little farther south. We're in Patagonia!"

"Really? I didn't know Spencer Hotels had a location down there."

"We don't. But Eben's considering it. He wants to capitalize on the high-end ecotourism trend so we're scouting locations. Chloe is having a blast. Just yesterday we went horseback riding through scenery so incredible, you can't imagine. You should have seen her up on that horse, just like she's been riding her whole life."

Sage's love for her stepdaughter warmed Anna's heart. When she and Sage inherited Brambleberry House, she used to be so envious of Sage for her vivid, outgoing personality.

Sage was much like Abigail in that every time she walked into a room, she walked out of it again with several new friends.

Anna never realized until they had become close friends how Sage's exuberance masked a deep loneliness.

That was gone now. Sage and Eben—and Chloe— were genuinely happy together.

"Sounds like you're having a wonderful time."

"We are. And how are things there? What's going on with the trial? I tried to call a few times last week to check in and got your voice mail."

"I know. I got your message. I'm sorry I haven't called you back. I've just been busy…"

Her voice trailed off and she sighed, unable to lie to her friend. "Okay, truth. I purposely didn't call you back."

"Ouch. Screening my calls now?"

"Of course not. You know I love you. I just…I didn't really want to talk about the trial," she finally admitted.

"That bad?"

The sympathy in Sage's voice traveled all the way across the phone line from Patagonia and tears stung behind her eyes.

"Not at all, if you enjoy public humiliation."

"Oh, honey. I'm so sorry. I should have been there. I've been thinking all week that I should have just ignored you when you said you didn't want either Julia or me to come with you. You're always so blasted independent but sometimes you need to have a friend in your corner. I should have been there."

"Completely not necessary. We're on the homestretch now. The defense should wrap up Monday, with closing arguments Tuesday, and a verdict sometime after that."

"I'm coming home," she said after that short delay. "I should be there with you, at least for the verdict."

"You absolutely are not!"

"You're my friend. I can't let you go through this on your own, Anna."

"I can handle it."

She would rather have her tongue chopped into little pieces than admit to Sage how very much she longed for her friends to lean on right now.

"You handle everything. I know. And usually you do a marvelous job at it. But you shouldn't have to bear this burden by yourself."

"If you cut short your dream trip to Patagonia with your family on my account, I will never forgive you, Sage Benedetto-Spencer. I mean it. You and Eben have already done more than enough."

"I should be there."

"You should be exactly where you are, horseback riding through incredible scenery with your husband and daughter."

Sage was silent for a moment and Anna thought perhaps the tenuous connection had been severed. "And you have to deal with a new tenant in the middle of all this, too. He's arriving any day now, isn't he?"

She rolled a pencil between her fingers. "Actually, he showed up a few days ago."

"And...?" Sage prompted.

"And what?" she said, stalling.

"What's he like?"

She had a wild, visceral image of his mouth on hers, of those strong muscles surrounding her, of his skin, warm and hard beneath her exploring fingertips.

How should she answer that? He was gorgeous and stubborn and infuriating and his kiss was magic.

"I don't really know. He's only been there a few days. So far everything has been...fine."

It was a vast understatement and she could only be grateful Sage was thousands of miles away and not watching her out of those knowing eyes of hers that missed nothing.

"Any sign of Abigail since your wounded soldier showed up or is she giving him a wide berth?"

"No ghostly manifestations, no. Everything has been quiet on the paranormal front."

"What about Conan? Does he like him?"

"Well, he did try to attack him last night in my apartment, but other than that, they get along fine."

"Excuse me? He attacked him? Our fierce and mighty watchdog Conan, who would probably lick an intruder to death?"

She sighed, wishing she'd kept her big mouth shut. Sage was far too perceptive and Anna had a sudden suspicion she would read far more into the situation.

"He and Conan went hiking yesterday on Neah-Kah-Nie Mountain and Lieutenant Maxwell fell and was scraped up a bit. He's already got an injury from a helicopter crash so it was hard for him to tend his wounds by himself but he's the, uh, prickly, independent type. He wasn't thrilled about me having to bandage his cuts. But Conan and I can both be persuasive."

"Okay, now things are getting interesting. Forget some stupid old trial. Now I want to know everything about the new tenant. Tell me more."

"There's nothing to tell, Sage. I promise."

Other than that she had kissed him and made of fool of herself over him and then spent the night wrapped in feverish dreams that left her achy and restless.

"What does he look like?"

Anna closed her eyes and was chagrined when his image appeared, hazel eyes and dark hair and too-serious mouth.

"He looks like he's been in a hospital too long and is hungry for fresh air and sunlight. Conan adores him and is already extremely protective of him. That's what last night was about. Conan didn't want him to go up the stairs until I'd taken a look at his swollen ankle."

"And did you? Get a good look, I mean?"

Better than she should have. "Sage, drop it. There's nothing between me and Lieutenant Maxwell. I'm not interested in a relationship right now. I can't afford to be. When would I have the time, for heaven's sake, even if I had the energy? Besides, I obviously can't be trusted to pick out a decent man for myself since my judgment is so abysmal."

"That's why you need to let Abigail and Conan do it for you. Look how well things turned out for Julia and for me?"

Anna laughed, feeling immeasurably better about life, as she always did after talking to Sage. "So what you're saying is that a fictitious octogenarian spirit and a mixed-breed mutt have better taste in men than I do. Okay. Good to know. If I ever decide to date again—highly doubtful at this point in my life—I'll bring every man home to Brambleberry House before the second date."

They talked a few moments longer, then she heard Chloe calling Sage's name. "You'd better go. Thanks for calling, Sage. I promise, I'll call you as soon as I know anything about the verdict."

"Are you sure you don't want me there?"

"Absolutely positive. When you and Eben and Chloe come back to Cannon Beach at Easter, we'll have an all-nighter and we can read the court transcripts together."

"Ooh, can we do parts? I've got the perfect voice for that weasel Grayson Fletcher."

She pitched her voice high and nasal, not at all like Gray's smooth baritone, but it still made Anna laugh. "Deal. I'll see you then."

She hung up the phone a few moments later, her heart much lighter as she focused on all the wonderful ways her life had changed in the last year.

Yes, she'd had a rough few months and the trial was excruciatingly humiliating.

But she had many more blessings than hardships. She considered Sage the very best gift Abigail had bequeathed to her after her death. Better than the house or the garden or all the antique furniture in the world.

The two of them had always had a cool relationship while Abigail was alive, perhaps afflicted by a little subtle rivalry. Both of them had loved Abigail and perhaps had wanted her affection for themselves.

Being forced to live together in Brambleberry House had brought them closer and they had found much common ground in their shared grief for their friend. She now considered Sage and Julia Blair her richest blessings, the two best friends she'd ever known.

She had a beautiful home on the coast, she had close friends who loved and supported her, she had two businesses she was working to rebuild.

The last thing she needed was a wounded soldier to complicate things and leave her aching for all she didn't have.

Chapter Eight

Few things could send his blood pumping like a heavy storm roiling in off the ocean.

Max walked along the wide sandy beach with Conan on his leash, watching the churn of black-edged clouds way out on the far horizon. Even from here, he could see the froth of the sea, a writhing mass of deep, angry green.

It wouldn't be here for some time yet but the air had that expectant quality to it, as if everything along the coast was just waiting. Already the wind had picked up and the gulls seemed frantic as they soared and dived through the sky, driven by an urgency to fill their stomachs and head for shelter somewhere.

At moments like this, Max sometimes wondered if he should have picked a career in the coast guard.

He could have flown helicopters there, swift, agile

little Sikorsky Jayhawks, flying daredevil rescues on the ocean while waves buffeted the belly of his bird.

He had always loved the ocean, especially *this* ocean—its moods and its piques and the sheer magnificence of it.

Conan sniffed at a clump of seaweed and Max paused to let him take his time at it. Though he didn't want to admit it, he was grateful for the chance to rest for a moment.

Considering his body felt as if it had been smashed against the rocks at the headland, he figured he was doing pretty well. A run had been out of the question, with his ankle still on the swollen side, but a walk had helped loosen everything up and he felt much better.

The ocean always seemed to calm him. He used to love to race down from the house the moment Abigail returned to Brambleberry House from picking him up at the airport in Portland. She would follow after him, laughing as he would shuck off his shoes and socks for that first frigid dip of his toes in the water.

Max couldn't explain it, but some part of him was connected to this part of the planet, by some invisible tie binding him to this particular meshing of land and sea and sky.

He had traveled extensively around the world during his youth as his mother moved from social scene to social scene—in the days before Meredith sent him to military school. He had served tours of duty in far-flung spots from Latin America to Germany to the gulf and had seen many gorgeous places in every corner of the planet.

But no place else ever filled him with this deep sense of homecoming as he found here on the Oregon coast.

He didn't quite understand it, especially since he had spent much longer stretches of time in other locations. When people in social or professional situations asked him where he was from, as Anna had done at breakfast the other day, he always gave some vague answer about moving around a lot when he was kid.

But in his heart, when he thought about home, he thought of Brambleberry House and Cannon Beach.

He sighed. Ridiculous. It wasn't his. Abigail had decided two strangers deserved the place more and at this point he didn't think he could do a damn thing about it.

If his military career was indeed over, he was going to have to consider his options. Maybe he would just buy a fishing boat and a little house near Yachats or Newport and spend his days out on the water.

It wasn't a bad scenario. So why couldn't he drum up a little more enthusiasm for it, or for any of the other possibilities he'd been trying to come up with since doctors first dared suggest he might not ever regain full use of his arm?

He flexed his shoulder as he watched the gulls struggle against the increasing wind. They ought to just give up now, he thought, before the wind made it impossible for them to fly. But they kept at it. Indeed, they seemed to revel in the challenge.

He sighed as his ankle throbbed from being in one place too long. He felt weaker than a damn seagull in that headwind right now.

"Come on, Conan. We'd better head back."

The dog made a definite face at him but gave one last sniff in the sand and followed as Max led the way back up the beach toward Brambleberry House.

The storm clouds were edging closer and he figured they had maybe an hour before the real fun started.

Good. Maybe a hard thunder-bumper would drive this restlessness out of him.

He was grateful for his fleece jacket now as the temperature already seemed to have dropped a dozen degrees or more, just in the time since they set off.

The moment he opened the beach access gate at Brambleberry House, Conan bounded inside, barking like crazy as if he had been gone for months.

Max managed to control him enough to get the leash off and the dog jumped around with excitement.

"You like storms, too, don't you? I bet they remind you of Aunt Abigail, right?"

The dog barked in that spooky way he had of acting as if he understood every word, then he took off around a corner of the house.

As Max followed more slowly, branches twisted and danced in the swell of wind, a few scraping the windows on the upper stories of the house.

He planned to start a fire in the fireplace, grab the thriller he had been trying to focus on and settle in for the evening with a good book and the storm.

Yeah, it probably would sound tame to the guys in his unit but right now he could imagine few things more enjoyable.

A quick image of kissing Anna Galvez while the storm raged around them flashed through his mind but he quickly suppressed it. Their kiss had been a one-time-only event and he needed to remember that.

"Conan? Where'd you go, bud?" he called.

He rounded the corner of the house after the dog, then stopped dead. His heart seemed to stutter in his chest at the sight of Anna atop a precarious-looking wooden ladder, a hammer in her hand as she stretched to fix something he couldn't see from this angle.

The first thought to register in his distinctly male brain was how sexy she looked with a leather tool belt low on her hips and her shirt riding up a little as she raised her arms.

The movement bared just the tiniest inch of skin above her waistband, a smooth brown expanse that just begged for his touch.

The second, more powerful emotion was sheer terror as he noted just how far she was reaching above the ladder—and how precarious she looked up there fifteen feet in the air.

"Have you lost your ever-loving mind?"

She jerked around at his words and to his dismay, the ladder moved with her, coming away at least an inch or more from the porch where it was propped.

At the last moment, she grabbed hold of the soffit to stabilize herself and the ladder, and Max cursed his sudden temper. If she fell because he had impulsively yelled at her, he would never forgive himself.

"I don't believe I have," she answered coolly. "My ever-loving mind seems fairly intact to me just now."

"You might want to double-check that, ma'am. That wind is picking up velocity with each passing second. It won't take much for one good gust to knock that ladder straight out from under you, then where will you be?"

"No doubt lying bleeding and unconscious at your feet," she answered.

He was not going about this in the correct way, he realized. He had no right to come in here and start issuing orders like she was the greenest of recruits.

He had no right to do anything here. He ought to just let her break her fool neck—but the thought of her, as she had so glibly put it, lying bleeding and unconscious at his feet filled him with an odd, hollow feeling in his gut that he might have called panic under other circumstances.

"Come on down, Anna," he cajoled. "It's really too windy for you to be safe up there."

"I will. But not quite yet."

He wasn't getting her down from there short of toppling the ladder himself, he realized. And with a bad ankle and only one usable arm right now—and that one questionable after the scrapes and bruises of the day before—he couldn't even offer to take her place.

"Can I at least hold the ladder for you?"

"Would you?" she asked, peering down at him with delight. "I'm afraid I'm not really fond of heights."

She was afraid of heights? He stared at her and finally noticed the slight sheen of sweat on her upper lip and the very slightest of trembles in her knees.

A weird softness twisted through his chest as he thought of the courage it must be taking her to stand there on that ladder, fighting down her fears.

"And so to cure your phobia, you decided to stand fifteen feet above the ground atop a rickety wooden ladder in the face of a spring storm. Makes perfect sense to me."

She made a face, though she continued hammering away. "Ha ha. Not quite."

"Well, what's so important it can't wait until after the storm?"

"Shingles. Loose ones." She didn't pause a moment in her hammering. "We need a new roof. The last time we had a big storm, the wind curled underneath some loose singles on the other side of the house and ended up lifting off about twenty square feet of roof. The other day I noticed some loose shingles on this side so I just want to make sure we don't see the same thing happen."

"Couldn't you find somebody else to do that for you?"

She raised an eyebrow. "Any suggestions, Lieutenant Maxwell?"

"You could have asked me."

She finally stopped hammering long enough to look down at him, her gaze one of astonishment as she looked first at his arm in the blasted sling, then at his ankle.

He waited for some caustic comment about his current physical limitations. Instead, her lovely features softened as if he'd handed her an armload of wildflowers.

"I…thank you," she said, her voice slightly breathless. "That's very kind but I'm sort of in the groove now. I think I can handle it. I would appreciate your help holding the ladder while I check a couple of shingles on the porch on the east side of the house."

He wanted to order her off the ladder and back inside the house before she broke her blasted neck but he knew he had no right to do anything of the sort.

The best he could do was make sure she stayed as safe as possible.

He hated his shoulder all over again. Was he going to have to spend the rest of his life watching others do things he ought to be able to handle?

"I'll help you on one condition. When the wind hits

twenty knots, you'll have to stop, whether you finish or not."

She didn't balk at the restriction as she climbed down from the ladder. "I suppose you're going to tell me now you have some kind of built-in anemometer to know what the wind speed is at all times."

He shrugged. "I've been a helicopter pilot for fifteen years and in that time I've learned a thing or two about gauging the weather. I've also learned not to mess around with Mother Nature."

"That's a lesson you learn early when you live on the coast," she answered.

She lowered the ladder and he grabbed the front end with his left hand and followed her around the corner of the house. The house's sturdy bulk sheltered them a little from the wind here but it was still cold, the air heavy and wet.

"I thought you said you kept a handyman on retainer," he said as together they propped the ladder against one corner of the porch.

She smiled. "No, you're the one who said I should. I do have a regular carpenter and he would fix all this in a second if he were around but he's been doing some work for my friend Sage's husband on one of Eben's hotels in Montana."

"Your friend's married to a hotel owner?"

He pretended ignorance while his stomach jumped as she ascended the ladder again.

"Yes. Eben Spencer owns Spencer Hotels. His company recently purchased a property here in town and that's how he met Sage."

"She's the other one who inherited Brambleberry House along with you, right?"

She nodded. "She's wonderful. You should meet her in a few weeks. She and Eben bought a house down the coast a mile or so and they come back as often as they can but they travel around quite a bit. She called me this afternoon from Patagonia, of all places!"

She started hammering again and from his vantage point, he had an entirely too clear view of that enticing expanse of skin bared at her waist when she lifted her arms. He forced himself to look away, focusing instead on the Sitka spruce dancing wildly in the wind along the road.

"Does she help you with the maintenance on the house?"

"As much as she can when she's here. And Julia helps, too. The two of us painted my living room right after Christmas."

"She's the one who lives on the second floor, right? The one with the twins."

"Right. You're going to love them. Simon will probably talk your leg off about what it's like to fly a helicopter and how you hurt your shoulder and if you carry a gun. Maddie won't have to even say a word to steal your heart in an instant. She's a doll."

His heart was a little harder to steal than that. Sometimes he wondered if he had one. And if he did, he wasn't sure a little girl would be the one to steal it.

He'd never had much to do with kids. He couldn't say he disliked them, they just always seemed like they inhabited this baffling alien world he knew little about.

"How old are the twins?" he asked.

"They turned eight a month ago. And Sage's stepdaughter Chloe is nine. When the three of them are together, there's never a dull moment. It's so wonderful."

She loved children, he realized. Before he'd gotten to know her a little these last few days, that probably would have surprised him. At first glance, she had seemed brusque and cool, not at all the sort to be patient with endless questions or sticky fingers.

But then, Anna Galvez was proving to be full of contradictions.

Just now, for instance, the crisp, buttoned-down businesswoman he had taken her for that first night looked earthy and sexy, her cheeks flushed by the cold and the exertion and her hair blown into tangles by the wind.

He wasn't interested, he reminded himself. Hadn't he spent all day reminding himself why kissing her had been a huge mistake he couldn't afford to repeat?

"There. That should do it," she said a moment later.

"Good. Now come down. That wind has picked up again."

"Gladly," she answered.

He held the ladder steady while she descended.

"Thank you," she said, her voice a little shaky until her feet were on solid ground again. "I'll admit, it helped to know you were down there giving me stability."

"No problem," he answered.

She smiled at him, her features bright and lovely and he suddenly could think of nothing but the softness of her mouth beneath his and of her seductive heat surrounding him.

They stood only a few feet apart and even though the wind lashed wildly around them and the first few drops of rain began to sting his skin, Max couldn't seem to move. He saw awareness leap into the depths of her eyes and knew instinctively she was remembering their kiss as well.

He could kiss her again. Just lean forward a little and all that heat and softness would be in his arms again...

She was the first one to break the spell between them. She drew in a deep breath and gripped the ladder and started to lower it from the porch roof while he stood gazing at her like an idiot.

"Thanks again for your help," she said, and he wondered if he imagined the tiniest hint of a quaver in her voice. "I should have done this last week. I knew a storm was on the way but I'm afraid the time slipped away from me. With an old place like Brambleberry House, there are a hundred must-do items for every one I check off."

She was talking much more than she usually did and seemed determined to avoid his gaze. She obviously didn't want a repeat of their kiss any more than he did.

Or at least any more than he *should*.

"Where does the ladder go?"

"In the garage. But I can return it."

He ignored her, just hefted it with his good arm and carried it around the house to the detached garage where Abigail had always parked her big old Oldsmobile. Conan and Anna both followed behind him.

Walking inside was like entering a time capsule of his aunt's life. It looked the same as he remembered from four years ago, with all the things Abigail had loved. Her potting table and tools, an open box of unpainted china doll faces, the tandem bicycle she had purchased several years ago.

He paused for a moment, looking around the cluttered garage and he was vaguely aware of Conan coming to stand beside him and nudging his head under Max's hand.

"It's a mess, I know. I need to clean this out as soon as I find the time. It's on my to-do list, I swear."

He said nothing, just fought down the renewed sense of loss.

"Listen," she said after a moment, "I was planning to make some pasta for dinner. I always make way too much and then feel like I have to eat it all week long, even after I'm completely sick of it. Would you like some?"

He was being sucked into Anna's life, inexorably drawn into her web. Seeing Abigail's things here only reminded him of his mission here and how he wasn't any closer to the truth than he'd been when he arrived.

"No," he said. "I'd better not."

His words sounded harsh and abrupt hanging out there alone but he didn't know how else to answer.

Her warm smile slipped away. "Another time, then."

They headed out of the garage and he was aware of Conan glaring at him.

The sky had darkened just in the few moments they had been inside the garage and it now hung heavy and gray. The scattered drops had become a light drizzle and he could see distant lightning out over the ocean.

"I should warn you we sometimes lose power in the middle of a big storm. You can find emergency candles and matches in the top drawer in the kitchen to the left of the oven."

"Thanks." They walked together up the front steps and he held the door for her to walk into the entryway.

He headed up the stairs, trying not to favor his stiff ankle, but his efforts were in vain.

"Your ankle! I completely forgot about it! I'm an

idiot to make you stand out there for hours just to hold my ladder. I'm so sorry!"

"It wasn't hours and you're not an idiot. I'm fine. The ankle doesn't even hurt anymore."

It wasn't quite the truth but he wasn't about to tell her that.

He didn't want her sympathy.

He wanted something else entirely from Anna Galvez, something he damn well knew he had no business craving.

Upstairs in his apartment, Max started a fire in the grate while his TV dinner heated up in the microwave.

The wind rattled the windowpanes and sent the branches of the oak tree scraping against the glass and he tried to ignore the delicious scents wafting up from downstairs.

He could have used Conan's company. After spending the entire day with the dog, he felt oddly bereft without him.

But he supposed right now Conan was nestled on his rug in Anna's warm kitchen, having scraps of pasta and maybe a little of that yeasty bread he could smell baking.

When the microwave dinged to signal his own paltry dinner was ready, he grabbed a beer and settled into the easy chair in the living room with the remote and his dinner.

Outside, lightning flashed across the darkening sky and he told himself he should feel warm and cozy in here. But the apartment seemed silent, empty.

Just as he was about to turn on the evening news,

the rocking guitar riff of "Barracuda" suddenly echoed through his apartment.

Not tonight, Mom, he thought, reaching for his cell phone and turning it off. He wasn't at all in the mood to listen to her vitriol. She would probably call all night but that didn't mean he had to listen.

Instead, he turned on the TV and divided his attention between the March Madness basketball games and the rising storm outside, doing his best to shake thoughts of the woman downstairs from his head.

He dozed off sometime in the fourth quarter of what had become a blowout.

He dreamed of dark hair and tawny skin, of deep brown eyes and a soft, delicious mouth. Of a woman in a stern blue business suit unbuttoning her jacket with agonizing slowness to reveal lush, voluptuous curves…

Max woke up with a crick in his neck to find the fire had guttered down to only a few glowing red embers. Just as she predicted, the storm must have knocked out power. The television screen was dark and the light he'd left on in the kitchen was out.

He hurried to the window and saw darkness up and down the coast. The outage was widespread, then.

From his vantage point, he suddenly saw a flashlight beam cutting across the yard below.

His instincts hummed and he peered through the sleeting rain and the wildly thrashing tree limbs to see two shapes—one human, one canine—heading across the lawn from the house to the detached garage.

What the hell was she doing out there? She'd be lucky if a tree limb didn't blow over on her.

He peered through the darkness and in her flashlight beam he saw the garage door flapping in the wind. They must not have latched it quite properly when they had returned the ladder to the garage.

Lightning lit up the yard again and he watched her wrestle the door closed then head for the house again.

He made his way carefully to his door and opened it, waiting to make sure she returned inside safely. Only silence met him from downstairs and he frowned.

What was taking her so long to come back inside?

After another moment or two, he sighed. Like it or not, he was going to have to find out.

Chapter Nine

She loved these wild coastal storms.

Anna scrambled madly back for the shelter of the porch, laughing with delight as the rain stung her cheeks and the churning wind tossed her hair around.

She wanted to lift her hands high into the air and spin around wildly in a circle in some primitive pagan dance.

She supposed most people would find that an odd reaction in a woman as careful and restrained as she tried to be in most other areas of her life. But something about the passion and intensity of a good storm sent the blood surging through her veins, made her hum with energy and excitement.

Abigail had been the same way, she remembered. Her friend used to love to sit out on the wraparound porch facing the sea, a blanket wrapped around her as she watched the storm ride across the Pacific.

Since moving to Brambleberry House nearly a year ago, Anna tried to follow the tradition as often as she could. Sort of her own way of paying tribute to Abigail and the contributions she had made to the world.

Conan shook the rain from his coat after their little foray to the garage and she laughed, grateful she hadn't removed her Gore-Tex parka yet. "Cut it out," she exclaimed. "You can do that on that side of the porch."

The dog made that snickering sound of his, then settled into the driest corner of the deep porch, closest to the house where the rain couldn't reach him.

Conan was used to these storm vigils. She would have thought the lightning and thunder would bother him but he seemed to relish them as much as she did.

Her heart still pumped from the wild run to the garage as she grabbed one of the extra blankets she had brought outside and used a corner of it to dry her face and hair from the rain.

Lightning flashed outside their protected haven and she shivered a little as she grabbed another quilt and wrapped it around her shoulders, then headed for the porch swing that had been purposely angled into a corner to shelter its occupants as much as possible from the elements.

She had barely settled in with a sigh and rattle of the swing's chains when thunder rumbled through the night.

Before it had finished, Conan was on his feet, barking with excitement.

"Settle down, bud. It's only the storm," she assured him.

"And me."

She gasped at the male voice cutting through the night and quickly aimed her flashlight in the direction of it. The long roll of thunder must have muffled Max's approach. He stood several feet away, looking darkly handsome in the distant flashes of lightning.

Her heart, already racing, began to pump even faster. This had nothing to do with the storm and everything to do with Lieutenant Maxwell.

"Is everything okay out here?" he asked, coming closer. "I saw from my window when you went out to the garage to close the door. When I didn't hear you come back inside, I was worried you might have fallen out here or something."

He was worried about her? A tiny little bubble of warmth formed in her chest but she fought down the reaction. He didn't mean anything by it. It was just simple concern of one person to another. He would have been just as conscientious if Conan had been out here in the storm.

More so, maybe. He loved her dog, while she was just the annoying landlady who wouldn't leave him alone, always inviting him to dinner and making him help her nail down loose shingles.

"I'm fine," she finally answered, unable to keep the lingering coolness from her voice after his abrupt refusal to share pasta with her earlier. "Sorry I worried you. I was just settling in to watch the storm. It's kind of a Brambleberry House tradition."

"I remember," he answered.

She gave him a quizzical look, wondering what he meant by that, though of course he couldn't see her expression in the dark.

"You remember what?" she asked.

An odd silence met her question, then he spoke quickly. "I meant, I remember doing the same thing when I visited the coast several years ago. A coastal storm is a compelling thing, isn't it?"

He felt the same tug and pull with the elements as she did? She wouldn't have expected it from the distant, contained soldier.

"It is. You're welcome to join us."

In a quick flash of lightning, she saw hesitation flicker over those lean features—the same hesitation she had seen earlier when he had refused her invitation to dinner.

Never mind, she almost said, feeling stupid and presumptuous for even thinking he might want to sit out on a cold porch swing in the middle of a rainstorm.

But after a moment, he nodded. "Thanks. I was watching the storm from upstairs but it's not quite the same as being out here in the thick of things, is it?"

"I imagine that's a good metaphor for the life of an army helicopter pilot."

"It could very well be."

"There's room here on the swing. Or you could bring one of the rockers over from the other side of the porch, but I'm afraid they're a little damp. This is the safest corner if you want to stay out of the rain."

"Says the voice of experience, obviously."

After another odd, tense little moment of hesitation, he sat down on the swing, which swayed slightly with his weight.

The air temperature instantly increased a dozen degrees and she could smell him, spicy and male.

Lightning ripped through the night again and her blood seemed to sing with it—or maybe it was the intimacy of sitting out here with Max, broken only by the two of them wrapped in a warm cocoon of darkness while the storm raged around them.

They settled into a not uncomfortable silence, just the rain and the thunder and the occasional creak and rattle of the swing's chains.

"Are you warm enough?" she asked. "I only brought two blankets out and one is wet but I've got plenty more inside."

"I should be okay."

"Here. This one should be big enough for both of us." She pulled the blanket from around her shoulders and with a flick of her wrists, sent it billowing over both of them.

Stupid move, she realized instantly. Stupid and naive. It was one thing to sit out here with him, enjoying the storm. It was something else indeed to share a blanket while they did it. Though they weren't even touching underneath it except the occasional brush of their shoulders as they moved, it all still seemed far too intimate.

He made no move to push the blanket off, though, and she couldn't think of a way to yank it away without looking even more foolish than she already must.

"I imagine you've seen some crazy weather from the front seat of a helicopter," she said in an effort to wrench her mind from that blasted kiss the day before.

"A bit," he answered. "Sandstorms in the gulf can come up out of nowhere and you have to either play it through or set down in the middle of zero visibility."

"Scary."

"It can be. But nothing gets your heart thumping more than trying to extract a wounded soldier in poor weather conditions in the midst of possible enemy machine-gun fire."

"You love it, don't you?"

He shifted on the swing, accompanied by the rattle of creaky chains. "What?"

"Flying. What you do."

"Why do you say that?"

She shrugged. "I don't know. Your voice just sounds… different when you talk about it. More alive."

"I do love it." He paused for a long moment as the storm howled around them. "I did, anyway."

"What do you mean?"

This time, he paused so long she wasn't sure he would answer her. She had a feeling he wouldn't have if not for this illusive sense of intimacy between them, together in the darkness.

When he spoke, his voice was taut, as hard as Haystack Rock. "The damage to my shoulder is…extensive. Between the burns and the broken bones, I've lost about seventy percent range of motion and doctors can't tell me whether I'll ever get it back. Worse than that, the infection damaged some of the nerves leading to my hand. At this point, I don't have the fine or gross motor control I need to pass the fitness test to remain a helicopter pilot in the army."

"I'm so sorry." The words sounded ridiculously lame and she wished for some other way she could comfort him.

"I'm damn lucky. I know that."

He spoke quietly, so softly she almost didn't hear him over the next rumble of thunder. "The flight medic and my copilot didn't walk away from the crash."

"Oh, Max," she murmured.

He drew in a ragged breath and then another and she couldn't help it. She reached a hand out and squeezed his fingers. He didn't seem in a hurry to release her hand and they sat together in the darkness, their fingers linked.

"What were their names?" she asked, somehow sensing the words were trapped inside him and only needed the right prompting to break free.

"Chief Warrant Officer Anthony Riani and Specialist Marybeth Shroeder. Both just kids. Marybeth had only been in country for a couple of months and Tony's wife was pregnant with their second kid. They both took the brunt of the missile hit on that side of the Black Hawk and probably died before we even went into the free fall."

She couldn't imagine what he must have seen, what he had survived. She only knew she wanted to hold him close, touched beyond measure that he would share this with her, something she instinctively sensed he didn't divulge easily.

"The crew chief and I were able to get the wounded soldier we were transporting out before the thing exploded. We kept him stable until another Black Hawk was able to evacuate us."

"Was he okay? The soldier?"

"Oh. Yeah. He was a Humvee gunner hit by an improvised explosive device. He lost a leg but he's doing fine, home with his family in Arkansas now."

"That's good."

"Yeah. We were both at Walter Reed together for a while. He's a good man."

He finally let go of her fingers and though she knew it was silly, she suddenly felt several degrees cooler.

"I can't complain, can I?" he said. "I've still got all my pieces and even with partial function, I should eventually be able to do almost anything I want. Except fly a helicopter in the United States Army, I guess. It's looking like I'll probably have to ride a desk from now on or leave the military."

"A tough choice. What will you do?"

He sighed. "Beats me. You have any ideas? Flying helicopters is the only thing I've ever wanted to do. I never wanted to be some hotshot fighter jet pilot or anything fancy like that. Just birds. I'm not sure I can be content to sit things out on the sidelines."

"What about being a civilian pilot?"

He made a derogatory sound. "Doing traffic reports from the air or flying executives into the city who think they're too busy and important for a limousine? I don't think so."

"You could do civilian medevacs."

"I've thought about it. But to tell you the truth, I don't know that I'm capable of flying anything at this point, civilian or military. Or if I ever will be. We're in wait-and-see mode, according to the docs, which genuinely stinks when you're not a very patient person."

The storm seemed to be passing over, she thought. The lightning flashes were slowing in frequency and even the rain seemed to be easing. She didn't want this moment to end, though. She was intensely curious about this man who had survived things she couldn't even imagine.

"I'm sure you'll figure it out, Max. My friend Abigail used to say a bend in the road is not the end, unless you fail to make the turn. You just need to figure out which direction to turn. But you will."

"I'm glad one of us has a little faith."

She smiled. "You can borrow mine when you need

it. Or Abigail's. She carried enough faith and goodness for all of us and I'm sure some still lingers here at
Brambleberry House."

He was again silent for a long time. Then, to her
shock, he reached for her hand again and held on to it
as the storm continued to simmer around them. They sat
for a long time like that in the darkness, while Conan
snored in the corner and the storm gradually slowed
its fury.

Anna's thoughts were scattered but she was aware of
overriding things. She was more attracted to him than
any man in her entire life. To his strength and his courage and even to his sadness.

He had been through hell and though he hadn't directly said it, she sensed he suffered great guilt over
the deaths of his crew members and she wanted to ease
his pain.

She was also, oddly, aware of the scent of freesia
drifting over the earthy smell of wet leaves and the
salty tang of the sea.

If she were Sage or Julia, she might think Abigail
was making her opinion known that Harry Maxwell
was a good man and she approved.

She couldn't believe Abigail was here in spirit. Abigail had been such a wonderful person that Anna
couldn't believe she was anywhere but in heaven, probably doing her best to liven up things there.

But at times, even she had to admit Abigail seemed
closer than at others. The smell of freesia, for instance,
at just the moment she needed it. She tried to convince herself Abigail had loved the scent so much it
had merely soaked into the walls of the house. But that
didn't explain why it would be out here in the middle of

a March rainstorm—or why she thought she caught the glitter of colorful jewels out of the corner of her gaze.

She shivered a little, refusing to give in to the urge to turn her head. Max, sitting too close beside her to miss the movement, misinterpreted it. "You're freezing. We should probably head in."

"I'm not. It's just…" She paused, feeling silly for even bringing this up but suddenly compelled to share some of Sage and Julia's theory with him. "I should probably confess something here. Something I should have told you before you rented the apartment."

He released her hand abruptly. "You're married."

She laughed, though it sounded breathless even to her. "No. Heavens, no. Not even close. Why would you even think that?"

"Not even close? Didn't you say you were engaged once?"

"Yes, years ago. I'm not close to being married right now."

"What happened to the engagement?"

She opened her mouth to tell him it was none of his business, then she closed it again. He had shared far more with her than just the painful end to an engagement that should never have happened in the first place.

"He decided he wanted a different kind of woman. Someone softer. Not so calculating. His words. At least that's what he wrote in the note he sent with his sister on the morning of what was supposed to be our wedding day."

She knew it was ridiculous but the memory still stung, even though it seemed another lifetime ago.

"Ouch."

His single, abrupt word shocked a laugh out of her. "It's been years. I rarely even think about it anymore."

"Did you love him?"

"I wouldn't have been a few hours away from marrying him if I didn't, would I?"

"Seems to me a hard, calculating woman like you wouldn't need to love a man in order to marry him. My mother never did and she's been married five times since my father died."

Now that revealed a wealth of information about his life, she thought. All of it heartbreaking.

"I'm not hard or calculating! I loved Craig. With every ounce of my twenty-four-year-old heart, I loved him. That first year afterward, I was quite certain I would literally die from the pain of the rejection. I couldn't wait to move away from my friends and family in Utah and flee to a place where no one knew me or my humiliating past."

"What's humiliating about it? Seems to me you had a lucky escape. The guy sounds like a jackass. Tell me the truth. Can you imagine now what your life would have been like if you had married him?"

She stared, stunned that he could hit right to the heart of things with the precision of a sharpshooter. "You are so right," she exclaimed. "I would have been completely miserable. I was just too young and stupid to realize it at the time."

It was a marvelously liberating discovery. She supposed she had known it, somewhere deep inside, but for so long she had held on to her mortification and the shame of being jilted on her wedding day. Somehow in the process, she had lost all perspective.

That day had seemed such a defining moment in her life, only because she had allowed it be, she realized.

She had become fearful about trusting anyone and had learned to erect careful defenses to keep people safely on the perimeter of her life. She had focused on her career, on first making By-the-Wind successful as Abigail's manager, then on building the company after she purchased it from her and then adding the second store to further cement her business plan.

Though she didn't think she had completely become what Craig called her—hard, calculating, driven—she had certainly convinced herself her strengths lay in business, not in personal relationships.

Maybe she was wrong about that.

"So if you're not married, what's your big secret?"

She blinked at Max, too busy with her epiphany to follow the trail of conversation. "Sorry. What?"

"You said you had some dark confession to make that you should have told me before I rented the apartment."

"I never said dark. Did I say dark?"

"I don't remember. I'm sure it was."

"No. It's not. It's just…well, rather silly."

"I could use more silly in my life right now."

She smiled and nudged his shoulder with hers. "All right. What's your opinion on the paranormal?"

"I'm not sure I know how to answer that. Are we talking alien visitations or bloodsucking vampires?"

"Neither. I'm talking about ghosts. Or I guess ghost, singular. As in the ghost that some residents of Brambleberry House believe shares the house with us. My friend Abigail."

"You're saying you think Abigail still walks the halls of Brambleberry House."

"I didn't say *I* believed it. But Sage and Julia do. They won't listen to reason. They're absolutely convinced she's still here and that Conan is her familiar, I guess you could say. She works through him to weave her Machiavellian plans. Though I don't really know if one should use that word when all her plans seem to be more on the benevolent side."

The rain had slowed and a corner of the moon peeked out from behind some of the clouds, lending enough light to the scene that she could clearly see his astonished expression.

He stared at her for an endless moment, until she was quite certain he must believe her barking mad, then his head rocked back on his neck and he began to laugh, his shoulders shaking so much the swing rocked crazily on its chains and Conan padded over to investigate.

She had never seen Max so lighthearted. He looked years younger, his features relaxed and almost happy. She could only gaze at him, entranced by this side of him.

The entire evening, she had been trying to ignore how attracted she was to him. But right now, while laughter rippled out of him and his eyes were bright with humor, the attraction blossomed to a hot, urgent hunger.

She had to touch him. Just for a moment, she told herself, then she would go back inside the house and do her best to rebuild her defenses against this man who had survived horrors she couldn't imagine but who could still find humor at the idea of a ghost and her dog.

Her heart clicked just like the rain on the shingles she had just fixed as she drew in a sharp breath, then leaned forward and brushed her mouth against his.

Chapter Ten

Her mouth was warm and soft and tasted like cinnamon candy.

For all of maybe three seconds, he couldn't seem to move past the shock of it, completely frozen by the unexpectedness of the kiss and by the instant heat that crashed against him like those waves against the headland.

He forgot all about his amusement at the idea of his aunt Abigail using a big, gangly dog to work her schemes from the afterlife. He forgot the rain and the wind and the vow he had made to himself not to kiss her again.

He forgot everything but the sheer wonder of Anna in his arms again, of those soft curves beside him, of her scent, sweet and feminine, that had been slowly driving him insane all evening long as she sat beside him, tugging at him until his senses were filled with nothing but her.

Her arms twisted around his neck and he deepened the kiss, breathing deeply of that enticing, womanly scent and pulling her closer until she was nearly on his lap.

For the first time since he had sat down on the porch swing next to her, he was grateful for the blanket around them. Now it was no longer a curse, lending an intimacy he didn't want. Instead, the blanket had become a warm, close shelter from the cold air outside, drawing them closer.

Nothing else existed here but the two of them and the wild need glittering between them.

Kissing her again had a sense of inevitability to it, as if all day he had been waiting for only this. Suspended in a state of hungry anticipation to once again feel her hands in his hair, her soft curves pressed against him, the rapid beat of his heart.

Since the first time he kissed her, his body had been aching to have her in his arms again. That's why he had punished his ankle with a long walk on the shore, why he had spent the morning at the gym he'd found in Seaside working on his physical therapy exercises, why he had done his best to stay away from Brambleberry House all day.

Now that he had rediscovered the wonder of a woman's touch—*this* woman's touch—he couldn't manage to think about anything else. And even when he wasn't consciously thinking about it, his subconscious had been busy remembering.

This was better than anything he might have

dreamed. She was warm and responsive, her mouth eager against his.

It was an intense and erotic kiss, just the two of them alone in the night in this warm shelter while the storm battered the coast around them, and he wanted it to go on forever.

Still, he had a vague awareness even as their bodies heated that the storm was calming—or at least moving farther inland, leaving them behind. The lightning strikes became more infrequent, the rolling thunder more distant.

He didn't care. Nothing else mattered but having her in his arms, slaking this raging thirst for her.

She moved a little, her soft curves brushing against his sling, but she quickly drew back.

"Sorry," she exclaimed.

"You don't have to be careful. I'm sorry my arm is in the way."

"It's not. I'm just afraid of hurting you."

"Let me worry about that."

"Are you? Worried about it, I mean?"

"What red-blooded male in his right mind would worry about a stupid thing like a cast on his arm right now?" he murmured against her mouth.

Her low laugh sent chills rippling down his spine.

"Do that again," he said.

In the darkness, she blinked at him. "Do...what?"

"Laugh like that. I would have to say, Ms. Galvez, that was just about the sexiest sound I've ever heard."

"You're crazy," she said, though she gave a self-conscious laugh when she said it and he thought he just might be content to sit there all night letting his imagination travel all sorts of wicked roads inspired by the sound.

"I must be. That's what six months in an army hospital will get you."

"I'm so sorry you had to go through that," she whispered. "I wish I could make everything okay."

To his shock, she planted a barely there kiss on the corner of his mouth then one on the other side. It was a stunningly sweet gesture and he felt something hard and tight that had been inside him for a long time suddenly break loose.

Had anyone ever shown such gentle compassion to him? He sure as hell couldn't remember it. To his dismay, tears burned behind his eyelids and he wanted to lean into her and just lose himself in her touch.

A fragile tenderness wrapped around them like Aunt Abigail's morning glory vines. He pulled her more firmly on his lap, solving the quandary of his cast by lifting the whole thing out of the way and resting his arm against her back as she nestled against his chest.

They kissed and touched for a long time, until he was aching with need, until she was shivering.

"Are you cold?"

Her laugh was rough. "Not even close."

Still, even as she said the words, she let out a long breath and he sensed her withdrawal, though she didn't physically pull out of his arms.

"This is crazy, Max. What are we doing here? This isn't...I don't do this kind of thing. I...we barely know each other."

He was having a hard time making his addled brain think at all but the still-functioning corner of his mind knew she was absolutely right. He had only been here a few days and in that time, he had been anything but honest with her.

But he didn't agree when she said she barely knew him. Right now, he felt as if she knew him better than anyone else alive. He had told her things he hadn't been able to share with the shrinks at Walter Reed.

"I don't know what this thing is between us but I'm fiercely attracted to you."

She let out a shaky breath and pulled out of his arms with a breathless little laugh. "Okay. Good to know."

"But then, you probably figured that out already."

"I believe I did, Lieutenant. And, uh, right back at you. So what do we do about it?"

He had a number of suggestions, none of which he was willing to share with her.

Before he could answer at all, the porch was suddenly flooded with lights as the electricity flashed back on.

Her eyes looked wide and shocked and she slid away from him on the porch swing as Conan gave a resigned-sounding sigh.

"Is that some kind of message?" Max asked with a rueful laugh. "Maybe the ghost of Brambleberry House is subtly telling us it's time to go inside."

"Ha. Doubtful. If I bought in to Sage and Julia's theory, Abigail's ghost would more likely be the one who cut the power in the first place," she muttered.

"You didn't tell me they had a theory about the ghost. I just figured she maybe wanted to hang around and make sure you treated her house the way she wanted."

He couldn't quite imagine Abigail as a malicious poltergeist. Not that she didn't love a little mischief and mayhem, but she wouldn't have caused it at any inconvenience or expense to someone else.

Though he might have expected things to be awkward with the heat and passion that still sparkled between them, he felt surprisingly comfortable with Anna.

He enjoyed her company, he realized. Whether they were talking or kissing or sitting quietly, he found being with her soothing, as if she settled some restless spirit inside him in a way nothing else ever had.

"Abigail was always a bit of a romantic," Anna answered. "She would have enjoyed setting the scene like this. The rain, the storm. All of it."

While he was trying to picture his aunt working behind the scenes as some great manipulator, Conan ambled off the porch steps and out in the misting rain.

"You don't really think some...ghost had anything to do with what just happened, do you?"

"I'm afraid my feet are planted too firmly on the ground for me to buy in to the whole thing like Sage and Julia do. And besides, while I firmly believe Abigail could have done anything she set her mind to, cutting off power along the entire coast so the two of us could..." Her voice trailed off and he was intrigued to see color soak those high, elegant cheekbones. "Could make out is probably a little beyond her capabilities."

Just as she finished speaking, the porch lights flickered off for maybe two seconds before they flashed back on again.

When they did, her eyes were bright with laughter.

"I wish you could see your face right now," she exclaimed.

He scanned the porch warily. "I'm just trying to figure out if some octogenarian ghost is going to come walking through the walls of the house any minute now with a bottle of wine and a dozen roses."

She laughed. "I don't believe you have anything to worry about. I've never seen her and I don't expect to."

Her smile faded and her dark eyes looked suddenly wistful, edged with sadness. "I wish Abigail *would* walk through that wall, though. I wish you could have known her. I think you would have loved her. She was…amazing. That's the only word for it. Amazing. She drew everyone to her in that way that very few people in the world have. The kind of person who just makes people around her feel happy and important, whether they're billionaire hotel owners or struggling college students."

"She must have been a good friend."

"More than that. I can't explain it, really. I just think you would have loved her. And I *know* she would have adored you."

"Me? Why do you say that?"

"She was always a sucker for a man in uniform. She was engaged to marry a man who died in Korea. He was her one true love and she never really got over him."

He stared. "I never…" Knew that, he almost said, but caught himself just in time. "How do you know that?"

"She told me about him once and then she never wanted to talk about him again," Anna answered. "She said he was the other half of her heart and the best person she'd ever known and she had mourned his loss every single day of her life."

Why had Abigail never told him anything about a lost love? He supposed it might not be the thing one confided in a young boy. What bothered him more was that he had never once thought to ask. He had always assumed she loved her independent life, loved being able to come and go as she pleased without having to answer to anyone else.

He found it terribly sad to think about her living in this big house all these years, mourning a love taken from her too soon.

"I would think a heartbreak like that would have given her an aversion to military men."

Anna shook her head, her eyes soft. "It didn't. I know she had a nephew in the military. I don't even know what branch but she was always so proud of him."

"Oh?"

"Her Jamie. I never met him. He didn't visit her much but she was still crazy about him. Abigail was like that. She loved wholeheartedly, no matter what."

Her words were a harsh condemnation, and the hell of it was, he couldn't even defend himself. He might not have visited Abigail as often as he would have liked, but it wasn't as if he had abandoned her.

They had stayed in touch over the years, he just hadn't been as conscientious about it while he was deployed.

"She sounds like a real character," he said, his voice gruff.

She flashed him a searching look and opened her mouth but before she could speak, Conan bounded back up the porch steps and shook out his wet coat on both of them.

Max managed to pull the blanket up barely in time to protect their faces.

"Conan!" she exclaimed. "Cut that out!"

The dog made that snickering sound he seemed to have perfected, then sauntered back to the corner.

"If you're looking for a signal to go inside, I believe

that's a little more concrete than some ghostly manifestation."

"You're probably right," he said, reluctance in his voice.

"You're welcome to stay out here longer. I can leave the lantern and the blankets."

"I'd rather have you."

The words slipped out and hovered between them. "Sorry. I shouldn't have said that. Forget it."

She blinked. "No, I—I…"

She looked so adorably befuddled in the glow from the porch light—and just so damn beautiful with that thick, glossy dark hair and that luscious mouth—that he couldn't help himself.

One more kiss. That's all, he promised himself as he pulled her closer.

She sighed his name and leaned into him. She was small and curvy and delicious and he couldn't seem to get enough.

He touched the warm, enticing skin above the waistband of her jeans. She gave a little shuddering breath and he felt her stomach muscles contract sharply. Her mouth tangled with his and she made a tiny sound of arousal that shot straight to his gut.

He feathered his fingers along her skin, then danced across it until he met an enticing scrap of lace. He curved his thumb over her and felt her nipple harden. She arched into him and a white haze of hunger gnawed at him, until all he could think about was touching her, tasting her.

She gasped his name.

"I need to stop or I'm afraid I won't be able to."

"To what?"

He gave a raw laugh and kissed her mouth one last time then leaned his forehead against hers, feeling as breathless as if he were a new recruit forced to do a hundred push-ups in front of the entire unit.

He wanted to take things further. God knew, he wanted to. But he knew it would be a huge mistake.

"To stop. I don't want to but I'm afraid what seems like a brilliant idea right now out here will take on an entirely different perspective in the cold light of morning."

After a long moment, she sighed. "You're probably right."

She rose from the porch swing first and though it was one of the toughest things he had ever asked of himself, he helped her gather the blankets and carry them inside the foyer.

"Good night, Anna," he said at her apartment door. "I enjoyed the storm."

"Which one?" she asked with a surprisingly impish smile.

He shook his head but decided he would be wise not to answer.

His last sight as he headed up the stairs to his apartment was of Conan sitting by Anna's doorway looking up at him, and he could swear the dog was shaking his head in disgust.

His TV had switched back on when the power returned and some Portland TV weatherman was rambling on about the storm that was just beginning to sweep through town.

He turned off the noise then went to the windows, watching the moonlight as it peeked between clouds to dance across the water.

What the hell was he going to do now?

Anna Galvez was no more a scam artist than his aunt Abigail.

He didn't know about Sage Benedetto but since he had come to trust Abigail's judgment about Anna, he figured he should probably trust it with Sage as well.

Anna had loved his aunt. He had heard the vast, unfeigned affection in her voice when she had talked about her, when she had told him how she wished he could have known Abigail.

She loved Abigail and missed her deeply, he realized. Maybe even as much as he did.

He would have to tell her the truth—that he was Abigail's nephew and had concealed his identity so he could basically spy on her.

After the heated embrace they had just shared, how was he supposed to come clean and tell her he had been lying to her for days?

It sounded so ugly and sordid just hanging out there like that, but he knew he was going to have to figure out a way.

As was often the case after a wild coastal storm, the morning dawned bright and cloudless and gorgeous.

Anna awoke in her bed in an odd, expectant mood. She rarely slept with the curtains pulled, so that she could look out at the sea first thing in the morning. Today, the waves were pale pink frothed with white.

Conan must have slept in. He was usually in here first thing in the morning, begging for his run, but she supposed the late-night stormwatching had tired him out.

She wished she could say the same. She had tossed and turned half the night, her body restless and aching.

She sighed and rolled over onto her back. She was *still* restless and achy and she was very much afraid Harry Maxwell had ruined stormwatching for her for the rest of her days. How could she ever sit out on the porch watching the waves whip across the sky without remembering the heat and magic of his arms?

Blast him, anyway.

She sighed. No. It wasn't his fault. She had known she was tempting fate when she kissed him but she hadn't been able to control herself.

She wanted a wild, passionate fling with Harry Maxwell.

She drew in a shaky breath. How was that for a little blunt truth first thing in the morning?

She was fiercely attracted to the man. More attracted than she had ever been in her life. She wanted him, even though she knew he would be leaving soon. Maybe *because* she knew he would be leaving soon.

For once in her life, she didn't want to fret or rehash the past. She wanted to live in the heady urgency of the moment.

She blew out a breath. Even if she ever dared tell them—which she wouldn't—Sage and Julia would never believe she was lying here in her bed contemplating such a thing with a man she had only known for a matter of days.

How, exactly, did one go about embarking on a fling? She had absolutely no idea.

She supposed she could take the direct route and go upstairs dressed in a flimsy negligee. But first she would have to actually go out and *buy* a flimsy negligee. And then, of course, she would have to somehow find the courage to put it on, forget about actually having the guts to walk upstairs in it.

She sighed. Okay, she didn't know exactly how she could work the logistics of the thing.

"But I *will* figure it out," she said aloud.

Conan suddenly barked from the doorway and she felt foolish for talking to herself, even if her only witness was her dog, who didn't seem to mind at all when she held long conversations with herself through him.

"Thanks for the extra half hour," she said to the dog.

He grinned as if to say *you're welcome,* then headed to the door to stand as an impatient sentinel, as was his morning ritual. She knew from long experience that he would stay there until she surrendered to the inevitable and got dressed to walk him down the beach.

This morning she didn't make him wait long. She hurried into jeans and a sweatshirt then pulled her hair back into a ponytail and grabbed her parka against the still-cold March mornings.

Conan danced on the end of his leash as she opened the door to Brambleberry House, then even he seemed to stop in consternation.

The yard was a mess. The storm must have wreaked more havoc than she'd realized from her spot on the seaward side of the house. The lawn was covered with storm debris—loose shingles and twigs and several larger branches that must have fallen in the night since she was certain she would have heard them crack even from the other side of the house.

Okay, she was going to have to put her tentative seduction plans for Harry Maxwell on the back burner. First thing after walking Conan, she was going to have to deal with this mess.

Chapter Eleven

She cut Conan's walk short, taking him north only as far as Haystack Rock before turning back to head down toward home and all the work waiting for her there.

At least it was an off-season Sunday, when her schedule was more flexible. As a small-business owner, she always felt as if she had one more thing she should be doing. But one of the most important things Abigail had taught her was to be protective of her time off.

You've got to allow yourself to be more than just the store, Abigail had warned her in the early days after she purchased By-the-Wind. *Don't put all the eggs of yourself into the basket of work or you're only going to end up a scrambled mess.*

It wasn't always possible to take time off during the busier summer season, but during the slower spring and winter months she tried to keep Sundays to herself to recharge for the week ahead.

Of course, cleaning up storm debris wasn't exactly relaxing and invigorating, but it was better than sitting in her office with a day full of paperwork.

Her mind was busy with all that she had to do as she walked up the sand dunes toward the house. She let Conan off his leash as soon as she closed the gate behind her and he immediately raced around the corner of the house. She followed him, curious at his urgency, and was stunned to find Max wearing a work glove on his uninjured hand and pushing a wheelbarrow already piled high with fallen limbs.

Her heart picked up a pace at the sight of him greeting Conan with an affectionate pat and she thought how gorgeous he looked in the warm glow of morning, lean and lithe and masculine.

"Hey, you don't have to do that," she called. "You're a renter, not the hired help."

He looked up from Conan. "Do you have a chain saw?" he asked, ignoring her admonition. "Some of these limbs are a little too big to cart off very easily."

"Abigail had a chain saw. It's in the garage. I'm not sure when it was used last, though, so it's probably pretty dull."

She hesitated, trying to couch her words in a way to cause the least assault to his pride. "Um, I hate to bring this up but don't you think your shoulder might make running a chain saw a little tough?"

He looked down at the sling with frustration flickering in his eyes, as if he had forgotten his injury.

"Actually, she also had a wood chipper," she added quickly. "I was planning to just chip most of this to use as mulch in the garden in a few weeks' time. The machine is pretty complicated, though, and it's a two-person job. To tell you the truth, I could use some help."

"Of course," he answered promptly.

She smiled, lost for just a moment in the memory of all they had shared on the porch swing the night before.

She might have stood staring at him all morning if Conan hadn't nudged her, as if to remind her she had work to do.

"Let me just find my gloves and then we can get to work."

"No problem. There's plenty out here to keep me busy."

She hurried inside the house and headed for the hall tree, where she kept her extra gardening gloves and the muck boots she wore when she worked out in the garden.

The man had no right to look so gorgeous first thing in the morning when she could see in the hall mirror that she looked bedraggled and windblown from walking along the seashore.

The idea of a casual fling had seemed so enticing this morning when she had been lying in bed. When she was confronted with six feet of sexy male in a denim workshirt and leather gloves, she wondered what on earth she had been thinking.

She had a very strong feeling that a casual fling with a man like Lieutenant Maxwell would turn out to be anything but casual.

Not that a fling with him seemed likely anytime in the near future. He had seemed like a polite stranger this morning, in vivid contrast to the heat between them the night before.

She sighed. It was a nice fantasy while it lasted and certainly helped take her mind off Grayson Fletcher and the misery of the trial, which would be resuming all too soon.

When she returned to the yard, she couldn't see Max anywhere. But since Conan was sprawled out at the entrance to the garage, she had a fairly solid idea where to find him.

Inside, she found him trying to extricate the chipper, which was wedged tightly behind an old mattress frame and a pile of two-by-fours Will had brought over to use on various repairs around the house.

The chipper had wheels for rolling across the lawn but it was still bulky and unwieldy. She stepped forward to give him a hand clearing a path. "I know, this garage is a mess. With every project we do on the house, we seem to be collecting more and more stuff and now we're running out of places to put it all."

"You'll have to build a garage annex for it all."

She smiled. "Right. A garage for the garage. Sage would love the idea. To tell you the truth, I don't know what else to do. I hate to throw anything away. I'm so afraid we'll toss an old lamp or something and then find out it was Abigail's favorite or some priceless antique that had been in her family for generations."

"You can't keep the house like a museum for her."

"I know. She wouldn't want that and what little family she had doesn't seem to care much about maintaining their heritage. But I still worry. My parents brought very little with them from Mexico when they came across the border. Their families were both poor and didn't have much for them to bring but sometimes I wish I had more old things that told the story of my ancestors and what their lives might have been like."

An odd expression crossed his features and he opened his mouth to answer but before he could, she pulled the last obstacle out of the way so they could pull out the chipper.

"Here we go. That should give us a clear path."

They pulled the chipper out of the chaotic garage and into the sunshine while Conan watched them curiously.

"Any idea how to work this thing?" Max asked.

She smiled. "A year ago, my answer to that question would have been a resounding no, but I've had to learn a few things since I've been at Brambleberry House. This home ownership thing is not for the weak or timid, I'll tell you that much. I've become an expert at removing wallpaper, puttying walls, even wielding a toilet snake. This chipper business is easy compared to that."

For the next two hours, they worked together cleaning up the yard while Conan lazed in whatever dappled bit of sunbeam he could find. It was a gorgeous, sunny early spring day, the kind she always considered a gift from above here in Oregon.

When the fallen branches were cleared and the beautiful wood chips from them stored at the side of the garage for a few more weeks until she had time to prepare the flower beds, Max helped her gather up the loose shingles and replace the gutter that had blown down.

"Anything else we can do?" he asked when they finished and were sitting together on the porch steps taking a breather.

"I don't think so. Not right now, anyway. It's an endless job, this home maintenance thing."

"But not a bad way to spend a beautiful morning."

She smiled, enjoying his company immensely. Even with only one good hand, he worked far harder than most men she knew. He carried heavy limbs under one arm and though he quickly figured out he couldn't push the wheelbarrow with one hand without toppling it over, he ended up dragging out Abigail's old garden wagon and pulling the limbs and wood chips in that.

"I used to hate gardening when I was a kid," she told him. "My parents always had a huge vegetable garden. We would grow peppers and green beans and sweet corn and of course we kids always had to do the weeding. I vowed I was going to live in a condominium the rest of my life where I wouldn't have to get out at the crack of dawn to pick beans."

"But here you are." He gestured to the house.

"Here I am. And you know something weird? Taking care of the garden and yard has become my favorite part of living here. I can't wait until the flowers start coming out in a few weeks. You will be astonished at Abigail's garden. It's a magic place."

He made a noncommittal sound, as if he wasn't quite convinced, and she smiled. "I guess you don't have much opportunity for gardening, living in base housing as you said you've done."

"Not in the army, no," he said in what she had come to think of as his cautious voice. "Various places I've stayed, I've had the chance to do a little but not much."

"You can do all you want at Brambleberry House while you're here. All hands are welcome in Abigail's garden, experienced or not."

"I'll keep that in mind."

Conan brought over a sturdy twig they must have missed and dropped it at his feet. Max obliged him by picking it up and tossing left-handed for the dog to scamper after.

It was a lovely moment and Anna found she didn't want it to end. "Do you feel like a drive?" she asked suddenly.

"With a specific destination involved or just for the ride?"

"A little of both. I need to head down to Lincoln City to drop off some items that were delivered by mistake to the store up here. I'd love some company. I'll even take you to lunch at my favorite restaurant at Neskowin Beach on the way down. My way of paying you back for your help today."

"You don't owe me anything for that. I didn't do much."

She could have argued with him but she decided she wasn't in the mood to debate. "The offer's still open."

He shifted on the step and looked up at the blue sky for a long moment and then turned back at her with a rather wary smile. "It *is* a gorgeous day for a drive."

She returned his smile, then laughed when Conan gave two sharp barks, whether from anticipation or just plain excitement, she couldn't guess. "Wonderful. Can you give me about half an hour to clean up?"

"Only half an hour?"

She grinned at him as she climbed to her feet. "Lieutenant, I grew up with three brothers in a little house with only one bathroom. A girl learns to work her magic fast under those circumstances."

She was rewarded with a genuine smile, one that warmed her clear to her toes. She hurried through her shower and dressed quickly. And though she would have liked to spend some time blow-drying her hair and fixing it into something long and luxurious and irresistible, she had to be satisfied with pulling it into a simple style, held away from her face with a yellow bandeau that matched her light sweater.

She did take time to apply a light coat of makeup, though even that was more than she usually bothered with.

"It's not a date," she assured Conan, who sat watching her with curious eyes as she applied eyeliner and mascara.

This is not a date and I am not breathless, she told herself when the doorbell rang a few moments later.

She answered the door and knew that last one was a blatant lie. She felt as if she were standing on the bluffs above Heceta Head with the wind hitting her from every side.

He wore Levi's and a brushed-cotton shirt in a color that matched the dark spruce outside. Hunger and anticipation curled through her insides.

"Do you need more time?" he asked.

"Not at all. I only have to grab my purse. Oh, and Conan's leash. Are you okay with him coming along? He pouts if I leave him alone too long."

"I expected it."

That was one of the things she appreciated most about him—his wholehearted acceptance of her dog.

Conan raced ahead as they headed out to her minivan and waited until she opened the door. His customary spot was in the passenger seat but he seemed content to sprawl out in the cargo area this trip, along with the boxes she had carefully strapped down the day before.

She backed with caution out of the driveway and waited until they were on the road heading south before she spoke. "I know you've been at least as far south as Neah-Kah-Nie Mountain. Have you gone farther down the coast?"

"Not this trip," he answered. "It's been several years."

"I've been driving to Lincoln City two or three times a week for nine months and I still never get tired of it."

"Is that how long you've had the store there?"

She nodded, then fell silent, remembering her starry dreams of last summer, when she had first opened the second store. She had wanted so desperately for the store to succeed and had imagined opening a third and maybe even a fourth store someday, until everywhere on the coast, people would think of By-the-Wind when they thought of books and unique gift items.

Now her dreams were in tatters and most days when she drove this road, she arrived with tight shoulder muscles and her stomach in knots.

"Did I say something wrong?" Max asked, and she realized she had been silent for a good mile or more.

"No. It's not you. It's just…"

She hesitated to tell him, though the trial was certainly common knowledge.

No doubt he would hear about it sooner or later and it was probably better that she give him the information herself.

Her hands tightened on the steering wheel. "My professional life is a mess," she admitted. "Once in a while I'm able to forget about it for an hour or so at a time but then it all comes creeping back."

She was almost afraid to look at him to gauge his reaction but she finally dared a quick look and found his expression unreadable. "Want to talk about it?"

"I don't want to ruin your enjoyment of the spectacular coastal scenery with such a long, boring, sordid story."

"Can a story be boring and sordid at the same time?"

The tongue-in-cheek question surprised a laugh from her when she least expected to find much of anything amusing. "Good point."

And a good reminder that she shouldn't take herself so seriously. She hadn't lost any team members to enemy fire. She hadn't been shot down over hostile territory or suffered severe burns or spent months in the hospital.

This was a tough hurdle and professionally and personally humiliating for her but it wasn't the end of the world.

She didn't know where to start and she didn't want to look like an idiot to him. But he had been brutally honest with her the night before and she suddenly found she wanted to share this with Max.

"I trusted the wrong person," she finally said. "I guess the story all starts with that."

Could the woman make him feel any more guilty, however unwittingly?

As Max listened to Anna's story of fraud and betrayal by the former store manager of her Lincoln City store, shame coalesced in his gut.

She talked about how she had been lied to for months, how she had ignored warning signs and hadn't trusted her gut.

How was Max going to tell her he had lied about his identity?

He had a strong suspicion her past experience with

this charlatan wasn't going to make her the forgiving sort when he came clean.

"So here we are six months later," she finally said. "Everything is such a disaster. My business is in shambles, I've got suppliers coming out of the woodwork with invoices I thought had been paid months ago and worse, at least two dozen of my customers had their credit and debit cards used fraudulently. It's been a months-long nightmare and I have no idea when I'll ever be able to wake up."

Max remembered his speculation when he read the sketchy information online about the trial that maybe she had been involved in the fraud, a partner who was letting her manager take the fall while she reaped the benefits.

The thought of that now was laughable and he was sorry he had even entertained the idea. She sounded sick about the trial, about the fraud, especially about her customers who had suffered.

"You said this Fletcher jerk has been charged?"

"Oh, yes. That's part of the joy of this whole thing, out there in the public eye for everyone to see what an idiot I've been."

"It's not your fault the guy was a scumbag thief."

"No. But it is my fault I hired the scumbag thief to mind my store and gave him access to the personal information of all my customers and vendors who trusted me to protect that. It's my fault I didn't supervise things as closely as I should have, which allowed him more room and freedom to stick his fingers in as many pies as he could find."

"That's a lot of weight for you to bear."

"My name is the one on the business license. It's my responsibility."

"When will the trial wrap up?"

"This week, I think. Closing arguments start tomorrow and I'm hoping for a quick verdict soon after that. I'll just be so glad when it's over."

"That bad?"

She shrugged and tried to downplay it but he saw the truth in her eyes. "Every day when I walk in the courtroom, I feel like they ought to hand me a dunce cap and a sign to hang around my neck—World's Biggest Idiot."

"You've sat through the entire trial?"

"Every minute of it. Grayson Fletcher stole from me, he stole from customers, he stole from my vendors. He took my reputation and I want to make sure he pays for it."

He had seen seasoned war veterans who didn't have the kind of grit she possessed in order to walk into that courtroom each day. He was astonished at the soft tenderness seeping through him, at his fierce desire to take her hand and assure her everything would be okay.

He couldn't do it. Not with his own deception lying between them.

"Anna, I need to tell you something," he said.

"What?" For just an instant, she shifted her gaze from the road, her eyes wary and watchful.

"I haven't been…" Honest, he started to say, but before the words were out, Conan suddenly interrupted him with a terrible retching sound like he had a tennis ball lodged in his throat.

Until this moment, the dog had been lying peacefully in the cargo area of the minivan but now he poked his head between the driver and passenger seats, retching and gagging dramatically.

"Conan!" she exclaimed. "What's going on, bud? You okay?"

The dog continued making those horrible noises and Anna swerved off the road to the wide shoulder, turned off the van and hurried to the side to open the sliding door.

Conan clambered out and walked back and forth a few times on his leash. He gagged once or twice more, then seemed to take care of whatever had been bothering him.

A moment later, with what seemed like remarkable nonchalance, he headed to a clump of grass and lifted his leg, then wandered back to the two of them, planted his haunches in the grass and looked at them expectantly.

Anna watched him, a frown on her lovely features. "Weird. What was that all about?"

"Carsick, maybe?" Max suggested.

"Conan's never carsick," she answered. "I swear, he has the constitution of a horse."

"Maybe he just needed a little fresh air and a convenient fern."

"So why the theatrics? Maybe he just needed attention. Behave yourself," she ordered the dog as she let him back into the back of the vehicle.

Conan grinned at both of them and Max could have sworn the dog winked at him, though of course he knew that was crazy.

"We're almost to Neskowin and my favorite place," Anna said as she returned to the driver's seat. "Are you ready for lunch?"

He still needed to tell her he was Abigail's nephew. But somehow the time didn't seem right now.

"Sure," he answered. "I'm starving."

"Trust me, you're going to love this place. Wait until you try the chili shrimp."

He couldn't remember the last time he had permitted himself to genuinely relax and have fun.

In the military, he had been completely focused on his career, on becoming the best Black Hawk pilot in his entire division. And then the last six months had been devoted to healing—first the burns and the fractures, then the infection, then the nerve damage.

All that seemed a world away from this gorgeous stretch of coastline and Anna.

While they savored fresh clam chowder and crab legs at a charming restaurant with a spectacular view, they watched the waves roll in and gulls wheel overhead as they laughed and talked.

She told him about growing up with three older brothers in Utah and the trouble they would get in. She told him about her father dying in an industrial accident and her mother's death a few years later from cancer.

She talked about her brother the biologist who lived in Costa Rica with his wife and their twin toddler girls, who knew more Spanish than they did English and could swim like little guppies. About her brother Daniel, a sheriff back home in Utah and his wife, Lauren, who was the only physician for miles around their small town and about her brother Marc, whose wife had just left him to raise their two little boys on his own.

He would have been content just to listen to her talk about her family with her hands gesturing wildly and her face more animated than he had seen it. But she seemed to expect some conversation in return.

Since he didn't think she'd be interested in the stepsiblings he had barely known even when his mother had been married to their respective fathers, he told her instead about his real family. About his army unit and learning to fly his bird, about night sorties when it was pitch-black beneath him as they flew over villages with no electricity and he felt like he was flying over some lunar landscape, about the strength and courage of the people he had met there.

After lunch, they took a short walk with Conan along the quiet, cold beach before continuing the short trip to Lincoln City.

Though he had been careful not to touch her all day, he was aware of the heat simmering between them. He would have to be dead to miss it—the kick of his heartbeat when she smiled, the tightening of his insides when she laughed and ran after Conan on the beach, the burning ache he fought down all day to kiss her once again.

She was the most beautiful woman he had ever known but he couldn't find any words to tell her so that didn't sound corny and artificial. As they reached the busy outskirts of Lincoln City, he watched, fascinated, as his lighthearted companion seemed to become more focused and reserved with each passing mile.

By the time they drove into a small district of charming storefronts and upscale restaurants and pulled up in front of the cedar-and-brick facade that said By-the-Wind Two, she seemed a different person.

"You can wait here if you'd like," she said after she had turned off the engine.

"I'd like to see your store, if that's okay with you,"

he said. There was a much smaller likelihood of anyone recognizing him as Abigail's nephew in Lincoln
City than if he'd gone into the original By-the-Wind, he
figured. Beyond that, he really did want to see where
she worked.

"Can I carry something for you?" he asked.

"I've got six boxes here. They're extremely fragile so we would probably be better off making a few
trips rather than trying to haul everything in at once,"
she said.

He picked up a box with his good arm and followed
her to a side entrance to the store, which she unlocked
and propped open for them. They carried the boxes
into what looked like a back storage room then they
made two more trips each, the last one accompanied
by Conan.

After they set down the last boxes, Anna led the way
into the main section of the store.

He looked around with curiosity and found the shop
comfortable and welcoming, very much in the same
vein as Aunt Abigail's Cannon Beach store. Something
jazzy and light played on a hidden stereo system and
the wall sconce lighting in the bookstore area made all
the books seem mysterious and enticing. Plump chairs
invited patrons to stay and relax and apparently they
did. Several were occupied and he had the feeling these
were regular customers.

A long-haired gray cat was curled up atop a low coffee table in one corner. Conan hurried immediately over
to the cat and Max braced himself for a confrontation
but the two of them seemed to have an understanding.

The cat sniffed, gave him a bored look, then sauntered away just as a woman with a name badge that

indicated she worked at the store caught sight of them and hurried over to greet Anna.

She looked thin and athletic, with long, salt-and-pepper hair pulled back in a ponytail and round wire-rim glasses that didn't conceal her glare.

"Excuse me, what are you doing here? Get out."

Anna tilted her head, much as the long-haired cat had done. "Last I checked, I still own the place."

The older woman all but shook her finger at her. "This is supposed to be your day off, missy. What do I have to do, hide your van keys so you take some time off?"

Anna laughed and hugged the other woman. "Don't nag. I know. I just brought the shipment of blown glass floats that was delivered to the other store. They're all in the back waiting to be stocked. You should see them, they're every bit as gorgeous as the few samples we received. I was afraid I wouldn't have time to drop them off before court tomorrow and I know they're already a week overdue."

"We would have gotten by without them for another day or two."

"I know, but it was a lovely day for a drive. Sue Poppleton, this is my new tenant, Lieutenant Harry Maxwell."

The woman gave him a friendly, curious smile, then turned back to Anna. "Since you're here, do you have five minutes to help me figure out what I'm doing wrong when I try to cancel a preorder in the system?"

"Of course. Max, do you mind just hanging out for a moment?"

"Not at all," he answered.

He headed for a nearby display of local travel books

and was leafing through one on local history when he heard the front door chime. He didn't think much about it, until he realized the entire section of the store had gone deadly quiet.

Chapter Twelve

"Get out," he heard Anna say with a coldness in her voice Max had never heard before.

Conan growled suddenly—whether at her tone or at something else, Max had no idea but he now burned with curiosity.

Not knowing quite what to expect, he stepped away from the display so he could get a clear view of the door.

The man standing just inside the store didn't look threatening at all. He was one of those academic-looking types with smooth skin, artfully tumbled hair, intense eyes behind scholarly looking glasses. Exactly the sort one might expect to find sitting in a bookstore on a Sunday afternoon with a double espresso and the *New York Times* crossword puzzle.

So why the dramatic reaction? Conan was standing in front of Anna like he was all set to rip the man apart and even her employee looked ready to start chucking remaindered books at his head.

The guy seemed completely oblivious to their animosity, his gaze focused only on Anna.

"Come on, Anna. Cut me a break here. I was across the street at the coffee shop and saw your van pull up. I left an excellent croissant half-eaten in hopes you might finally give me a chance to explain."

"I don't need to hear any explanations from you. I need you out of my store right now."

Her voice wobbled, just a little, but in that instant Max figured it out. This must be the bastard who had screwed her over.

He took a step forward, thinking he could probably knock the guy out cold with one solid left hook, but he paused. Maybe it would be better to see how things played out.

Besides, she looked as if she had plenty of help.

"Call off your mutt, will you?"

The dog Max had never seen do anything but enthusiastically lick anyone who so much as looked at him still stood in a protective stance in front of Anna, low growls rumbling out of him.

"I ought to let him rip your throat out after what you've done."

"Come on, baby. Don't be like this."

He raked a hand through his hair and gave Anna what Max figured he probably thought was some kind of melting look.

Anna appeared very much frozen solid. "Like what?" she asked quietly. "Like a woman who finally found her brain about six months too late and figured out what a *cabrón* you are."

Max didn't know much Spanish but he'd heard that particular term in the army enough to know it was not a particularly affectionate or flattering one.

Sue chortled, which seemed to infuriate the man even more. His face turned ruddy beneath his slick tan and he took a step forward, only to pause when Conan growled again.

His mouth hardened but he stopped. "How long did you have to practice that injured victim act you played so well in court when you testified?"

"Act?" Anna's voice rose in disbelief.

"Come on. You knew what was up the whole time. You just preferred to look the other way."

Anna drew in a shaky breath and even from here, Max could see the fury in her eyes. "Get out. That is your last warning before I call the police. I'm sure the judge will just love to find out you've been in here harassing me."

"Careful, babe. Harassment is an ugly word. You don't want to be throwing it around casually. Of course, sometimes it's a perfectly appropriate word. The exact one, really. Like when a business owner coerces an employee to sleep with her."

Her features paled and she looked vaguely queasy. "I never slept with you, thank the Lord."

"She didn't coerce you into anything and you know it, you disgusting piece of vermin," Sue snapped, and Fletcher blinked at her as if he'd forgotten she was there.

"Every single employee of By-the-Wind could testify about how you were the one constantly putting out the vibe, hitting on her every time she turned around," she went on. "Sending her flowers, writing poems on the employee bulletin board, taking credit for everybody else's ideas just so you could convince her you were Mr. Wonderful."

Anna drew in a deep breath, not looking at all thrilled by the other woman's defense of her. Instead, her color flared even higher. "Uh, Sue, maybe you should start unpacking those floats I brought so you can make sure none of them shattered in transit."

The other woman looked reluctant to leave but something in Anna's gaze must have convinced her to go. With one last glare at Grayson Fletcher, she headed for the stockroom.

As soon as she was out of earshot, Anna turned back to the man. "You are way out of line."

He shrugged. "Maybe. But if, say, I spoke to the local newspaper reporter covering the case, I could probably spin things exactly my way. You wouldn't look like the sainted victim then, would you?"

Anna opened her mouth to retort, but he cut her off before she could. "Of course, I could always keep my mouth shut, under the right circumstances."

"What circumstances?"

He shrugged. "If I *am* convicted on these bogus charges, maybe, just maybe, you could see your way clear to testifying on my behalf in the sentencing hearing."

She narrowed her gaze. "That sounds suspiciously like blackmail."

"Another ugly word. That's not it at all. I would just think in the interest of making things right, you would want to tell the judge you've had second thoughts and have had time to look at things a little differently," he said calmly.

She gazed at him for a long time. Just before Max

was ready to step forward and kick the guy out of the store, she spoke in a quiet, determined voice.

"Go to hell, Grayson. Of course, I can comfort myself with the thought that by this time next week that's exactly where you're going to find yourself—the hell that passes for the Oregon State Penitentiary in Salem."

The other man's face turned a mottled red, until any trace of anything that might have been handsome turned ugly and mean. He took another step forward, not even stopping when Conan barked sharply.

"You should have left things alone." His low, intense voice dripped with rancor. "I would have paid everything back eventually. I was working on a plan. I tried to tell you that, but you were too damn uppity to listen. Well, you'll listen to me now. I have enough dirt on you that I can ruin you. You harassed me, you assaulted me, you threatened to fire me if I didn't sleep with you. That's the story I'm going to be feeding the pretty little local reporter. And then you framed me to hide your own crimes. When my civil suit is done, you're going to be lucky if I leave you with so much as a comic book. I'll take this store and your other one and that damn house you love so much. Then where will you be? A stone-cold bitch left with nothing."

She seemed to freeze, to shrink inside herself. Max, however, did not. He stepped away from the shelves and faced the other man down.

"Okay, time's up, bastard."

Anna lifted shocked eyes to his, as if she'd forgotten his presence. Max had dealt with enough of Fletcher's type in the military that he wasn't at all surprised to see his bullying bluster fade when confronted with direct challenge.

"Says who?" he asked warily.

"Between me and the dog, I think it's safe to say we can both make it clear you've outstayed your welcome."

Fletcher looked between Conan and Max, as if trying to figure out which of them posed the bigger threat, then he gave a hard laugh, regaining a little of his aplomb. "What are you going to do? Club me with your cast?"

Max gave the same grim, dangerous smile he used on recalcitrant trainees. "Try me."

The four of them stood in that tableau for several long seconds until Conan barked sharply, as if to add his two cents to the conversation. Fletcher stared at them again then gave Anna one last look of sheer loathing before he turned and stalked out of the store.

She wanted to die.

To walk down to the beach and dig the biggest, deepest hole she could manage and just bury herself inside it like a geoduck clam.

Bad enough that she had been caught unawares by Grayson and had stood there like an idiot letting him rant on and on with his damning—but completely ridiculous—allegations.

How much worse was it that Max had been a party to her disgrace?

Not exactly the best way to seduce a man, to show him unmistakable evidence what an idiot she was. When she remembered how she had actually thought she was coming to care for that piece of dirt, she just about thought she would be sick.

"Well, that was the single most humiliating ten minutes of my life."

Max moved closer and she alternated between wanting to bury her face in her hands so she didn't have to look at him and wanting to curl against that hard chest of his.

"You have no reason to feel humiliated. I'm the one who should feel humiliated. I didn't even get one good swing with my cast."

His disgruntled tone surprised a shaky laugh out of her. "I'm sure you can still chase him down at the bakery with his half-eaten croissant," she said. "Or send Conan over to bring him back."

"That kind of instant problem solving must be why you're the boss."

She laughed again, then realized her knees were wobbling. "Excuse me, I need to sit down."

She plopped down on the nearest couch, still fighting the greasy nausea in her belly, the sheer mortification that she had once been stupid and gullible enough to be attracted to a slimy worm like Grayson Fletcher.

"I told you my life was a mess."

"You've still got By-the-Wind."

"For now."

"Any chance he can make good on those threats?"

She sighed and pressed a hand to her stomach. Sexual harassment. How low could the man stoop?

"He can try, but there's absolutely no evidence backing him up. I refused to even date him for months. I didn't want any appearance of impropriety. The other employees can all confirm that. But he was so damn persistent and I was…flattered. That's what it comes down to. I only dated him for a month, but I swear I never slept with him."

Oh, why couldn't she keep her mouth shut? Did she really need to share that particular detail with Max?

"Then don't worry about it. I know his type. He's all bluff and bluster up front but the minute you confront him, he runs away like the rat he is."

"I'm just sorry you were tangled up in the middle."

"Funny, I was just thinking how glad I am that I was here to back you up."

She stared at him for a long moment, at the solid strength of his features, the integrity that seemed so much a part of him. The contrast between a sleazy, dishonest slimebag like Grayson Fletcher and this honorable soldier who had sacrificed so much for his country and still bore the scars for it was overwhelming.

"Thank you," she whispered.

With a full heart, she leaned across the space between them to kiss him softly. Compared to their heat and passion of the night before, this was just a tiny kiss of gratitude, just a slight brush of her lips against his, but it rocked her clear to her toes.

She was crazy about this man. She was aware she had only known him a few days but she was in serious danger of falling head over heels.

She eased away from him, feeling shaky and off balance.

"You're welcome," he murmured, and she wondered if she imagined that raspy note in his voice.

"What did I miss?"

At the sound of her employee's voice, Anna tried to collect her scattered wits. She took a deep breath and found Sue had come out of the stockroom carrying two of the colorful glass floats.

"Not much. He's gone."

"Good riddance. I don't care what you say, I'm calling the cops the next time he has the nerve to come in here."

"Sounds like a plan," Anna said. "Did I answer what you needed to know on canceling an order?"

"Yes. And now you need to get out of here and enjoy the rest of your day off." Sue had on that bossy mother-hen voice that Anna was helpless to fight. "Go have some fun. You deserve it."

She rubbed her hands on her slacks and turned back to Max as a customer came up to Sue and asked her for help locating an item.

"You're welcome to look around more if you'd like."

"I think I'm done here," he answered.

"Are you ready to go home, then?"

A strange light flickered in his eyes and she wondered at it, until she remembered his transitory life. The concept of home probably wasn't one he was used to considering.

"Good idea," he said after a moment, and his words were punctuated by Conan barking his approval.

Dusk was washing across the shore as they reached the outskirts of Cannon Beach and the setting sun cast long shadows across the road and saturated everything with color.

Brambleberry House on its hill looked graceful, welcoming, with its gables and gingerbread trim and the wide porch on all sides.

"I love coming home this time of day," she said as she pulled into the driveway. "I know it's silly but I always feel like the house has been waiting here all day just for me."

"It's not silly."

"Abigail used to say a house only comes alive when it's filled with people who love it." She smiled, remembering. "She used to have this quote on the wall. 'Every house where love abides and friendship is a guest, is surely home, and home, sweet home, for there the heart can rest.'"

He was quiet for a long time, gazing as she was at the house gleaming in the fading sunlight. "You do love it, don't you?" he asked, finally breaking the silence.

"With my whole heart. Rusty pipes, loose shingles, flaking paint and all."

"She knew what she was doing when she left it to you, didn't she?"

It seemed an odd question but she nodded. "I hope so. Sometimes I'm overwhelmed with the endless responsibility of it, especially when the rest of my life seems so chaotic right now. I have no idea why she left things as she did and bequeathed Brambleberry House to Sage and to me out of the blue, but I love it here. I can't imagine ever leaving."

He let out a breath, his eyes looking suddenly serious in the twilight. "Anna—"

Whatever he intended to say was lost when Conan began barking urgently from the cargo area of the van, as if he had expended every last ounce of patience.

She laughed. "Sorry. That sounds dire. I'd better take him down the beach a little to work out the kinks from the car ride. You interested?"

She thought she saw frustration flicker across his features but it was quickly gone.

"Sure. I've got kinks of my own to work out."

Conan leaped out of the van as soon as she hooked on his leash and practically dragged her behind him in his eagerness to mark every single clump of sea grass on the beach trail.

Just before they reached the wide stretch of beach, Max reached for her hand to help her around a rock and he didn't let go. They walked hand in hand with Conan ahead of them and warmth fluttered through her despite the cool spring wind.

She didn't want to the day to end. Even with the humiliation of the encounter with Gray Fletcher, it had been wonderful, the most enjoyable day she'd spent in longer than she could remember.

Conan obviously didn't share her sentiments, however. The dog could usually run for miles along the beach at any time of the day or night. But though he had been so insistent earlier, as soon as he had taken care of his pressing need, now he didn't seem nearly as enthusiastic to be walking. One moment he planted his haunches stubbornly in the sand, the next he tried to tug her back the direction they had come.

The third time he tried the trick, she gave a tug on the leash. "You don't know what you want, do you?"

"As a matter of fact, I do."

She looked over at Max and found him watching her in the fading sunlight, a glittery look in his hazel eyes that made her catch her breath.

"I was talking to Conan," she murmured. "He's being stubborn about the walk. I think he's ready to go back."

"Not yet," Max said quietly.

Before she could ask him why not, he pulled her against him as the sun slid farther down the horizon.

All the heat and wonder they had shared the night before during the storm came rushing back like the tide and she couldn't seem to get enough of him.

She tried to be careful of his sling and his arm but he lifted the sling out of the way so he could pull her against his chest.

He kissed her for long moments, until they were both breathing hard and the sun was only a pale rim on the horizon.

"If we keep this up, we're going to be stuck down here in the dark and won't be able to find our way back."

"Conan will lead the way," she murmured against his mouth. "He hasn't had dinner yet."

He laughed roughly and kissed her again. She wrapped her arms around his waist, a slow heat churning through her. She couldn't seem to get close enough to him, to absorb his hard strength and the safe harbor she felt here.

She didn't know how long they stood there accompanied by the murmur of the sea, a salty breeze eddying around them. She would have been quite content to stay all night if Conan hadn't finally barked with thinly veiled impatience.

The moon had started to rise above the coastal range, a thin sliver of light, but all was dark and mysterious around them.

"I guess we should probably head back."

She couldn't see his features but she was quite sure she sensed the same reluctance that was coursing through her.

Somehow she wasn't surprised when he pulled a flashlight from his keychain in the pocket of his leather bomber. He was a soldier, no doubt prepared for anything.

"I don't have night-vision goggles with me so this will have to do," Max said. He reached for her hand

and they walked back up the beach toward Bramble-berry House, whose lights gleamed a welcome in the darkness.

Her insides jumped wildly with nerves and anticipation. She didn't want this to end but how could she possibly scramble for the courage to tell him she wanted more?

They said little as they made their way back home. Even in his silence, though, she sensed he was withdrawing from her, trying to put distance between them again.

Her instinct was confirmed when they reached the house. She unlocked her apartment and opened the door for Conan to bound inside to find his food. She and Max stood in the foyer and she didn't miss the tight set of his features.

Desperate to regain the fleeting closeness, she drew in a shaky breath and lifted her mouth to his again.

After a moment's hesitation, he returned the kiss with an almost fierce hunger, until her thoughts whirled and her body strained against him.

After a long moment, he wrenched his mouth away. "Anna, I need to tell you something."

Whatever it was, she didn't want to hear it. Somehow she knew instinctively it was something she wouldn't like and right now she couldn't bear for anything to ruin the magic of this moment.

"Just kiss me, Max. Please."

He groaned softly but after a moment's hesitation he obliged, tangling his mouth with hers again and again until nothing else mattered but the two of them and the fragile emotions fluttering in her chest.

"I have been trying to figure out all day how to seduce you," she admitted softly.

His laugh was rough and strummed down her nerve endings. "I think it's safe to say you don't have to do anything but exist. That's more seduction than I can handle right now."

She smiled with the heady joy rushing through her. He made her feel delicate and beautiful, powerful in a way she had never known before.

"Come inside," she said, her voice soft.

He froze and she knew she didn't mistake the indecision on his features. "Anna, are you sure?"

"Please," she murmured.

With a ragged sigh, he yanked her against him and an exultant joy surged through her.

This was right. She was crazy about him, she thought. Head-over-heels crazy about this man.

She knew he wasn't going to be here forever, that he wanted to return to active duty as soon as possible and she would be alone again.

But for now, this moment, he was hers and she wasn't going to waste this precious chance fate had handed her.

A soft, silken spell wove around them as they kissed their way inside her bedroom.

The rest of her house was tasteful and subdued, all whites on wood tones. Her bedroom was different. It was soft and feminine, with lavenders and greens and yellows.

How was it possible that Max could seem so overwhelmingly masculine amid all the girly stuff, the flounces and frills? she wondered. He had never seemed so dangerously, enticingly male.

She led the way to her bed, with its filmy white hangings and mounds of pillows. Max looked at the bed for a moment then back at her and his expression was raw with desire.

"I should probably warn you I haven't done this in a while. I've been redshirted for a while with my injury and before that I was in a country where there wasn't a hell of a lot of opportunity for extracurricular activities."

She couldn't seem to think with these nerves skating through her. "Good to know. I haven't, either. My engagement ended five years ago and I haven't been with anyone else."

His eyes darkened, until the pupils nearly obscured the green-gray of the irises.

"I don't know if I can take things slowly. At least not the first time."

She smiled. "Good."

He gave a rough laugh and kissed her again, then lowered her to the bed. "As much as I want nothing more than to take hours undressing you and exploring every inch of that glorious skin, I'm a little clumsy with buttons right now. With this damn cast, I can barely work my own."

"I've got two hands," she answered. Her fingers trembled a little as she slowly worked the buttons of her shirt and pulled her arms free. At least she had worn one of her favorite bra-and-panty sets, a lacy creation in the palest peach.

He swallowed hard. "I definitely don't think I can take things slowly."

He pressed his mouth to her bared shoulder, then trailed kisses along the skin just above the scalloped edge of her bra. She shivered, arching against him as he slid a hand along the bared skin at her waist then up until he touched her intimately through the lace.

She wanted more. She wanted to feel his skin on hers. He must have shared her hunger because he pulled the sling off, revealing the cast underneath that ran from his wrist to just above his elbow and began working the buttons of his shirt.

"Let me help," she said.

He leaned back to give her more access and she helped him out of his shirt and then went to work on the snaps on his Levi's.

"I can take it from here," he told her.

In moments, they were both naked and he was everything she might have dreamed, all hard muscles and lean strength.

Then she caught her first view of the full extent of his injuries and her heart turned over in her chest.

For some reason, she had thought the damage was contained to his arm and shoulder. But rough, red-looking burns spread out from his collarbone to his pectoral muscles on the right side, crisscrossed by scars that were still blinding white against his skin.

"Oh, Max," she breathed.

Regret slid across his features. "I should have kept my shirt on. I'm so used to it by now I forget how ugly it is."

"No. No, you shouldn't have. I am so sorry you had to go through that."

She pressed her mouth just above the raw-looking skin at the spot where his shoulder met his neck, then again in the hollow above his collarbone.

"Does it hurt?"

He looked as if he wanted to deny it but he finally

shrugged. "Sometimes. Right now, no. Right now, all I can think about is the incredibly sexy woman in my arms. Come up here and kiss me."

"Absolutely, Lieutenant," she said with a smile and settled in his arms.

They kissed and touched for a long time, exploring all the planes and hollows and secret places while those tensile emotions twisted through her, wrapping her closer to him.

He said he couldn't take things slowly but it seemed to her their teasing and touching lasted for hours. At last, when she wasn't sure she could endure another moment, he braced above her on his left forearm and he entered her.

She gasped his name and tightened her arms around him, hunger soaring inside her like bright, colorful kites on the wild air currents of the beach.

Had she ever known this sense of wonder, the feeling of completion, that scattered pieces of herself had only right this moment fallen into place?

She was floating higher and higher, her heart as light as air as he moved inside her, slowly at first and then faster, his mouth hard and urgent on hers with a possessive stamp that thrilled her to the core.

She held tight to him, her body rising to meet his, and then he pushed slightly harder and she gasped suddenly as she broke free of gravity and went soaring into the air.

He groaned her name, then with one last powerful surge he joined her.

Oh, heaven. This was heaven. She held him tightly as a delicious lassitude slid over her.

Chapter Thirteen

Abigail would have approved.

Anna lay next to Max, her arm across him, feeling his chest rise and fall with each slow, steady breath as he slept. Pale moonlight filtered in through her open window and played across his features, and she thought how vulnerable he looked in sleep, years younger than the hard-eyed soldier he appeared at times.

Abigail would have loved him. She didn't quite know why she was so certain but somehow she knew her friend would have been quick to include him in the loose circle of friends that Sage had called her lost sheep—people who were lonely or tired or grieving or who just needed to know someone else believed in them.

Max would have been drawn into that circle, whether he wanted it or not. Abigail would have taken him in, would have filled him with good food to ease all the hollows from those months in the hospital. If he ended up leaving the army, Abigail would have been right there helping him figure out his place in the world.

He made a soft sound in his sleep and her arm tightened around him. She rested her cheek against his smooth, hard chest, astonished at the sense of peace she found here in his arms, the tenderness that seemed to wind through her with silken ties.

She was in love with him.

The truth shimmered through her, bright and stunning, and she drew in a sharp breath, astonished and suddenly terrified.

Love. That wasn't in the plan. She was supposed to be having a casual fling, nothing more. The man had made no secret of his plans to leave as soon as he could. This whole situation seemed destined for disaster.

He wasn't the stick-around type. He couldn't have made that more plain. He had told her himself that he considered his base in Iraq more of a home than anywhere else he had lived. She remembered how sad that had seemed when he told her. It was even more tragic now that she had come to know him better, since she had seen a certain yearning in his eyes when he looked at Brambleberry House.

He needs a home. A place to belong. That's what he's always needed.

The words whispered into her mind and she frowned. Why on earth would such a thought even enter her mind, let alone with such firm assurance? It made absolutely no sense, but she couldn't shake the unswerving conviction that Harry Maxwell needed Brambleberry House, maybe more even than she did.

She couldn't make him stay. She knew that with the

same conviction. She might want him to, with sudden, fierce desperation, but she couldn't hold him here.

When his shoulder healed, he would return to his unit, to his helicopter, and would go wherever he was needed, no matter how dangerous.

Even if his arm didn't heal as well as he hoped, she couldn't see him sticking around. Brambleberry House was a temporary stop on his life's journey and there was nothing she could do to change that.

She sighed, just a tiny breath of air, but it was enough to awaken him. Watching him come back to consciousness was a fascinating experience. No doubt it was the soldier in him but he didn't ease into wakefulness, he just instantly blinked his eyes open.

Her brothers always told her she did the same thing—one minute, she could be in deep REM sleep, the next she was wide-awake and ready to rock and roll.

They used to tease her that she slept with the proverbial one eye open, as if she was afraid one of them would sneak into her room during the night and steal her dolls. Not that she ever had many, but could she help it if she liked to protect what little she had from pesky older brothers?

"Hi," Max murmured, a sexy rasp to his voice, and Anna forgot all about brothers and dolls and sleeping.

"Hi yourself." She smiled, determined to savor every single moment she had with him. Why waste time wishing he could be a different sort of man, the kind who might be happy rattling around an old house like this for the rest of his life?

"Have I been asleep long?"

She shook her head. "A half hour, maybe."

"Sorry. I didn't mean to doze off on you."

"I didn't mind. It was…nice." A major understatement, but she wasn't about to risk scaring him off by revealing just how much she had treasured a quiet moment to savor being in his arms.

He gazed down at her, an oddly tender expression in his hazel eyes that stole her breath and left her stomach doing cartwheels again.

"It has been. Everything. I never expected this, Anna. You have to know that."

She smiled, her heart full and light. "I didn't, either. But a gift can be all the more rare and precious when it's unexpected."

"Is that more of Abigail's wisdom?"

"No. Just mine."

With surprising dexterity, he tugged her with his left arm so she was lying across his chest, then he twisted his hand in her hair so he could angle her mouth to meet his kiss. "You are a wise woman, Anna Galvez."

She smiled. "I don't know about that. But I'm learning."

They kissed and touched and explored for a long time there in the dark, quiet intimacy of her room. At last he pulled her atop him, letting her set the pace.

Their first union had been all heat and fire. This was slower, sweet and sexy and tender all at the same time.

I love you.

She almost blurted the words just before she found release again, but she caught them in her throat before she could do something so foolish.

He wasn't ready to hear them yet—and she wasn't sure she was ready to say them.

It took a long time for his heartbeat to slow back to anything resembling a normal pace. He lay in the dark watching the moonlight dance across the room and listening to Anna breathe beside him.

The soft tenderness seeping through his insides scared the hell out of him.

This wasn't supposed to happen. He wasn't supposed to care so much. But somehow this woman, with her tough shell that he had discovered hid a fragile, vulnerable core, had become fiercely important to him.

She soothed him. He didn't know how she did it but these last few days with her had been filled with a quiet peace he only now realized had been missing since his helicopter crashed.

He had been so damn restless since he was injured. But with Anna, the future didn't seem like a scary place anymore. She made him think he could handle whatever came along.

Except telling her the truth.

He let out a long, slow breath, guilt pinching away at the tranquility of the moment. He had to tell her Abigail was his aunt. The very fact that he was lying in her bed having this conversation with himself while she was naked and warm in his arms was evidence that he had allowed the deception to go on far too long.

But how, exactly, was he supposed to tell her that now? She would be furious and hurt, especially after they had shared this.

He stared up at the ceiling, trying to figure out his options. He ached at the idea of hurting her but he couldn't see any way out of it. Maybe it would be best all the way around if he just left town before this could go on any further.

She would be hurt and baffled if he suddenly disappeared. But what would hurt her more—wondering why he left or discovering he had deceived her, that he had slept with her under false pretenses?

What he had done was unconscionable. He could fool himself that his intentions had been honorable, that he had only wanted to make sure Abigail had been competent in her last wishes when she left the house to Anna and Sage Benedetto. He had been compelled to do something, if only to assuage his own guilt over his negligence these last few years.

Then he had come to Brambleberry House and Anna had made Abigail's French toast for him and bandaged his wounds and kissed him senseless and everything had become so damn tangled.

He hated the idea of leaving her. It seemed the height of cowardice, especially after what they had shared tonight. But what would cause the least harm to her?

"Will you come with me next week when the verdict is read?"

Her voice in the darkness startled him and he shifted his gaze from the ceiling to see her watching him out of those huge dark eyes.

"I thought you were asleep," he said.

"No. I was just thinking."

"About the trial?"

"Sorry. Everything comes back to that right now. I'll be so glad when it's over."

He kissed her forehead, pulling her into a more comfortable position. "It's been rougher on you than you let on, hasn't it?"

She didn't answer but he thought her arms tightened around him. "I've been okay. I have. I just…I think I could use someone else in my corner during the verdict. Would you come?"

Like his aunt, Anna was a strong, independent woman. He had a feeling asking for anything was difficult for her. The fact she had asked him to stand by her touched him deeply.

He could stay a few more days. He owed her that, and perhaps giving her the support she needed at this critical time would be a small way to atone for his deception.

"Yeah. Sure. I'll come with you," he answered. "And if he's found not guilty, we've always got clubbing him senseless with my cast to fall back on as Plan B."

She laughed and kissed him. He pulled her close, pushing away the chiding voice of his conscience for now.

A few more days of this sweet, seductive peace. That's all he wanted. Surely that wasn't too much to ask.

"Are you ready for this?" Max asked her three days later as they sat on a park bench outside her store in Lincoln City enjoying the afternoon sunshine, the first since Sunday.

She made a face, her stomach fluttering with nerves. "Do I have a choice?"

"You always have a choice. You could just forget the whole thing and catch the next fishing boat out of town. Or I could make a phone call, get us a helicopter in here to fly us down the coast to an excellent crab shack I've heard about in Bandon."

"You're not helping."

He gave her an unrepentant grin and she couldn't help thinking how much lighter he had seemed these last few days. The occasional shadow still showed up in his gaze but he laughed more and seemed far more comfortable with the world.

The time they'd spent together since Sunday night had seemed magical. She never would have expected it, but the last two days of the trial passed with amazing swiftness. Even listening to the defense's closing arguments, where she had been painted as everything from an incompetent manager to a corrupt manipulator, hadn't stung as much as it might have a few days earlier.

Now she saw it for what it was—Grayson's desperate ploy to escape justice.

Between the trial and trying to stay on top of administrative duties at both stores, her days had been as packed and chaotic as always.

But the nights.

They had been sheer heaven.

When she returned to Brambleberry House Monday night, Max and Conan had been waiting for her with what he called his specialty—take-out Chinese. After dinner, Max started a fire in her fireplace and read a thriller with Conan at his feet while Anna did payroll and caught up on paperwork.

Eventually she gave up trying to concentrate with all this heat jumping through her insides. She had joined him on the couch and Max had tossed her reading glasses aside and kissed her while rain clicked against the window and Conan snored softly beside them. Later—much later—she had fallen asleep holding his hand.

Tuesday had been largely a repeat, except he had grilled steaks for her out in the rain while she held an umbrella over his head and laughed at the picture he made in one of Abigail's frilly flowered aprons.

That was the moment she knew with certainty that what she felt for him wasn't some passing infatuation, that she was hopelessly in love with him—with this wounded soldier with the slow smile and the secrets in his eyes.

She had no idea what she was going to do about it—except for now, she was going to live in the moment and enjoy every second she had with him.

Her cell phone rang suddenly and she jumped and stared at it.

"Are you going to get that?" Max asked.

"I'm working up to it."

She knew it must be the prosecutor, calling to tell her the verdict was in and about to be read.

The jury had been deliberating for four hours and Max had been with her for two of those hours. She had called him as soon as the jury had started deliberations and he had rushed down to Lincoln City immediately, even after she told him it might be hours—or possibly days—before the jurors reached a verdict.

She was immeasurably touched that he had kept his promise to come with her when the verdict was read—and she was grateful now as she answered her phone with fingers that trembled.

"Hello?" she said.

"They're back," the prosecutor said. "Can you be here in fifteen minutes?"

"Yes. I'll be right there."

She hung up the phone and sat, feeling numb and shaky at the same time.

Max reached for her hand. "Come on. I'll drive your car. We can come back for mine."

He kept his hand linked with hers as they walked into the courthouse. "What will you do if he's exonerated?" he asked, the question she had been dreading.

A few days ago, she was quite certain that possibility would have devastated her. But she had learned she had a great deal in common with Abigail's favorite sea creatures. Like the by-the-wind sailors her store was named for, she would float where fate took her and manage to adapt. Even on that fishing boat Max joked about.

"I'll survive," she said. "What else can I do?"

He squeezed her fingers and didn't let go as they walked into the courtroom and sat down.

So much of her life the last several months had been tied up with this trial but in the end, the verdict was almost anticlimactic. When the jury foreman read that jurors had found Grayson Fletcher guilty on all counts of fraud, Anna let out a tiny sob of relief and Max immediately wrapped her in his arms and kissed her.

Max stayed by her side as she hugged the prosecutor, who had worked so tirelessly for conviction, and as she received encouraging words from several others in the community who had come to hear the verdict.

She finally allowed herself to glance at Grayson and found him looking pale and stunned, as if he couldn't quite believe it was real. A tiny measure of pity flickered through her, even though she knew he deserved the consequences for what he had done.

Still, she wasn't going to hold a grudge the rest of her life, she decided. Life was just too short for her to be bitter and angry at being duped.

"We need to celebrate," Max said after they left the courtroom. "I'm taking you to dinner tonight. Where would you like to go?"

"The Sea Urchin," she said promptly, without taking even a moment to think about her answer. "Sage's husband owns it and since it's a Spencer Hotels property, of course it's fabulous. The food there is unbelievable. The best on the coast."

"I love a woman who knows what she wants."

If only he truly meant his words, she thought, then pushed the thought away. She was deliriously happy right now and she wasn't going to spoil it by worrying about the future.

She had a hard-and-fast rule never to use her cell phone while she was driving except in an absolute emergency, especially on the sometimes curvy coastal road, but she was severely tempted as she drove her van home from Lincoln City to phone everyone in her address book to give them the happy news.

She restrained herself, focusing instead on following Max's SUV, since they had both driven down separately, and trying to contain the happiness bubbling through her.

Still, even before she had a chance to greet Conan, her cell phone rang the moment she walked in the door at Brambleberry House. She grinned when she saw Sage's name and number on the caller ID.

"All right, that's just spooky. How did you know the verdict was in?" she asked, without even saying hello.

Sage shrieked. "It is? I had no idea! Sue called me from the store hours ago when the jury went out for deliberation. I was just checking the status of things since I haven't heard from you. Tell me!"

Anna took a deep breath, thinking again how her life had changed since she inherited this house. A year ago, she would have had no one to share this excitement with except her employees. Now she had dear friends who loved her. She was truly a lucky woman.

"Guilty. Guilty, guilty, guilty!"

"Yes!" She heard Sage shouting the news to Eben and even over the phone, Anna could hear her husband's delighted exclamation.

"Oh, that's wonderful news. I hope they throw the book at the little pissant."

"This, from the world's biggest bleeding heart?" she teased.

"I care about things that deserve my time and energy," Sage said primly. "Grayson Fletcher does not."

"True enough," Anna replied.

"Oh, I'm so happy. I'm only sorry I wasn't there. With Julia gone, too, you're not going to have anyone to celebrate with!"

"Am, too," she answered. "For your information, I'm going to the Sea Urchin for dinner with Max."

There was a long, pregnant silence on the other end of the phone. "Max? Upstairs Max?"

Anna smiled, wondering how he would react to that particular nickname. "That's right."

"All right. What other secrets have you been keeping from me, you sly thing?"

Anna grimaced. She probably shouldn't have let that slip. But now that she had, she knew she wouldn't be able to fool Sage for long. "Nothing. Well, not much, anyway. It's just that Upstairs Max has been spending most of his time downstairs the last few days," she finally confessed.

That long pause greeted her again. "So does Conan like him?"

"Adores him. He treats him like his long-lost best friend."

"And have you smelled any freesia lately?'

Anna made a face. "Cut it out. Abigail's not match-making in this situation. She must be taking a break."

"Or maybe he's not the one for you."

Her heart gave a sharp little tug. "Of course he's not," she answered promptly. "He's only here a short time and then he's leaving again. I know that perfectly well."

"Are you sure?"

She wasn't certain of anything, other than that she was fiercely in love with Harry Maxwell. But she wasn't about to reveal that little tidbit of information to Sage.

"You know I'm going to insist on a full report from Julia as soon as she gets back. And the minute we get back to the States, I'm coming up there, even if I have to use up all my carbon offsets for the year."

"Sage, honey, stop worrying about me, okay? You don't have to come up here to babysit me. Max is a wonderful man and I know you'll love him. But I also know this is only temporary. I'm fine with that."

After she hung up the phone some time later, those words continued to echo through her mind. Had she ever lied to Sage before? She couldn't remember. This one was a doozy, though. She wasn't fine. No matter how cool and sophisticated she tried to be about things, she knew she would be devastated when he left.

And he would leave. She knew that, somewhere deep inside of her, with a certainty she couldn't explain. Her time with him was limited. Even now, he could be pre-paring to leave.

Fight for him. He needs you.

The words whispered through her mind, so strong and compelling that she looked around the room to find a source.

He needs you.

The smell of freesia floated across the room and Conan looked up from his rug, thumped his tail on the floor, then went back to sleep.

Anna shivered, her heart pounding, then she quickly caught herself before her imagination went crazy. That's what happened when she talked to Sage. She lost every ounce of common sense and started believing in ghosts.

Not that it was bad advice. If she loved Max, shouldn't she be willing to fight for the man?

Starting tonight, she decided, and went to her closet for her favorite dress, a shimmery sheath in pale green that made her dark skin and hair look exotic and sultry.

She might not have a matchmaking ghost on her side, but she could take control of her own fate.

Max wouldn't know what hit him.

Chapter Fourteen

Max rang the doorbell to Anna's apartment, aware of the sense of foreboding in his gut.

He was going to tell her tonight after dinner. No more excuses. He had put things off far too long and the time had come to confess everything. Maybe she would be so happy at the guilty verdict that she would be in a forgiving sort of mood.

Or maybe she would evict him and throw all his belongings out of her house.

He hoped not. He hoped she would find it in her to understand his motives. But either way, he owed her the truth.

Conan barked behind the door and a moment later, it swung open, revealing a vision in pale green.

From the first time he saw her, Max had considered

Anna Galvez beautiful, with those huge brown eyes and her glossy dark hair and classically lovely features.

But right now she was truly breathtaking.

She had piled her hair up in a loose, feminine style, with curls dripping everywhere. She wore a sexy dream of a dress with a low back that showed off fine-boned shoulders and all that luscious skin of hers. She also wore more jewelry than he'd seen on her—a diamond choker and matching bracelet and slim, dangly earrings that glittered in the foyer light.

She looked lush and sensual and he wanted to stand in the foyer of Brambleberry House all night just looking at her.

"Wow," he murmured. "You look incredible. I know that sounds completely lame but I can't think of another word for it."

"Incredible is good." She smiled. "Come in. I'm just about ready."

He wanted to devour her but he was afraid of messing up perfection so he stood inside the doorway while she picked up a filmy scarf from a side table and wrapped it around her shoulders, then grabbed one of those tiny little evening bags women managed to cram huge amounts of paraphernalia into.

Conan padded over to her wearing one of his pathetic take-me-with-you looks. The dog brushed against her and Max held his breath. Meredith—hell, most women he knew—would have gone ballistic to have dog hairs on one of her fancy party dresses but Anna simply laughed and scratched the dog's chin.

"I'm sorry, bud, but you know you can't go with us to the Sea Urchin. You wouldn't want to. You'd be bored senseless, I promise. But we'll be back later and we'll play then."

The dog heaved a massive sigh and headed for his favorite rug, but in that instant, that tiny interaction, Max felt as if the entire house had just collapsed on top of him.

Emotions washed through him, thick and raw and terrifying, and for an instant of panic, he wanted to turn on his heels and walk out of Brambleberry House and just keep on going.

He was in love with Anna Galvez. Not because she was achingly beautiful or because she made his heart race and the blood pool in his gut.

But because she was strong and courageous and smart and she made him believe in himself again.

He was in love with her. How the hell had that happened?

One minute, his life had been going along just fine. Okay, maybe not perfect. His shoulder problems were proving to be a major pain and he had no idea if he would still be in the army in a few weeks. But he had been dealing with the setbacks in his own way.

And then this woman, with her stubborn independence and her brilliant smile and her ambitious dreams, had knocked him on his butt. She talked to her dog and she knew her way around a wood chipper and she filled his soul with a peace he never realized had been missing.

"Max? Is everything okay?"

How long had he been staring at her? Too long, obviously. He drew in a ragged breath and realized she was watching him with concern while Conan seemed to be grinning at him.

"Yeah. Yeah. Fine. You just dazzle me."

He could tell she thought he was talking about her appearance and he decided not to correct the misconception.

"Thank you." She smiled. "The jewelry is Abigail's. She never went anywhere, even to the grocery store, without glittery stuff dripping from every available surface. She used to tell me, 'My dear girl, a woman my age has to use every available means at her disposal to distract the eye from all these wrinkles.'"

He could hear Abigail saying exactly that and he suddenly missed his aunt desperately.

"You don't need any jewels," he said. "You're stunning enough without them. The most beautiful woman I've ever known."

Her mouth parted slightly as her eyes softened. "Oh, Max," she whispered. "I do believe that's the sweetest thing anyone has ever said to me."

"It's the truth," he said gruffly.

She smiled with stunning sweetness and stepped forward to press her mouth against his.

His heart seemed to flop around in his chest like a rockfish on the line and he could barely breathe around the tenderness inside him. He kissed her, almost desperate with the need to touch her, taste her, burn every moment of this in his mind.

The magic he always found with her began to coil and twine around them and he closed his eyes as she wrapped her arms around his neck, holding him as if she couldn't bear to let go.

He was wondering just how long it might take for her to fix herself up again if he messed up all this perfection when Conan suddenly barked urgently and raced to the door.

A moment later, he heard the front door to the house open and children's laughter echo through the house.

Anna pulled away from him with a startled gasp, then her face lit up with joy. If she was breathtaking before, right now with her eyes bright and a wide smile lighting her features, she was simply staggering.

"They're back!" she exclaimed.

He couldn't seem to make his brain work. "Who?"

"Julia and the twins! Oh, this just makes this entire day perfect. Come on, you've got to meet them."

She looked a little windblown from the passion of their kiss but she linked her hand with his and opened the door. Conan rushed out first, just about tripping over his feet in his rush to greet two dark-haired children who were starting up the stairs, their arms loaded with backpacks.

"Conan!" both children shouted, dropping their bundles and hurrying back down the stairs.

The dog barked and jumped around them, licking first one and then the other while the boy and girl giggled and hugged him.

"Hey, I need a little of that love."

"Anna Banana!"

The little boy jumped up from hugging the dog and launched himself at Anna. She gave him a tight hug then turned to gather the less rambunctious girl to her as well.

"How are you, my darlings? I know you've only been gone a week, but I swear you've grown a foot in that time! What have you been eating, Maddie? Ice cream for breakfast, lunch and dinner?"

The girl giggled and shook her head. "Nope. Only for breakfast and lunch. We had pizza and cheeseburgers the rest of the time."

"You've been living large in Montana, haven't you?"

"We had tons of fun, Anna! You should have come with us! We went on a horseback ride and we went sledding and skiing and then we went to Boise and visited Grandma and Grandpa for three whole days," the boy exclaimed.

The girl—Maddie—dimpled at her. "You look superpretty, Anna. Are you going to a ball?"

Anna smiled and hugged her again. "No, sweetheart. Just to dinner at Chloe's dad's hotel."

"Ooh, will you bring me a fortune cookie?" the boy asked. "I love their fortune cookies."

"I'll see what I can do," Anna promised, just as a slim blond woman tromped through the door carrying a suitcase in each arm. She dropped them as soon as she walked into the foyer and saw Anna greeting the children, and Max watched while the two women embraced.

"I just heard. Sage just called me. Oh, Anna, I'm so happy about the guilty verdict. Will is, too."

"Yeah," Maddie said with a grin. "You should have heard him yelling in the car. My ears still hurt!"

Anna laughed and looked behind them. "Where is Will?"

"He's getting the rest of our luggage off the roof rack. He should be here in a moment."

The woman glanced over Anna's shoulder at Max and though she gave him a friendly smile, he thought he saw a kind of protective wariness there. It made him wonder what Anna might have told her friends about him.

"Hi," she said. "You must be Harry Maxwell."

The false name scraped against his conscience like metal on metal. He didn't know what to say, loath to perpetuate the lie any more than he already had.

Anna saved him from having to come up with a response. "I'm sorry," she exclaimed with a distracted laugh. "I was so happy to see you all again, I forgot my manners. Max, this is Julia Blair and her children Maddie and Simon. Julia, this is Lieutenant Harry Maxwell."

He nodded hello, then reached forward to shake Julia's outstretched hand.

"We're interrupting something, aren't we?" she said. "You both look wonderful and you're obviously on your way out."

"We're heading to the Sea Urchin to celebrate the verdict," Anna said.

"We can do it another time," Max offered. "I'm sure you two probably want to catch up."

"No, go on. Keep your plans," Julia said. "We can catch up later tonight over tea when the kids are in bed."

Max said nothing, though he thought with fleeting regret of the last two nights when he had slept with her in his arms.

"I was going to shut Conan in my apartment while we're at dinner but you're certainly welcome to take him upstairs with you. I'm sure he'll be so much help while you're trying to unpack."

"Thanks," the other woman said dryly.

"Let me help you with your luggage," Max said.

Julia gave a surprised glance at his omnipresent sling. "You don't have to do that."

"You'd better let him," Anna said with a laugh. "The man doesn't take no for an answer."

"Doesn't he?" Julia murmured.

Max felt his face heat and decided he would be wise to beat a hasty retreat. He picked up one of the suitcases and carried it up and set it on the landing outside the second-floor apartment. He was just heading back down for the second suitcase, when he heard a male voice from the foyer below.

"We were only gone eight days. Why, again, did we need all these suitcases?"

Max froze on the stairway, his heart stuttering. He knew the owner of that voice.

And worse, the man knew him.

"Wow, Anna. You look fabulous!"

Anna beamed at Will Garrett, who lived three houses down. Will was not only a gifted carpenter who had done most of the renovation work on Brambleberry House but, more importantly, he was a dear friend.

"I would say the same for you if I could see you behind all the suitcases," she said with a laugh.

"Here. How's that?" He set down the luggage and pulled her into a close hug. She hugged him back, her heart lifting at the smile he gave her. Every time she saw Will, she marveled at the changes in him these last six months since he and Julia had fallen in love again.

Before Julia and her twins came to Brambleberry House, Will had been a far different man. He had been lost in grief for his wife and daughter who had been killed in a car accident three years ago.

Anna had grieved with him for Robin and Cara. She and Sage—and Abigail, before her death—had worried for him as he pulled away from their close circle of friends, drawing inside himself in the midst of his terrible pain.

They had all rejoiced when Julia moved in upstairs and they learned she had been his first love, when they were just teenagers.

The two of them had rediscovered that love and together, Julia and her twins had helped Will begin to heal.

"I heard the good news about that idiot Fletcher," Will said, too low for the children to overhear. "I couldn't be happier that he's finally getting what's coming to him. Maybe now you can put the whole thing behind you and move forward."

She thought of the progress she had made, how she had brooded far too long about everything. Her perspective had changed these last few days, she realized, thanks in large part to Max.

She *was* ready to move forward, to refocus her efforts on saving both stores. Through hard work, she had built something good and worthwhile. She couldn't just give up all that because of a setback like Gray Fletcher.

She looked up and saw Max standing motionless on the stairs. She smiled up at him, awash in gratitude for these last few days and the confidence he had helped her find again.

"I need to introduce you to our new tenant. Will, this is—"

He followed her gaze and suddenly his eyes lit up. "Max! What are you doing here?"

Max walked slowly down the stairs and Anna frowned when Will gave him that shoulder tap thing men did that seemed the equivalent to the hug of greeting she and Julia had shared.

"Why didn't anybody tell me you were living up-stairs? This is wonderful news. Abigail would have been thrilled that you've finally come home."

Anna stared between the two men. Will looked de-lighted, while Max's expression had reverted to that stony, stoic look he had worn so often when he first arrived at the house.

Her pulse seemed unnaturally loud in her ears as she tried to make sense of this new turn of events. "I don't understand," she finally said. "You two know each other?"

"Know each other? Of course!" Will exclaimed. "We hung out all the time, whenever he would visit his aunt. A couple weeks every summer."

"His...aunt?"

Will gave her an odd look. "Abigail! This is her nephew. The long-lost soldier, Max Harrison."

Anna drew in a sharp breath, her solar plexus con-tracting as if someone had socked her in the gut. She stared at Max, who swallowed hard but didn't say any-thing.

"That's impossible," she exclaimed. "Abigail's neph-ew's name was Jamie. Not Harry or Max. *Her Jamie.* That's what she always called him."

"My full name is Maxwell James Harrison. Abigail was the only one who called me Jamie."

She was going to hyperventilate for the first time in her life. She could feel the breath being slowly squeezed from her lungs. "Max Harrison—Harry Maxwell. I'm such an idiot. Why didn't I figure it out?"

"I can explain if you'll let me."

Lies. Everything they shared was lies. She had kissed

him, held him, slept with him, for heaven's sake. And it had all been a lie.

She pressed a hand to her stomach, to the nausea curling there. First Grayson and now Max. Did she wear some invisible sign on her forehead that said Gullible Fool Here?

All her joy in the day, the triumph of the guilty verdict, the fledgling hope that she could now regain her life seemed to crumble away like leaves underfoot.

Julia, with her usual perception, must have sensed some of what was racing through Anna's head. She quickly stepped in to take control of the situation.

"Will, kids, let's get these suitcases out of the entryway and upstairs to the apartment. Come on."

The children grumbled but they grabbed their backpacks and trudged up the stairs, Conan racing ahead of them in his excitement at having them all back.

In moments, the chaos and bustle of their homecoming was reduced to a tense and ugly silence as she gazed at the man she thought she had fallen in love with.

Most people call me Max. She remembered his words, which very well might have been the only honest thing he had said to her since he moved in.

She moved numbly back into her apartment, only vaguely aware that he had followed her inside.

A hundred thoughts raced through her head but she could only focus on one.

"You lied to me."

"Yes," he answered. Just that, nothing else.

"What am I missing here?" she asked. "Why would you possibly feel like you had to lie about your relationship with Abigail and use a false name?"

He rubbed a hand at the base of his neck. "It was a

stupid idea. Monumentally stupid. All I can say is that it seemed like a good idea at the time."

"That tells me nothing! Who wakes up in the morning and says, 'gosh, I think I'll create a false identity today, just for kicks'?"

"It wasn't like that."

"Then explain it to me!"

Her hands were shaking, she realized. This felt worse than the slick, greasy feeling in her stomach when her accountant had discovered the first hint of wrongdoing at the store. She was very much afraid she was going to be sick and she did her best to fight down the nausea.

"I was stationed in Fallujah when Abigail died. I didn't even know she died until several months later."

"Wrong!" she exclaimed. "Sage notified Abigail's family. I know she did! Not that it did any good. Not a single family member bothered to come to her funeral."

"Sage notified my mother. Not the same thing at all. I told you my relationship with my mother is difficult at best and she never liked Abigail. The only reason she let me come here all those summers was because she thought Abigail was loaded and would eventually leave everything to me. Meredith didn't think to mention to me that Abigail had even died until two months after the fact, and then only in passing."

"How can I believe anything you tell me?"

He closed his eyes. "It's true. I loved Abigail. I doubt I could have swung leave to attend a great-aunt's funeral but I would have moved heaven and earth to try."

"So how do we get from here to there?"

He sighed. "My mother is between husbands, which means that, as usual, she's short on cash. She suddenly remembered Abigail had this house that was supposed to be worth a fortune and she seemed to think it should have come to me, as Abigail's only living relative. And of course, to her by default if something happened to me in the Middle East. Imagine her dismay when she found out Abigail had left Brambleberry House to someone else. Two strangers."

The nausea roiled in her stomach, mostly that he could speak of his own mother regarding his possible demise with such callousness. "This was about money?"

"I don't give a damn about the money!" he said, with unmistakable vehemence. "My mother might but I don't. This was about making sure Abigail knew what she was doing when she left the house and its contents to two complete strangers."

"Strangers to you, maybe, but not to Abigail!" Anna's temper flared with fierce suddenness. "She was our friend. Sage and I both loved her dearly and she loved us. Obviously more than she loved some nephew who never even bothered to visit her."

He drew in a sharp breath. "It was a little tough to find time for social calls when I was in the middle of a damn war zone!"

She had hurt him, she realized. She wanted to take back her words but how could she, when her insides were being ripped apart by pain?

She loved him and he had lied to her, just like every other man she'd ever been stupid enough to trust.

She could feel hot tears burning behind her eyes and she was very much afraid she was going to break down in front of him, something she absolutely could not allow. She blinked them back, focusing on the anger.

"Let me get this straight. You came here because you thought I was some kind of scam artist? That Sage and I had schemed and manipulated our way into Abigail's life so she would leave us the legacy that should have been yours."

He compressed his mouth into a tight line. "Something like that."

"And where did sleeping with me fit into that?"

Chapter Fifteen

Her words hovered between them, a harsh condemnation of his actions these last few days. In her eyes, he could see her withdrawal, the hurt and fury he fully deserved.

Why had he ever been stupid enough to think coming to Cannon Beach was a good idea? He thought of the events he had set into motion by that one crazy decision. He hated most of all knowing he had hurt her.

"Everything between us has been a lie," she said, her voice harsh.

"Not true." He stepped forward, knowing only that he needed some contact with her, but she took a swift step back and he fought hard to conceal the pain knifing through him.

"I never expected any of this to happen. I only intended to spend a few weeks running recon here, getting the lay of the land. I just wanted to check things out, make sure everything was aboveboard. I felt like I owed it to Abigail because..."

Because I loved her and I never had a chance to say goodbye.

"Well, my reasons don't really matter. I swear, I tried to keep my distance but you made it impossible."

"What did I do?"

"You invited me to breakfast," he said simply.

You fixed up my scrapes and bruises, you listened with compassion when I rambled on about my scars, you kissed me and lifted me out of myself.

You made me fall in love with you.

The words clogged in his throat. He wanted desperately to say them but he knew she wouldn't welcome them. He had lost any right to offer her his love.

"I figured out a long time ago that you genuinely cared about Abigail and there was nothing underhanded in you and Sage Benedetto inheriting Brambleberry House."

"Well, that's certainly reassuring to know. Was that before or after you slept with me?"

"Anna—"

"So tell me, Max. As soon as you figured out I wasn't some con artist, why didn't you tell me who you were?"

He raked a hand through his hair. "I wanted to, a hundred times. I tried, but something always stopped me. The dog. The storm. I don't know. It just never seemed like the right time."

He sighed, wishing she would give him even the tiniest of signals that she believed any of this. "And then after we made love, I felt like we were so entangled, I didn't know how to tell you without hurting you."

Her laugh was bitter and scorched his heart. "Far easier to go on letting stupid, oblivious Anna believe the fantasy."

"You're not stupid. Or oblivious. I deceived you. Though I might have thought I had good intentions, that I owed something to Abigail's memory, it was completely wrong of me to let things go as far as they did."

She said nothing and he scanned her features, looking for any softening but he saw nothing there but pain and anger. "I never meant to hurt you," he said.

She stood in a protective stance with her shoulders stiff, and her arms wrapped tightly around her stomach, and he didn't know how to reach her.

"Isn't it funny how people always say that after the fact?" she said, her voice a low condemnation. "If you truly never meant to hurt me, you should have told me you were Abigail's nephew after you kissed me for the first time."

He had no defense against the bitter truth of her words. She was absolutely right.

He had no defense at all. He was wrong and he had known it all along.

"I'm sorry," he murmured, hating the inadequacy of the words but unable to come up with anything better. He should leave, he thought. Just go before he made things worse for her.

He headed to the door but before he opened it, he turned back and was struck again by how beautiful she was. Beautiful and strong and forever out of his reach now.

"Aunt Abigail knew exactly what she was doing when she left Brambleberry House to you," he said, his voice low. "She would have hated to see me sell this house she loved so much and she must have known that with my career in the army, I wouldn't have been able to give it the love and care you have. You belong here, in a way I never could."

He closed the door softly behind him and headed slowly up the stairs, every bone in his body suddenly aching to match the pain in his heart.

That last he had said to her was a blatant lie, just one more to add to the hundreds he had told.

She belonged here, that much was truth. But he couldn't tell her that these last few days, he had begun to think perhaps he could also find a place here in this house that had always been his childhood refuge.

The words to the poem she had quoted echoed through his memory. *Every house where love abides and friendship is a guest, is surely home, and home, sweet home, for there the heart can rest.*

His heart had come to rest here, with Anna. She had soothed his restless soul in ways he still didn't quite understand. He had come here hurting and guilty over the helicopter crash and the deaths of his team members, wondering what he could have done differently to prevent the crash.

He had been frustrated about his shoulder, worried about the future, grieving for his team and for Abigail.

But when he was with Anna, he found peace and comfort. She had helped him find faith again, faith in himself and faith in the future.

The thought of walking away from her, from this place, filled him with a deep, aching sorrow. But what choice did he have?

He couldn't stay here. He had made that impossible. He had been stupid and selfish and he had ruined everything.

* * *

"How is it humanly possible for one woman to be such a colossal idiot when it comes to men?"

Two hours after Max walked out of her apartment, Anna sat in Julia's kitchen. The children were in bed, exhausted from their journey, and Will had returned to his own home down the beach, the house where he and Julia would live after their marriage in June.

"That is a question we may never answer in our lifetimes." Sage's voice sounded tinny and hollow over the speakerphone.

"Sage!" Julia exclaimed, a frown on her lovely features.

"Kidding. I'm kidding, sweetheart. You know I'm kidding, Anna. You're not an idiot. You're the smartest woman I've ever met."

"So why do I keep falling for complete jerks?"

Conan whined from his spot on the kitchen rug and gave her a reproving look similar to the one Julia had given the absent Sage.

"Are you sure he's a complete jerk?" Julia's voice was quiet. "He is Abigail's nephew, after all, so he can't be all bad. I've been wracking my memory and I think I might have met him a time or two when we stayed here during the summers when I was a girl. He always seemed very polite. Quiet, even."

"I'm afraid I never met him so I can't really offer an opinion either way," Sage said on the phone. "He came to stay several years ago before he shipped out to the gulf but I was on a field survey down the coast the whole time. I do know Abigail always spoke about him in glowing terms, but I figured she was a little biased."

Anna remembered the solid assurance she had experienced several times that Abigail would have approved of Max and her growing relationship with him. It hadn't been anything she could put her finger on, just a feeling in her heart.

Fight for him. He needs you.

She suddenly remembered those thoughts drifting through her mind earlier in the evening when she had been preparing for the celebration that hadn't happened.

She was almost certain that had been a figment of her imagination. But was it possible Abigail had been trying to give her some kind of message?

She hated this. She couldn't trust him and she certainly couldn't seem to trust herself.

"He lied to me, just like Gray and just like my fiancé. With my history, how can I get past that?" she asked out loud as she set her spoon back in the bowl of uneaten ice cream.

She hadn't had much of an appetite for it in the first place but now the cherry chocolate chunk tasted terrible with this bitterness in her mouth.

"Maybe you can't," Sage said.

Julia said nothing, though an expression of doubt flickered over her features.

"You don't agree?" Anna asked.

The schoolteacher shrugged. "Do I think he should have told you he was Abigail's nephew? Of course. Deceiving you was wrong. But maybe he just found himself in a deep hole and he didn't know how to climb out without digging in deeper."

"And maybe he should have just buried himself in the hole when he got down far enough," Sage said.

Though Anna knew Sage was only trying to offer her support, she suddenly found she wanted to defend him, which was a completely ridiculous reaction, one she quickly squashed.

"I've been lied to so many times. I don't know if I forgive that."

"You're the only one who can decide that, honey," Julia said, squeezing her fingers. "But whatever you do, you know we're behind you, right?"

"Ditto from the Patagonia faction," Sage said over the phone.

Though she was quite certain it was watery and weak, Anna managed a smile. "Thank you. Thank you both. As tough as this is, I'm grateful I have you both."

"And Conan and Abigail," Sage declared. "Don't forget them."

The dog slapped his tail on the floor at the sound of his name but didn't bother getting up.

"How can I?" she said. She and Julia were saying goodbye and preparing to hang up when Sage suddenly gasped into the phone.

"The letter! We've got a letter for Abigail's nephew, remember?"

"That's right," Anna exclaimed. "I completely forgot it!"

"What letter?" Julia asked.

"From Abigail," Anna explained. "She left it as part of her estate papers for her great-nephew. Her Jamie."

"It was another of those weird conditions of her will," Sage added. "He could only receive it if and when he arrived in person to Brambleberry House. I was all in favor of mailing it to him in care of the army but Abigail's attorney stipulated her wishes were quite clear. We weren't even supposed to tell him about it until he showed up here."

"Why was she so certain he would come back to Brambleberry House after her death? Especially since she had gone to such pains to leave the house to you two, leaving him with no reason to return at all?" Julia asked with a puzzled frown.

"I don't know. I wondered that myself," Anna admitted.

She remembered how sad she had thought it that Abigail seemed so desperate for her nephew, who hadn't visited her much when she was alive, to come here, even after her death.

"She was right though," Sage said. "Just like she always was. He came back, just as she seemed to know he would."

Anna shivered at the undeniable truth of the words.

"You have to give it to him," Sage continued. "Do you know where it is?"

"In the safe in my office," she answered promptly. "I kept it there with all the other estate documents."

"I'd give anything to know what's in that letter. What do you think Abigail had to say to him?" Sage asked.

Anna wondered the same thing after she and Julia had said goodbye to Sage and she had returned downstairs to her own apartment and retrieved the letter from her safe.

She sat looking at the envelope for a long time, at Abigail's familiar elegant handwriting and those two words. *My Jamie.*

For the first time, she allowed herself to look at this from Max's perspective. He said he had loved his aunt and she knew she had hurt him tonight when she said Abigail must not have loved him enough to leave the house to him.

It had been a cruel thing to say, especially since she knew from the way Abigail talked about her nephew that she had adored him.

What would Anna have done if a beloved elderly relative had left a valuable legacy to two strangers? She probably would have been suspicious as well. Of course, she would have wanted to find out the circumstances. But would she have lied about her identity to investigate?

She couldn't answer that. She only knew that some of her anger seemed to be subsiding, drawing away from her like low tide.

She gazed at the letter. *My Jamie.* She was going to have to give it to him, but she knew she couldn't go knocking on his apartment door. She wasn't ready to face him again. Not yet. Maybe in the morning, she would be more in control of her emotions.

Still, some instinct told her she needed to deliver this tonight, whether she faced him or not. Praying she wouldn't encounter him wandering around in the dark, she moved quietly up the stairs and slipped the letter through the narrow crack under the door.

There you go, Abigail, she thought, and was almost certain she felt a brush of air against her cheek.

The task done, she stood for a long moment on the landing outside his apartment, her emotions a tangled mess and her heart a heavy weight in her chest.

Max backed his SUV out of the Brambleberry House driveway just as the sun crested the coast range. His duffel and single suitcase were in the backseat and the letter that had been slipped under his apartment door was on the seat beside him.

He knew the letter was from Abigail. Who else? Even if he hadn't recognized her distinctive curlicue handwriting, he would have known from only the name on the outside.

My Jamie.

He had stared at that envelope, his heart aching with loss and regret. It even smelled like her, some soft, flowery scent that made him think of tight hugs and kisses on the cheek and summer evening spent in the garden with her.

Finally he had stuck it in the pocket of his jacket and walked down the stairs of Brambleberry House for the last time.

He knew of only one place he wanted to be when he read her final words to him. It seemed fitting and right that he drive to the cemetery to pay his last respects before he left Cannon Beach. He had been putting it off, this final evidence that Abigail was really gone, but he knew he couldn't avoid the inevitable any longer.

He found the cemetery and drove through the massive iron gates under winter-bare branches. Only when he was inside looking at the rows of gravestones, surrounded by tendrils of misty morning fog, did he realize he had no idea where to find his aunt's plot amid the graves.

At random, he picked a lane and parked his SUV halfway down it then started walking. He had only gone twenty feet before he saw it, a tasteful headstone in pale amber marble under a small statue of an angel, with her name.

Abigail Elizabeth Dandridge

Someone had angled an intricate wrought-iron bench there to look over the grave and the ocean beyond it.

Anna? he wondered. Somehow it wouldn't have surprised him. It seemed the sort of gesture she would make, practical and softhearted at the same time.

He sat at the bench for a long time, until the damp grass began to seep through his boots and the wrought-iron pressed into the back of his thighs. He wasn't quite sure why he was so apprehensive to read Abigail's final words to him.

Maybe because of that—because it seemed so very final. Silly as it seemed, he hated that this was the last time anyone would call him the nickname only she had used.

Finally he opened the envelope. A tiny key fell out, along with several pieces of cream vellum. He frowned and pocketed the key then unfolded the letter, his insides twisting.

My dear Jamie,

I suppose since you're reading this, it means you have come home to Brambleberry House at last. I say home, my dear, because this is where you have always belonged. During the rough years of your childhood, while you were off at military school, even when you were off serving your country with honor and courage, this was your home. You have always had a home here and I hope with all my heart that you have known that.

By now you must be thinking I'm a crazy old bat. I'm not so sure you would be wrong. I want you to know I'm a crazy old bat who has loved you dearly. You have been my joy every day of your life.

So why didn't I leave you the house? I'm sure you're asking. If you're not, you should be. I nearly did, you know. Since the day you were born, I planned that you would inherit Brambleberry House when I left this earth. Then a few years ago, something happened to change my mind.

I began to want something more for you than just a house. You see, houses get dry rot or are bent and broken by the wind or can even crumble into the ocean.

Love, though. Love endures.

I knew love when I was a girl, a love that stayed with me my entire life. Even though the man I loved died young, I have carried the memory of him inside me all these years. It has sustained me and lifted me throughout my life's journey.

I wanted the same for you, my Jamie. For you to know the connection of two hearts linked as one. So I began to scheme and to plot. You needed a special woman, someone smart and courageous, with a strong, loving heart.

I knew from the moment I met Anna, she was perfect for you.

He stopped and stared at the gravestone as a chill rippled down his spine. Impossible. How could Abigail have known from beyond the grave that he would find Anna, that he would fall in love with her, that he would feel as if his heart were being ripped out of him at the idea of walking away from her? With numb disbelief, he turned his attention back to the letter.

I wanted you to meet her, Jamie. To see for yourself how wonderful she is. I thought if I left you the house outright, you would quickly sell it and return to the army, leaving all you could have found here behind without a backward glance.

Anna and Sage would watch over my house with loving care, I knew. And I also knew that if I left the house to them, eventually you would come home to find out why. I thought perhaps when you did, you would find something far more valuable here than bricks and drywall and a leaky roof.

It was a gamble—a huge one. I only wish I could be there to see if it paid out. Of course, there was always a chance you might fall for Sage, but I had other plans for her, plans that didn't include you.

I can't even contemplate the eventuality that you might not fall for Anna. You are too smart for that—or at least you'd better be!

Please know that my dearest wish is that you will find joy, my darling Jamie.

All my love, forever,

Abigail.

P.S. In case you're wondering, the key is to a safe-deposit box at First National Bank of Oregon where you will find record of my investment portfolio. The proceeds are all to go to you, as the legal documentation in the safe deposit will attest and my attorney can confirm. I've played the market well over the years and I believe you'll find the value of my portfolio far exceeds the worth of an old rambling house on the seashore. I pray you will put my money to good use somewhere, even if I'm wrong about you and Anna being perfect for each other.

He stared at the letter for a long, long time, there in the cemetery with only the wind sighing in the trees and a pair of robins singing and flitting from branch to branch as they prepared their spring nest.

All these years, he had no idea his great-aunt was a sly, manipulative rascal.

He ought to be angry at her for luring him here. She had set him up, had played him every step of the way.

Instead, he laughed out loud, then couldn't seem to stop. He laughed so hard the robins fluttered into the sky, chattering angrily at him for disturbing their work.

"Oh, Abigail," he said out loud. "You are one in a million."

How could he be angry, when her actions had been motivated only by love for him? And when she was absolutely right?

Anna was a smart, courageous woman with a strong, loving heart. And she was perfect for him.

He couldn't just walk away from her, from the chance to see if he could find what Abigail wanted so much for them both.

He was gone.

Anna sat on the porch swing where Max had held her so tenderly the night of the storm and gazed out at the sleeping garden, at the rose bushes with their naked thorns and the dry husks of daylily leaves she hadn't cut down in the fall and the bare dirt that waited in a state of anticipation for what was to come.

He was gone and she was quite certain he wouldn't be back. His SUV was gone when she awoke and when she had let Conan out, she had found the key to his apartment hanging on her doorknob, along with a simple note.

I'm so sorry, he had written, without even signing his name.

The morning was cold, with wisps of fog coming off the sea to curl through the trees and around the garden. She shivered from it. She really should go inside and get ready for work but she couldn't seem to move from the porch swing.

Conan, his eyes deep with concern, padded to her and placed his head in her lap.

Just that tiny gesture of comfort sent the first tear trickling down her cheek, then another and another until she buried her face in her hands and wept.

She gave into the storm of emotions for only a few moments before she straightened and drew in a shaky breath, swiping at the tears on her cheeks. Of course he was gone. What did she expect? She had made it quite clear to him the night before that she couldn't forgive him for lying to her. Did she expect him to stick around hoping she would change her mind?

Would she have?

It was a question she didn't know the answer to. This morning, her anger had faded, leaving only an echo of hurt that he had maintained the deception even after they made love.

Julia's words kept running through her head.

Maybe he just found himself in a deep hole and he didn't know how to climb out without digging in deeper.

Yes, he had lied about his identity. But she couldn't quite believe everything else was a lie. He had stood up to Grayson for her that day in the store, he had come with her to the verdict, had held her hand when she was afraid, had kissed her with stunning tenderness. What was truth and what was a lie?

She loved him. That, at least, was undeniably true.

She let out one last sob, her hands buried in Conan's fur, then she straightened her spine. He was gone and she could do nothing about it. In the meantime, she had two businesses to run and a house to take care of. And now she needed to find a new tenant for her third-floor apartment so she could pay for a new roof.

Conan suddenly jerked away from her and went to the edge of the porch, barking wildly. She turned to see what had captured his attention and her heart stuttered in her chest.

Max walked toward her through the morning mist, looking lean and masculine and dangerous in his leather bomber jacket with his arm in the sling.

The breath caught in her throat as he walked toward her and stopped a half-dozen feet away.

"I made you cry."

"No, you didn't. I never cry."

He raised an eyebrow and she lifted her chin defiantly. "It's just cold out here and my allergies must be starting up. It's early spring and the grass pollen count is probably sky-high."

Now who was lying? she thought, clamping her teeth together before she could ramble on more and make things worse.

"Is that right?" he murmured, though he didn't look as if he believed her for an instant.

"I thought you left," she said after a moment.

He shrugged. "I came back."

"You left your key and vacated the apartment."

Where did this cool, composed voice of hers come

from? she wondered. What she really wanted to do instead of standing out here having such a civil conversation was to leap into his arms and hold on tight.

He shrugged, leaning a hip against the carved porch support post. "I changed my mind. I don't want to leave."

"Too bad. You can't walk out on a lease agreement and then waltz back in just because you feel like it."

Amusement sparked in his hazel eyes. Amusement and something else, something that had her pulse racing. "Are you going to take me to court, Anna? Because I have to tell you, that would look pretty bad for you. I would hate to pull out the pity card but I just don't see how you could avoid the ugly headlines. 'Vindictive landlady kicks out injured war veteran.'"

She bristled. "Vindictive? *Vindictive?*"

"Okay, bad choice of words. How about, 'Justifiably angry landlady.'"

"Better."

"No, wait. I've got the perfect headline." He slid away from the post and stepped closer and her pulse kicked up a dozen notches at the intent look in his eyes.

"How about 'Idiotic injured soldier falls hard for lovely landlady.'"

"Because only an idiot would be stupid enough to fall for her, right?"

He laughed roughly. "You're not going to make this easy on me, are you?"

She shrugged instead of answering, mostly because she didn't quite trust her voice.

Just kiss me already.

"All right, this is my last attempt here. How about

'Ex-helicopter pilot loses heart to successful local business owner, declares he can't live without her.'"

Conan barked suddenly with delight and Anna could only stare at Max, her heart pounding so loudly she was quite certain he must be able to hear it. She didn't know quite how to adjust to the quicksilver shift from despair to this bright, vibrant joy bursting through her.

"I like it," she whispered. "No, I love it."

He grinned suddenly and she thought again how much he had changed in the short time he'd been at Brambleberry House.

"It's a keeper then," he said, then he finally stepped forward and kissed her with fierce tenderness.

Tears welled up in her eyes again, this time tears of joy, and she returned his kiss with all the emotion in her heart.

"Can you forgive me, Anna? I made a mistake. I should never have tried to deceive you and I certainly shouldn't have played it out so long. I never expected to fall in love with you. That wasn't in the plan—or at least not in *my* plan."

"Whose plan was it?"

"I've got something to show you. Something I'm quite sure you're not going to believe."

He eased onto the porch swing and pulled her onto his lap as if he couldn't bear to let her go. She was going to be late for work, Anna thought, but right now she didn't give a darn. She didn't want to be anywhere else in the world but right here, in the arms of the man she loved.

"I'm assuming you're the one who slipped the letter from Aunt Abigail under my door."

She nodded. "She was quite strict in her instructions

that you not receive it until you returned to Brambleberry House in person. Sage and I didn't understand it
but the attorney said that was nonnegotiable."

"That's because she was manipulating us all," he answered. "Here. See for yourself."

He handed her the letter and she scanned the words
with growing astonishment. By the time she was done,
a single tear dripped down the side of her nose.

"The wretch," she exclaimed, then she laughed out
loud. "How could she possibly know?"

"What? That you're perfect for me?"

Her gaze flashed to his and she saw blazing emotion
there that sent heat and that wild flutter of joy coursing
through her. "Am I?" she whispered, afraid to believe it.

"You are everything I never knew I needed, Anna.
I love you. With everything inside me, I love you. Abigail got that part exactly right."

She wanted to cry again. To laugh and cry and hold
him close.

*Thank you, Abigail. For this wonderful gift, thank
you from the bottom of my heart.*

"Oh, Max. I love you. I think I fell in love with you
that first morning on the beach when you were so kind
to Conan."

He kissed her, his mouth tender and his eyes filled
with emotion. "I'm not the poetry type of guy, Anna.
But I can tell you that my heart definitely found a home
here, and not because of the house. Because of you."

This time her tears slipped through and she wrapped
her arms around him, holding tight.

Just before he kissed her, Anna could swear she heard
a sigh of satisfied delight. She opened her eyes and was
quite certain that over his shoulder she caught the glitter

of an ethereal kind of shadow drifting through the garden, past the edge of the yard and on toward the beach.

She blinked again and then it was gone.

She must have been mistaken, she thought, except Conan stood at the edge of the porch, looking in the same direction, his ears cocked.

The dog bounded down the steps and into the garden. He barked once, still looking out to sea.

After a long moment, he barked again, then gave that silly canine grin of his and returned to the porch to curl up at their feet.

Epilogue

It was easy to believe in happy endings at a moment like this.

Max sat in the gardens of Brambleberry House on a lovely June day. The wild riot of colorful flowers gleamed in the late-afternoon sunlight and the air was scented with their perfume—roses and daylilies and the sweet, seductive smell of lavender that melded with the brisk, salty undertone of the sea.

Julia Blair was a beautiful bride. Her eyes were bright with happiness as she stood beside Will Garrett under an arbor covered in Abigail's favorite yellow roses while they exchanged vows.

The two of them were deeply in love and everyone at the wedding could see it. Max was glad for Will. He had been given a small glimpse from Abigail's letters over the years of how dark and desolate his friend's life had been after the deaths of his wife and daughter. These last three months, Anna had shared a little more of Will's grieving process with Max and he couldn't imagine that kind of pain.

From what he could tell, Julia was the ideal woman to help Will move forward. Max had come to know her well after three months of living upstairs from her. She was sweet and compassionate, with a deep reservoir of love inside her that she showered on Will and her children.

"May I have the rings, please?" the pastor performing the ceremony asked. Then he had to repeat his request since Simon, the ring bearer and best man, was busy making faces at Chloe Spencer.

"Simon, pay attention," his twin sister hissed loudly. To emphasize her point, she poked him hard with the basket full of the flower petals she had strewn along the garden path before the ceremony.

"Sorry," Simon muttered, then held the pillow holding the rings out to Will, who was doing his best to fight a smile.

"Thanks, bud," Will said, reaching for the rings with one hand while he squeezed the boy's shoulder with the other in a man-to-man kind of gesture.

As Will and Julia exchanged rings, Max heard a small sniffle beside him and turned his head to find Anna's brown eyes shimmering with tears she tried hard to contain.

He curled his fingers more tightly around hers, and as she leaned her cheek against his shoulder for just a moment, he was astounded all over again at how very much his world had changed in just a few short months.

She had become everything to him.

His love.

When the clergyman pronounced them man and wife and they kissed to seal their union, he watched as the tears Anna had been fighting broke free and started to trickle down her cheek.

He pulled a handkerchief from the pocket of his dress uniform, and she dabbed at her eyes. For a woman who claimed she never cried, she had become remarkably proficient at it.

She had cried a month earlier when Sage Benedetto-Spencer told them she and Eben were expecting a baby, due exactly on Abigail's birthday in November.

She'd cried the day the accountant at her Lincoln City store told her they were safely in the black after several record months of sales.

And she had cried buckets for him when, after his latest trip to Walter Reed a month ago, he had come to the inevitable conclusion that he couldn't keep trying to pretend everything would be all right with his shoulder; when he had finally accepted he would never be able to fly a helicopter again.

Max could have left the army completely at that point on a medical discharge, but he had opted instead only to leave active duty. Serving part-time in the army reserves based out of Portland would be a different challenge for him, but he knew he still had much to offer.

The ceremony ended and the newly married couple was immediately surrounded by well-wishers—Conan at the front of the pack. Though he had waited with amazing patience through the service, sitting next to Sage in the front row, the dog apparently had decided he needed to be in the middle of the action.

Conan looked only slightly disgruntled at the bow tie

he had been forced to wear. Maybe he knew he'd gotten a lucky reprieve—Julia's twins had pleaded for a full tuxedo for him but Anna had talked them out of it, much to Conan's relief, Max was quite certain.

"What a gorgeous day for a party." Sage Benedetto-Spencer approached them with her husband. "The garden looks spectacular. I've never seen the colors so rich."

"Your husband's landscape crew from the Sea Urchin did most of the work," Anna said.

"Not true," Eben piped in, wrapping his arms around his wife. "I have it on good authority that you and Max had already done most of the hard work by the time they got here."

Max considered the long evenings and weekends they had spent preparing the yard for the ceremony as a gift—to himself, most of all. Here in Abigail's lush gardens as they'd pruned and planted, he and Anna had talked and laughed and kissed and enjoyed every moment of being together.

He loved watching her, elbow-deep in dirt, Abigail's floppy hat on as she lifted her face to the evening sunshine.

Okay, he loved watching her do anything. Whether it was flying kites with the twins on the beach or throwing a stick for Conan in the yard or sitting at her office desk, her brow wrinkled with concentration as she reconciled her accounts.

He was just plain crazy about her.

They spoke for a few more moments with Eben and Sage before Anna excused herself to make certain the caterers were ready to start bringing out the appetizers for the reception.

When she still hadn't returned a half hour later, Max went searching for her.

He found her alone in the kitchen of her apartment, which had been set up as food central, setting bacon-wrapped shrimp on etched silver platters. Typical Anna, he thought with a grin. Sure, the caterer Julia and Will had hired was probably more than capable of handling all these little details, but she must be busy somewhere else and Anna must have stepped in to help. She loved being involved in the action. If there was work to be done, his Anna didn't hesitate.

She was humming to herself, and he listened to her for a moment, admiring the brisk efficiency of her movements, then he slid in behind her with as much stealth as he could manage. She wore her hair up and he couldn't resist leaning forward and brushing a kiss along the elegant arch of her bared neck, just on the spot he had learned, these last few months, was most sensitive.

A delicate shiver shook her frame and her hands paused in their work. "I don't know who you are, but don't stop," she purred in a low, throaty voice.

He laughed and turned her to face him. She raised her eyebrows in a look of mock surprise as she slid into his arms. "Oh. Max. Hi."

He kissed her properly this time, astonished all over again at the little bump in his pulse, at the love that swelled inside him whenever he had her in his arms.

"It's been a beautiful day, hasn't it?" she said, soft joy in her eyes for her friends' happiness.

"Beautiful," he agreed, without a trace of the cynicism he had expected.

His own mother had been married six times, the most

recent just a few weeks ago to some man she'd met on a three-week Mediterranean cruise. With his childhood and the examples he had seen, he had always considered the idea of happy endings like Julia and Will's—and Sage and Eben's, for that matter—just another fairy tale. But this time with her had changed everything.

"Anna, I want this," he said suddenly.

"The shrimp? I know, they're divine, aren't they? I think I could eat the whole platter myself."

"Not the shrimp. I want the whole thing. The wedding, the flowers. The crazy-spooky dog with the bow tie. I want all of it."

She blinked rapidly, and he saw color soak her cheeks. "Oh," she said slowly.

He wasn't going about this the right way at all. He had a feeling if Abigail happened to be watching she would be laughing her head off just about now at how inept he was.

"I'm sorry I don't have all the flowery words. I only know that I love you with everything inside me. I want forever, Anna." He paused, his heartbeat sounding unnaturally loud in his ears. "Will you marry me?"

She gazed at him for a long, drawn-out moment. Through the open window behind her, he was vaguely aware of the band starting up, playing something soft and slow and romantic.

"Oh, Max," she said. She sniffled once, then again, then she threw herself back into his arms.

"Yes. Yes, yes, yes," she laughed, punctuating each word with a kiss.

"A smart businesswoman like you had better think this through before you answer so definitively. I'm not much of a bargain, I'm afraid. Are you really sure you'll be happy married to a weekend warrior and high-school physics teacher who's greener at his new job than a kid on his first day of basic training?"

"I don't need to think anything through. I love you, Max. I want the whole thing, too." She kissed him again. "And besides, you're going to be a wonderful teacher."

Of all the careers out there, he never would have picked teaching for himself, but now it seemed absolutely right. He had always enjoyed giving training to new recruits and had been damn good at it. But high-school students? That was an entirely different matter.

Anna had been the one who'd pointed out to him how important the teachers at the military school Meredith sent him to had been in shaping his life and the man he had become. They'd been far more instrumental than his own mother.

Once the idea had been planted, it stuck. Since he already had a physics degree, now he only had to finish obtaining a teaching certificate. This time next year, he would be preparing lesson plans.

It wasn't the path he had expected, but that particular route had been blown apart by a rocket-fired grenade in Iraq. Somehow this one suddenly seemed exactly the right one for him.

He couldn't help remembering what Abigail used to say—*A bend in the road is only the end if you refuse to make the turn.* He was making the turn, and though he couldn't see it all clearly, he had a feeling the path ahead contained more joy than he could even imagine.

He rested his chin on Anna's hair. Already that joy seemed to seep through him, washing away all the pain. He couldn't wait to follow that road, to spend the rest of his life with efficient Anna—with her plans and her ambitions and her brilliant mind.

Suddenly, above the delectable smells of the wedding food, he was quite certain he smelled the sweet, summery scent of freesias.

"Do you think she's here today?" Anna asked him.

He tightened his arms around her, thinking of his aunt who had loved them all so much. "Absolutely," he murmured. "She wouldn't miss it. Just as I'm sure she'll be here for our wedding and for the birth of our children and for every step of our journey together."

Anna laughed softly. "We'd better hold on tight, then. If Abigail has her way, I think we're in for a wild ride. A wild, wonderful, perfect ride."

* * * * *

We hope you enjoyed reading

NEVER LET GO

by *New York Times* bestselling author
SHERRYL WOODS and

A SOLDIER'S SECRET

by *USA TODAY* bestselling author
RaeAnne Thayne

Both were originally
Harlequin® Special Edition® series stories!

Discover more heartfelt tales of family, friendship
and love from the Harlequin® Special Edition
series. Romance is for life, and these stories
show that every chapter in a relationship has
its challenges and delights, and that love can be
renewed with each turn of the page.

⊕ HARLEQUIN®

SPECIAL EDITION

**Look for six new romances every month
from Harlequin Special Edition!**

Available wherever books are sold.

www.Harlequin.com

NYTHSE0813

***

"I'm perfectly capable of shoveling my own driveway."

Abby felt something jolt inside her as the man's dark gaze roved over her. Lordy. He really *was* handsome.

"But you don't have a shovel."

"My grandfather had a snowblower," she said. "I didn't have a good way to move it here so I sold it." Along with most everything else that her grandparents had owned.

The reality of it all settled like a sad knot in her stomach.

"So you'll get another blower," the man was saying. "But for now—" he waggled the handle "—this is it." He pushed a long swath of snow clear from the driveway.

"Mr. uh—"

"Sloan."

At last. A name. "Mr. Sloan, if you don't mind lending me the shovel, I can do that myself. I'm sure you've got better things to—"

"Just Sloan. And no. I don't have better things to do. So go back inside. As soon as you can pull your car up in the driveway, I'll leave you to it."

She flopped her hands. "I can't stop you?"

"Evidently not." He reached the end of the driveway, pitched the snow to the side with enviable ease and turned to make another pass in the opposite direction. At the rate he was going, the driveway would be clear in a matter of minutes.

She ought to be grateful. Instead, she just felt inadequate.

She went back inside. The fire had already started warming the room. Abby sat down on the floor next to her little brother and pulled off her coat. "Why don't we leave the rest of our unpacking until later and get the television hooked up?"

She turned away from him only to stop short at the sight of Sloan standing inside the door. She hadn't even heard him open it.

"Driveway's clear."

"Thank you. I'll have to figure out a way to return the favor."

His dark eyes seemed to sharpen. "That might be interesting." Then he smiled faintly and went out the door again, silently closing it after him.

***

Don't miss A WEAVER BEGINNING
by USA TODAY *bestselling author Allison Leigh.*

Available October 2013 from
Harlequin® Special Edition wherever books are sold.

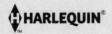

SPECIAL EDITION

Life, Love and Family

Save $1.00 on the purchase of

A WEAVER BEGINNING

by Allison Leigh,

available September 17, 2013 or on any other
Harlequin® Special Edition® book.

Available wherever books are sold, including most bookstores,
supermarkets, drugstores and discount stores.

Save
$1.00

on the purchase of
A WEAVER BEGINNING
by Allison Leigh,
available September 17, 2013,
or on any other Harlequin® Special Edition book.

Coupon valid until December 10, 2013. Redeemable at participating retail outlets
in the U.S. and Canada only. Limit one coupon per customer.

52610921

Canadian Retailers: Harlequin Enterprises Limited will pay the face value
of this coupon plus 10.25¢ if submitted by customer for this product only. Any
other use constitutes fraud. Coupon is nonassignable. Void if taxed, prohibited
or restricted by law. Consumer must pay any government taxes. Void if copied.
Nielsen Clearing House ("NCH") customers submit coupons and proof of sales to
Harlequin Enterprises Limited, P.O. Box 3000, Saint John, NB E2L 4L3, Canada.
Non-NCH retailer—for reimbursement submit coupons and proof of sales directly
to Harlequin Enterprises Limited, Retail Marketing Department, 225 Duncan Mill
Rd., Don Mills, ON M3B 3K9, Canada.

5 65373 00076 2   (8100)0 11860

U.S. Retailers: Harlequin Enterprises
Limited will pay the face value of this coupon
plus 8¢ if submitted by customer for this
product only. Any other use constitutes fraud.
Coupon is nonassignable. Void if taxed,
prohibited or restricted by law. Consumer must
pay any government taxes. Void if copied. For
reimbursement submit coupons and proof of
sales directly to Harlequin Enterprises Limited,
P.O. Box 880478, El Paso, TX 88588-0478,
U.S.A. Cash value 1/100 cents.

® and TM are trademarks owned and used by the trademark owner and/or its licensee.
© 2013 Harlequin Enterprises Limited

NYTCOUP0813

REQUEST YOUR FREE BOOKS!

2 FREE NOVELS
FROM THE ROMANCE COLLECTION
PLUS 2 FREE GIFTS!